BUC

PAID IN BLOOD

BUCKHORN:
PAID IN BLOOD

WILLIAM W. JOHNSTONE

with J. A. Johnstone

PINNACLE BOOKS
Kensington Publishing Corp.
www.kensingtonbooks.com

PINNACLE BOOKS are published by

Kensington Publishing Corp.
119 West 40th Street
New York, NY 10018

PUBLISHER'S NOTE
Following the death of William W. Johnstone, the Johnstone family is working with a carefully selected writer to organize and complete Mr. Johnstone's outlines and many unfinished manuscripts to create additional novels in all of his series like The Last Gunfighter, Mountain Man, and Eagles, among others. This novel was inspired by Mr. Johnstone's superb storytelling.

All Kensington titles, imprints, and distributed lines are available at special quantity discounts for bulk purchases for sales promotions, premiums, fund-raising, educational, or institutional use. Special book excerpts or customized printings can also be created to fit specific needs. For details, write or phone the office of the Kensington sales manager: Kensington Publishing Corp., 119 West 40th Street, New York, NY 10018, attn: Sales Department; phone 1-800-221-2647.

PINNACLE BOOKS, the Pinnacle logo, and the WWJ steer head logo are Reg. U.S. Pat. & TM Off.

ISBN-13: 978-0-7860-3803-9
ISBN-10: 0-7860-3803-9

First printing: August 2016

10 9 8 7 6 5 4 3 2 1

Printed in the United States of America

CHAPTER 1

When Joe Buckhorn emerged from the livery stable and spotted the town marshal striding in his direction, he couldn't suppress a twinge of apprehension.

Looked like trouble was coming his way already.

Buckhorn had only just arrived in the town of Forbes, Texas. With the sun hanging low in the afternoon sky and the place looking peaceful and sort of welcoming from the knob of a distant hill, he'd decided he would ride in for a good meal and a cold beer, maybe a bath, and then a night's sleep in a soft bed before moving on in the morning. He wasn't wanted for anything and wasn't looking for trouble.

But the lingering memory of times past, when his business and the interests of the law had often been at cross purposes, tended to make him leery whenever he saw somebody wearing a badge headed his way.

Not that the badge-toter in this case looked particularly menacing. He was on the short side, had more than a few years on him, was potbellied and bespectacled, and sported a high-crowned, cream-colored

Stetson that appeared at least one size too large so that it rested on the tops of a pair of jug ears.

As if in acknowledgment of his mild appearance, the man walked with somewhat tentative steps rather than the bold, clear-out-of-my-way strides that marked the bullying tactics of too many law enforcers in small settlements across the West. And, if Buckhorn wasn't mistaken, it sounded as if the man was humming a soft tune as he came down the street.

Buckhorn was still trying to decide what to make of this vision when the livery proprietor, a fellow named Hobbs, came out of the barn and stepped up to stand beside him. Chewing on a long piece of straw that poked out one corner of his mouth, Hobbs said, "Okay. Here comes Elmer now."

"Elmer?"

"Elmer Dahlquist. Our town marshal."

"I see the badge. You expectin' him?"

Hobbs cut Buckhorn a sidelong look.

"Well, yeah. I sent my boy to fetch him right after you rode up."

Buckhorn looked puzzled for a moment before working that expression into a scowl.

"You sayin' you called the law on me?"

Hobbs felt the heat from those narrowed eyes and cleared his throat, then said, "No, sir. Not like that, not the way you make it sound—I just let Elmer know you'd showed up, the way he asked some of us business owners to keep an eye out for."

Buckhorn was growing more confounded and annoyed by the minute.

"The marshal had business owners around town

on the lookout for me to show up?" he asked. "What the hell for?"

"Probably be simpler," Marshal Dahlquist said as he drew closer to the two men, "if you just went ahead and let me explain, Mr. Buckhorn. You *are* Joe Buckhorn, ain't that right?"

"That's right," Buckhorn said, still with the scowl in place. "But I don't understand what makes you so doggone interested in me."

A wan smile came and went on the marshal's round face.

"Me, personally? I got no special interest in you at all. Not as long as you behave yourself and don't cause no trouble while you're in town. My interest in you is strictly on account of this telegram I got a couple days ago."

Dahlquist produced a folded piece of paper from his shirt pocket, unfolded it, held it out to Buckhorn. In the dimming light of early evening, Buckhorn saw that it was from a man named Tolliver, addressed to Dahlquist.

Be a favor if you'd stay on the lookout for a Joe Buckhorn who might be passing your way. Hired gun, but not wanted by the law. Part Indian. Wears a bowler hat. Rancher here named Danvers has need of his services. Let me know if he comes around. I'll have Danvers wire him there direct. Thanks.

When Buckhorn lifted his eyes after he was done reading, Dahlquist said, "Thad Tolliver is a sheriff farther west and south some. Good man. Works out of the town of Barkley. Don't know this Danvers personally, but I've heard the name. Runs a big ranching operation in that area."

"Big enough to have the local sheriff acting as a messenger boy for him, it seems," observed Buckhorn.

"Don't know about that. Like I said, Tolliver has always been a good man, so I got no problem doing him this favor. You familiar with him or Danvers, either one?"

"Can't say I am."

"Well, at least one of 'em seems to know something about you. Enough to describe you and want to hire your, ah, 'services,' as the message says."

"I've been doin' what I do for a while now," Buckhorn replied. "Long enough for folks to have heard about me and long enough for me to know how to stay on the right side of the law. As far as the description . . . how many big, ugly Indians do you run across wearing a bowler hat and packing a six-gun they look like they know how to use?"

"You make a point there," Dahlquist said.

There was no denying that Buckhorn's appearance tended to leave a lasting impression. Tall, lean, solid looking; crow's wing-black hair and skin bronzed to a deep reddish-brown hue that spoke clearly of the Indian blood in him; hawklike facial features that most would consider to be on the homely side although a surprising number of women seemed to find them intriguing. All decked out in a brown suit jacket and matching vest, neatly knotted string tie, and topped off with a rakishly tilted bowler.

At first glance he might be mistaken for a whiskey drummer or some such—but nobody would maintain that assessment for very long. Not after closer consideration of the hardness around his eyes or the way the Frontier Colt .45 pistol hung loose and ready in the well-worn holster on his hip.

"I guess the only question left now," Dahlquist went on, jabbing a finger to indicate the paper Buckhorn was still holding, "is how you want to respond to that? I'm sure Virgil Holmes, who runs our telegraph office, has closed up shop for the day. But he's a pretty amenable fella, especially after he has a good meal in him. Once I know he's finished supper, I could ask him to send a response to Tolliver and probably have something direct to you from Danvers back in the morning. Unless none of it is any interest to you, then we can just forget the whole thing."

Buckhorn didn't have to think on it for very long. His last job, moneywise, hadn't worked out nearly as well as he'd expected. So if a big Texas rancher had a new proposition to make, he was willing to hear the man out.

As far as Dahlquist's friendly offer to help speed things along by providing a little extra go-between service, there was a part of Buckhorn that wanted to take him up on it. But at the same time there was also part of him that stubbornly hated being beholden to anybody. He had wrestled with that pride many times in his life, and pride usually won.

So his response was, "I'd be obliged for the chance

to hear what this Danvers has to say, Marshal. But I sure hate to step on your telegraph man's suppertime, not to mention yours. I can wait until morning to respond to this message from the sheriff myself, then see what Danvers comes back with."

"Nonsense. I still got my evening rounds to make and it won't take Virgil but two shakes to send that telegram. You wouldn't be stepping on our time to amount to nothing. You see, Mr. Buckhorn, folks in and around Forbes are real friendly that way—to each other and to strangers passin' through alike." Here the marshal showed another brief smile, this one a bit toothier than before. "And when it comes to hired guns like yourself passin' through—meaning no disrespect to you personally, mind you—I figure our best chance to keep things that way is for me to help move situations like this along."

Now it was Buckhorn's turn to smile as he said, "You know, Marshal, I think that was about the most pleasant get-your-ass-out-of-town speech I ever heard."

Dahlquist held up an admonishing finger.

"Nobody said anything about kicking anybody out of town. Just helping to move the situation along, like I said, that's all."

"Well, I guess I can't hardly blame you for that. And since all I ever intended was to stop for the night anyway, reckon we're both aimed in the same direction." Buckhorn handed back the telegram. "If you'll contact that sheriff over in Barkley, I'd appreciate it. Suppose I can count on you lookin' me up in the morning when you've heard something back?"

"Bright and early."

Buckhorn gestured toward one of the buildings across the street.

"Sign over there says Hotel and Restaurant. That's where you'll find me."

"Fine place. I recommend it. See you there in the morning."

CHAPTER 2

In the Star Hotel dining room, Buckhorn enjoyed a fine meal of steak with all the trimmings, washed down by a couple of cold beers and then followed by coffee and a generous slice of just about the best peach pie he'd ever tasted.

When he was done eating, he was directed to a back room on the hotel side where a tub of fresh, hot water was waiting. While he soaked and scrubbed, his clothes and boots were taken for a good brushing.

If anyone had an issue with him being part Indian, Buckhorn saw no sign of it. No sidelong glances or veiled, hostile stares. It appeared Marshal Dahlquist had it right about the folks in his town being real friendly.

In his second-floor room, Buckhorn hung up his freshly brushed outer clothes. He'd changed to clean socks and long johns downstairs and now he took a fresh shirt from his war bag, which he hung with the other garments he'd dress in tomorrow. The dirty items he stuffed down at the bottom of the war bag, telling himself that he'd have to remember to look up a laundry service in Barkley or whatever the next town was that he landed in for any length of time.

Early in his profession as a hired gun, Buckhorn had done some bodyguard work for a rich man whose attention to grooming and attire had left a lasting impression. Buckhorn decided he would pattern his own way of dressing after much of what he'd seen practiced by that wealthy man and others in his circle.

As the son of a "tame" Indian father and a white trash mother who'd abandoned them both when Joe was only six years old, his beginning had been a shabby one. The years that followed with his remaining parent were grim, as Albert Buckhorn took to drink and feeling sorry for himself until he staggered into the middle of the street and got trampled by a runaway freight wagon.

That left Joe facing almost a decade of abusive, filthy living on the reservation where his father's people didn't want any more to do with an orphaned half-breed than the white folks in town did.

As a young man, he had left that miserable existence behind and soon discovered that he was good with a gun, but people still regarded him as little better than a cur. If he wanted to climb to a better station in life, he told himself, then he would start by dressing the part. And he'd adhered to that goal ever since.

Tonight, settled into his room at the Star Hotel, Buckhorn was feeling pretty good. Full belly on the inside, boiled and scrubbed clean on the outside, the prospect of a new job on the horizon. The big, soft-looking, fresh-smelling bed beckoned him, and he could hardly wait to stretch out. But first, he decided, he wanted to let in some cool night air.

The room's single window was tall and narrow, opening onto an elongated balcony that ran across the front of the hotel building. After first dimming the bedside lantern so he would not be silhouetted against a background light, Buckhorn went to the window and prepared to crack it open a few inches.

Looking down on Forbes's main street, softly illuminated by a series of oil lanterns hung on posts at well-placed intervals, he saw Marshal Dahlquist strolling unhurriedly along on the opposite side, stopping to check and make sure the front doors of each of the buildings he came to were securely locked.

Buckhorn made a little bet with himself that, when he got the window open, he'd be able to hear the marshal softly humming a tune as he went along. It wasn't very often you ran across somebody who seemed so content in his work.

Buckhorn pushed aside the window's gauzy curtains. An instant before he twisted the lock tab that would allow the bottom half of the window to be raised, the roar of a heavy caliber gun split the night. Buckhorn jerked back a half step. The sound of the gunshot came from somewhere very close—outside and directly under the balcony, the way it sounded.

Across the street, Elmer Dahlquist's oversized hat flew off and went spinning one way while the marshal made a dive in a different direction. Buckhorn watched the little man hit the ground and go scrambling with surprising nimbleness toward a thick-walled water trough. As he squirmed in behind the tank he grabbed his pistol.

Two more shots boomed. One slug tore a deep gouge in the dirt, throwing up a geyser of dust and grit right behind where Dahlquist's heels had been digging a moment earlier. The second one *whapped!* loudly against the side of the trough.

After spinning and snatching his Colt out of the holster and gunbelt he'd hung on a bedpost, Buckhorn turned back and used the noise of those latest blasts to cover the sound of him throwing the window open wide. He slipped over the sill and onto the balcony, creeping shadow-quiet in his stocking feet.

Below, somewhere in the blackness beyond the reach of the streetlamps at the mouth of an alley running beside the hotel, a voice called out.

"I've got you right where I want you, Dahlquist, you son of a bitch! I've got seven years of payback built up in my craw, and now it's time to settle accounts for what you did to me and my little brother Varliss. I ventilated your stupid hat and now I'm gonna do the same to your damn head!"

"Who is that talking, you ambushin' skunk?" Dahlquist wanted to know. "You got something to settle with me, let's step on out in the street and do it face to face. Like men!"

"The hell with that! I like things just the way they are," the gunman in the alley called back. To emphasize his words he fired again and sent another round hammering against the water trough.

Dahlquist popped out long enough to reach around one end of the tank and snap off two shots, shooting blindly into the inkiness of the alley.

"Stretch out like that again, you old bastard, and see what it gets you," the ambusher mocked.

Having crept to the end of the balcony, Buckhorn eased forward to peer over the railing. It took his vision a moment to adjust, but then, in the murkiness below, he could make out the man shooting at the marshal. He was hunkering behind an enormous rain barrel, an angular specimen clad in a pair of one-strap overalls, lace-up work shoes, and a slouch hat. He was doing his shooting with a long-barreled rifle, a modified Spencer carbine turned into a buffalo gun, probably .56 caliber.

Ordinarily, Buckhorn made it a point never to stick his nose in a situation unless his life was in danger or he had been hired to get involved. But there were times, like now, when a fella had to make exceptions. Elmer Dahlquist had gone out of his way to be fair and friendly, something a half-breed rarely ran into. On top of that, Buckhorn loathed ambushers and back shooters.

Another exchange of shots crackled back and forth across the street. Once again the water trough took a hit, and its contents sloshed and slopped over the edges. Many more impacts like that from the buffalo gun and the tank was liable to rupture wide open, Buckhorn knew.

"Mighty good shootin' to be able to hit this big ol' tank from clear across the street. You must've been target practicin' for those seven years," Dahlquist taunted. Then: "Wait a minute. Seven years? And a brother named Varliss . . . Is that you over there, Clyde Byerby?"

"Give the man a great big see-gar!" crowed the shooter in the alley. "Too bad you ain't never gonna get the chance to enjoy it, Dahlquist, 'cause I'm gonna blow apart your smoke puffer like a melon dropped from a church steeple."

Buckhorn could have easily leaned over the balcony and fired down on the ambusher before the man ever knew he was there. Could have killed him with one shot. But the varmint's own words about dropping a melon from on high gave Buckhorn another idea—one he had a hunch Marshal Dahlquist would be far more approving of.

"You blamed fool, Clyde," Dahlquist called. "You couldn't have got out of prison more'n a couple weeks ago. So now you're gonna shoot me and land yourself right back in?"

"They'll never put me in the pen again," Clyde said. "If I can't make it across the border after I've done for you, they'll have to cut me down. But no matter, however it turns out, at least I'll have squared things with you!"

While this exchange was taking place, Buckhorn was silently on the move. A row of brightly painted clay pots holding cactus rose plants sat along the railing of the balcony. Buckhorn hefted the nearest of these and found it to have what he judged to be sufficient weight.

Setting his Colt aside, he picked up the potted cactus and carried it over to the end of the balcony. Held at arm's length, it was almost directly above Clyde Byerby. When the man snugged the buffalo gun to his shoulder again and braced very still, getting ready to trigger another round, Buckhorn released the pot.

He scored a direct hit.

The pot struck the top of the target's head with a

dull *clunk!* and, mashing flat the slouch hat, broke apart like flower petals opening. Clay shards fell away, spilling clumps of dirt and pieces of cactus down over the ambusher's shoulders and back. Byerby went limp, arms falling loosely to his sides, rifle slipping from his grasp, body sagging against the big rain barrel like a pile of soiled laundry.

When Buckhorn was satisfied he had knocked the man cold, he straightened up behind the railing and called across the street to Dahlquist, "War's over, Marshal. You can come claim your prisoner now."

Dahlquist peeked cautiously above the edge of the water trough, and then he, too, stood up. He still held his pistol at the ready. The front of his clothes were soaked and there was a smudge of mud on one cheek. Lifting his chin to gaze up at the hotel balcony, he said, "Is that you, Buckhorn?"

"None other."

Now that the shooting had stopped, lights started appearing in the windows of living quarters over some of the businesses lining the street. Two or three men emerged tentatively from the front of the saloon down in the next block, and Buckhorn thought he could hear a sudden scurry of activity downstairs in the lobby of the hotel.

"What did you do to Byerby?" Dahlquist wanted to know.

"He found out he was allergic to cactus rose plants. You'd better get over here and slap some cuffs on him before he regains consciousness. I'll be down as soon as I get some pants on."

* * *

By the time Buckhorn made it down through the lobby and out to the street—after donning not only his pants but also his boots and gunbelt—quite a crowd had gathered in front of the alley next to the hotel. There was an edge of annoyance in Elmer Dahlquist's normally mild tone as he tried to answer jabbering questions as politely as he could while alternately barking orders in an attempt to keep the scene under control.

When he spotted Buckhorn shouldering his way through the crowd, the marshal's frown fell away. Smiling, he said, "Here's the man of the hour now. Ladies and gentlemen, I give you Joe Buckhorn—not only a hired gun of wide renown, but well on his way to becoming one of the most feared potted plant-slingers in the West."

There was actually a smattering of applause from some of those present, thinking the marshal was truly being serious. Most of the others just looked a bit puzzled.

Unruffled by the good-natured rib, Buckhorn came to stand before the marshal and said, "I may quit carrying a six-gun altogether, soon as I've perfected a brace of holsters so's I can pack a potted plant on each hip."

Dahlquist's expression turned serious.

"Well, you sure got the job done with one tonight," he said for everybody to hear. "And you just may have saved my life in the process. For that I'm mighty grateful."

"Trouble is," Buckhorn said, gesturing to the shredded Stetson Dahlquist had retrieved from the middle of the street and now stood fidgeting with, "I wasn't in time to save that fancy hat of yours."

"This old thing?" Dahlquist said, continuing to worry the Stetson between his hands. "It was a gift from my late wife, just before she passed on. Special ordered from some fancy haberdashery in Dallas." A lingering sadness touched his face for a moment before he realized it, and he quickly covered it with a wry twist of his mouth. "Anybody could see the blamed thing was a mile too big, but I didn't have the heart to hurt her feelings by not wearing it. And after she was gone, well, I just kept on wearing it. Reckon I've got cause to buy one that fits proper now."

"Reckon so," Buckhorn agreed in a somber tone. "The right hat's a serious thing for a man."

CHAPTER 3

Shortly past noon on the following day, Buckhorn rode out of Forbes and headed southwest toward Barkley County and the Danvers ranch that reportedly occupied a large percentage of it.

In an exchange of telegrams earlier that morning, he had gotten the basic details of the job he was being offered, what it would pay, and a sweetener in the form of a promise for a healthy up-front fee that would be waiting for him if he could come right away. Buckhorn had wired back his acceptance of the job and his assurance that he was on his way.

Elmer Dahlquist, wearing a new hat that fit much better but unfortunately did nothing to hide his jug ears, had shown up at the livery stable to see him off.

"Still don't see why you don't wait and start out fresh in the morning," he'd said. "You ain't gonna make it all that far before sundown catches you."

"You said Barkley County is about a day-and-a-half ride," Buckhorn reminded him. "I knock off the half part today, I've got a chance of being there by tomorrow night. You read the sense of urgency in those wires from Danvers. Sounded like time was pretty important."

Dahlquist sighed and said, "Yeah, I guess you're right."

"Besides, speaking of time—yesterday you were pushing for me to make my time here as short as possible. Now you're suggesting I stay extra." Buckhorn smiled. "Make up your doggone mind."

"Havin' somebody save your life changes a fella's outlook considerable."

"Aw, come on," Buckhorn said, starting to feel more than a little uncomfortable from all the praise that had been heaped on him by that point. "I helped you out of a tight, yeah. But there's no way of knowing that I saved your life. Hell, you would have figured out a way to handle that Byerby character."

"Not if he'd've blasted apart that blamed water trough—which he was on the verge of doin' with that big old buffalo gun, and you know it."

"The only thing I know for sure," Buckhorn said, "is that all that shootin' was keeping me from getting a good night's sleep. So I was able to help quiet things down. By the way, what are you gonna do with that varmint?"

"Byerby? Send his ass back to prison if I have any say in the matter," Dahlquist huffed. "I tried to help the blamed fool the first time around. I couldn't keep his brother Varliss from being hanged, but I spoke up at Clyde's trial and he served prison time instead. Look what it got me!"

"More important," Buckhorn said solemnly, "look what it *damn near* got you. Don't go soft and speak up for him no more. Let the ungrateful dog rot behind bars."

"Don't worry. I might be a sentimental old fool sometimes," the marshal assured him, "but never twice over the same thing."

"Once can be enough to get you killed. Best to tighten up all the way around," Buckhorn advised him as he swung into the saddle and pointed his steeldust to the west and some south.

"I'll work on that. Wishin' you luck on your job over in Barkley. You ever come back around these parts, stop by. You'll always be welcome in my town."

Words like those were damn seldom handed out to somebody in Buckhorn's line of work, and a half-breed to boot. Hearing them made the gunman feel strange inside. But then he remembered his own advice.

"See? Right there," he said over his shoulder. "You're too damn sentimental for your own good."

"Don't worry," Dahlquist called after him. "I see you comin', I'll hide all the potted plants."

CHAPTER 4

He held the steeldust to a steady pace throughout the balance of the day, across rolling, treeless plains interrupted occasionally by lonely, flat-topped buttes or sudden, twisting canyons that made Buckhorn think of gouges torn in the earth by a giant, ragged fingernail.

As darkness descended, Buckhorn stopped and made camp near the base of one of the buttes where a row of stubborn pines had taken root. After seeing to his horse's needs, he got a small fire going and boiled a pot of coffee. Along with a cup of the bitter brew, he ate the two beef sandwiches he'd purchased from the hotel restaurant before leaving Forbes.

When he was done eating, he poured himself a second cup of coffee, liberally doctoring this one with sugar. Then he set the pot off the coals and left the fire to fade as he stretched out on his bedroll with the sweetened coffee and willed himself into a relaxed state that would eventually allow sleep to come.

He thought about the job he was headed to take on. It sounded a bit more complex and intriguing than most of the work that had been coming his way of late. Usually he found himself hiring out to serve as a menacing presence on one side (ordinarily the most aggressive one, sometimes the most desperate) in a range war or land grab, or to body-guard some rich individual who'd gained his wealth by ruthless means but then didn't have the guts to face retaliation from those he'd stomped all over to get it.

In the past, Buckhorn hadn't given much thought to the rightness or wrongness of which side he was on, or what those he represented might have done to get to a point where they needed his services. All he cared about was the money. And that included doing whatever it took to earn it.

More recently, however, after a failed, tragic love affair and a brush with death, he'd done some re-evaluating of the kind of man he had become—and didn't particularly like what he saw.

He'd done some things that had almost certainly taken him past the point of redemption, Buckhorn figured. One of the reasons he loathed ambushers and back shooters so much—like that ungrateful Byerby cur back in Forbes—was because, at the bottom of the low things he had done in his past dealings, was to once or twice take part in those kinds of tactics himself.

But that didn't mean he couldn't still make a try at cleaning up his act from here on out. Yet he also had to face the reality that he was really only qualified to do one thing: gun work. So that meant setting his sights on taking jobs where he was on the *right* side of a dispute . . . as best as he could tell. Sometimes that wasn't as clear-cut as a body might figure.

This situation he was heading into down Barkley way, though, seemed straightforward enough. The telegrams from P. Danvers, the man who was hiring him, spoke of being "plagued" by rustlers. What was more, there was mention of Danvers's youngest son having "gone missing." That figured in as the real clincher for Buckhorn and was cemented by the final line of Danvers's last telegram: *My son's life may hang in the balance. Please hurry.*

Feeling good about the *rightness* of what he was about to take on, Buckhorn drifted into as deep and untroubled a sleep as he'd experienced in a long time.

A hot, dry wind blew up early the next morning and nudged Buckhorn and his steeldust along through much of the day. It caked them with dust and grit and parched their throats, but they kept on at the same steady pace as the previous day.

The wind became gustier in the afternoon, interrupted partly by the land becoming more broken, rockier. This was primarily due to the tail end of a low, brownish mountain range reaching down from the north. The buttes and canyons became more frequent, sometimes connected by stony ridges. Clumps of cottonwood, pine, and ash dotted the slopes here and there and they crossed a couple of narrow streams, also running down out of the mountains.

Buckhorn saw the way ahead of them rising on a gradual slope, and he somehow sensed that before too long it was going to drop off into a low valley or bowl where they would find the town of Barkley. He patted the steeldust's neck and muttered, "Not much farther, boy . . . I don't think."

The words were barely past his lips before the first bullet sizzled through the air scant inches from the tip of his nose, close enough so that Buckhorn felt the heat of the passing slug. The delayed *crack!* of a distant rifle came a moment later, and then more bullets were whining all around him.

One of the slugs thudded high into the steeldust's neck, and the stricken beast went down almost instantly. Buckhorn kicked out of his stirrups and rolled free as the horse collapsed. He stayed close enough to use the big body for cover as he skinned his Winchester out of its saddle scabbard and hunkered down to make a fight of it.

More bullets pounded into the horse's carcass.

Buckhorn snatched his canteen from the saddle and put it down where it wouldn't be at risk for getting hit. With water and plenty of ammunition he figured he could hold out until nightfall if he had to. For the time being, he just stayed low and let the bushwhackers blast away while he tried to make a better assessment of his predicament.

He was being fired on by two riflemen. They were concealed on a jagged spine of rock to his north, positioned on either side of the spine's peak about twenty yards apart. The elongated rock formation was the tail of a higher, more solid mass, reaching down and tapering off completely near where Buckhorn had been riding when the first shot cut through the air. In back of and to either side of the intended target was all open space, nothing but gravel and short prairie grass. No back door.

Buckhorn swore under his breath.

The gunsmoke haze from the two shooters, seen by him as he'd pitched from his falling horse, indicated where they were. But that didn't gain him a hell of a lot, not when it failed to reveal the shooters themselves. What's more, in those jagged rocks there looked to be plenty of other places for them to shift to. Firing back at the smoke haze where they had been was likely just a waste of ammo.

Not to mention the fact that—since his position was fixed and they already had it sighted in—any attempt to return fire on his part would mean dangerously exposing himself.

Buckhorn swore again.

The shooting became sporadic and then stopped altogether. Everything turned quiet, except for intermittent gusts of that hot wind, blowing dust and softly rattling grains of sand.

Buckhorn stayed very still. His ambushers were undoubtedly reloading, but what about after that? Was there a chance they might think one or more of their rounds had hit him? That he was lying here wounded . . . or maybe even dead?

In his mind, he replayed his reactions after that first bullet had nearly snipped off the end of his nose. The way he'd grabbed his rifle as the horse went down was an instinctive act that could mean anything or nothing. And plenty more rounds had slammed in after that. When he grabbed the canteen it had been dangling down within easy reach, so there was a good chance that movement had gone unnoticed.

After that, he'd just burrowed in tight against the dead horse and let them blaze away.

True, he'd hit the dirt with every intention of blazing back the first chance he got . . . but he hadn't. Not yet. And now he was glad he hadn't. Because he was beginning to think that his best chance to make it out of this might be for his would-be assassins to think they already had him dead or gravely wounded. That would leave them two choices: they could elect to simply ride off and assume their job was done, or they could come closer to investigate, make certain.

Buckhorn continued to stay very still, except for the way his grip tightened on the Winchester and how his teeth became bared in a wolflike smile. He'd settle for his ambushers making either decision . . .

But having them move in for an up-close look at their handiwork and thus provide him the chance to demonstrate just how alive he still was would definitely suit him better.

CHAPTER 5

"I think he's dead. Don't you figure he must be dead?" Billy Crandall asked as he crouched low in a rocky seam, feeling his legs start to cramp. "Ain't a blamed thing moved down there in a half hour or more. He's *got* to be dead."

"Maybe, maybe not," drawled Red Grainley, also crouched in the jagged rocks a few yards away. "He's half Injun, remember. Those red devils can be mighty sneaky."

"Well, they can't out-sneaky a bullet, can they?" Billy insisted. "I'm pretty sure I hit him at least twice when he went flyin' outta that saddle. He never moved after that."

"We never *saw* him move. There's a difference. He fell outta sight behind the horse, but that don't mean he's dead. He ain't never seen us at all, but that don't make us dead, does it?"

"He ain't ever poked his head up to try and look for us."

"Same difference. We ain't seen him move, he ain't seen us move. Don't necessarily make any of us dead."

"We each pumped over a dozen rounds of lead at him. *There's* the difference. And, like I also said, I'm—"

"I know, I know. You're *pretty sure* you *maybe* hit him a time or two. Well, I didn't see no sign of it."

"You callin' me a liar?" Billy demanded, hackles clearly raised.

"Calm the hell down, kid. Let's fight one fight at a time, okay?" Red said wearily. "I didn't mean to sound like I was doubtin' your word. All I'm sayin' is that I, for one, ain't in no hurry to sashay down there on the *chance* that redskin is dead. That leaves the chance he might still be alive, too, and if we get in a hurry to expose ourselves to him, then it could turn out mighty bad for us."

Nobody said anything more right away. Then, after a few beats, Billy muttered, "I guess you're right. We got to be careful and smart about this. But I'm gettin' awful tired of just squattin' here like a hen on an egg, especially with that hot wind blowin' sand against the side of my face until it's about scraped raw."

"Nerves, kid," Red told him. "If that redskin down there *is* still alive, that's what he's countin' on . . . wearin' down our nerves."

"Well, for my part, I don't mind sayin' he's doin' a damn good job of it."

Buckhorn could hear the men up in the rocks talking, though he could only make out a few inter-mittent words. Enough to know they were growing impatient, and that was good for him.

In slow, careful movements, he dipped his fingers in some of the sticky blood seeping from the steel-dust's wound and smeared it strategically onto himself. If the men came to examine whether or not he was dead, the blood would help give them some initial visual assurance, put them a little more at ease if they moved in for a closer examination . . . at which point Buckhorn was poised to show them the last thing they wanted to see—or ever *would* see in their miserable lives.

On the other hand, if they just came close enough to pump some additional rounds into him to guarantee their work . . . well, then it would turn out differently. But that was the risk he was setting himself up for. All he could do now was let the string play out.

Several more minutes passed, until this time it was Red Grainley who allowed the waiting to get to him.

"Nuts to this. Maybe you're right, kid," he said. "Us just squattin' here like a couple of layin' hens is gettin' us nowhere. Especially if that stinkin' redskin has been layin' down there dead all this time."

"You sayin' we're gonna go make sure?"

"We ain't gonna just ride away and leave it to chance. I won't be no part of playin' it that way."

"No. No, a-course not." But all of a sudden Billy didn't sound quite so confident anymore.

"We'll work our way down slow. Keep our rifles ready and keep a space between us, same as we got now," Red said. "If there's some kind of trickery waitin' for us, we'll be too far apart for him to get us both without one of us havin' the chance to even the score."

Billy licked his lips and nodded.

"Right. Like I said before . . . careful and smart."

They began working their way down the rocky spine, each keeping to their side of the peak, staying several yards apart from one another. Expressions grim, rifles raised and ready, eyes locked on the fallen horse, alert for any sign of movement from the man hidden behind it. The only sounds were the puff of their anxious, labored breathing and the scuff of their boots against the rocks and the gusts of sand-rattling wind.

As Red and Billy reached the point where the rocks began to taper off before spreading out to the flat openness where the horse lay, they moved a little wider apart for a ways. Then, gradually, when they had almost reached the fallen animal, they converged somewhat, coming in at slight angles from either end.

The sprawled man came into the sight of each of them. His body was twisted in a rather awkward way, one shoulder and arm jammed tight—almost *under*— the back of the steeldust. Its rider lay totally still, his bowler hat spilled a few feet from his head, shiny black hair fanned out on the sandy ground. Behind his splayed legs, the Winchester he'd yanked free instinctively now lay partly dusted over by the wind. Bright scarlet blood was streaked across the man's reddish-bronze cheek and splashed thickly over one shoulder.

"I told you I blasted him. I knew I did," said Billy in a kind of hushed awe at his own perceived accomplishment.

"You sure did, kid. You blasted him good."

Now Billy sneered and said, "Shame a good horse had to get killed, too."

At which point a deep, seemingly disembodied voice responded, "Yeah. The horse didn't like it much, either."

As poised and ready as the two riflemen thought they were, the unexpected voice froze them for a moment.

That was all the time Buckhorn needed to roll back from the way he had his gun arm jammed tight against the steeldust and bring into play the Colt he held gripped in his fist.

Swinging his arm according to where their voices had indicated them to be, he fired first on Red, then on Billy. Two .45 rounds pumped into each, all four triggered in the span of scarcely more than a second. All four scored chest hits that sent puffs of dust and spurts of blood erupting outward on impact.

The two ambushers crumpled at the knees and toppled backward, hitting the ground dead without making a sound or coming anywhere close to getting off a shot of their own.

CHAPTER 6

"Nope. Same for this one. I don't recognize him, either."

Thad Tolliver straightened from the stooped-over position he had assumed in order to examine the faces of the two dead men tied facedown over the back of the bay horse. He put both hands to the small of his back, bracing it as he straightened up.

Tolliver was a big man, closing in on fifty, tall and thick through the chest and shoulders, running to a bit more of the same in his gut. He had sand-colored hair, mutton-chop sideburns, and a broad, open face that seemed inclined toward friendliness but looked like it could flush with anger almost as easily. It wasn't a face made for hiding his feelings.

Tolliver aimed that face at Joe Buckhorn now and said, "You have no idea who they are, either. That right?"

"Never saw 'em before in my life, not until they tried to bushwhack me," Buckhorn said. "Just like I told your deputy."

The deputy he referred to, one Harold Scanlon, a

gangling young man with bristly, prematurely white hair and a perpetually earnest expression on his narrow face, shook his head in exasperation.

"I might have seen these jaspers around town a time or two," Scanlon said. "But not very often and not any time recent, I don't think. Either way, I got no idea as to names or where they come from."

"Don't worry about it. Maybe something more will come to you," the sheriff told him.

The three men were talking in a narrow, bare alley behind the sheriff's office in the town of Barkley. Scanlon, who was manning the office when Buckhorn showed up leading the corpse-laden horse, had first sent somebody to fetch the sheriff and then suggested they move around here to the back rather than stay out front on the street. It was full dark. Light pouring out of the office's open back door, aided by a pair of lanterns hung on upright posts, gave the scene a reasonable amount of illumination.

"We can hardly remember, let alone keep track of every cowpoke who drifts in and out of town," Tolliver said. "Especially the ones who don't make themselves memorable by causing any trouble."

"Well this pair sure showed themselves *capable* of making trouble—leastways they tried," Buckhorn pointed out. "You're gonna do some follow-up asking around about them, aren't you?"

Tolliver gave him a look.

"You trying to tell me how to do my job?"

"Not necessarily," Buckhorn said. "But I think I've got the right to take an interest. I couldn't hear everything they said back and forth to each other up in the rocks, but I heard enough to know they were layin' for me in particular—not just anybody who happened along. Their whole purpose was to kill me. If it wasn't robbery or revenge, that means somebody must have sent 'em. Hired 'em. And there's a good chance that anybody who'd pay once and have it fail, might very likely pay for another try. So you can see why I'd be more than a little interested in some background on these two."

Tolliver paused, considered what Buckhorn had said, then replied, "I guess that makes sense. But it also follows that a fella like you could have *hombres* gunnin' for you from just about anywhere, right? I mean, for reasons that have nothing to do with your coming here."

"True enough, as far as it goes," said Buckhorn. "But my sense was that these varmints were *waitin'* for me, not so much comin' *after* me." He shrugged. "But that's just a hunch. All the more reason, though, to see if you can come up with some idea where they're from, how they might fit in."

"You search the bodies for identification or anything?" Tolliver asked.

Buckhorn shook his head.

"Didn't take the time. As it was, roundin' up their horses and getting them loaded onto one had me plenty pressed for makin' sure I could find the town before it got too dark."

The sheriff turned to his deputy and said, "All right, Harold, here's what I want you to do. Take these bodies over to Schmidt, the undertaker. Don't stop and talk to anybody on the way, don't answer no questions, don't speculate on nothing you've heard here, you understand? If Schmidt is still eating supper, tell him I said it can wait. Mine got interrupted, his can, too. You stick around while he's shucking these bodies down. Collect everything he takes off them, from their pockets and so forth. Make note of any tattoos or other marks on either of the dead men. Then bring the whole works, along with their saddlebags, back here. Got all that?"

"Got it, Sheriff."

Tolliver scrunched his face thoughtfully and added, "Come to think on it, if I ain't here when you get back, check over at the Hotel Alamo dining room. Me and Mr. Buckhorn might be over there."

"Got it," Scanlon said again.

The young deputy led the horse out of the alley and disappeared.

Tolliver turned back to Buckhorn, saying, "I got my supper interrupted, like I said. And since you're fresh in off the trail, I figure you haven't eaten in a while yourself. So, if you'd care to join me, we can kill two birds with one stone—you having your supper and me finishing mine. As a bonus, the Hotel Alamo serves some of the best vittles around. What's more, since we're conducting official business, I'll turn the price of the meals in for the county to pick up the tab."

The irony of how much time he was spending lately in the cordial company of law enforcement officials wasn't lost on Buckhorn. While he'd only once ever officially been a wanted man, and that was some years back up in Colorado Territory, his line of work had gained him a certain notoriety over time that naturally caused lawmen in the know to eye him warily whenever he came around. And he did the same in reverse. As a result, he made it a point to try to keep as clear of badge-toters as he could.

But now, right on the heels of the time spent in Forbes with Marshal Dahlquist, here he was rubbing elbows with Sheriff Tolliver as soon as he arrived in Barkley—a lawman who'd not only just seen two dead bodies delivered to his doorstep by Buckhorn, but who also had full knowledge that Buckhorn's whole purpose in coming here was to hire out his gun.

The offer of a good meal was nonetheless inviting, and the reason Buckhorn was inclined toward turning it down had nothing to do with Tolliver's badge. The thing was, since he had arrived in town much later than expected, there was another matter he felt needed tending to first.

"That's a mighty temptin' offer and don't think I'm not grateful, Sheriff," he said to Tolliver. "But I know you're well aware of what brings me to your town and, since I got sort of delayed getting here, I figure I'd better—"

"I'm way ahead of you, Buckhorn," Tolliver cut him off, smiling as he did so. "What you're saying is that, before you do anything else, you feel obligated to check in with Mrs. Danvers and let her know you've arrived, right? You're probably about to ask me for directions to her ranch. Well, I can do better than that. You see, in anticipation of you showing up and her wanting to meet with you as soon as possible, she came into town and is staying right at the Alamo. As a matter of fact, that means we could kill *three* birds with one stone. You and me could have our supper and I could have somebody from the hotel staff send for Mrs. Danvers so that—"

Now it was Buckhorn's turn to do some interrupting.

"Wait a minute. You keep saying 'she' and 'Mrs.' In Forbes, when I agreed to take this job, I was exchanging telegrams with a 'P. Danvers.' I figured it was a man. You saying I'm hiring my gun out to a woman?"

Tolliver's smile widened.

"Oh, yeah. Pamela Danvers—the Widow Danvers, that is—she's a woman all right. One hell of a woman."

CHAPTER 7

One look at Pamela Danvers as she entered the Hotel Alamo dining room made it quickly evident why Sheriff Tolliver had used the words he did to describe her. She was indeed quite a woman, the kind who made an immediate and powerful impact on any man with red blood pumping through his veins.

Buckhorn quickly sensed about her a confident and comfortable awareness of herself, therefore making any added affectations or pretenses totally unnecessary. Simply put, she was strikingly beautiful; she knew it, accepted it, and left everyone else to deal with that fact as they wished.

Average height, lustrous dark hair, the kind of figure that no choice of apparel could keep from revealing to be voluptuous, and flashing, intelligent, challenging eyes of a distinct lavender hue. Faint lines at the corners of those eyes hinted at the maturity of her years—around fifty, Buckhorn judged—yet somehow that only added to her grace and allure.

As she passed through the room toward where the

two men awaited, all eyes—men and women alike—followed her.

When she neared their table, Tolliver and Buckhorn rose.

She smiled and greeted the sheriff simply with, "Thad." Then she extended her right hand and said, "And you must be Mr. Buckhorn. I am Pamela Danvers."

On the infrequent occasions he'd had reason to do so, Buckhorn always found it rather awkward to shake hands with a woman. It felt no less so now, except in this case he discovered the hand he took in his gripped back with surprising firmness and strength.

Tolliver stepped around and held a chair for Mrs. Danvers to seat herself. She then quickly motioned the two of them back into their own chairs.

"I see you both are taking your supper," she said, noting the meals that had just arrived for the two men. "I ate earlier, so please don't let me stop you from enjoying the excellent fare here. Coming from a ranching family, I assure you I've carried on more than one dinner conversation where the words were spoken around mouthfuls of good food."

"I had my supper interrupted," the sheriff tried to explain, "and Buckhorn here, having been on the trail, hadn't eaten at all yet. So, since we weren't sure how long before you'd be coming down, we—"

"It's all right, Thad. I understand. Just go ahead and eat." Then, after looking around, the Danvers woman added, "Although, before we actually get into any serious discussion, I have to wonder out loud is right here in public the best place for us to talk?"

"We can go somewhere else if you insist. But I

figure here is convenient and as good as any," Tolliver answered, having already covered the same ground with Buckhorn. "It isn't very crowded this evening and I asked for this corner table, away from what few other diners there are. If the place starts to fill up, we can always move. But, for now, nobody will overhear anything we have to say. They already know most of it anyway. And anything new that comes out of this, they're likely to find out soon enough."

"Very well. I guess you're right."

When a waitress came over to inquire if she wanted anything, Mrs. Danvers ordered some tea. After the waitress departed, Mrs. Danvers said to Tolliver and Buckhorn, "Once I've had my tea and you gentlemen have finished eating, perhaps you'll join me in an after-dinner drink. I usually have some brandy or wine of an evening, a habit my late husband and I developed and one I've continued since Gus's passing."

"Certainly sounds inviting," Tolliver said. "But I'll have some follow-up matters to take care of on account of those bodies Buckhorn brought in, and then my normal late rounds to do after that. So I'd better pass."

"Mr. Buckhorn?"

"First of all, how about just calling me Buckhorn— or Joe, if you'd rather? Pretty rare for a half-breed to get called 'mister.' As for the drink, I'd be honored to join you. I don't know about brandy, but wine would be good. Saw whiskey get the better of my father—yet another Indian who couldn't handle his firewater—so I tend to give hard liquor in general a pretty wide berth. Some wine or a cold beer now and then is about it."

Pamela Danvers regarded him for a moment before asking, "Do you always do that—work so hard to clarify the Indian heritage in you? Do you think I may not want to hire you because of your bloodline?"

Buckhorn frowned.

"I wasn't aware I was laying it on overly thick about my Indian blood. It just sort of fell into what the conversation was covering. As far as whether or not you'd change your mind about hiring me because I'm a half-breed . . . well, it wouldn't be the first time I've run into something like that. I'd survive. But, since you contacted me on account of my reputation, I figured you already knew that part and didn't have a problem with it."

"And you'd be exactly right," Pamela declared. "As for the rest of it, me apparently reading too much into your words, you'll have to pardon me. But now let us back up to before any of that—What did you say, Thad, about Mr. Bu—er, Joe—bringing in some bodies?"

Tolliver grinned around the forkful of beefsteak he'd just put in his mouth. "I was wondering how long you were going to leave that slide. Probably be best to just let, er, Buckhorn tell the story."

"Unless or until we learn more about the identities of those two skunks," Buckhorn said when Pamela's gaze shifted expectantly to him, "there's not a whole lot to tell. Earlier this afternoon, some miles before I got to town, two men tried to ambush me. Came close enough to kill my horse, as a matter of fact. But after waitin' 'em out for a spell, letting their nerves and impatience get the better of their caution, I was able to turn the tables on them. Didn't have much choice but to bring them in facedown over a saddle."

"Good Lord," Pamela said. "And no one knows who these men are?"

"Were," Tolliver corrected her gently. "But no, nobody recognizes them. Leastways not me, Deputy Scanlon, or Joe. But we're working on trying to scrounge up identities for one or both of 'em."

"And you have no idea *why* anyone would want to ambush you?" Pamela asked Buckhorn.

"Oh, I can think of plenty of folks who'd like to see me ambushed and dead. But none from any time recent and none I'd figure to be in this area. I didn't know I'd be headed this way myself until a couple of days ago."

"How about these troubles of yours somehow being behind the attempt, Pamela?" said Tolliver. "It's certainly no secret about the rustling problem you've been having and your claims that Dan Riley is behind it."

"Nor is it any secret that my claims are accurate, even if the law can't prove them!" Pamela responded quickly and with some heat.

Tolliver sighed patiently and continued, "And word is spreading more and more about Jeff having gone missing and how you decided to hire somebody from the outside to help get to the bottom of things. So it wouldn't be so hard to figure that maybe somebody on the other end—whether it's one person or maybe two, depending on if the rustling and Jeff's disappearance is connected or not—decided not to waste any time getting rid of your hired gun and making you all the more upset and desperate."

"There's just one thing wrong with that," Pamela said, eyes blazing and mouth twisting in a momentarily unflattering way. "I don't get desperate. I get all the more determined to get even and come out on top!"

CHAPTER 8

The waitress reappeared with Pamela's tea, allowing everybody a few moments to calm down and some of the tension to ease.

When the waitress had left, Buckhorn said evenly, "There's a couple more things wrong with the notion of that ambush coming from somebody wanting to stop me from hiring on with Mrs. Danvers. Mostly the same reasons I named as why it likely wasn't somebody from my past. Word might've got around about Mrs. Danvers lookin' to hire *somebody* to come in and lend a hand. But how could they have known it was me? Not to mention when I was due in and which direction I'd be comin' from?"

Tolliver pursed his lips thoughtfully and said, "Those are fair points."

"Unless," Buckhorn offered, "somebody's got a real talkative telegraph operator, either here or back in Forbes. They're the only two who had all the details. And as far as the fella back in Forbes, I don't know how he could have gotten word ahead, strictly on his own, for somebody to be waitin' for me."

Tolliver and Pamela shook their heads in unison.

"Sam Beckel, our operator here, is so tight lipped you couldn't drive a chisel between his flappers with a sledgehammer if he didn't want to open up," said Tolliver. "Believe me, I've tried to get information out of him as a lawman and, without a court order, even I got nowhere."

"I can vouch for Sam, too," Pamela agreed. "Nothing like we're talking about leaked from him." Once again those lavender eyes settled on Buckhorn and regarded him as if with renewed interest. "Let me add, Joe, how encouraged I am that you not only have already proven your prowess with a gun—as evidenced by the way you survived that ambush—but how you are now demonstrating a quick, analytical mind. I think I made an excellent choice in contacting you. I already feel better with you on my side."

Buckhorn actually felt himself flush under the praise. He hoped it didn't show and then thought, wryly, for once the deep copper color of his face might be coming in handy. He replied, "I appreciate the kind words, ma'am. I'll try to keep measuring up to them, for your sake and my own. A man who's *just* good with a gun won't last long if he doesn't have some brains to back it up."

"Recognizin' that," Sheriff Tolliver put in, "is another sign that Pamela has got it right about you, Buckhorn. Lord knows I've seen my share of gunslicks come and go over the years who tried to do all their thinking with their gun hand. Their kind never lasted long, like you said. Not on my account, I don't mean— I never considered myself anywhere near the category of a fast gun. But there usually are other ways to hold your ground if, as you say, you take time to use your head."

"You've done a good job as sheriff here in Barkley, Thad. Everybody knows that," Pamela assured him. "But there's only so much you *can* do with no town marshal and only two deputies to cover both the town and the whole wide county."

Tolliver's eyes remained on Buckhorn.

"With all that said, you must still find yourself wondering why I'm being so cooperative about Pamela hiring an outsider like you to come in and get involved."

"I figure you got your reasons," Buckhorn said. "Mrs. Danvers probably just ran down most of 'em."

Tolliver nodded and said, "Yeah, I guess she did at that. A man has to know his limitations, Buckhorn, and I'm not too proud to admit mine. Just like admitting I'm no faster than average with a gun. You think I wouldn't like to be the one to round up those rustlers who are raisin' hell all through my jurisdiction and seem to be gettin' bolder and bolder with each passin' month?"

"If you'd concentrate on a single *person*, you could wrap up all or most of your problems in one fell swoop," Pamela said rather haughtily.

"Yeah, I know, Pamela. If I believed like you that every foul deed in the territory, short of maybe poison ivy, was the fault of Dan Riley, then things would be a lot simpler. Trouble is, I can't go on just bitterness and a gut feeling like you want me to. I'm hampered by pesky little details like motive and opportunity and proof."

Pamela lifted her teacup and said only "Hmpf!" before taking a sip.

Buckhorn cleared his throat and tried to steer things back in line with where he might fit in.

"You say there are a number of other ranches around besides Mrs. Danvers's?"

"Half a dozen or so, yeah. None near as big as Pamela's Circle D, but they all run fair-size crews. And, in anticipation of your next question, yes they've been hit by rustlers, too. They haven't lost as many head, but that sort of stands to reason since their operations are smaller to begin with."

"With widespread trouble like that," said Buckhorn, "I'm surprised you didn't try callin' in the Texas Rangers."

"Thad did just that," Pamela answered. "We had a ranger show up a while back, a young man by the name of Peck. But he only stayed around for a few days. He got called away to help with some kind of bigger trouble down along the border. We haven't heard from him since, and I, for one, don't miss him a bit."

Tolliver grinned tolerantly.

"Pamela has the same stubborn streak as her late husband. I don't know if it was always just naturally in their blood or if it got added to from the two of 'em being together. But the Danvers way is to handle things as independently as possible."

"You're damned right it is," Pamela said. "It's the Danvers way and it's a good way."

Buckhorn felt a corner of his mouth quirk up slightly. He said, "I guess me bein' a hired hand and therefore on your payroll ain't the same as a ranger."

"Same here," Tolliver joined in, his grin still in place. "You know, me being just the local law dog and all."

"Oh, stop it, you two," Pamela said. "Of course you each represent outside help of a sort. But it's different. I can discuss and reason with you, like we're doing now. That ranger was as cold and secretive as a damp old cave deep in the ground. Not once in the whole time he was here did any of us know what he was doing or thinking. And then suddenly he was gone and left us no better informed than when he got here."

"Yeah, that part's true enough," Tolliver agreed, his grin finally fading. "I understood he had to take off kinda urgent-like, but I'll admit I was more than a little rankled that he didn't take time to give me, the local law, even the bare bones as far as any kind of report on what he'd found."

"From everything I've seen and heard," Buckhorn said, "the rangers don't take a back row to anybody when it comes to showing a streak of independence—except from their own, of course—as far as how they go about handling a situation."

Tolliver grunted.

"That was sure the case with the one who showed up here."

Buckhorn's brows furrowed some as he fixed his gaze on Pamela Danvers.

"I guess that makes it about as good a time as any to mention that my way is usually to run on a sort of loose rein, too, when it comes to most jobs I take. If that's gonna be a problem, I reckon we better settle on some guidelines before we go much farther."

Pamela lowered her cup of tea after taking a sip and said, "I'll naturally want some sort of periodic reports on whatever progress you're making. But, considering the way you've presented yourself so far, I don't see a problem with allowing you, as you say, 'a sort of loose rein.'"

"That's good to hear."

"I guess it would also be a good time to finish makin' it clear where I stand on your involvement, Buckhorn," spoke up Tolliver. "Whatever arrangement you arrive at with Pamela is, of course, between the two of you. From the standpoint of the local law, I'd appreciate my own occasional update on any developments. You handled yourself well by coming directly to my office after your trouble on the trail. You need to follow that example and let me know as soon as possible if any more shooting is necessary."

Buckhorn tipped his head and said, "Fair enough."

"Good," said Pamela. "Now we can proceed with . . ."

She let her words trail off at the sight of Deputy Scanlon entering the dining room and plodding purposefully in their direction.

CHAPTER 9

"Sorry I ain't got more to report, Sheriff," Scanlon stated, a tone of genuine regret ringing in his voice. "But me and Schmidt went all through those two varmints' stuff and came up with next to nothing. They each had a few coins in their pockets, only a couple dollars total. And one of 'em had a deck of playin' cards, the kind that have . . . uh, pardon me for mentionin' this, ma'am . . ." His eyes darted briefly, nervously to Pamela Danvers and then dropped to look at the floor as his cheeks flushed red with embarrassment. "The kind with naughty pictures on the backs. That was about it. Nothing to identify 'em."

"You did your best, Scooter," Tolliver consoled him. "You can't help it if there was nothing there to find."

"What about their saddlebags?" Buckhorn asked. "Did you check them?"

Scanlon nodded.

"Yeah, we did. Wasn't much there, neither. A handful of jerky and a couple badly withered apples in one of 'em; some corn dodgers, a half-used plug of tobacco, and a can of peaches in the other."

Buckhorn cut his gaze to the sheriff and said, "A lack of supplies like that tells me they didn't travel very far to get to the ambush spot and didn't figure on traveling very far after they were done doin' what they came for. I'd say that makes them local. Wouldn't you agree?"

Tolliver frowned thoughtfully.

"A couple local boys that nobody recognizes. That's both puzzling and troubling."

"Not if they were sent by that rat Dan Riley," said Pamela. "You know he's got an outlaw pack gathered around him. He keeps them hidden away like the light-fearing vermin they are, so why should it be a surprise that, when he turns a pair of them loose, nobody recognizes them?"

"But that brings us right back to how Riley, or anybody else we can think of, would know it was me who was on the way and which way I'd be coming," Buckhorn pointed out.

Scanlon said, "Could it be, since they were so low on supplies and all, they were just a couple of saddle tramps after all? Lookin' to ambush anybody who came along for whatever they could steal?"

Tolliver shook his head.

"No, we already covered that. Buckhorn is convinced they came strictly to kill and, from what he overheard when they were talking back and forth up in the rocks, it was him they wanted."

"Why does everyone *refuse* to accept the obvious?" Pamela said somewhat shrilly. "Who else could be behind it but Dan Riley? I don't know how he found out the things he needed to know, but it *had* to be him. Nothing else makes sense."

"I'll go along with that much. There's a lot about this that doesn't make sense," said Tolliver, his mouth pulling into a hard, straight line. "But, damn it, Pamela, I'm not willing to jump to the conclusion that it's the work of Riley just because you *want* it to be."

Eyes blazing once more, Pamela responded, "No, it's becoming more and more apparent you're not willing to jump at anything when it comes to confronting Dan Riley. In fact, if you drag your feet any more, the sheriff's office is liable to end up with a moat around it."

Color rose in the sheriff's cheeks and there was a flash of fire in his eyes, too, as he said, "That is a hell of a thing for you to say to me! It's unfair and untrue and you damn well know it."

Where this heated exchange would have gone next was left unanswered due to another interruption in the form of someone else approaching the table. All eyes shifted as awareness spread of the man walking up behind Deputy Scanlon.

The newcomer was a tall, rawboned *hombre*, well over six feet, with faded blue, seen-it-all-before eyes set deep in a narrow face under a gnarled ledge of brows and above a drooping mustache, both shot with streaks of iron gray. He was clad in range clothes that had seen more than a little wear and bore the dust of recent time on the trail.

But, more than any of that, what drew the focus of those tracking his advance was the star-in-circle badge of a Texas Ranger pinned prominently on the man's shirtfront.

"Pardon the intrusion, folks," said the ranger in a low, even voice as his eyes swept the faces around the table. "I just got into town and a fella down the street said he thought he saw the sheriff head this way." His gaze came back to Tolliver and settled there. "My name's Lyle Menlo. I'm with the Texas Rangers. Don't mean to step on your meal, Sheriff, but when you're done and have a free moment, I'd be obliged to have a few words with you."

Tolliver pushed back from the table and stood up, extending his hand.

"Name's Thad Tolliver, Ranger. Welcome to Barkley. Wish you'd've wired you were coming, I would have been on the lookout and not made you have to hunt me down."

"Don't worry about it," said Menlo, grasping the offered hand.

Tolliver introduced Deputy Scanlon and the two men also shook hands. Then the sheriff added, "And my tablemates are Mrs. Pamela Danvers and Mr. Joe Buckhorn."

Menlo pinched his hat brim to Pamela, pointedly made no move to shake hands with Buckhorn.

"Pleased to meet you, ma'am . . . Buckhorn."

"Actually, as you can see," said Tolliver, gesturing to his empty plate, "you caught me just as I finished eating. Since it appears you've been on the trail a while and probably want to catch a meal for yourself, not to mention making overnight accommodations, the least I can do is spare you the time you need without delay."

"I'd appreciate that," Menlo said. "Perhaps we can go to your office where we can talk in private."

"If you want." The sheriff hesitated. "However, if you're here on the matter of the rustling and some of the other crimes we've had around here lately, as I suspect, then you'd probably be interested to know that Mrs. Danvers has a very direct interest in that. The rustling part, that is. In fact, it was the main topic of the discussion we were having when you showed up. You see, Mrs. Danvers owns the biggest cattle spread in the county and has been hit harder than anyone by the rustlers."

Menlo nodded and said, "Yes, I recognized the Danvers name. The Circle D spread, right?"

"That's correct," said Pamela. "How is it you're familiar with my name and our brand?"

"One of my fellow rangers spent some time hereabouts a while back, didn't he? Young fella named Kirby Peck?"

"That's right."

The old ranger shrugged.

"I read the report he turned in about the troubles you're havin' around here. I've got a copy of his notes, been studyin' 'em." Menlo tapped his shirt pocket, and there was the crinkly sound of folded paper from inside. "That's how I already know quite a few details and associated names when it comes to what's been going on."

"In that case," Tolliver said, "as far as anything learned from observations made by Peck, you've got me at a disadvantage. For whatever reason, young Peck didn't see fit to share a blasted thing with me. It didn't help that he got called away so suddenly and urgently, but still . . ."

"Are you saying you've been sent to take over where Peck left off?" Pamela asked.

"That's the general idea, ma'am."

"Why didn't Peck come back himself?"

Menlo's expression went flat.

"He couldn't, ma'am. That piece of urgent business he got called away on didn't turn out so good for him. He's dead."

Pamela averted her eyes and her expression saddened. She said, "I . . . I never really got to know him. None of us did. But I'm truly sorry to hear about his passing."

"Appreciate you saying so, ma'am. He was a good kid. Well on his way to bein' a fine man. But everybody dies. It was his time."

Tolliver cleared his throat and said to Menlo, "We can go over to my office now, if you're ready."

The old ranger made no reply, merely nodded. He and Tolliver excused themselves and started away. Scanlon plodded after them. After a couple steps, however, Menlo stopped and turned back to face the table where Pamela and Buckhorn still sat.

Menlo's eyes came to rest on Buckhorn.

"Funny thing," he said. "I've read through Peck's notes two or three times now and I don't recall seeing a mention of your name anywhere."

"Not surprising," Buckhorn responded. "I wasn't around back then."

Menlo considered this for a moment. Then he gave another curt nod and turned away again.

CHAPTER 10

Later that night, Joe Buckhorn lay on the bed of his second-floor hotel room, rolling the details of the Danvers job around in his head. It was even more complex than the first impressions he'd gotten from the telegrams exchanged when he was back in Forbes. And that was without the added complication presented by the unexpected arrival of Lyle Menlo, the Texas Ranger.

When Buckhorn had tried to suggest to Pamela Danvers—after Menlo and the local lawmen left the pair of them alone in the hotel dining room—that the ranger's involvement might negate further need of his services, she had refused to listen to any such notion.

As far as the rustling, she'd said, she would welcome Menlo going ahead and trying to bring that to a stop. That was the kind of thing the rangers could get to the bottom of better than almost anybody.

But she was adamant that the matter of her missing son, the details of which had barely been discussed up to that point, was something she still wanted Buckhorn to take the point on.

"Jeff is my youngest. He's twenty-two," she had told him. "He's tall and strong, an excellent horseman, can work cattle with the best—all the things you'd expect for a young man born to a big ranching operation. But there is also a gentle side to him that is far less common. There is sparse evidence of same, I daresay, in his older brother Micah. Nor was Jeff's father, my late husband Gus, known for his compassion and gentle ways . . . although I alone can attest that he *did* have his moments of tenderness."

At the last, Pamela had paused briefly to smile a fleeting, faraway smile before continuing.

"Most others, however, saw only the hard, stern, driven side of Gus. Something he cultivated to a certain extent, often saying that you didn't build a ranch like the Circle D wearing kid gloves."

"Did Jeff make any attempt to try and hide his contrasting nature?" Buckhorn had asked, using a little gentleness of his own to nudge the conversation back on track.

Pamela shook her head.

"No. Not at all. Nor, as far as I know—other than frequent jabs from his brother, who took delight in ribbing Jeff about his gentle nature—did he suffer any consequences for it. In fact, I think most people, even the other ranch hands, genuinely liked Jeff just the way he was."

Buckhorn couldn't help noticing that Pamela's references to Jeff seemed to slip back and forth between present and past tense. The always on-guard part of him wondered if this was merely due to stress or if it was an indicator of something more. But, for the time being, he wasn't ready to let his thoughts go very far down that trail. First, he wanted to hear the rest of what Pamela had to present about how Jeff had gone missing and what she figured Buckhorn could do about it.

Toward that end, he again nudged her along by saying, "Do you think Jeff's gentler ways somehow figures in to him being missing?"

"In a manner of speaking, yes. There's no doubt about it," Pamela had responded flatly. "More accurately, the overall romantic outlook that his gentleness is a part of was the key factor. You see—and this is something I've revealed to no one else save for a very close inner circle—Jeff initially left of his own accord. He ran away to be with a young woman he'd fallen in love with . . . Eve Riley, the daughter of Dan Riley, the thieving, rustling, back-stabbing scoundrel I loathe above any other!"

This revelation had surprised Buckhorn nearly as much as the sight of a Texas Ranger marching into the hotel dining room earlier.

"And you know this how?" he'd asked.

"He left me a note." Pamela had squeezed her eyes shut for a moment and then recited from memory: "*Mother . . . I've gone to be with Eve. We are in love and plan to marry. We know that neither you nor her father will understand and so to avoid the added strain our love would put on an already ugly situation we are going away together. Try not to worry. I will contact you shortly to let you know I am safe. Love . . . Jeff.*"

After opening her eyes again and expelling a breath to regain composure, Pamela had continued, "That was almost two weeks ago. I haven't heard a peep from him since. Three days after he'd been gone was when I asked Thad to circulate word that I was seeking you or someone in your line of work."

"How was he fixed for money? Do you know if he took any with him?"

"Jeff has his own bank account. He made a substantial withdrawal two days before he left. He did not close the account, however; it still has some money left in it."

"That seems like a promising sign."

"I chose to believe so."

"Since he had money, maybe Jeff and the Riley girl got on board a stagecoach or train to put some quick distance between themselves and this area."

"It's possible," Pamela conceded with reluctance.

"How about things from Eve Riley's end? I'm guessing her father wouldn't like the pairing of his daughter with your son any better than you do?"

"Who knows how someone like Dan Riley is likely to feel? On one hand, I can't imagine he would be in favor of it. On the other, knowing how upsetting it would be to me, the evil bastard might relish the idea."

"According to Jeff's note, it doesn't sound like either him or Eve expected approval from her father," Buckhorn had pointed out. "And that's your biggest concern, ain't it? You're thinking that Riley might somehow have got wind of what the two lovebirds were planning and clamped down to stop them from running off. If that's the case, then Jeff possibly got hurt or is maybe just being held captive. That about the size of it?"

Anguish gripping her lovely features, Pamela had said, "It is my deepest fear. I can imagine no other reason why Jeff hasn't contacted me by now. Much as I dread it, being injured or restrained are the only possibilities I can think of."

"How about a ransom note?"

"Nothing. But, more than a money demand, it would be like Dan Riley to find greater satisfaction knowing I was left twisting in the wind, agonizing helplessly with no way of being certain."

"Has anyone at least confronted Riley? Asked him if he's seen anything of Jeff, made some kind of inquiry about his daughter?"

"I wouldn't give the brute the pleasure of seeing my distress firsthand," Pamela had replied, a flash of fire once more blazing in her eyes. "Sheriff Tolliver rode out to Milt Riley's place—that's Dan's brother and where Dan and Eve now live since the passing of Celeste, Dan's late wife and Eve's mother. No one actually sees Dan around there very much, though. The standard story is that he's gone on cattle-buying trips or other business. Everybody knows that's just another way of saying he and his group of hardcases are off on another rustling raid or some other piece of outlawry—like that stage robbery the other day."

Buckhorn recalled Tolliver mentioning a stage-coach robbery in passing. He said, "You figure that was the work of Riley's bunch?"

"None other. And I'm not the only one who thinks that way. It all points toward them expanding in their activities and boldness."

"Yet nobody's ever been able to prove anything by catching them red-handed."

The fire was still in Pamela's eyes when she said, "Not yet. But I'm holding out renewed hope for Ranger Menlo to have some success on that front."

"When Tolliver went out to Milt Riley's place, I take it he got the usual runaround about brother Dan being away on business?"

"Precisely."

"How about the daughter Eve? Was she present?"

"Conveniently, she was traveling with her father on this occasion."

"Any other attempts to try and figure out which way Jeff might've gone or to try and spot any fishy shenanigans around the Riley ranch?" Buckhorn wanted to know.

"My son Micah sent men out on various pretenses to scour the countryside in every direction for some sign of Jeff. Nothing. Also, since we have amongst our crew two men who formerly scouted for the army, Micah assigned them on two or three different nights to watch the Riley ranch. Again, unfortunately, they came back with nothing to report."

Pushing on persistently, Buckhorn had said, "Going back to the possibility that the two runaways might have boarded a stagecoach or train . . . did Tolliver check the passenger lists for any of the lines running out of surrounding towns?"

"Really, Mr. Buckhorn," Pamela had responded with a heavy sigh of annoyance. "I'm beginning to think that you're working nearly as hard to avoid the obvious as I accused Thad of doing. The answers to what happened to my son lie no further than with that devil's spawn, Dan Riley. I insist you concentrate there, at least at the start, if you're going to undertake this job for me."

Buckhorn neither liked nor responded well to ultimatums. But the woman's very clear, very deep anguish touched him. Just as the plaintive tone of the final words in the telegram from her that he'd gotten in Forbes—*"My son's life may hang in the balance"*—had played such a big part in drawing him here to begin with. Plus, he admitted to himself grudgingly, it sounded like she probably had it right in believing that her son's prolonged disappearance was tied in some way to Dan Riley.

So he'd taken her advance payment and agreed to stick with the job, to sleep on it overnight in order to see if he could come up with some fresh plan for finding and exploiting a chink in the shield surrounding Riley.

All of which brought him to the point he was at now . . . alone in his room, not yet having discerned any kind of chink and therefore not yet having any kind of plan, and feeling too restless to settle into sleep.

Not the worst start to a job he'd ever experienced, he told himself, but hardly the most promising, either . . .

CHAPTER 11

Eventually, Buckhorn drifted into a fitful slumber.

As it turned out, that was a good thing. Maybe a lifesaving thing.

He was always a light sleeper, attuned on some instinctive level for the slightest out-of-place sound, quick to react when such triggered his inner alarm. That probably would have kicked in again tonight as it had a number of times in the past.

But on this occasion it wasn't necessary because he happened to be more or less awake between bouts of tossing and pillow-mangling when he heard the scuff of a boot on the bare hallway floor outside his door.

In an instant, he was fully awake and in that same heartbeat of time his .45 was snatched from the bedside nightstand and clamped firmly in his right fist. He raised himself on his left elbow and locked his gaze on the narrow, horizontal sliver of light that leaked in under the door from a lantern out in the hall.

The shape of the straight-backed wooden chair he had hooked under the knob was murky and somewhat grotesque looking. The door was locked, but there was always the chance that some varmint with a confiscated passkey might be prepared for that.

As Buckhorn watched, two smudges of shadow interrupted the bar of light under the door—at a distance apart matching approximately where a man's feet would be planted. A floorboard creaked. Ever so slowly, the knob soundlessly turned partway in one direction until it met resistance, then did the same in the other direction. A floorboard creaked again and the smudges of shadow disappeared as whoever was out there took a step back.

Everything turned very quiet.

Buckhorn held his breath. He could feel the slightly accelerated thump of his heart.

A faint rustling of the curtain over the room's only window—propped open in keeping with Buckhorn's habit of letting in some fresh air whenever he slept indoors—drew his attention. He tried to recall what the front of the Hotel Alamo looked like, what he had seen outside the window when he propped it open earlier. There was no balcony out there like there'd been at the hotel in Forbes, he was sure of that.

But there *was* a slanted, rough-shingled band of roofing that extended out over the boardwalk down at ground level. It wasn't much, but it would be enough for somebody who was sure-footed and sufficiently determined to venture out upon it.

Buckhorn continued to lie very still and listen intently. He didn't sense any further movement from out in the hall or on the strip of roofing outside his window. But his internal alarm bells were nevertheless clanging loudly. He was convinced that whoever had so slyly tried his doorknob in the first place was still on the prowl somewhere close by. Failing at the door, the prowler might be considering a try at coming in through the window. Or, if there was more than one, they might try catching him between them.

Buckhorn slipped silently from the bed. He knelt beside it long enough to fashion the blankets and wadded-up pillow into a long, lumpy shape that, in the heavily shadowed murkiness, would at a quick glance pass for a human form. It was an old trick that had probably failed as often as it worked, but it was worth a try all the same.

Then, scooting on his butt and bare feet, he moved around to the foot of the bed and positioned himself there, back pressed to the wall. This placed him out of direct line with both the door and the window yet provided clear sight of each.

After that, Buckhorn half sat/half squatted and waited with all the patience instilled in him by the Indian blood coursing through his veins.

A quarter hour, maybe slightly less, passed before anything happened. When it did, it came with shattering suddenness.

The twin roar of a double-barreled shotgun started the ball, the simultaneous discharges blasting out a pumpkin-sized pattern all around the doorknob. An eruption of lead and wood slivers and roiling blue gunsmoke exploded into the room. Had it not been for the chair lodged under the knob, the latter would have been torn away and the door would have slammed violently open.

As it was, the knob clung precariously by a twisted bolt or two and the door continued to hang within its frame, though just barely, mostly propped by the chair whose vertical back struts were now reduced to shredded twigs.

While the room was still shivering from the shotgun blast, the outline of a second shooter appeared in the window. The sound of breaking glass announced a pistol barrel knocking out a higher, larger opening through which an arm was thrust with the pistol gripped menacingly at its end. The gun barked three times in rapid succession, the slugs screaming across the room and punching into the lumpy form on the bed.

As the shooter in the window was getting off his third round, Buckhorn began firing back. He, too, triggered his Colt three times—the difference being that each of his slugs hit flesh and bone rather than merely wadded-up bedding. The man in the window emitted a thin yelp, his shape jerking with each impact, before he twisted away and toppled off the narrow strip of roof.

In the meantime, the shotgunner was kicking and beating wildly against the riddled door, attempting to force his way into the room. A thick arm thrust through the opening made by the double-barreled blast, yanking and twisting to remove the remains of the wedged chair.

Buckhorn could have easily emptied his Colt through the already destroyed door and put down this threat as well. In fact, his first inclination was to do just that. But then he remembered all the unanswered questions from the ambush earlier in the day, and he decided that trying to take the shotgunner alive might be a useful thing.

Surging to his feet, he rushed around the end of

the bed and charged the door. As the remaining shreds of the chair were swept away and what was left of the door started to swing inward, Buckhorn led with his shoulder and hurled his full weight and momentum against it, ramming it back against the would-be intruder. An enraged curse bellowed from the man.

The abused door could no longer hold up. With a screech of twisting hinges and several sharp cracks as the slab of flimsy wood broke into pieces, the whole thing gave way and collapsed out into the hall from the force of Buckhorn's charge. The former shotgunner was knocked off balance and fell underneath what was now little more than a pile of rubble. Buckhorn landed on top.

What followed was a frantic, awkward struggle with Buckhorn fighting to maintain his balance atop the broken pieces of door and the man underneath thrashing wildly to try and fling him off. As the thick arm reaching through the hole in the door had indicated, the shotgunner was an oversized specimen, massive through the chest and gut and strong as an ox.

When a slice of broad, ugly face made even uglier by an expression of furious anger was revealed between broken, shifting pieces of the rubble, Buckhorn didn't hesitate to pound down on it with the barrel of his Colt. Blood spurted from the ox's nose, but rather than being stunned by the clubbing, it only served to infuriate him more. Issuing another thunderous roar, the ox shoved straight upward with both powerful arms and at the same time arced his massive body.

Buckhorn was lifted into the air and tossed to one side like a sack of corn shucks. He landed hard and went rolling. The Colt flew from his grasp. He dug in his heels to halt the roll, then scrambled to his feet as fast as he could. The ox was rising, too, shedding broken pieces of wood like a buffalo shivering off shards of winter sleet.

Buckhorn's eyes swept frantically, trying to spot his gun. Failing to see it, he knew that the worst thing he could do was allow the ox to stand up all the way and get his balance set.

Buckhorn launched himself once again straight for the shotgunner. He lowered his head and rammed with as much momentum as he could generate right into the bulging gut. At the same time he threw first a left hook and then a right hook into the big man's ribs.

There was some give to the gut as the top of Buckhorn's head sank into it. He had the satisfaction of hearing a great whoosh of air being expelled outward. But the ox's ribs felt as unyielding as iron rods under Buckhorn's hammering fists. Still, the big man was staggered, the back of his head and shoulders clunking loudly as they were driven into the edge of the door frame.

Buckhorn tried going upstairs with his punches, starting with a hard uppercut aimed at the big man's jutting, whiskered chin. If the blow had landed, it surely would have taken a toll. At the last second, however, the ox jerked his head to one side and Buckhorn's fist only grazed a flabby cheek. The miss pulled Buckhorn off balance and left him open for the ox to hook a thick arm around his middle and once more fling him away with enough force to lift his feet off the ground.

Buckhorn crashed against the back wall of the hallway and barely managed to stay upright when his feet again touched the floor. He was still groping to find his balance when the ox shoved away from the door frame and came at him with fists doubled together in a sweeping roundhouse aimed at tearing his head off. In response, rather than continuing to hold himself upright, Buckhorn dropped into a low crouch, letting the intended blow pass over his head. The ox's doubled fists struck the wall with pulverizing impact, knocking loose great chunks of plaster and chalky dust.

Knowing instinctively that an attempted stomping would come next due to the position he'd placed himself in, Buckhorn pitched forward into a somersault that carried him out to the middle of the hallway. He scrambled once more to his feet as the ox wheeled to face him, lips curled in a menacing, animal-like snarl.

As Buckhorn pushed himself up from the floor, his hand touched the cold steel of an object that could give him a badly needed edge in this desperate confrontation. It wasn't his Colt, which he would have preferred because he knew for certain there were unfired rounds in it, but the double-barreled Greener that had been used to blast apart the hotel room door was almost as good.

The only problem was that he had no way of knowing if it had been reloaded. With only a split second to calculate before the ox charged, Buckhorn decided there hadn't been enough time for that before the big man had begun tearing at the door barehanded. Still, even if as only a club, the Greener felt good as he closed his hands around it.

As expected, the ox came charging at him. The fact he seemed undeterred by the sight of Buckhorn now wielding the Greener was a pretty good indicator the weapon held only spent cartridges. That might have been somewhat more reassuring if the ox wasn't also showing the same indifference toward the threat of the shotgun being used as a club.

But Buckhorn was undeterred, too, when it came to doing exactly that. He got set as the ox rushed, cocking the Greener over his right shoulder, gripping the twin barrels, fiercely intent on making the walnut stock a skull-splitter if he could find the right opening. Taking the ox alive was no longer a chief concern of Buckhorn's—keeping himself that way *was*.

The big man's rush came at surprising speed, crushingly powerful arms reaching out ahead, fingers clawed to rip or ball into smashing fists, a string of curses on his lips. Buckhorn was braced and ready but he knew the collision was going to be terrific.

At the last instant, however, one of the ox's feet slipped on an unstable piece of the rubble, causing his balance and momentum to shift ever so slightly. This was enough to allow Buckhorn's reflexes to gain a tiny slice of an advantage and to react ahead of those reaching arms and hands, slipping up in between. This time when Buckhorn swung an uppercut it wasn't with his fist—it was with the butt of the Greener, driving it devastatingly hard to the point of the ox's chin.

The big man's head snapped back even as the momentum of his lunging body continued to carry him forward. Spit and blood and chips of broken teeth flew from his mouth. His knees buckled and his upper body tipped steadily downward until he finally flopped heavily to the floor.

Even though he'd landed the telling blow, Buckhorn couldn't completely escape the ox's rush. He was knocked to one side and down and the Greener, caught between the victim's now-flailing arms, was wrenched from Buckhorn's grasp.

Buckhorn rolled onto his stomach and again scrambled to get back to his feet. As he did so, his eyes at last fell on the .45 that had been knocked from his grasp what seemed like an eternity ago. He stood up, feeling newly revitalized with the Colt returned to his fist. He also felt relieved by the assumption he would look around and find the ox knocked senseless.

But to his shock and amazement, he saw that wasn't the case. Sprawled in the middle of the hallway, rolled onto one hip and propped on his left elbow, the big man was not only still conscious but appeared ready to continue making a fight of it. Blood streamed from his mouth and nose, and his eyes were decidedly glazed over, but they still held an intense, hateful glare aimed directly at Buckhorn.

What was more, his right hand was reaching inside the front of the vest he wore, clawing frantically to withdraw something—a weapon of some sort, Buckhorn had to figure.

The words coming between gasps for breath, Buckhorn shook his head and said, "Don't try it, man. You don't have a chance." He raised the Colt. "It's over. Whatever you're reaching for, let it drop."

But it became clear beyond any doubt that surrender wasn't in the big man's makeup. As quick as his dazed condition would allow, he jerked from inside the vest a short-barreled revolver that looked like a toy in his giant fist. But it wasn't a toy. If given the chance, its sting would deliver death as certain as any other gun.

Buckhorn was past handing out any more chances to the ox. He said, "You damn fool," and then triggered the Colt's remaining rounds into the man.

CHAPTER 12

Despite the lateness of the hour, the Hotel Alamo and the street out in front of it were swarming with activity.

During the time he'd been locked in battle with the ox, which actually hadn't lasted that long no matter how it seemed, Buckhorn was reasonably sure that anyone within earshot of what was taking place had shown the sense to keep their heads down. After he'd dispatched the big man, an exhausted Buckhorn had dragged himself back to his room where he sat on the edge of the bed and promptly reloaded his Colt.

That done, he placed the gun on the mattress beside him for as long as it took to pull on his britches, boots, and gunbelt. It was while he was doing this that he'd heard the first indications—the scurry of feet, the murmur of voices—of others venturing forth to see what the ruckus was about.

Once he was dressed, Buckhorn had taken his Colt and headed downstairs. He knew the ox was dead but he wasn't sure about the man he'd blasted out of the window. It didn't seem likely the window shooter could have survived the bullets and the fall, but it wasn't a loose end Buckhorn wanted to leave dangling.

Down on the street, a crowd of onlookers was gathering, its makeup consisting mostly of hotel staff and guests along with a handful of patrons drifting down from the saloons in the next block. They all edged back to give Buckhorn plenty of room when he showed up and walked over to examine the sprawled form of the window shooter. Checking him out didn't take a lot of time or effort; he was definitely dead.

Buckhorn was still standing over the fallen man, .45 held at his side, when a lean, square-jawed young fellow wearing a deputy's badge shouldered his way through the ring of onlookers. The newcomer's eyes swept the scene, then came to rest on Buckhorn.

"Just hold it right like you are, mister. Don't move." Out of the corner of his eye, Buckhorn could see the deputy's hand settle on the grips of the six-shooter holstered on his right hip. "Toss that gun. Then step away."

Buckhorn didn't want any more trouble, but neither was he feeling in an especially tolerant mood.

"Best make up your mind, son," he said. "You want me to stand still or do you want me to back away?"

"Just watch your mouth and do as you're told."

Buckhorn stood very still for a long moment. Then he said, "No, I don't believe I'm in the mood to toss my iron. I'll holster it, real slow like. That'll have to do."

A flush spread over the deputy's smooth face, partly anger and partly bewilderment.

"Now see here, mister, you'd better—"

Before he got the rest of it out, a new presence and

a new voice emerged from the growing crowd of gawkers.

"Bud McKeever! What in the world do you think you're doing?" Pamela Danvers demanded, stepping forth clad in a maroon dressing gown, ink black hair spilling loosely around an expression of fierce disapproval. "Stop accosting this man! Can't you see that he's not the one in the wrong here? He only defended himself against an assault on his room."

"How can you be so sure?" McKeever said stubbornly. "Getting to the bottom of all the shooting is what I'm trying—"

The young deputy got interrupted again, this time by the hotel's front desk clerk, a man named Wellfleet.

"Mrs. Danvers is right, Bud. Two men—that one layin' there and another one up in the second-floor hallway—attacked Mr. Buckhorn in his room. I heard the shotgun blast that started the ruckus and, once you look at the way things are laid out, you can see plain enough how it went. Mr. Buckhorn is lucky to be alive."

"Plus," Pamela added stonily, "Buckhorn is an associate of mine. I personally vouch for his behavior."

By now the young deputy was showing signs of getting plenty flustered. When Sheriff Tolliver suddenly appeared, hatless and outer shirt stripped away, suspender straps flopping limply at his sides, the look of relief on McKeever's face was undeniable.

"What in blazes is going on? What happened here?" the sheriff barked irritably.

"There's been a shooting, sir," McKeever answered.

"You think I haven't figured out that much?"

Tolliver jerked his scowl from the deputy and planted it on Buckhorn. "Why am I not surprised to find you in the middle of it? I thought I warned you about more gunplay in my town."

"Reckon you didn't spread your warning wide enough," Buckhorn told him. Then, jerking a thumb to indicate the man lying in the dirt, he added, "Seems like this jasper and another one upstairs didn't get the message."

"The one upstairs dead, too?"

"He sorta insisted on it."

"Any chance you know who they are this time?"

Buckhorn shook his head and said, "Never seen either of 'em before in my life."

Tolliver bared his teeth in a grimace.

"Jesus. The way you go around killing people, seems you could at least go to the trouble of getting to know one of 'em once in a while before you stop their clocks."

"Maybe I'll hand out business cards or put up fliers—asking all no-good skunks to kindly introduce themselves before they commence tryin' to stop *my* clock. How would that be?"

"He's got kind of a mouth on him," McKeever said.

Tolliver cut him a look.

"What about you? You know this dead *hombre*?"

"Can't say I do."

"The one upstairs?"

"Ain't been up there yet," McKeever answered. "I only just got here ahead of you."

"Well, get up there then. Have a look and see if you happen to recognize that one," Tolliver said gruffly. "Get the nosy parkers out of the way while you're at it, and keep that hallway clear until I get there. Crazy fools will be dippin' their damn hankies in the blood for souvenirs if we don't keep 'em back. Where's Harold Scanlon? Anybody seen him?"

"He ain't showed up yet. Not around here," Wellfleet said.

Tolliver raked his scowl over the nearest faces in the crowd until he locked on the round mug of a portly middle-aged man in a white shirt with garters on its sleeves.

"You, Tom Rogan. Go find Scanlon and tell him to get his butt over here. Then go fetch Schmidt, the undertaker. Tell him to bring his wagon, we got some more work for him."

Rogan's head bobbed obligingly as he said, "Sure thing, Sheriff. Right away."

After Rogan had hurried off, Tolliver faced the encircling crowd again and flailed his arms, waving them back.

"Give me some breathing room here, folks! Back up a little. Godamighty, this ain't no doggone carnival show. Have a smidge of respect for the dead, even if he only was an ambushing rat."

With a good deal of grumbling, the crowd receded a few steps.

Only Pamela Danvers stood her ground, even came forward some to say, "You need to calm down, Thad. You're acting awfully distraught."

"And why shouldn't I? I've had four dead men dumped in my lap in less than twenty-four hours. That's hardly grounds for keeping calm, Pamela."

"It doesn't mean you have the right to snap people's heads off or give yourself a stroke on top of it."

While this exchange was going on, Buckhorn finally got around to holstering his .45. When he turned and started to go back inside the hotel, Tolliver was quick to stop him.

"Hold it. Where do you think you're going?"

Buckhorn gestured.

"Back up to my room. What used to be my room, that is, what's left of it. I want to gather up my personal belongings before everybody and his brother starts roaming around up there. Then I'll be needing a different place to finish the night, one without a busted door and window and a bed ventilated by bullet holes."

"As an associate of Mrs. Danvers, we can sure fix you up with that, Mr. Buckhorn," Wellfleet assured him. "And you have my personal apology for all the trouble and inconvenience. That's hardly the normal treatment experienced by guests of the Alamo Hotel."

"And hardly the shape I make a habit of leaving my hotel rooms in," Buckhorn replied. He tipped his head toward the dead man. "But you'll have to take up the matter of damages with either this gent here, or his partner."

Wellfleet's expression seemed uncertain as to whether or not Buckhorn might be making an attempt at wry humor. Either way, he wasn't showing any sign of being amused by the thought of a damaged room.

"You go ahead and tend to your personal effects," the sheriff said to Buckhorn. "If my deputy has any questions about it, have him come to the window and I'll set him straight on it being okay with me."

"Me and him didn't exactly hit it off," Buckhorn pointed out. "I have to bring him to the window, I might be tempted to toss him down so you can tell him a little more direct."

"Haven't you had enough exercise for one day?" Tolliver said.

Buckhorn shrugged.

"Reckon so. But he's a proddy one, and I'm not exactly in a patient mood."

"I'll go ahead of Mr. Buckhorn and make sure Deputy McKeever knows his coming up is okay with you, Sheriff," offered Wellfleet. "Even if no one else has, *I* certainly have seen quite enough belligerence and damage for one night."

"Obliged to you for doing that, Wellfleet," said Tolliver. Then, to Buckhorn: "Go on and collect your stuff, get settled in a different room. But don't get too comfortable. I still need to go over with you the exact details of what happened here."

"I hope you don't intend to interrogate Joe too far into the night," Pamela said. "Especially after what he's been through already. We have plans for him to accompany me out to my ranch first thing in the morning."

"All the more reason to get this wrapped up tonight," Tolliver said. "I can't let him gun down two men and then ride out of town without getting a proper statement on the events of the shooting." He looked at the body lying in the street, grunted, and shook his head. "Especially considering the others directly involved are hardly in any condition to talk about it."

"You'll get your statement, Sheriff. Come around whenever you're ready," Buckhorn told him. Then, grinning wryly, he added, "Try not to keep me waitin' too long, though. As *you* can see, I need to log all the beauty sleep I can get."

CHAPTER 13

Buckhorn was sitting at the writing desk in his new room when the knock came at the door. Scattered on the desktop before him was his disassembled Frontier Colt. Close by, at the corner of the desk, in keeping with Buckhorn's habit never to be caught without quick access to an armed and ready weapon, was a short-barreled Colt Lightning chambered for the same .45 caliber rounds as the Frontier model.

His fist closing on the Lightning, Buckhorn called, "Who's there?"

"It's Sheriff Tolliver. I've got Ranger Menlo with me."

The latter caused a look of mild surprise to register momentarily on Buckhorn's face. Calling, "Just a minute," he rose and walked over to remove the chair wedged under the doorknob. He carried the Lightning down at his side.

"Come ahead on in, Sheriff."

The door opened slowly and the two lawmen entered. Buckhorn stood off center of the doorway until they were all the way inside.

"Don't have a lot of room in here for entertaining visitors," Buckhorn said. "But grab a seat where you can find one and sit down."

"We'll try not to take up too much of your time," said Tolliver as he settled on the edge of the bed.

Menlo took the writing desk chair where Buckhorn had been sitting before their arrival. The old ranger ran his eyes over the gun parts spread out on top of the desk.

"Always a good idea to make time for taking care of the tools of your trade," he remarked.

"A practice I try to follow," agreed Buckhorn. "Especially after I take a fool notion to use my shooter like a hammer for trying to pound knots on the buffalo-headed skull of somebody like that big fella back in the hallway. I was making sure nothing important got bent."

"You shot him three times smack in the face," Tolliver reminded all present. "I'd say that should have been a pretty good indication the weapon's aim was still okay."

"That was only from a couple feet away. Not far enough to really say for sure. Everything looks okay, but when I get outside of town tomorrow, I figure on doing some distance shooting to make certain."

Tolliver smiled wanly and said, "I like the sound of that 'outside of town' part."

"Far as pounding knots on the head of Ace Ringwold," Menlo said, "you ain't wrong in thinking there'd be about as much risk to the object doin' the pounding as to that ornery noggin of his. From what I saw, though, those .45 slugs you favor didn't have no trouble drillin' through."

Buckhorn scowled.

"Wait a minute. You saying you know the identity of that big ox who tried to shotgun me?"

"Bespeaking of the lowlifes my job too often brings me in contact with, yes, that is true," Menlo answered.

"Ain't that something?" said Tolliver. "The ranger here strolled up and was able to recognize both of your attackers quick as a finger snap."

"Although you didn't simplify it any with the way you shot Ringwold in the face," Menlo added. "But given Big Ace's general size and shape and the fact I'd run across him not too long ago, there wasn't much doubt. And seein' as how the one down in the street was Bill Moonfield, Ace's longtime running pard, well, that pretty much clinched it."

"I never heard those names before in my life, just like I never saw the two jackasses packing them around," Buckhorn said. "So that still doesn't explain why the hell they came gunnin' for me . . . unless you know the answer to that, too, Mr. Ranger?"

Menlo pushed out his lips and twisted his mouth around some before replying, "Ain't necessarily crazy about your attitude or the lack of respect you're showin' for this badge of mine. But after what you got put through this evening, reckon you got the right to know what was behind it. And, I gotta admit, anybody who could get caught cold by a couple of hardcases like Ringwold and Moonfield and come out of it with their skin still intact has to be pretty near half-rough. Can't help but admire that in a man."

Buckhorn sat down in the chair he'd been using to jam the door and waited for the old ranger to continue.

"Like I said, I had a run-in with those two varmints not far back. Less than a week ago, in fact, down in a town called Tilted Rock. I knew they was on a half dozen different wanted dodgers. So I slapped the cuffs on and turned 'em over to the local sheriff. Arranged with him to hold 'em in his jail and send out telegrams for those who had claim to come get 'em for trial. I knew the trouble here had been hanging fire for too long, so I didn't want to take time to haul 'em back myself."

Menlo paused for a moment, frowning deeply over the sequence of events he was relating, then went on. "Thinkin' back, I reckon I should have given closer consideration to that Tilted Rock sheriff. I'm figuring now he either was incompetent or crooked. Maybe a bit of both. I got no way of knowing if Ringwold and Moonfield busted their way out or bribed that fool in some way. But it's plain enough they got clear of his jail . . . and headed after me."

"And caught up with you here in Barkley?"

"So it would seem."

Buckhorn leaned forward in his chair.

"If you're leading up to saying they somehow mistook me for you, then they must've suffered from powerful bad eyesight—too bad to have ever trailed you here to begin with."

"I'm suggesting they mistook you for me, it's true," said Menlo confidently. "But not as a result of *visually* mistakin' us for one another."

"What else is there?"

Menlo smiled somewhat smugly.

"They knew I had gotten into town late. They *expected* I would check into a hotel for the night. Since Barkley has only one—the Alamo—they somehow snuck a peek at the guest register. They didn't see my name there but they saw yours, Buckhorn. And since you were the only guest registered this date . . . let's face it, the Alamo's business doesn't exactly seem to be thriving . . . I can only guess they must have figured I signed in under a false name. It's not real common, but it's also not unheard of for a ranger to show up in a trouble spot and work undercover for a while until he's got a firsthand feel for the lay of the land."

It seemed a little farfetched, but Buckhorn was grudgingly able to follow the way Menlo was thinking.

"So the two hardcases looking to settle their score with *you*, set their sights on *my* room because they thought you were the one inside," he said. "But where were you instead?"

Menlo did that twisty thing with his mouth again before answering.

"I guess we all have our personal rituals . . . or habits, you might call them. Like you taking extra care with your guns. One of mine, it happens, is a dislike for feeling bottled up or cornered when I first arrive in a new town. If I spend any length of time and I get a little used to a place, it mostly goes away. At first, though—I reckon partly because I spend so much time out on the trail anyway—I don't like being hemmed in by four strange walls. So, for the first night or two, I usually spread my bedroll on the outskirts somewhere and sack out where I got some openness around me and I don't get that bottled-up feeling."

"And that's where you were tonight?"

Menlo jabbed a thumb.

"Not too far out back of the jailhouse. Close enough to hear the shootin' and the ruckus when it all busted loose. I crawled outta my bedroll and came out into the street with the rest of the folks who were scurrying for a look-see. You can't imagine what a surprise it was when I spotted that first body on the ground and recognized it as Bill Moonfield." He clapped a palm to the back of his neck and gave it a good rubbing. "Even at that, it took a while for me to start piecing it together. But after I heard how there was another fella, a great big one, layin' dead upstairs and how Buckhorn had blasted his way clear of the crossfire they tried to lay on him . . . well, once I made my way inside and got a look at the hotel register, then I had it figured out."

"It's a convoluted tale, nobody can say otherwise to that. But it's the only one that makes any sense, and it's sure as blazes more than we had to begin with," said Sheriff Tolliver. A corner of his mouth lifted wryly. "Maybe we ought to have you go take a look at those two other mystery ambushers who made a try for Buckhorn earlier in the day, Ranger. Might be you could identify them, too."

"I'll pass," Menlo said wearily. "I'm still chapped over Ringwold and Moonfield being on my back trail for a day or two and me not havin' a clue they were there. What's more, what if those ones from earlier turn out to be fugitives also on the run from the rangers for some past deed? Buckhorn here might start to get the notion he's got to go around cleanin' up leftover ranger business. How do you think that'd make me feel?"

Buckhorn arched a brow and said, "Everybody has their cross to bear. How do you think it makes me feel to get mistaken for a Texas Ranger?"

CHAPTER 14

Buckhorn rose early the next morning, ate a quick, simple breakfast of boiled eggs, toast, and coffee, then claimed his horse from the livery stable and rode out of town to conduct some personal business.

The animal he took from the livery was a dappled gray stud he had confiscated from one of the ambushers who'd managed to kill his other horse at the start of yesterday's attempt on his life. Buckhorn had gotten a limited feel for the gray during the trip on into town, after he'd dispatched its previous owner along with his partner. He liked the way the animal handled well enough to strike a bargain with Sheriff Tolliver for its purchase. If anybody came around making a counterclaim on the animal and thereby revealed an association with the *hombre* who'd been riding him before, then Buckhorn would be more than happy to deal with that individual as well.

Ahead of his scheduled ten a.m. meeting with Pamela Danvers, Buckhorn was looking to confirm a couple of things. One, he wanted to do some test-firing with his re-assembled Frontier Colt to make certain—as a backup to his visual inspection—that its action and accuracy were still as true as ever after what he'd put it through last night.

Two, he wanted to see how the gray reacted to gunfire, both from someone on his back as well as in generally close proximity. Somebody in Buckhorn's line of work couldn't afford to leave to chance that his gun might be adversely affected, even in the slightest, or that his horse might bolt from fright if shooting broke out in its presence.

About a mile and a half outside town, Buckhorn came to a broad, shallow valley that seemed a likely spot to conduct the activities he had in mind.

For starters, he shook out the long lasso from his saddle. He secured one end to the horn, the other he tied around the base of a sturdy looking sapling growing on a slope of the canyon. Buckhorn didn't want to find out the hard way that the gray was easily spooked by having it take off unrestrained at the first blast of a cartridge. Since the horse was only just getting used to him, as he was to it, there was no telling how far or to where it might run. And the prospect of losing his saddle and gear on top of possibly having to walk all the way back to town was not an attractive thought.

Buckhorn didn't waste any time getting his first indication of the gray's nerves. As soon as he'd tied the lasso to the sapling, he wheeled sharply, drew the Colt, and fanned four rapid-fire shots toward the low rim of the canyon. The gray's rear end skittered slightly to one side, but otherwise he held his ground nicely.

"Good boy," Buckhorn walked over and told him, accompanying the words with some encouraging pats and strokes of the thick, strong neck. As he did this,

Buckhorn felt the poke of the Colt Lightning where it was thrust in his belt at the small of his back.

Odd as it might sound, this was a comforting discomfort. When burning powder and concentrating on target shooting, a man periodically found himself with nothing but spent cartridges in his shooting iron. For somebody like Buckhorn, getting caught with an empty gun—even in a remote location and even if only momentarily—could be a fatal oversight. For that reason, he never allowed himself to begin a session of target practice without first arming himself with a fully loaded backup never meant to be part of the shooting except in case of emergency.

As he reloaded the Frontier model he had just fired, Buckhorn's eyes scanned the canyon rim where he'd aimed his shots. There had been a row of smallish, jagged rocks up there that were his targets. None of them remained now.

The corners of Buckhorn's mouth quirked in a ghost of a smile. So far, so good. Initial testing showed promise that his gun still shot true and the horse he'd chosen didn't appear skittish.

For the next half hour, Buckhorn went through an established regimen of shooting. Some of it was from a fast draw, some taking a bit more time for accuracy at a distance. Some was with his Winchester rather than the handgun. Some was from a standing position, some lying flat on his stomach, some from horseback.

In all instances, his speed and accuracy were as sharp as ever. Never completely satisfactory to Buckhorn, but nevertheless enough for him to concede he wasn't losing anything.

Through it all, the dappled gray held his ground as

well or better than could have been hoped for. By the end, Buckhorn had become convinced the animal must have been trained as a military mount at some point. In fact, even though he couldn't remember the last time he'd ever bothered naming a horse, he took to calling this one "Sarge" for its impressive, steady reliability.

Once Buckhorn had satisfied himself as far as everything he'd come here to test and it was time to start thinking about heading back, he took a few minutes to just relax. He drank deeply from his canteen, poured a hatful for Sarge to also partake of, then stretched out in the shade of a cluster of young trees while the gray munched on a nearby patch of graze. The sun was a simmering white blob in a cloudless sky, building toward a mighty hot day by the look of it.

Buckhorn's thoughts lingered only briefly on events of the previous day and evening. There were a few dangling strings still left from that tangle, but by and large he was willing to put most of it behind and good riddance. What he was ready to focus on was what lay ahead—the missing Danvers son, Jeff, and what it might take to dig out whatever or whoever was behind his disappearance.

"Hello there, Powder-burner! Can you hold your fire long enough for a stove-up ol' cowpuncher to meander on through?"

Buckhorn glided instantly, smoothly to his feet, hand dropping to rest on the grips of his holstered Colt. Walking toward him, across the flat center of the shallow valley, he saw an elderly gent leading a gleaming black mare hitched to a handsomely outfitted buggy.

The man's right hip appeared permanently jutted outward in an awkward way, and he walked with a pronounced limp that was almost painful to watch. Inasmuch as the buggy seat was empty and the horse seemed to be plodding along just fine, Buckhorn couldn't figure out why the "stove-up" man was making his way on foot—although the act didn't seem to be producing the discomfort it looked like it should and he was actually moving along at a fairly good clip.

As the stranger drew nearer, Buckhorn shifted his gaze and scanned the canyon rim on all sides.

The limping man smiled and said, "Don't worry. I'm not some kind of decoy sent to distract you for a raiding party waitin' to sweep down as soon as you relax your guard."

"All right. Who are you, then?" Buckhorn said rather bluntly.

"Already told you. I'm a stove-up ol' cowpuncher. Name's O'Binion. Miles O'Binion. Mean anything to you?" The old-timer squinted expectantly in conjunction with the question.

Buckhorn studied him a minute longer more before answering. Somewhere between fifty and sixty, average height although he might have stood near six feet if not for the way his bad hip twisted him to one side. Alert, intelligent eyes and an air of wiry strength in spite of his physical limitations. Clad in standard range clothes but with boots that didn't show the usual wear and scuffing, a hogleg holstered butt-forward on his good hip, and a cleanly shaven face that bore the deep seams of having withstood many strong winds and plenty of hard weather . . . though maybe not so much recently.

For all that, neither O'Binion's name nor his appearance meant anything to Buckhorn. He said as much.

O'Binion shrugged and said, "Not altogether surprisin', I guess. Could have gone either way. Just thought she might've mentioned me is all."

"'She'?" Buckhorn echoed. "You thought who might have mentioned you?"

"Why, Mrs. Danvers. The widow, Miss Pamela." O'Binion jutted out his chin and did some extra scrutinizing of his own. "Less'n I miss my guess by a powerful ways, you *are* the gunman she sent for, ain't you? Fella by the name of Duckworth or some such?"

"Buckhorn. Joe Buckhorn."

"Yeah, that's it. I'm plumb terrible at rememberin' names. Don't take no offense by it, I sometimes butcher the handle of folks I've known for twenty years. You can butcher my name right back if it makes you feel better. But most folks just call me 'Obie.'"

"Okay, Obie," Buckhorn said. "Butchered handles aside, how is it you know about me by any name?"

"On account of there ain't a whole lot concernin' Miss Pamela that I *don't* know about, buster. I'm what they've took to callin' the 'handyman' around the Circle D. I was in on it practically from the beginnin' with Gus hisself. Ramrodded the whole shebang for him when things started really takin' off. Then *this* happened"—O'Binion smacked a fist against his deformed hip—"and I had to give up those chores to somebody else. But Gus kept me on, as has his widow since his passin'."

"As their handyman."

"That's the size of it. Meanin' I do a little bit of everything, not too much of nothing. Also meanin' that, among other things—even though Miss Pamela can ride like the wind when she's of a mind to—I generally drive her back and forth between the ranch and town. Which is where I'm headed now, to pick her up and bring her back home. But I guess you already know that, don't you? That she's coming back home this morning, I mean. If you *are* Buckburn, that is."

"Buck*horn*. And yes, I'm aware she's going back to the ranch this morning. I'll be accompanying her, as a matter of fact. I just didn't know she had a buggy coming to pick her up."

Obie pulled a watch on a long chain from his pocket and checked the time.

"Yeah, and I'm gonna be late if I don't get a move-on. Good thing I left plenty early so's it gave me the chance to stop and enjoy the shootin' show you just put on. Whooee! That was something to see."

Buckhorn felt a little funny hearing that. He didn't like going through his routine with somebody watching. More than that, he didn't like anybody watching him when he didn't know they were there. Like Ranger Menlo had said about being unaware he was being trailed on his way to Barkley, it chapped.

"You saw the whole thing?" Buckhorn asked.

"Most of it. I heard you when you was just gettin' started, so I reined up before I came around the corner of that slope back a ways. Crawled down from the buggy and came forward on foot to have a look-see. I held off on account of I figured you might not go ahead with everything if you knew somebody was lookin' on."

"It rankles me that I didn't know you were there."

"Aw, don't get sore about it," Obie told him. "I know the lay of the land around here like the back of my hand. I ought to; I rode it a thousand times. Know it good enough so's back in the day I even managed to dodge an Injun war party or two due to knowin' every hill and gully where I could squirt outta sight. And that ain't no mean feat, let me tell you."

"No, I don't suppose it was."

Obie grinned.

"Heck, in a manner of speakin', I guess I sorta did it again, didn't I? Well, partly anyhow. I mean, seein's how you're only *partly* Injun."

In spite of himself, Buckhorn felt a faint grin tugging at his own mouth. He wasn't one who took to many people, and not very quickly on those rare occasions when he did. But there was something easily likable about this talkative old rascal.

"Gettin' back to the shootin' show itself," Obie went on. "What was that all about, anyway? Just practicin' your draw and accuracy and the like?"

"You got it."

"Tarnation, man. Didn't you get your fill of the real thing yesterday and last night with all the shootin' and ambush-escapin' you went through? I'd reckon any fella who blasted his way outta those scrapes could rightly figure his lead-throwin' skills was in good enough shape not to need any more practice."

"Hold it." Buckhorn frowned. "If you're just now comin' from the ranch, how do you already know about all that stuff?"

Obie chuckled and said, "They got a new saloon gal at the Twilight Palace in town. Mighty pretty little blonde, they tell me. At the ranch, we got a couple young wranglers with terrible urgent humps in their backs who laid eyes on her about the same time. Every night for the past couple weeks, when they oughta be huggin' their bunks for the sake of gettin' some rest to better face the next day's work that's gonna be waitin' for 'em, one or the other gets the notion to slip out and try to gain some ground with the blonde. But when he gets to the Palace, guess what? He finds the other poor hump-back lad either already there with the same notion, or ridin' in right on his tail to make sure there ain't no advantage gained."

"Surprised they haven't shot each other by now," Buckhorn muttered.

"Could come to that," Obie said with a fatalistic shrug. "Or, more likely, they're both gonna keel over from exhaustion due to burnin' the candle at both ends, get their dumb asses fired, then limp off with their tails tucked between their legs to go drown their sorrows at the Palace . . . only to discover that all along the blonde has already been claimed as the personal property of Dandy Don Frake, owner of the joint."

"Seems to be a lot of unrequited love going on around the Circle D," said Buckhorn.

"What's that?" Obie asked sharply.

Buckhorn waved him off.

"Never mind. Going back to the love-struck young wranglers who haven't figured out the score yet, I take it they were still in town last night when the ruckus broke out at the hotel? And they brought back to the ranch that tale, as well as the one about my earlier trouble on the trail?"

"Indeed they did."

"Layered thick with plenty of embellishment, I'll bet."

"That's what I figured when I first listened to the telling. But now I ain't so sure." Obie lifted his eyebrows. "After what I seen out here just a little bit ago, Powder-burner, I'd say you're the real goods. Could be there wasn't the need for much embellishment."

CHAPTER 15

They rode into Barkley together, O'Binion on the buggy, Buckhorn trotting alongside on Sarge. The old-timer jabbered much of the way, until they hit the main road for the final stretch and the dust kicked up by the buggy wheels finally caused him to close his yap for a while.

They'd barely rolled into town, however, when Obie started in again. As they pulled up before the Hotel Alamo, they spotted Pamela Danvers and Sheriff Tolliver through the front window of the dining room, taking a late breakfast together.

"There's another lovesick fool longin' for a heart that will never be his," Obie said. "What was that term you used a while back, Powder-burner—unrequested love or some such?"

"Unrequited," said Buckhorn.

"Yeah, that's the one. Say, how is it that a hired gun and a half-breed to boot—no offense, mind you—knows those kind of big words to fling around?"

Buckhorn, who generally *was* quick to take offense at any remark about his mixed blood, wondered fleetingly why he didn't mind so much when it came from Obie. He simply said, "Did a job for a fella once who read books all the time, worked at improving his mind. Didn't seem like a bad thing to aim at for myself. But whose unrequited love are you babbling about in this case?"

"Why, right there in the window. Ain't you got eyes? Thad Tolliver fell for Miss Pamela as soon as she was, well, available. Probably had feelings for her, like practically every other man in these parts, even before that. Back when she *wasn't* available on account of bein' a married woman. But as soon as that changed, Tolliver pretty quick-like stopped makin' any attempt to hide the way he felt."

"But she doesn't feel the same way about him?"

Obie grunted.

"Nope. She's in love with one man and one man only. Gus Danvers is a mighty hard act to follow, even after bein' dead for nigh on to six years now. Ain't sayin' there's anything wrong with the sheriff, he's a good man, too. He just ain't Gus."

"So Mrs. Danvers will stay in love with a ghost?"

"That's the way I see it."

Buckhorn saw something, too. He saw that Miles O'Binion was also in love with Pamela Danvers. Probably had been for even more years than Tolliver.

Eyeing the oldster shrewdly, Buckhorn said, "It's startin' to become clear to me that you don't miss much of anything that goes on in Barkley County. Mrs. Danvers might've been better off hiring *you* to find her missing son."

O'Binion's expression grew somber.

"You'd be wrong there, Powder-burner. That's one

thing I *don't* know about . . . and I'm kinda worried
over findin' out, no matter who gets to the bottom
of it."

Half an hour later, they were headed right back
out of town again. Once more Buckhorn rode alongside the buggy, only this time the latter held Pamela
Danvers in addition to O'Binion. Her presence, it
soon was evident, did little to quell his steady stream
of jabber. It was equally evident that the two of them
were thoroughly comfortable with each other—
harkening back to Obie's earlier claims about the
longevity and closeness of his relationship with the
Danvers family.

Given the stillness of the day and the fact that Obie
was holding to an easier pace than before, Buckhorn
and Pamela were also able to do some talking. Mostly
he listened as she told of the history of the area, how
she and her husband had come here almost as newly-
weds, their oldest son Micah still an infant, Jeff not yet
born; how they had struggled and sacrificed and
worked their fingers to the bone to get Gus's dream
off the ground. It couldn't have been clearer, from
the look on her face and the tone in her voice whenever she spoke of Gus, how proud she was of him and
how right Obie had been about the strength of her
enduring love for him.

Pamela also spoke of how O'Binion had been their
first hired hand and, she freely acknowledged, what
an important role he played in those early years of
helping to make the dream blossom and start to come
true. Obie interjected frequently and there was no

mistaking his own pride in what the Circle D had grown into and his part in helping that happen.

If Buckhorn had harbored any doubt about the vastness of the Danvers spread, it would have been dispelled by the time and distance they continued to eat up from when Pamela first indicated they had crossed onto Circle D range. And they still hadn't come in sight of the main house and outbuildings.

What they abruptly did come in sight of, though, as they crested another of the rolling, grassy hills that now dominated the terrain, was a group of three horsemen riding at a hard gallop straight toward them.

Buckhorn's reaction was to check Sarge's forward momentum, giving a tug on the reins with his left hand while his right dropped instinctively to thumb the keeper thong off the hammer of his Colt. Experience had taught him that the sight of riders coming fast could be cause for concern.

Catching Buckhorn's movement out of the corner of his eye, Obie clucked softly and said, "Take it easy, Powder-burner. They're friendly."

On the heels of this advisement, he began pulling back on the mare's reins and braking the buggy to a halt. Buckhorn checked his gray the rest of the way and brought him to a halt beside the stopped vehicle.

The riders kept advancing. One of them spurred out ahead of the other two and, as he drew nearer, Buckhorn could see a wide smile spread across his handsome face. Cutting his gaze over to the buggy seat, Buckhorn noted Pamela Danvers's lips widen in a matching smile. He realized then that the approaching lead rider was her oldest son, Micah.

This was confirmed a moment later when, after making a bit of a show out of galloping up close before reining his horse and wheeling it sharply before settling it beside the buggy, the smiling horseman greeted her by saying, "Good morning, Mother."

"Good morning to you, Micah," Pamela responded, still beaming.

"Wouldn't be such a good mornin' if you broke your horse's neck, jerkin' it around like that," grumbled Obie. "On the other hand, you might break your own fool neck, too. That might brighten things considerable."

"Obie! What a terrible thing to say," Pamela chided him.

"Aw, pay him no attention, Mother," Micah Danvers said. "Me and the old goat didn't see each other before he headed out earlier, and he doesn't feel his day is complete until he's had the chance to bitch at me about something."

"And you never fail to provide me plenty to bellyache about," Obie shot back. "By the way, watch your language around your mother."

Ignoring this exchange of barbs that Buckhorn judged must be a common thing, Pamela said, "Did you ride out to escort me the rest of the way in, Micah?"

Micah aimed a new, disarming smile at his mother. He was indeed a handsome rake, Buckhorn had to admit. Thirtyish, trim and solid looking, thick black hair like his mother's, and equally dark eyes rather than her lavender ones. A contribution from his father, evidently, capable of a smoldering gaze that looked like it could twinkle or turn dangerous just as easily as his smile switched on and off.

He was decked out in range clothes, but of much higher quality than standard and augmented by touches like gold piping on the shirt, pearl cuff links, a silver hat band, and more silver trimming on the tooled leather, cross-draw holster that held a gleaming, prominently displayed Peacemaker with pearl grips to match the cuff links. In short, a rich young pup not hesitant about flaunting his prominence and convinced he was tough enough to stand up to anybody who might take issue with it.

That was Buckhorn's read, and he was pretty sure the two of them wouldn't need to spend very much time together to discover that they tended to rub one another the wrong way.

In response to his mother's inquiry, Micah replied, "Well, it's certainly true I was hoping to run into you since I knew Obie had gone in to drive you back home. But, truth to tell, me and Hank and Dave here are mainly on our way into town to meet with the Texas Ranger we heard showed up there yesterday."

"Yes. It's true a ranger arrived in town last evening. It's not the same one as before; this is an older man named Menlo." Pamela's smile was gone now and a look of concern had fallen over her face. "What makes you in such a hurry to meet with him?"

Micah licked his lips and said, "Now I don't want you to work up a big concern over this. It's gonna be taken care of. But I have reason to think we're on the verge of getting hit by another rustling raid. So the ranger's timing as far as showing up here now could hardly be any better. That's what I want to talk to him about."

"What makes you think the rustlers are gettin' ready to hit again soon?" Obie wanted to know.

Micah started to answer but then stopped short. His eyes cut to Buckhorn, then back again.

"Maybe it's best," he said, "if we waited to discuss the details until after I see the ranger. Then we can go over them in private."

It took a moment for Pamela to catch on. When she did, she said, "If you're concerned about speaking freely in front of Joe, you needn't be. You can talk as openly in front of him as you can in front of the men riding with you."

"Hank and Dave are the ones who found what it is I want to talk to the ranger about. Plus, they ride for the Circle D brand and have for some time. Their loyalty is beyond question."

"And I vouch for Mr. Buckhorn. Now answer Obie's question and quit acting ridiculous."

"Ridiculous?" Micah echoed. "I'm not sure I'm the one acting that way, Mother. You know how cautious we've had to be with all the shenanigans going on around here lately." He jabbed a thumb in the direction of Buckhorn. "I don't know this stranger from a fresh-born calf. And neither do you, not really. I say it's only smart for us to—"

"You dare question my judgment?" his mother cut him off. "You heard me say I vouch for Mr. Buckhorn. You know full well that I have been in contact with him via telegram and by that means solicited his involvement in our problems. I asked him to come here, and, in case you haven't figured it out, I have subsequently hired him."

"Yeah, I'm not blind. I can see that much," Micah said. "And word already spread from town last night about your hired gun and how he blasted two men before supper and two more afterward for dessert. Big deal. So he's good with a gun. That don't necessarily make him honorable or trustworthy. You'll remember I was never in favor of you hiring somebody like him in the first place. And now that a Texas Ranger has showed up again, I see the need for him even less. Just a waste of money, if you ask me."

"Nobody did. Leastways not that I heard," said Buckhorn, speaking for the first time.

Micah's eyes narrowed.

"What did you say?"

The two *hombres* who had ridden up with Micah, a pair of individuals roughly the same age as him, exhibiting the lean, leathery appearance of men who'd lived the wrangler life for more than a few years, edged their horses forward a bit and slitted their eyes in the direction of Buckhorn as well.

"I think you heard me okay. But I'll say it again just to make sure you get the full drift," Buckhorn said. "Far as I can tell, your mother neither needed nor asked for your permission to hire me. From my standpoint, you for sure are no part of my arrangement with her. Now, if it makes it easier on everybody—and *if* that's the way your mother wants it—I'll trot off a ways so you can say your piece without worrying about me overhearing. But, from here on out, don't make a habit of trying to get in the way of me doin' my job."

"I don't know who the hell you think you are,

mister," Micah said, an angry flush spreading up his neck and flooding over his face. "But nobody rides onto Circle D land and tells me what I can and can't do."

"Seems to me somebody just did," Obie pointed out.

"You keep out of this, you old goat. Nobody asked for your two bits' worth."

"Just as nobody asked for yours," Pamela reminded her son. "Although you have every right to express your opinion when it comes to the business of running this ranch, you exercised that right some days back and I told you then I intended to go ahead and hire Mr. Buckhorn. That should have been the end of it. To air it again now is rude and uncalled for, and I suggest an apology is in order."

"To him?" Micah said, jerking his head to indicate Buckhorn.

"To everyone, if you wish. Your behavior is rude to all present."

"With the exception of you, Mother, all present can go to hell. The sun will never rise on a day when I apologize to a bunch of hired help, especially not a stinkin' red half—"

Once again Pamela stopped Micah from finishing what he'd been about to say. This time she did so by suddenly rising partway out of her seat and leaning forward, lunging to land a backhanded slap across his mouth. The blow was so quick and unexpected it caused Micah to jerk back and nearly tip from his saddle.

Quicker than the sound of the slap lasted, Buckhorn's Colt leaped to his fist. His arm extended outward at waist level and the gun muzzle swept over Micah and his two pals.

"Everybody just hold easy. Real easy," he said in a low, almost soothing voice.

"Joe!" Pamela said. "There's no need for that."

"Maybe not, maybe so. Just makin' sure," Buckhorn said.

"You'll allow him to hold a gun on me?" Micah wailed to his mother.

"You're the one who brought it on," Buckhorn told him. "I've killed men for taking that tone and calling me a half-breed. I'd like to think I've mellowed some in recent years, but you never can tell. Your mother may have just saved your life."

"Please," Pamela urged. "Holster the gun."

"It won't matter," said Obie. "If you young pups got eyeballs and half a brain between ya, you saw how fast that Colt came into play. He leathers it, don't get no fool notions that'll keep him from showin' you a second time. Not to put words in the Powder-burner's mouth, but I'm pretty sure you can count on that hogleg doin' some squealin' if it gets hauled out again."

Buckhorn gave a curt nod.

"What the old man said."

Then he slipped the Colt back into its holster.

A ripple of ragged tension passed through the scene. Nobody moved or spoke for several beats.

Until Buckhorn started backing Sarge away, saying, "I'll move on out of earshot so's the rest of you can finish talking . . ."

CHAPTER 16

When the Circle D ranch headquarters came into sight, it was every bit as sizable and impressive as Buckhorn had by then reckoned it would be.

The whole works was laid out in a sort of V formation, with the main house—a sprawling, flat-roofed, stone and wood construct—tucked into the inner point of the V, a tree-studded slope rising up on its back side. Angling away from the house, making up the two "legs" of the V, was a row of structures including corrals, various outbuildings, and an elongated bunkhouse. All appeared sturdy looking and in good repair.

On the way in, Buckhorn had gotten glimpses of longhorn cattle clustered among the grassy hills. At present, there were none visible around the headquarters though there were numerous holding pens that could have contained a large quantity. In nearby corrals, however, several dozen horses milled about.

Back on the trail, the discussion between Pamela and her son hadn't lasted for very long after Buckhorn separated himself so they were free to talk. Once finished, Micah and his companions tore off in a cloud of dust for town and Pamela and Obie had rolled on to where Buckhorn waited.

As the handyman reined the buggy up next to him, Buckhorn's eyes met the somewhat troubled gaze of Pamela and he asked, "Do I still have a job with you?"

"Of course," she'd answered promptly enough. "Although I must say that I don't entirely approve of the way you so promptly made your gun a part of that altercation. At the same time, however, I understand that the gun is part of who and what you are, and I also recognize that much of my disapproval stems from protective motherly instincts. I know that Micah can be headstrong and mouthy, even what some might call a bully on occasion. But none of that means I am prepared to see him shot."

"Understandable."

"When he returns home later on and has had a chance to cool down, I will talk to him and calm him down some more. I'm usually able to get him to listen to me, to reason . . . albeit grudgingly at times. I doubt I'll be able to coax out that apology, but I believe he'll come around otherwise. In his own way, he's just as worried about his brother as I am. If you can steer as clear of him as you're able in the meantime, I'd greatly appreciate it."

"I'll do my best," Buckhorn had promised her. "Most likely my search for Jeff will keep me mostly away from the ranch, anyhow."

"I think that would be beneficial. Micah's preoccupation with this perceived new rustling threat will help, too."

For the rest of the trip, they hadn't talked much

more. Buckhorn was naturally curious about whatever it was that had Micah so convinced another rustling raid was imminent, but he didn't push it. If the cattle stealing part of Pamela's problems was going to be handled by Micah and the legal authorities, headed by Ranger Menlo and probably backed by Sheriff Tolliver, then so be it. Buckhorn was going to have his hands full trying to unravel what was behind Jeff Danvers's disappearance and hopefully find a way to get the young man back home safe and sound.

One thing further that *was* decided on the way was overnight accommodations for Buckhorn. At first, Pamela revealed, she was going to invite him to stay in one of the main house's guest bedrooms. But in view of the friction now existing between him and Micah, that hardly seemed like a wise idea. Same for staying in the bunkhouse, inasmuch as veteran wranglers Hank and Dave had been part of the recent confrontation and likely would "poison the well" as far as the attitudes of the other hands toward Buckhorn.

It was Obie who spoke up and solved the problem by suggesting that Buckhorn bunk with him in the separate cabin where he lived in accordance to his long-standing special status with the Danverses. Stifling any mention of his concerns about ever getting any sleep, considering the handyman's near-constant jabbering, Buckhorn had said that would be fine with him. Pamela agreed, and so the matter was settled. The one addendum was her insistence that both Buckhorn and Obie would join her for dinner later, in the main house.

* * *

"Well, here she is. Home sweet home," announced Obie as he ushered Buckhorn into his cabin. "Nothing fancy, but it suits me real fine. Gives me my privacy and more room for me and my bum hip to shuffle around 'thout bumpin' into the other fellas or their gear over in the crowded bunkhouse."

The cabin was a simple but functional layout. A good-sized single room, square in shape, with a kitchen area on one side, a small wooden table and three straight-backed chairs in the middle, a fireplace over against the opposite wall bracketed on one side by a cowhide-covered easy chair and on the other by a sling bed in a sturdy wood frame. Above the bed was a narrow loft accessible by a ladder reaching up from just off the kitchen.

Pointing, Obie said, "I've always got plenty of coffee, jerky, beans, and biscuits over in that cabinet by the stove. Feel free to help yourself for as long as you're here. For breakfast and my midday meal, I usually wander over and see what they're dishin' up in the grub shack on the other side of the bunkhouse. Of an evenin', I usually take my meal here. Except for once in a while—like tonight—when Miss Pamela invites me to the big house."

"Not a bad setup. Not bad at all," Buckhorn said sincerely.

Obie pointed again.

"There's a sleepin' pallet up there in the loft that you're welcome to use. Or, if you don't favor the climb—like I can't manage no more—you can spread your bedroll on the floor wherever it suits you, or stretch out in my big ol' chair if you want. I promise you'll find that mighty comfortable. Many's the time I doze off in it and sleep the night through."

"If it's all the same to you, that chair looks pretty inviting," said Buckhorn. It wasn't that the climb up to the loft bothered him; it was the confinement up there, the risk of getting trapped in that small a space, that he didn't like the thought of.

"Done and done," proclaimed Obie. "Go ahead and give 'er a try, see what you think."

Buckhorn took him up on the offer and found the chair indeed very roomy and comfortable. So much so, in fact, that he hated to crawl back out and join Obie at the table where a cup of thick black coffee was placed before him.

"Need any fixin's?" Obie wanted to know. "Got no cream, but I do have some sugar."

"This is fine."

"Yup. That's the way I like it, too. Straight and strong."

They each blew on their cupfuls of the strong, black brew, cooling the surface enough for cautious sips.

After he'd slurped down a couple swallows, Obie eyed Buckhorn and said, "You're a quiet cuss, ain't you, Powder-burner? Patient."

Buckhorn shrugged and said, "When it suits me."

"Uh-huh. But you ain't foolin' me." Obie took another loud slurp. "You're anxious to know what Micah saw that's got him so primed about another rustlin' raid comin' soon, ain't you?"

Buckhorn started to protest but then changed his mind. He didn't feel a pressing need to know what Micah was up to, yet he nevertheless was somewhat curious. Why talk himself out of learning something that might prove unexpectedly useful? So he said, "Well, since it was sorta dangled under my nose, then yanked away, yeah, I can't deny wondering about it some."

"I figured as much. I know your main interest now is supposed to be finding young Jeff, but you're probably thinkin' that the rustlin' that's been goin' on—especially if Dan Riley is the one behind it like Miss Pamela is so dead set on believin'—just might be tied in. Right?"

"Seems worth considering," Buckhorn said. "I don't know about the rustling part, but it's hard to leave out Riley since it's his daughter Jeff supposedly ran off with."

"One way or other, it's all tangled together."

"You sound awfully sure about that."

"I don't like coincidences."

"Me neither. But back up a minute. You said *if* Dan Riley is behind the rustling like Miss Pamela is so dead set on believing. Sounds like Riley's involvement is something you're not so sure of."

"You don't miss much, do you?"

"Tell me I'm wrong."

Obie drank some more of his coffee.

"I don't think you've heard the full story on Dan Riley. So let's back up a little farther yet and I'll fill you in. At one time, you see, Dan was the ramrod for the Circle D. I first hired him, as a matter of fact, when I held that position. He was a top hand right from the get-go. The Circle D was growin' steady all that time and Dan Riley fast became my right-hand man. When that ol' bull got me cornered in a holdin' pen and damn near killed me, it was Dan who finally drove him off. I got left with *this*"—Obie savagely whacked his right fist against his damaged hip—"but I never would've come out of it alive if not for Dan."

The old handyman paused to smile thinly before adding, "Sometimes, when I'm of a mood to feel sorry for myself, I ain't so sure whether he did me any favors or not . . . but that's for me to deal with."

"Pain and setbacks can seem like they get laid on awful thick at times," Buckhorn responded in an understanding tone. "But, generally speaking, coming out alive is usually for the best."

"Anyway," Obie continued with a faint sigh, "after I got took out of commission, Dan Riley was the logical choice to take over ramroddin' the outfit. He took right to it and did a helluva fine job. Him and Boss Gus really hit it off, too. I always stayed close to both of 'em, but the way the two of 'em carried on together actually kinda made me jealous.

"Dan got married to a gal from town. Celeste, her name was. Wasn't long before daughter Eve came along. Miss Pamela and Boss Gus were her godparents. After the baby, though, Celeste fell to poor health. She never lived to see her daughter's second birthday. Mighty sad times around here after that. We all got Dan through it. Miss Pamela and her housekeeper-cook Helga—she's still aboard; you'll meet her at dinner later on—helped with the raisin' of little Eve. She grew up a rough and tumble tomboy, but on the outside as pretty as a palomino colt."

"So she was raised with the Danvers boys?" Buckhorn asked.

"In a manner of speakin'. She was quite a bit

younger than them, remember. They mostly didn't want nothing to do with her back then."

"From the sound of it, though, I guess that changed. Leastways where Jeff is concerned."

"Yeah, that's what things do. Change." An abrupt gloominess seemed to have crept into Obie's voice. A moment later it became evident why, where his thoughts had gone. "One of the biggest changes we all had to go through . . . one of the worst . . . was when Boss Gus took sick and died." He hung his head over his cup of coffee and shook it slowly back and forth. "Never been through a rougher time than that."

Not wanting to let the oldster get too mired in grief, Buckhorn prodded him a bit by saying, "And then, afterwards, is when Dan Riley turned bad?"

"Not right away. But in time, yeah. It was almost as hard to believe as it was to accept that Boss Gus was gone for permanent. But too many signs pointed that way. Missin' cattle, feeble excuses, descriptions that fit Dan to a tee for a fella offerin' to sell beef on the sly, money traceable to Dan that he shouldn't't've oughta had. Too many things piled up. Miss Pamela had no choice but to confront him. When he couldn't—or wouldn't—come up with any reasonable explanations, there wasn't nothing left for her to do but fire him."

"Yet," Buckhorn said, "you continue to have a hard time buying Riley as a rustler."

Obie lifted his face. There was still sadness pooling in his eyes, but there was also a hard edge of determination showing through.

"You spend enough time with a man, you go through all kinds of trouble and challenges with him—I'm talkin' wranglin' herd after herd of ornery cattle, sloggin' through seasons of the worst weather conditions you can think of, goin' gun to gun against for-real rustlers, even a skirmish or two with renegade Injuns—you make it through all that, you get a pretty doggone good feel for the fella who went through it alongside you. What he's made of, where he'll draw the line on what he will or won't do."

"And your feeling is that Riley wouldn't turn bad, wouldn't start rustlin' and cheatin' the Circle D brand."

"In spite of all the signs pointin' his way, I've never been able to swallow it all the way down."

"What about the other kinds of crime? Stagecoach robberies or such?"

"It'd be more of a possibility than turnin' on the Circle D. But not by much."

"More than any other critter, human beings can fool you. Take a turn for the worse plumb out of the blue. For reasons nobody else can ever figure."

Obie shook his head stubbornly. "For one thing, Dan never had no cause to. He had it made right like things was. Plenty of folks around—busybodies and nosy parkers partly, but others who weren't generally given to that sort of thing—speculated that Dan and Miss Pamela, seein's how they'd always been close-like and then had gone on to suffer the loss of their spouses, might even end up together some day. Man and wife."

"You?"

Obie shrugged and replied, "Never saw no outward sign of it. But things like that happen. They'd've made a right handsome couple. In a way, it would've almost seemed like a natural thing."

"Only it didn't go that way," Buckhorn summed up. "In fact, it eventually swung about as far away from anything like that as it could get."

"That's for sure. And all the while the rustlin' has continued and Miss Pamela's feelings toward Dan Riley have turned more and more bitter until seein' him caught and punished is almost like a . . . a . . . what's the word I want?"

"Obsession?"

"That's the one! Even though no kind of hard proof has ever turned up, Miss Pamela is so convinced, so obsessed, that it's almost like she'll never be able to rest in her own grave until she first sees Dan swing by his neck for betrayin' the Circle D and her and Boss Gus's memory like she's bound and determined he's done."

Buckhorn said, "Which brings us to the here and now, with her not only convinced Riley is behind the rustling but also insisting he might be somehow involved in Jeff's prolonged disappearance."

Obie got up and went to fetch the coffeepot. Bringing it over and refilling their cups, he said, "She's a hardheaded gal once she gets her mind made up. Maybe this new rustlin' raid that Micah thinks he's got sniffed out, especially if he gets the ranger's cooperation, will settle a thing or two."

"Maybe," Buckhorn allowed. "This thing that's got Micah so worked up . . . you were workin' your way around to tell me about it, remember?"

CHAPTER 17

Even with the sun in its afternoon descent and the ground he was covering cast in mottled shade, the day remained hot. Buckhorn passed the back of one hand across his forehead, wiping away sweat.

He was about ten miles from the ranch headquarters, making his way on foot along the crown of a weedy, tree-studded hogback. Sarge was tied downslope a ways back, grazing contentedly.

Obie had provided good directions and Buckhorn had found his way to this spot with minimal trouble. To the south and west of the hogback lay a large, flat meadow, oval in shape, of fresh spring grass. On the back side of the hogback, to the north, the ground quickly turned rocky and broken.

Under the direction of Micah Danvers, who was ramrodding the Circle D operation these days, the original plan had been to move a good-sized herd of longhorns into the lush meadow this very afternoon. The meadow was part of a piece of land the Circle D had acquired from a neighbor the previous winter, and Micah and his crew had been looking forward to grazing a herd of prime beef there the first chance they got.

Scouting ahead of the much-anticipated move, however, looking for any sign of cougars or wolves that might pose a threat to the herd, the two wranglers Hank and Dave had instead spotted some suspicious horse tracks up on the hogback. Upon reporting these to Micah, he'd ridden back with them to have a look for himself.

What was suspicious about the tracks was the fact that they were fresh and that no Circle D riders had been sent this way in weeks. And when they led away from the hogback, they disappeared into the broken land to the north, never showing any inclination of heading off east toward ranch headquarters.

What all of this had immediately signaled to Micah and his riders was that word had gotten out somehow about a herd being brought to this somewhat isolated graze, and as a result, some eager would-be rustlers had paid a visit to look the layout over and plan their raid. Subsequently, moving the herd in this afternoon was temporarily delayed and instead Micah and his boys headed for town to see if they could interest Ranger Menlo and/or Sheriff Tolliver in helping to set a trap.

When Obie had related these details to Buckhorn, the gunman, for some reason he couldn't fully explain, had felt a strong impulse to go check out the spot for himself. There were hours to kill before dinner, and Buckhorn had already been feeling restless, so he didn't put much effort into fighting the impulse.

The terrain was too rough for a buggy and Obie couldn't sit a horse with his bad hip, so it wasn't feasible for him to come along. But since he knew practically every inch of Circle D property, the directions he scribbled down were almost as precise as if he were right there pointing the way.

"Hard to believe Micah would be showin' back up out there from town in the time it'll take you to pay a visit from here. But in case he does," the old man had cautioned, "you make yourself scarce, you hear? I know you ain't afraid of him and I know skitterin' wide of trouble ain't exactly your way. But as a favor to me and for Miss Pamela's sake, don't push it when it comes to him if you can help it. Okay?"

"If it's that important to you, Obie, then I'll do my best not to," Buckhorn had said. "But is there something about Micah you're not telling me?"

"Besides the fact he's a petty, sneaky, snake-mean little bastard I wouldn't trust as far as I could throw that cookstove over there, you mean?" Obie's eyes swam with a mixture of remorse, anger, and maybe a hint of fear. "You don't know how much it pains me to say that about the firstborn of Boss Gus. But it's true. I fought admittin' it for a long, long time . . . until there was no gettin' around it anymore."

"Pamela said Micah lacks gentleness. That he's stern and driven like his father."

"Paugh! Micah's nothing like his father. Gus was stern and driven, true enough. Some called him ruthless, but that wasn't really accurate. He was always pushin' fierce-like to achieve the goal of makin' the

Circle D a success and couldn't abide anybody who wasn't willin' to work as hard as he did. Miss Pamela became a lot like him after Gus was gone, bent on makin' sure none of what he broke his hump for did any back-slidin'. But Micah ain't like either of his parents. He *is* ruthless. And he only cares about keepin' the Circle D big and successful for the sake of the personal power it gives him."

"Yet his mother can't see it."

"She's at that not-wantin'-to-admit-it place I was stuck in for so long."

"If she ever does realize it, it'll be a crushing blow."

"You think I don't know that? And if you ain't able to bring Jeff back into the picture, it'll hit her harder yet."

Buckhorn had frowned deeply at this.

"Jesus, old man, you don't hold back when it comes to heaping a heavy load on a fella, do you?"

"They say the Good Lord don't pile on more than a body can carry."

"Maybe not. I'm afraid me and the Good Lord haven't paid a whole lot of attention to one another for quite a spell now."

"Sorry to hear that, Powder-burner," was Obie's solemn response. Then he added, "But here's one more thing I want you to keep in mind about Micah. He ain't got nowhere near your skill with a gun. But he ain't no slouch, neither. And he'll always have two or three of his boot-lickin' *compadres* close by. He'll try to force your hand if you give him an opening, but he'll only do it if he figures he's got the deck stacked against you. Remember that."

* * *

The formative years spent on the reservation of his father's tribe, in spite of the misery and mistreatment he had to endure due to his mixed blood, had at least taught Buckhorn skills he'd honed and found use for long after he struck out on his own. Tracking was one of these.

As it turned out, however, finding and following the horse prints he'd come to investigate this afternoon hardly required any special knack. They were plain as could be.

The grass covering the crest of the hogback, unlike the lush growth down in the meadow, was short and coarse due to almost always being in the shade. And the ground sprouting it had enough clay content to take and hold very clear-edged prints. By separating from Sarge and proceeding on foot, Buckhorn was able to walk carefully enough and lightly enough to avoid adding any spoor of his own.

He found the tracks of four horses, just as described, ascending the elongated hump of ground from the north and retreating back the same way. Buckhorn could tell that the animals had stood mostly in one place for a time, probably while their riders gave the layout of the meadow a good looking over. They also moved back and forth for a few dozen yards in either direction, likely taking brief looks from other vantage points, before turning back the way they'd come.

Buckhorn also spotted where the Circle D men had ridden up for their own look-see—first two sets of tracks that would have been Hank and Dave; then joined by a third when they returned with Micah. They'd trampled over some of the initial tracks at first, until they took note of them and then got more careful. After that, although they never went to the trouble of dismounting and finishing their examination on foot, like Buckhorn, they nevertheless showed reasonable caution so as not to disturb the ground unnecessarily.

Once he'd given the hogback a good looking over, Buckhorn returned to where he'd left Sarge. He swung up into the saddle and rode the gray in a wide loop all around the perimeter of the meadow, looking for any additional sign that might be of interest.

He spotted nothing. Having completed the loop and finding himself once again on the back side of the hogback, where the tracks of the original riders came and went out of the broken land to the north, Buckhorn toyed with the idea of seeing how far he could follow them in that direction.

Hank and Dave had reported that they'd lost the sign fairly quickly in the rocks. Buckhorn was willing to bet he could stick with them a lot farther than that, but in the end there really was no point. He'd had no clear purpose for coming here in the first place, so it wasn't surprising he didn't feel like he'd accomplished much as a result, other than confirming the story Micah and his wranglers had told about finding unaccounted-for tracks at the spot where they were planning on pasturing a herd. And, given the history of cattle stealing already going on, the conclusion that these could be an indicator of more rustling being planned seemed hard to argue against.

As he pondered these things, Buckhorn came to another conclusion that he had trouble arguing against, even though it soured him to admit it. He *had* had a reason for coming out here after all, he realized. He came because he was looking for a way to kill some time rather than face Pamela Danvers's other problem, the one he'd agreed to focus on exclusively . . . the disappearance of her son Jeff.

While the tracks on the hogback were quite clear, that was hardly the case for any tracks leading toward Jeff. What happened to him after he took off on his "honeymoon"? Why hadn't he made any further contact with his mother? Was he still with Eve Riley, and if so, where might the two of them be?

Answers to these questions seemed as elusive as wisps of smoke caught on the wind, and Buckhorn felt at a loss where to begin, how to start snatching smoke back out of the air.

But you took the woman's money, he reminded himself grimly. *And her worry about her son's life "hanging in the balance" was a big part of what drew you here to begin with, made you feel like this might be a chance to cut yourself a slice of that redemption you claim to care about these days. You damn well can't run and hide from it now.*

A moment after these thoughts ran through his head, something turned up that he *did* have to duck and hide from—if he wanted to stay alive, that was. A rifle shot boomed from the northwest end of the hogback, where the trees grew the thickest and the hump of ground itself was rockier and more rugged. The wind-rip of the bullet cutting through the air was all too familiar and all too close.

Buckhorn pitched himself from the saddle and

went into a rolling scramble for cover. As he did so, he shouted "Sarge! Git!" Even if it meant giving up access to his own Winchester, he didn't want to risk having another horse shot out from under him, especially the gray he had so quickly grown fond of. At his command, Sarge bolted obediently away and was soon obscured by some nearby trees.

More bullets poured down, slicing the air and tearing into the ground, chasing Buckhorn as he clawed in behind the protection of an upthrust of ragged rocks. He bellied flat there, safe as long as he hugged close to the ground. But the bullets kept coming, whacking and ricocheting directly above his head now, spitting dirt and chunks of rock down on his back and shoulders.

Buckhorn had his Colt drawn and gripped securely in his fist. He swore under his breath. He was pinned down again, a predicament similar to the one he'd been in yesterday back on the trail. *Had it only been yesterday?* Damn, he was getting sick of people shooting at him!

Only this time he wasn't pinned quite as tight as before, when he'd been caught in the wide open. Here, with reasonable risk, he had the options of shifting to alternative cover or even making an escape . . . except for the fact that running wasn't exactly his style.

It was a single rifleman doing all the lead throwing. So far. That didn't mean there might not be others, though, maneuvering to make a try for him from a better angle.

But, for the time being, all Buckhorn had to focus

on was the one shooter. He didn't have him pinpointed beyond a puff of gunsmoke he'd caught a glimpse of as he sprang from the saddle, but at least that was something—enough for him to show the ambushing skunk that he intended to make a fight of it.

Reaching around the slab of rock he was ducked behind, making no attempt at careful aim, Buckhorn triggered three rapid-fire rounds toward where he'd seen the gunsmoke. Then he dropped back again and immediately began replacing the spent shells.

The burst of return fire quieted the rifleman briefly, but then he sent two more rounds pounding down. Okay, Buckhorn thought, the shooter liked to pour it on but seemed quick to let up when the lead was sailing back his way. Not necessarily unwise, but something Buckhorn might nevertheless be able to use to his advantage.

He twisted part way around and looked behind him. About half a dozen yards from where he lay there was a thick growth of underbrush with a couple of pine trees and a stout cottonwood butted up close on the back side. If he could make it there, he would not only gain fresh cover but he'd have some room to move and maneuver. The rifleman would no longer know exactly where he was.

Another slug tore into his rocky shield and spat dust and gravel down onto him. Buckhorn muttered another curse. This was getting old fast. It was time to make some changes.

Once again reaching suddenly around the end of the rock slab, Buckhorn snapped off another trio of shots, loosely aimed at the thickened layer of gunsmoke hanging in the air. Then, pivoting on his rump, while the ambusher was hopefully ducked low in response to the bullets sizzling his way, he got his feet under him and lunged in the direction of the underbrush and trees. A diving roll took him to where he wanted to be—just as the rifleman, responding quicker than Buckhorn had anticipated, sent a pair of slugs ripping and slapping through the bushes just above his head.

Buckhorn rolled again and then squirmed in behind the cottonwood.

While his hands reloaded the Colt as unerringly as if they had eyes of their own, Buckhorn scanned the situation from his new vantage point. He had effectively evened the odds. In fact, given his experience and skill at gunplay, he most likely had tipped things in his favor.

The rifle that had so busily been pumping lead at his pinned-down position had now abruptly gone silent, and Buckhorn couldn't help suspecting that the shooter might be coming to the same conclusion. The main thrust of an ambush was meant to be one-sided, to strike and kill suddenly from concealment without ever giving the target much of a chance.

When that failed and the situation was turned into the kind of confrontation the ambusher didn't have the guts to stage in the first place, then the whole thing was knocked out of kilter. The ambusher was left with the choice of sticking it out and attempting to finish the job or giving up and fleeing with the intent of perhaps trying again another time.

That might be the case here, Buckhorn thought.

But, then again, it might not. Until he was sure, he had to take the precaution that the rifleman was still hanging around, waiting for another opening, determined to complete what he'd set out to do.

Whichever way it went, Buckhorn was certainly not of a mind to just sit and wait to find out. He could be extremely patient when he had to. But given the choice—which he now had since he'd escaped from being pinned down—he'd far rather take the fight to an opponent than wait for it to be carried to him.

He began to move. Silently, smoothly, making his way from one clump of cover to the next, he worked his way along the eastern slope of the hogback. Every dozen or so yards he paused to listen intently and to sweep his gaze in a wide arc out ahead, alert for any sign of the ambusher also being on the move.

As a second choice, Buckhorn would have welcomed the sight of Sarge and his Winchester in the sheath strapped to the big gray's saddle. The Colt was plenty reliable, but the rifle would provide some added punch and range, especially if the ambusher tried to make a break for it.

Several minutes ticked by. Despite being swallowed by shade most of the time, Buckhorn was sweating freely. A steady trickle of moisture wormed down the back of his neck and formed a kind of gritty paste under his collar where the dust and rock fragments had spilled down earlier from the bullet strikes just above his head. He rolled his shoulders in discomfort and muttered another curse directed at the rifleman who'd sent those bullets his way.

Up ahead, the gunsmoke haze marking the spot

the rifleman was firing from had mostly dispersed now. But the spot remained a focal point for Buckhorn, even though the ambusher had in all likelihood shifted away from there. Nevertheless, Buckhorn continued to edge toward it.

Until he heard the abrupt whicker of a horse responding to spurs being roughly put to it, followed by the hammering thud of hoofbeats breaking into motion and rapidly picking up speed.

Buckhorn tensed, but only for a moment. He straightened partially out of his crouch, eyes straining to take in a broader view. His gaze swept across the spot where the smoke had been. Several yards beyond, he spotted traces of a boiling dust cloud kicked up by a running horse. No sign of animal or rider, just their dust. And the sound of the hoofbeats—fading fast now, headed away.

Buckhorn emerged the rest of the way into a clearing. His right hand hovered clawlike over the grips of his Colt. But if there was nothing to see, there was nothing to shoot. Not even his Winchester would have done him any good on an invisible target.

Buckhorn stood with his feet planted wide and his teeth bared in a grimace for a long moment, glaring after the diminishing swirls of dust. At length, he hacked up a mouthful of gritty phlegm and spat it to the ground. Then he turned and plodded off to go find Sarge.

CHAPTER 18

By the time Buckhorn rounded up the gray and made it back to Circle D headquarters, he barely had time to get cleaned up for dinner. He was grateful to find that while he was gone Obie had given his good jacket and pants a thorough brushing and had even put a fresh polish on his dress boots.

"Hope you don't mind me goin' into your war bag," the old handyman said. "You left it layin' open on the chair and those things were right on top. So, since I had some time on my hands and seein's how you like to dude up a bit, I figured I'd go ahead and take care of it for ya."

"Not a problem. I appreciate it," Buckhorn told him.

Which was true enough. But that didn't keep Obie's actions from adding to the pile of puzzles Buckhorn was already trying to make sense of.

On his ride back from the hogback and the attempted ambush there, one thought above all others had kept running through his mind. The only person who'd known he was going out there on such short notice had been O'Binion. Had Obie sent the ambusher after him? If so, why? If not, what else could explain the rifleman's presence and his attempt to plant a bullet in Buckhorn? Or did this most recent attack somehow fit in with the still unexplained earlier try back on the trail?

At the washstand Obie steered him to, already set with a basin, soap, towel, and a pitcher of fresh water, Buckhorn scrubbed away the sweat and grit from his scrambling around on the hogback. When he rinsed off the suds with repeated palmfuls of water scooped to his face he wished he could also rinse clear some of the clutter starting to build up inside his head.

He was usually very slow to put trust in anyone, even though he'd found himself leaning that way pretty easily with Obie. But then the question of who had known to send the latest ambusher after him came into play. And now, as the flip side to that, he had to ask himself why—if Obie *had* arranged the ambush attempt and as a result wouldn't be expecting Buckhorn to make it back—would the old-timer go to all the trouble of brushing and laying out his dress duds?

As he toweled dry, Buckhorn decided stubbornly that any doubts nagging him about the handyman weren't yet sufficient to outweigh the more positive feelings he'd initially developed. Still, as was second nature to him anyway, he would remain guarded.

In conjunction with that, he further decided he would not mention the hogback ambush to Obie or Pamela or anybody else. At least not yet. If anybody happened to let something slip, an indication of knowing about the incident, then that would not only give him something to pounce on but it might also provide a clue to making some of the other puzzle pieces fit.

Whether or not those pieces would connect to the rustling or to Jeff's disappearance Buckhorn had no way of knowing. But he had at least one tangible thread he could start pulling on first thing in the morning—following the trail of the fleeing ambusher to wherever it led from the hogback.

By the time he'd finally caught up with Sarge, the impending darkness of evening and the limited time he had to get back to the Circle D made Buckhorn choose to hold off on immediately pursuing the trail.

Buckhorn had no doubt he'd be able to pick up the trail of the ambusher in the morning. All he had to do in the meantime was get through the dinner in the main house and then wait for the rest of the night to pass.

"What do I have to do to get that damn half-breed shot!? Take care of it myself?"

Micah Danvers slammed the edge of his fist down hard on top of the scarred, cigarette-scorched table in the rear corner of the Crooked Spur Saloon. The beer mugs, glasses, and a half-full whiskey bottle adorning the table bounced and wobbled precariously from the force of the blow.

Dave Millard, seated across from Micah, reached quickly to steady the whiskey bottle.

"Take it easy, Micah!" he cautioned. "Better hold it down."

"I ain't holdin' nothing down," Micah snarled in response. "This is getting damned frustrating and I'm plenty sick of it. I send out three men—count 'em, *three*—and they can't manage to kill one lousy Indian."

"Doggone it, Micah," Dave said. "You want everybody in the joint to hear you?"

There was only a handful of other customers in the Crooked Spur that evening. Four of them were playing red dog at another round-topped table over by the front door, two others were holding up the bar while they sipped their beers and chewed the fat with the barkeep.

None of them appeared to be paying any attention to the men in the corner, but if you looked closely enough you could spot a certain rigidity in the backs of the card players that indicated what they really were doing was working hard at making it *look* like they weren't paying attention.

"To hell with what that bunch of lard-bottomed townies hears or don't hear," Micah said. "I say what I want when I want to say it."

"Maybe so," Dave allowed. "But, if you ever find somebody who *does* manage to kill Buckhorn for you, then one of those lard bottoms over there might remember what they heard and it could mean serious trouble."

"If that crack about findin' somebody who can manage the job on that redskin was aimed at me," said Hank Boynton, the third man seated at the table, who was still a little out of breath from having burst into the Crooked Spur only a few minutes earlier, "you can shove it up your pipe, Dave."

"You'd better try a turn at takin' it easy, too," Dave advised him. "I didn't mean nothin' personal by it, Hank. I was just sayin', that's all."

Hank scowled.

"Yeah, I heard what you was sayin'. If you think it's such an easy waltz around the dance floor, maybe you oughta take a crack at it yourself. I tell you that is one quick, lucky redskin." Hank's head sank lower and so did his voice. "I had him square in my sights yet somehow I missed my first shot. After that, the devil was everywhere and nowhere. I could tell he was circlin' on me through the bushes and trees . . . and I knew that if I stuck around much longer I'd be feelin' *his* sights on *me*—just ahead of a bullet that wasn't gonna miss."

Micah expelled a ragged breath. When he spoke, it was in a more controlled voice.

"That's okay, Hank. You did your best. I'm glad you didn't stick around long enough to get ventilated like that pair of so-called hardcases I brought in from Vermillion and sent after Buckhorn before he ever hit town. Luckily, they were new to the area so nobody recognized the carcasses he brought in. But that wouldn't hardly have been the case with you, Hank. If Buckhorn had plugged you and drug your carcass back to town it would have pointed straight to me."

One side of Hank's mouth tilted up ruefully.

"Gee, Micah, thanks for the deep concern over the me gettin' plugged part."

"Aw, you know what I mean. Of course you getting plugged would matter, too." Micah made a placating gesture. "It was a bad call on my part to even send you after that damn 'breed. I got too hasty, too eager. I knew damn well either my mother or that old bucket-mouth Obie would blab to Buckhorn about the tracks you two spotted on the hogback. And I had almost as strong a hunch that he'd want to go nosing around out there for himself."

"Turned out you had it figured exactly right," said Dave.

Micah shook his head.

"Yeah, but it was still a bad idea to send Hank and not only risk him but everything else, too, by failing to show a little more patience. Now that we've got that Texas Ranger willing to throw in with us on catching those rustlers and my mother is sending Buckhorn off on a wild goose chase after my kid brother, things are falling into place just fine without me taking unnecessary chances."

"You met with Ranger Menlo while I was gone after the 'breed?" Hank wanted to know.

"For a fact," Micah told him. "He liked my idea about planning a trap for the rustlers and jumped at the chance to be part of it. Him and the sheriff both. Menlo's going to meet us out there tomorrow afternoon, after we've moved the cattle into the meadow, so he can look things over and help us work out the final details."

Hank's eyes shone as he said, "Man, if you could catch Dan Riley and his cattle thieves red-handed, with a Texas Ranger right there in our corner, that would settle Riley's hash once and for all and really give you a grip on everything, Micah. Especially with Jeff out of the picture."

"In the picture or not," Micah snorted, "my tenderhearted little brother is of no consequence to me doing or getting whatever I want."

Dave poured some of the whiskey into a glass, knocked it back, then said, "What *is* the deal on Jeff, anyway? Where do you figure he's got to since he took off, and why ain't your ma or you or anybody else heard a peep out of him in all this time?"

"How the hell do I know where the little puke got to? And why should I care?" Micah reached for the bottle and took a swig directly from it. Lowering it, he added, "Okay. The truth on what I think where Jeffy's concerned? I think the young fool had his back so humped up over Eve Riley that he turned careless and got caught trying to sneak her out from under her old man's nose. I figure right about now—for aiming to spoil the delicate little bud he sees his daughter as— Dan Riley has chopped Jeffy into bite-sized little pieces and fed 'em to that pack of hogs his brother Milt keeps in a pen out back on his ranch."

Hank's face turned a little green and his lips twisted with distaste.

"Are you serious?"

Micah shrugged.

"Never can tell. Daddies get mighty testy about protecting the virtue of their little girls."

"But according to that note you told us Jeff left, he claimed Eve was *wanting* to go with him."

"That's the way *he* saw it. Maybe he was mistaken," Micah said. "Or maybe she did feel that way about him, but when Daddy caught 'em trying to run off together, she slipped into the innocent act and pleaded that she was being snatched away against her will. Wouldn't be the first time a little teaser pulled something like that. Not by a long shot."

"But Eve seems to've gone missin', too," Dave pointed out. "When you sent me and Hank to spy on Milt Riley's ranch to see if we could spot anything after Jeff went missin', there wasn't no sign of her anywhere around, either."

"Not hide nor hair," Hank confirmed. Then the green tint returned to his face. "Jesus. You don't think Riley would've done . . . you know, what you said before . . . to his own daughter, do you?"

"No. Of course not." Micah waved a hand dismissively. "But that don't mean he might not figure she deserved to be locked away for a spell. You know, like you do with a bitch dog in heat until you can make sure the studs have quit comin' around."

"Yeah, I guess that could explain it," allowed Dave.

"Look. We're spending way more time than I care to discussin' my roaming brother and his romantic inclinations. Whatever he's gone and stepped in, I don't give a damn about."

Micah took another swig of the whiskey. This time when he lowered the bottle, his mouth was stretched in a sly smile.

"Hell, since my mother has sicced the 'breed on finding little Jeffy, he's bound to go poking around the Rileys, right? With a little luck, maybe he'll ruffle the feathers of over-protective Daddy Dan and the two of them will get into it. Whatever else he is or isn't, Dan Riley is one rough old cob." The smile turned into a prolonged chuckle that bordered on becoming a giggle. "Wouldn't that be something? After all my fretting and our failed attempts to remove my mother's hired gun, maybe her mortal enemy will be the very one to solve our Injun problem for us!"

CHAPTER 19

Taking dinner that evening with Pamela and Obie in the handsomely appointed main house turned out to be considerably more pleasant than Buckhorn expected.

For starters, the meal itself—as prepared and served by Helga, a stout old German gal who'd been the Danverses' cook-housekeeper for years—was excellent. Roast beef, cabbage, sweet potatoes, fresh-baked rolls, and cherry pie for dessert, accompanied by cold buttermilk and rich, strong coffee. And then, a little later on, some red wine that Pamela said came from her late husband's private stock.

Buckhorn couldn't help thinking, as he sipped the wine and gazed upon his lovely and elegantly decked out hostess, that Gus Danvers not only had good taste but had been one damn lucky man.

Conversation during the meal had moments of intense seriousness when Pamela spoke of her missing son and expressed her hope and confidence that Buckhorn would somehow find him and bring him back safe and sound. For the most part, though, it was lighter in content. The comfortable banter between Pamela and Obie was easy to listen to, and in the process, Buckhorn heard plenty more stories about the formative days of the Circle D.

He would have liked to have heard more about Dan Riley and how things had gone so awry with him, but every time the talk seemed headed that way Pamela quickly showed signs of her anger and bitterness and Obie would steer things in a different direction.

In the midst of enjoying their wine, Micah showed up. He came barging in as soon as he returned from town. He'd obviously been drinking and his mood seemed every bit as surly as it had been at the close of that afternoon's encounter.

"Well, well, well," he said from the doorway to the dining room, mouth spread in a sneering grin. "Mother and her little helpers. What a charming sight to behold."

"That's more than I can say for you," Pamela was quick to respond. "You're drunk and you're clearly still bent on being as rude and obnoxious as possible. There's hardly anything charming about that."

Micah's sneer remained firmly in place as he said, "Yeah, well, even if the apple doesn't fall far from the tree, Mother, it can still roll off for a ways after it hits the ground."

"If you're comparin' yourself as an apple off the tree that was your pa," said Obie in a disgusted tone, "that's a laugh. You don't measure up no closer'n a shriveled-up bud on a branch."

"I already heard enough outta your mouth for one

day, you old gimp. Any more will be too much, and too much is liable not to be healthy for you."

A flush of anger flooded Obie's face and his gnarled hands balled into fists on top of the table.

"It's a damn good thing for you, you impertinent pup, that I *am* a stove-in ol' gimp. If it was otherwise, I'd've long ago give you the thrashin' your pa would have took care of himself if he was still around to see you earn it."

"It's easy to talk tough," Micah goaded him, "when you know you're safely in a position to never have to back it up."

It took all the restraint Buckhorn could muster to hold himself in check. For Pamela's sake, he'd promised to do his best to cut Micah some slack. But that didn't keep him from wanting to drive his fist square into that taunting sneer and knock it clean off the insolent brat's shoulders.

"I won't have this kind of belligerence in my house, at my dinner table," Pamela stated forcefully. "I won't stand for it!"

Still planted in the doorway, Micah appeared to sway somewhat unsteadily and his eyes took on a kind of bleary weariness.

"More and more lately," he said, "it seems like what you really can't stand, Mother, is me. I guess it's too bad that the wrong son went missing."

"Micah! What a dreadful thing to say."

"See what I mean? That's how I always come across to you—dreadful in both word and deed. Why try to deny it?"

Pamela's nostrils flared.

"I refuse to have this ridiculous conversation—"

"Ah, back to ridiculous," Micah interrupted. "Didn't we already cover that ground? Is ridiculous a step up or down from dreadful? Which do you consider it?"

"I consider it a moot point," Pamela said, fighting to keep her voice level. "Either way, I refuse to continue this discussion with you in your drunken condition. We clearly need to have a serious talk, but now is not the time or place."

Micah spread his hands in a conciliatory gesture and said, "At last, something we can agree on. This is also not the time or place for me to waste any more of my evening. I'll find an empty cot in the bunkhouse where I will be welcome to either sleep off my drunkenness—or perhaps deepen it. One way or other, it shall run its course. And then, Mother, we can indeed have our 'serious talk.'"

So saying, Micah turned and started from the doorway, holding himself in that rigid, carefully balanced manner of someone who is intoxicated to the point of unsteadiness but trying very hard not to show it. After a couple steps, he paused to say over his shoulder, "Never mind me. Go on back to whatever you were doing that made the charming scene I walked in on. Pretend I never showed up to rain on your little indoor picnic." And then he clomped out of the room and on out of the house.

The trio at the table sat in silence for several awkward moments until, in a notably strained voice, Pamela said, "My apologies for the abysmal behavior of my son. Thank you for speaking up on behalf of Gus and myself, Obie. And thank you, Joe, for staying out of it. I could tell it wasn't easy for you."

She took a swallow of her wine before continuing, "I don't know what has gotten into Micah lately. It troubles me and angers me, in equal parts. I want to lay it on a combination of stresses over the cattle rustling and concern about whatever's happened to Jeff added to the day-to-day responsibilities of ramrodding our outfit . . . but I fear there may also be something totally apart from those things."

"The boy's got some darkness down deep inside him," Obie said. "Ain't no gettin' around it."

"This is one time," Pamela replied, a forlorn smile appearing, then almost instantly fading, "that I wish you were less agreeable, dear Obie."

"If the rustlers go ahead and make a try on the herd being moved into that meadow and Micah's plan to catch them in the act works out," Buckhorn suggested, trying to toss in something a little more positive, "maybe that'll help set his head a little squarer on his shoulders."

Pamela's reaction was to shift her gaze questioningly back and forth between Buckhorn to Obie. Catching the gist of her unspoken inquiry, Obie said, "Yeah, it was me. I went ahead and told Powderburner about the curious tracks on the hogback and what had Micah so fired up about 'em, what he figured they must mean."

Buckhorn said, "Don't blame Obie. I was being nosy and pressured him into telling me what it was that had Micah spurring so hard to get to town. Hope you don't see me knowing about it as a problem."

"No, of course not," Pamela replied. "I should have gone ahead and explained it myself. I guess I was too preoccupied with other thoughts."

"As far as Micah's trip to town," Obie said, "he just came and went without mentionin' how his meetin' with that Texas Ranger went."

Frowning, Pamela said, "The fact he came back drunk doesn't seem like a good sign. If he wanted to get the ranger's cooperation, I hope he had more sense than to try and do it in that condition."

"If he met with the ranger at all," Buckhorn said, "he most likely did his drinking afterward. Nobody'd be dumb enough to do it the other way around."

Obie grunted.

"You're probably right. But that boy's actions ain't been overly bright lately."

"Now I wish *I* was the one who could disagree," Pamela said with a wistful sigh as she reached once more for her wineglass.

Buckhorn and Obie exchanged glances and an unspoken acknowledgment passed between them, signaling that now was probably a good point to call it an evening. When Obie suggested as much, Pamela seemed to welcome the notion.

"Please accept my apologies for the way things concluded," she said as she saw them to the door. "Prior to that, I, for one, had a most enjoyable time. I hope you did, too."

The two men heartily assured her they had and then took their leave.

Back in Obie's cabin, the old handyman didn't waste any time pulling a jug of corn whiskey out from one of the kitchen cabinets.

"With all due respect to Gus's 'special stock,' wine

ain't never done much of a job when it comes to satisfyin' my liquor appetite. But this genuine, double-rectified bust-head is guaranteed to do the job, and then some." He held the jug high. "Join me?"

"Got to pass. Me and that stuff don't mix well," Buckhorn told him. "But thanks, anyway."

Obie looked confounded. Then: "Oh. Well . . . You know, on second thought I don't reckon my old gizzard needs any of this panther juice poured over it tonight, neither. Micah's demonstration of tangle-footedness ain't exactly something needs copyin'."

"Hey, old-timer. You want to have yourself a night-cap, you go right ahead," Buckhorn said. "Don't hold back on account of me, you hear? If you had some more wine or a glass of cold beer, I'd be more than happy to join you. But whiskey ain't a taste I ever acquired or ever wanted to. Personal choice of mine, that's all. But don't let it stop you."

"You sure?"

"Said so, didn't I?"

Obie dug out a tin cup and tipped the jug over it, pouring a generous amount. Before lifting the cup to his lips, he frowned down into it for a long moment.

"Too bad I ain't got enough of this who-hit-John to drown that snotty damn Micah in."

"Be a waste of good whiskey, wouldn't it?"

"Not if it got the job done . . . or soaked some sense into that twisted-around thick head of his!"

Buckhorn watched the old man's throat muscles work as he gulped from the cup, and he knew that what he was really trying to drown was his own frustration and humiliation over no longer being physically capable of confronting Micah like he would have done back in the day.

Buckhorn felt pangs of mixed sorrow and anger, remembering how, as a little kid, he had watched his father use whiskey to try to drown *his* frustrations and limitations—in his case, never realizing or admitting that the whiskey itself was the problem holding him back more than anything. Not that Obie seemed anywhere near the hopeless boozehound that Buckhorn's father became, but the trip down that path always started by tipping up a bottle.

For that reason, Buckhorn was glad to see Obie restopper the jug and put it away once he had drained the cup.

"Don't know about you," Buckhorn said, removing his jacket and starting to unbutton his shirt, "but I think I'm ready to stretch out and give this big old chair of yours a serious try. No tellin' what tomorrow's gonna bring, but I'm sure it will prove to be interesting."

"Not much doubt about that," Obie agreed. "Reckon we'll find what, if anything, Micah was able to arrange with the ranger as far as layin' for those rustlers he figures are itchin' to make a move. From what you saw out there on the hogback, you think he might not be so far off the trail, eh?"

They'd only had the chance for a limited discussion of what Buckhorn had found on his visit to the area around the meadow, and even that was filtered through what the gunman was willing to reveal.

"I saw the tracks," he admitted again now. "If Micah and the other two are convinced they didn't come from Circle D riders, then, yeah, I'd have to go along with 'em belonging to somebody possibly up to no good."

"Like you said, whatever it turns out to be is likely to prove interestin'." Obie walked over to his bed and sat down on the edge. "As for your part, you'll be swingin' your attention mostly to huntin' for young Jeff, won't you?"

"That's the way Mrs. Danvers wants it."

"You got in mind how you're gonna go about it?"

"Still kinda wrestlin' with that, to tell you the truth. For starters I figure to go into town tomorrow and meet with Sheriff Tolliver, ask him to check out a couple things I think ought to be covered, and he's in a position to do it quicker and easier than I can."

Apart from failing to mention his intent to also follow the trail of the ambusher who'd made the try for him earlier, Buckhorn was telling the truth. No matter that Pamela thought it a waste of time, he was hoping he could convince Tolliver to check the passenger listings on any stagecoach runs or train departures from surrounding towns for the time frame matching when Jeff and Eve Riley might have used either as a means to put some distance between themselves and the general area.

"After that," Buckhorn continued, "I guess I'll be staking out Milt Riley's ranch. I know it's already been done, but maybe I can have better luck spotting something that looks like it could tie in."

"I got to hand it to you, Powder-burner," Obie said, reaching awkwardly, due to his bad hip, to pull off his boots. "You've got a thinkin' head on your shoulders as well as lightnin' in your gun hand. Not a combination you tend to see all that often. For quite a spell now I ain't been able to keep from fearin' the worst where young Jeff is concerned. But now, with you on the job, I got reason to hope maybe it can turn out better after all."

Buckhorn made a face. "There you go again, heaping too much in the way of expectations on me. Give it a rest, you old rascal. Remember, I'm just a hired gun. Nothing more, nothing less. Now get some sleep and let me do the same."

"You really think he might be good enough?" The eagerness in Micah Danvers's tone clearly conveyed what he hoped the answer would be.

Hank Boynton scuffed his feet on the ground, wanting to be careful about picking the right words for his response.

"No way of knowin' for positive. But he sure *seems* confident about it," he said. "And, even before this, I've heard the other fellas comment more than once on the way he wears that fancy tie-down rig of his. You know, how it looks like he sure knows how to use it."

"That don't amount to a hill of beans," Micah grumbled. "A rooster struts around wearin' spurs, too, but that don't mean he knows how to ride a horse."

"Yeah, but there's more to it than that," Dave Millard spoke up. "There's some of the fellas who've seen him shoot, too. Target practice and such. They say he's fast as blazes and mows down anything and everything he aims at."

Micah frowned thoughtfully.

He'd run into Dave and Hank on his way to the

bunkhouse. They, in turn, had been on their way to the main house to see him about the matter now under discussion.

One of the Circle D riders, it seemed, a man named Gonzalez, had heard about the hiring of Buckhorn and ever since had done little but make noise to the effect that *he* could handle such a job if he'd only been asked. The noise had steadily escalated to the point of him boasting he intended to challenge Buckhorn first thing in the morning and, after he outdrew and killed him, he would claim the hired gun job— and the big payday that came with it—for himself.

"Where's Gonzalez now?" Micah wanted to know.

"He turned in for the night," said Hank. "He's in his bunk, sleepin' like a baby. Can you believe that? Not nervous one damn bit."

"Whether it means anything as far as how good he might be, you sure got to give it to him for bein' a cool customer," allowed Dave.

The three men were leaning against a corral fence not too far from the bunkhouse and cook shack. A fat moon was on the rise, casting their shadows into long, distorted shapes.

"How long has Gonzalez been with us?" said Micah.

"Not too long. Only a few months."

"What does anybody know about him?"

"He mentioned to a couple of the boys that he got in some trouble down on the border before headin' up to these parts. Gave the impression he was sorta layin' low until things settle down back wherever he came from."

"So he's got no family around close?"

"Not that anybody knows of."

Micah was thoughtfully quiet again for a few seconds. Then his mouth slowly spread into a wide grin and he said, "You know what, boys? I think more and more luck is finally startin' to pile up on our side of the line. First, the ranger shows up just in time to help us stomp out those pesky rustlers. Then we hit on the notion of ol' Dan Riley risin' up to help us with our Injun problem. And now, from right under our noses, we got Gonzalez as plan B for takin' care of that damn 'breed."

"If he makes his play right away in the morning," Hank said, looking confused, "wouldn't that make Gonzalez plan A? And then, if it's still necessary, Riley would be plan B."

Micah chuckled tolerantly.

"Plan A, plan B—what the hell difference does it make? We'll call it our one-two punch if it makes you feel better. And you're right, if Gonzalez throws his punch in the morning and that gets the job done, then we won't have to worry about involvin' Riley at all. Fellas, I tell ya it's an embarrassment of riches!"

CHAPTER 20

Buckhorn reckoned that Obie's oversized easy chair was about as comfortable as any bed he could remember ever occupying. Half swallowed by it, he slept straight through the night. But from practically the first moment he woke the next morning, he sensed something in the air. Not danger exactly, not any kind of immediate threat. But trouble nonetheless. Something brewing. Like a sky thickening with the buildup of an oncoming storm.

He got to his feet and spent a minute stretching out the kinks from too many miles in the saddle and too many bedrolls spread on cold, hard ground—an accumulation amounting to more than just one night in the soothing chair could manage to erase. After buckling on his gunbelt and stomping into his boots, a routine that never varied no matter under what conditions he awoke and arose, Buckhorn went to the kitchen area to get some coffee going.

Once he had a fire crackling in a chamber of the cookstove and a pot starting to bubble over top of it, he stepped to the window and gazed out on the

Circle D spread. In contrast to his premonition about a gathering storm, shafts of butter-yellow sunlight slanted in, washing over him.

Although the clanking of the stove lid and the coffeepot didn't disturb Obie, the wafting aroma of the cooking coffee rousted the old-timer without Buckhorn having to say a word.

"Hallelujah and Glory-be," the old handyman declared as he clambered to a sitting position on the edge of his bed, "now *that* is the way to wake up of a mornin'. Lured by the sweet perfume of fresh-brewed coffee."

"You haven't tasted my coffee yet," Buckhorn warned him. "You might want to hold off on that praise."

"Paugh! When you've poured down as many gallons of burnt bean juice as I have over the years, Powder-burner, you'll come to conclude same as me that coffee is sorta like the warm embrace of a pretty gal. The worst I ever had, wasn't bad."

Buckhorn grinned.

"If you say so. I thought about gettin' some vittles going, too, but I didn't see much in the way of breakfast fixin's."

In between grunts and groans as he pulled his boots on, Obie said, "We'll get ourselves some chow over at the grub shack. That's where I usually take my breakfast. Cookie'll have plenty more coffee, too, but this here that you've brewed up will fuel us up for the hike over there."

Buckhorn glanced out the window again, at the cook shack only a short distance away.

"Good thing I made enough to stoke us for that long journey," he said.

The low-ceilinged cook shack was filled with a dozen or so raucous wranglers, the low rumble of overlapping conversations, and the smells of sweat, dust, and tobacco. Overriding it all was the mingled aroma of frying bacon, boiling coffee, and pancakes scorching on a griddle.

When Buckhorn and Obie walked in, everything stayed the same except for the low rumble of talk. All conversation stopped and suddenly the hiss of the frying bacon seemed very loud.

The gathering storm, Buckhorn thought to himself. Without changing his expression or turning his head, he cut his gaze first to one side of the room and then to the other, scanning faces and reading body language, looking for any sign of trouble coiled to spring loose.

Off to his right, seated with their backs to the wall, he spotted Micah Danvers and his men Dave and Hank. Their eyes met his and their expressions registered faint bemusement. *They knew something.*

Obie kept walking, slow but steady, down a middle aisle that ran between tables and benches on either side, making his way toward a particularly long table positioned across one end of the kitchen area. The top of the table was crowded with a stack of clean plates, eating utensils, and several pans of food. Buckhorn, walking behind Obie, glimpsed bacon, scrambled eggs, and flapjacks among other things; but mostly he continued to scan the faces and bodies surrounding him.

When they got to the edge of the table, a voice with a heavy Spanish accent rang out from behind them.

"You may go ahead and fill your plate, old one. Eat as much as you wish. For you, *raza*, it would only be a waste of good food. Because you are not going to live long enough to digest it."

Buckhorn took his time turning around. His gaze came to rest on a dark-skinned man of medium height standing in the middle of the aisle they had just walked down. The man's feet were planted wide, his eyes narrowed into dangerous, intensely focused slits. A tied-down holster of shiny black leather adorned with silver studs rode low on his right hip. A Colt with bleached white pearl grips rested loose in the holster. The man's right hand, covered by a skintight glove of the same shiny black leather as the holster, hovered close at his side, ready to hook and draw.

Buckhorn gave him an unhurried looking over, then said, "And *you* are the reason I'm not gonna live long enough to digest my breakfast. That the general idea?"

"That is *exactly* the idea."

"Since you're so certain of the outcome, I guess you obviously don't believe in the practice of allowing the condemned man a hearty final meal."

"Like I said, it would only be a waste of good food."

"What about you? Did you eat?"

"Yes, I did. It was very enjoyable." The dark-skinned man smiled. "Fortunately, I will have plenty of time to digest it."

Addressing Micah and his two cohorts, Obie said, "What's goin' on here? What's the big idea? You three set this up, didn't you?"

"Calm down, Obie," Micah said with a lazy smile. "You get yourself too worked up, your food ain't gonna digest good, either. No matter how long you got. As far as Mr. Gonzalez's issue with your friend Buckhorn, that's strictly his own doing. I'm hearing it play out for the first time, same as you."

Keeping his eyes fixed on Buckhorn, Gonzalez said, "I have no quarrel with the old one. But you should advise him that if he keeps blabbering to the point of annoying me, I may decide to change my mind."

A ghost of a smile played across Buckhorn's mouth.

"Comes to talking—or blabbering, as you say—the old gent is sorta hard to turn off."

"That is unfortunate."

"Comes to unfortunate," said Buckhorn, "I got no problem killing you, since you're working so hard to earn it . . . but before I do, care to explain the why of it?"

Gonzalez's eyes narrowed even more as he said, "The question of which of us is capable of killing the other is the whole point. Mrs. Danvers saw fit to hire you, an outside gun, when I was already right here, perfectly able to do anything you can. That offends me, plus it takes money that I could have earned and puts it in your pocket instead of mine. I intend to show her the error of her ways by demonstrating that I am faster and better than you. Then, when you have been removed, she will see the wisdom of hiring me in your place."

"That was quite a mouthful. For a minute there I thought you figured on talking me to death."

"The talking that counts most I do with the gun from my hip."

Now Buckhorn's eyes narrowed and turned as cold as two chips of black ice.

"Let's get to it then. You figure on slapping leather here, or do we step outside?"

By then, the other men in the room had edged back wide of the aisle where Buckhorn and Gonzalez stood faced off.

"You are a tall one, señor," Gonzalez said, one side of his mouth curling into a sneer, "but there is plenty of room right here for you to fall."

For those watching, it seemed like several heartbeats passed with the two men frozen in place, glaring at one another, poised for action. In reality, it only took a second before hands blurred, too fast for the eye to follow, streaking to draw and fire.

When the guns blasted, however, there was one big difference: Buckhorn's Colt was leveled and aimed, Gonzalez's had only just cleared leather and hadn't yet started to rise.

Buckhorn's slug struck just below Gonzalez's chin, snapping his head back and throwing a splash of exiting gore as the Mexican pitched backward and started to topple. It was only then that his gun spoke, trigger finger spasming reflexively in death, bullet ripping into the floorboards and spitting a harmless puff of dust and splinters.

That fast, it was over and done.

With the bluish gunsmoke still roiling in the air, Buckhorn swung the muzzle of his Colt and brought it to bear on Micah, Dave, and Hank.

"You wantin' any of this?" he demanded to know.

Three sets of hands shot into plain view, palms open and empty.

"Nothing doing here, mister," Micah was quick to assure him. "It's like I told Obie—all of that was strictly the crazy Mexican's play. You can leather that hogleg now. You, too, Obie."

For the first time, Buckhorn became aware that Obie had drawn his revolver and was sweeping it around the room, covering the gunman's back. Their eyes met. Buckhorn gave a simple nod, signaling his gratitude. Only then did they pouch their irons.

CHAPTER 21

"And if that wasn't enough," Micah Danvers was lamenting as he paced back and forth, "for the second time in two days he pointed a gun at me. Right there in front of all the other hands! Do you have any idea how undermining that could be to my authority over them, how damaging to their respect for me?"

"A man is dead, Micah," his mother replied in a strained voice. "Don't you think that should be of greater concern than your bruised ego?"

Micah stopped pacing and made an imploring gesture.

"That's exactly my point! A man is dead—because of the hired gun you brought into our midst. He killed one of our own! How are the other men going to react if we just let it go at that? What is Ranger Menlo going to think when he comes out to help with our rustling problem? If we accept and harbor a killer, what right do we have to complain about others breaking the law?"

They were gathered—Pamela, Micah, Obie, and Buckhorn—in the parlor of the main house. Less than an hour had passed since the shooting of Gonzalez. The body still lay where it had fallen in the grub shack, covered by a tarp. Dave and Hank had gone into town to fetch Sheriff Tolliver. It was expected and hoped that Ranger Menlo would also come.

"You seem to be conveniently forgettin'," Obie spoke up, "that Gonzalez forced Powder-burner's hand. He had a gun strapped on, too, and he called the tune that got him plugged. Unless you know something that nobody else has ever heard of, shootin' a man in self-defense ain't against the law and don't amount to murder. Not nohow."

"When one of the men is a professional killer," Micah objected, "and the other is a simple wrangler who's goaded into—"

"Goaded by who?" Obie wanted to know. "By you and those two boot-lickers who follow you around like a coupla pet dogs? I figured something like that right from the get-go."

"That's a damn lie," Micah said. "You heard what Gonzalez said. He was goaded by the fact an outsider—nothing more than a hired killer, I still claim him to be—was brought in to do work that could be handled by men we already have on our crew."

"So it's my fault then. Is that what you're saying?" Pamela asked. "Gonzalez is dead because I chose to seek out a professional rather than solicit some common cowpuncher to take on a complex, risky job—part of which may involve saving the life of your own brother?"

"What does a gunslick from clean outside the territory know about finding a missing person? We've had men who've lived around here all or most of their lives—me, Sheriff Tolliver, and more—who haven't found a single sign of what happened to Jeff. You think a complete stranger can come along and do a better job of it?"

"That's what I aim to find out," Pamela told him. "I originally hired him to look into the rustling problem also, if you remember. As a further reminder, no one you just named—and that includes you—has gotten very far in that regard, either."

"That's a cruel thing to say, Mother!"

"I'm just stating a fact," Pamela responded coolly. "But now that you've found those suspicious tracks and have gained the cooperation of Ranger Menlo, it appears you may be on the brink of making some welcome headway. I applaud you for that. And to avoid the potential complications that might come from too many fingers in the pie, you might like to know that I have asked Mr. Buckhorn to concentrate solely on Jeff's disappearance and leave the rustling problem to you and the ranger."

"Which means," Buckhorn said, addressing Micah and speaking almost for the first time since they'd come inside, "that as soon as the lawmen have come and gone and we're able to put this morning's business behind us, I figure to be heading out for some reconnoitering that ought to steer the pair of us real wide from each other."

"That's the best news I've heard since you showed up in these parts," Micah replied bluntly.

"Might come as a shock, but serving up good news to you hasn't exactly been a priority of mine."

"All right, that's enough," Pamela was quick to interject. "One thing for certain, you two being far enough apart that I won't have to listen to you constantly snapping at each other's throats will be good news to *my* ears."

Although disappointing to Micah and his cronies perhaps, it came as not much of a surprise to anybody else that the inquiry by Sheriff Tolliver and Ranger Menlo into Gonzalez's death was quickly determined to have been a clear case of self-defense.

Nevertheless, as the body was being loaded by Undertaker Schmidt and an assistant onto a wagon to be hauled back to Barkley for burial in the town cemetery, Menlo motioned Buckhorn aside and said to him, "Dead bodies seem to pile up around you like partners flock to a pretty gal at a square dance."

"Not like I'm advertising for a turn on that particular kind of dance floor," Buckhorn replied. "I'm not partial to music played to the tune of flying lead."

"All the same, you seem to have learned the steps pretty well," Menlo said. "It's a good thing your work keeps you on the drift. You was to settle in one place for very long, you'd turn it into a ghost town. Speakin' of which, how long you figure to be hangin' around these parts?"

"Don't have a very clear feel for that just yet. This is only the start of my second full day, remember."

"I understand that with me on hand to help with the rustling situation you're going to be concentrating on finding the missing Danvers boy."

"That's the way Mrs. Danvers wants it."

"That's kinda outside your normal range of services, ain't it? Or have you taken up detective work of late?"

"Man's got to change and evolve else he's apt to go stale," Buckhorn said. "I've got some ideas on how to go about getting a lead or two."

"Anything you'd care to share?"

Buckhorn took his time responding. When he did, he told the ranger his idea about checking the surrounding area's stage and train passenger lists for the days shortly after Jeff Danvers's disappearance.

Menlo was pursing his lips thoughtfully by the time he'd heard him out.

"Sounds like some pretty good thinkin'," he allowed. "Matter of fact, it sounds like something Sheriff Tolliver should already have done by now."

"Sort of what I thought."

As they talked, the ranger and the gunman were leaning against a hitch rail down a ways from the front of the main house. Most of the Circle D wranglers, having been kept available for questioning by the lawmen, were still milling around the front of the grub shack, smoking cigarettes and drinking coffee. Up closer to the main house, Sheriff Tolliver and Pamela stood with their heads together in what appeared to be a very intense conversation.

Menlo's gaze hung on the sheriff and the widow for a moment and then cut back to Buckhorn.

"What's your read on the sheriff?" he asked abruptly.

That shoved Buckhorn's eyebrows up more than a little bit.

"You're askin' *me*?"

"You've got a head on your shoulders that works for more than just holdin' up that fancy hat, don't you?" The ranger dismissed the rhetorical question with a shrug. "Okay. I'll give you mine first. I think the sheriff is basically a good man. Honest and well intentioned. But not overly bright and in a fog too much of the time on account of the Widow Danvers. He's got two deputies that fall pretty much along the same lines, except maybe for bein' in a fog over the widow. That's my take from the short time I've been here. And, for what it's worth, that was also the general impression left in his notes by Kirby Peck, the young ranger who spent some time here before me. Maybe I came into it with a bias after readin' his words, but I don't think so. I think I'd've seen it about the same regardless. Now. What say you?"

"To be honest, I don't know that I've thought it through quite that far. On the other hand, I can't say I've got anything to argue against those observations, either."

"Uh-huh." Menlo regarded Buckhorn closely for a long moment. "I took a read on you pretty quick, too. Then, since I recognized your name and description, though only vaguely, I sent out some telegrams to do a little follow-up checkin'."

"This should be interesting."

"No papers turned up on you."

"There's never been any."

"Still and all, there was a time—and not all that long ago—when you were considered little more than a hired killer. You sold your gun to the highest bidder, and pretty soon people standin' against your employer started turning up dead. Sometimes it was a face-on shootout like this deal here today. Other times, though there was never any way to prove for sure you were involved, it was nothing short of a gundown, flat-out murder."

Menlo kept regarding him close. Buckhorn met his eyes, said nothing.

"Then something changed," the ranger went on. "You kept hiring out your gun, just as you're doing here. But random killings with your name hinted at being attached to 'em seemed to stop. The shootings and killings you've been associated with lately have been either acts of self-defense or as part of protecting your employer. What turned you? What's different?"

"You're the one telling the tale. All I can say, like I already told you, is that a man has to—"

"I know, a man's got to change and evolve else he's apt to turn stale." Menlo glanced over to the wagon with Gonzalez's body loaded on it, then back to Buckhorn again. "Five men shot and killed, all in self-defense, all in only a couple of days. I'd say you've got a ways to slide before you have to worry about turnin' stale."

"There a point to all this, Ranger?" Buckhorn wanted to know.

Menlo glanced around some more. He seemed to consider something for a long moment before saying, "We stand here palaverin' much longer, we're gonna draw attention and suspicion. There's enough of that going on around here already. But I *do* want to go over some more things with you. You willin' to meet up with me somewhere later on?"

Buckhorn didn't see where he had much choice.

"Reckon so," he said.

Menlo nodded.

"Good. They're gonna delay movin' that cattle herd to the meadow for another day, not until morning. How about we meet there, after I've gone back to town with the sheriff and then had a chance to slip away again. Say about an hour past noon. You know the spot I'm talkin' about. That hogback above the meadow where somebody tried to ambush you again?"

CHAPTER 22

"Well, there goes Gonzalez, toes up," said Dave Millard as his gaze followed the undertaker's wagon rolling away, flanked by the sheriff and the ranger on horseback and the tarped body of Gonzalez stretched out on the wagon bed. "And, over yonder, still standin' big as life, is that hard-to-kill damn half-breed."

Micah Danvers didn't bother looking after the departing wagon, but he did cut his gaze to where Buckhorn and Obie were heading into the latter's cabin.

"Not only walkin' around big as life," he said bitterly, "but hardly leaned on at all by those two law dogs we just had here. What was up with that? A low-down hired gun, and a half-breed to boot, and they treat him with kid gloves like some kind of respectable citizen. On top of that, the ranger ended up shootin' the breeze with him for the longest spell, practically like they was the best of pals."

"What was that all about?"

"I don't know. But I didn't like seeing it, I know that."

Dave took a hard final drag on the butt of a cigarette, dropped it to the dusty ground, and mashed it under the toe of his boot.

"So where does that leave us?" he said, the words coming out in a stream of smoke. "Guess we can say plan A has officially fizzled and we're ready to move on to plan B, right? Or is it C or D we're up to by now?"

Micah aimed a fierce scowl in Dave's direction and said, "What kind of snotty remark is that?"

"Calm down, calm down." Dave was quick to try to deflect the testiness he'd poked into. "All I meant was how stubborn—or lucky—Buckhorn is about not dyin'."

Micah gritted his teeth.

"I wish I could believe it *was* nothing but luck. But that heathen has got more going for him than just that. You saw—or no, you probably didn't, since it was so damn fast—how he outdrew Gonzalez. And that Mexican was no slouch, you had to give him that. Plus, Buckhorn's been every bit as quick and slick when it came to dodgin' the ambushes we tried to set up for him."

"Boy, you don't have to tell me," agreed Hank. "If only I hadn't missed that first shot when I made my try. But after that, like I told you, he was like a doggone ricochetin' bullet, bouncin' every which direction faster than I could keep up with."

The three of them were standing in front of the bunkhouse. There was nobody else around, the other wranglers having finally been sent off to go about their day's chores, so they were able to talk freely.

"So what are you sayin', Micah?" Dave asked. "You ain't ready to give up on trying to get rid of Buckhorn, are you?"

Glaring off at nothing in particular, Micah answered, "No. We can't do that now, even if I was of a mind to. We've poked at him too much. He don't strike me as the type who's gonna shrug it off and go away until he's dug up some answers."

"So what, then?"

"Like you said a minute ago—plan B. Since my mother has him zeroed strictly on trying to track down Jeff, that means he's bound to go sniffing around the Rileys. Which means, like we talked before, he'll also be bound to draw the attention and anger of ol' Dan. So there's still the chance our Injun problem might end right there. At the very least, it should keep Buckhorn out of our hair for a while."

"And in the meantime," said Hank, "we'll be coming at Riley over this new rustling thing. And we'll have both the sheriff *and* the ranger on our side."

Micah nodded as his mouth curved into a thin smile.

"With a little luck of our own—something we're by-God overdue for, says I—if Dan Riley does for Buckhorn and the ranger and Tolliver help us do for Riley, we could end up clearing the board of our two biggest problems."

But then the smile faded as Micah thought again about how Buckhorn and the ranger had spent so much time talking together. He wished he knew what the hell that had been about . . .

* * *

Pamela Danvers stood alone in the parlor of the main house.

She often did this when stressed or deep in reflection. Above the cold fireplace she stood facing hung a large, intricately detailed painting of her and her late husband, Gus. They had originally posed as depicted there for a photographer. Later, as a surprise for Pamela on the occasion of their twenty-fifth wedding anniversary, Gus had arranged for a painter out of Galveston to take a copy of the tintype and reproduce it on canvas, complete with rich colors. For Pamela, the pose and the painting represented the high point of her life. Only a couple of months after the anniversary celebration, Gus was diagnosed as having a cancer in his stomach; by the following anniversary date, he was gone.

Except for the days immediately surrounding Gus's death and funeral, Pamela seldom wept. The hard years of forging a marriage, raising two sons, and working side by side with Gus to build the Circle D into the grand ranch it had become had steeled her into a stoicism and determination that rivaled even Gus's.

These moments of intense solitude, when she went either far inside herself or sometimes felt transported up into that painting on the wall, where she could again draw strength from having Gus beside her, were the closest she came to giving herself over to despair. But, even then, it only lasted for a short time. Pamela would not allow it to grip her any longer.

This current set of problems was only making her so distraught because of the ways it involved her two sons—the exposure of the petty, insolent, mean-spirited sides of Micah she had somehow never noticed before, and the absence of gentle, soothing Jeff.

Curiously, and troubling in its own way, was the fact that the main source of solace she found herself relying on wasn't the fawning Thad Tolliver, or the ever-faithful old Obie, or even the crusty Texas Ranger Menlo.

It was Joe Buckhorn. A hired gun. A half-breed.

If anybody was going to find a way to bring back Jeff and sort out the rustling and all the rest . . . on some instinctive, intuitive level, Pamela knew it was going to be Buckhorn.

"That hogback above the meadow where somebody tried to ambush you again yesterday."
Those words from Ranger Menlo kept running through Buckhorn's head, and no matter how many times he replayed them or how many different angles he tried to consider them from, they remained just as disconcerting as when he'd first heard them.

How did the old lawman know about the incident? Had he told anyone else? Could it be that, for some crazy reason, Menlo had staged it himself? But how could he know Buckhorn was going to be there? And what reason would he have for opening fire—to try to scare him off? Surely not to actually try to kill him; if that were the case, he'd hardly forewarn Buckhorn and then invite him back for another try, would he?

On the other hand, that would make about as much sense as some of the other questions and possibilities swirling around this situation.

"What's the matter, Powder-burner?" Obie wanted to know. "You're pickin' at your food and scowlin' off into space like some lovesick schoolboy. Or is it pluggin' that loudmouth Mexican that's botherin' you?"

They were seated at the table in Obie's cabin over tin plates of scrambled eggs and bacon, their interrupted breakfast that Obie had gone back and fetched from the grub shack.

"Naw, it's got nothing to do with the Mexican. He got what he was asking for, and that's that," Buckhorn answered. "I'm just rolling some things around inside my head, that's all. I'll be riding out of here in a little bit to try and get a line on young Jeff, and I really don't have much to work with."

"You don't think you'll get any answers out of Dan Riley?" said Obie.

Buckhorn turned it right back on him by asking, "Do you?"

Obie averted his eyes. He looked down at his plate and concentrated on stabbing a piece of bacon. After he'd popped it in his mouth and begun to chew, he said, "You already know how I feel about Dan. But you can't *not* talk to him about it. Nobody else has yet, not directly. They've skulked around and spied, but nobody's gone up to him, face to face, and flat out asked him if he knows anything about Jeff."

"Why not?"

"Miss Pamela won't have it. That's how bitter she is toward Dan—she sees it that any kind of direct approach like that would amount to crawlin' to him and askin' for his help. I even offered to be the one to do it, but she barely let me get the offer out of my mouth."

Buckhorn frowned.

"Well, I figured to start out by doing some skulking and spying on the Riley spread myself. Looking for some sign of either Jeff or Eve. But sooner or later I fully expected to also take a run at Riley himself. Wasn't something we discussed in so many words, but Mrs. Danvers never told me *not* to try anything like that."

"Don't bring it up, then," Obie advised. "Should it come up later, it sounds to me like a clear-cut case of better to ask forgiveness than permission. Or maybe Miss Pamela has finally come to her senses about it and sees that, if you're gonna do the job she's hired you to do, you're gonna *have* to talk to Dan."

"The other side of the coin, from what I've heard, is that Riley tends to make himself scarce whenever anybody does come around. Supposedly always off on some kind of business trip or some such. No reason to expect he won't try the same thing with me. Sounds like you might be somebody he'd make an exception for, though. Comes down to it, you willing to run some interference for me?"

Obie puffed out his cheeks and released a gust of air.

"Whew. For me, that'd be goin' *direct* against Miss Pamela's wishes. But, what the hell, somebody's got to stand up to the damn fool stubbornness bein' showed by her and Dan both. Yeah, if you need me to, I'll side you on that."

"Obliged," Buckhorn said for the second time in little more than an hour, expressing his gratitude to a man who only yesterday he'd half suspected of maybe playing a hand in the hogback ambush . . . and who he still couldn't be certain had not.

CHAPTER 23

Buckhorn hung back in a stand of pine trees and watched the approach of Lyle Menlo along the near edge of the meadow. His gaze swept wider and farther, scanning for signs of anyone else. When he was satisfied the ranger was alone, he nudged Sarge out into an open area atop the crest of the hogback.

Knowing his movement and emergence into the open had caught the attention of Menlo, Buckhorn called out no greeting. When Menlo reached a point where he was directly down slope from where Buckhorn again sat his horse, it was the ranger who spoke first.

"Even though I got here a mite early, I figured I'd find you waitin'."

"Wouldn't have it any other way," Buckhorn replied.

"Uh-huh. You alone?"

"Wouldn't have *that* any other way, either."

Menlo nodded and said, "Good." He touched his heels to the sides of his mount, and the animal obediently climbed the slope until its rider reined it to a halt alongside Buckhorn and Sarge.

"Not too far from here is where that ambusher opened up on you, ain't it?" said Menlo, matter-of-factly.

Buckhorn regarded him, not saying anything right away. Then: "Okay. I've let it gnaw at me long enough, so I'll go ahead and ask. How the hell do you know about that ambush attempt, and why haven't you said anything to anybody else? Or have you?"

Menlo grinned.

"You were pretty cool about holding it in. But then, when you finally decide to let go, it really comes a-pourin', don't it?"

Buckhorn waited, continuing to pin the ranger with a hard stare.

Menlo put away the grin and said, "All right. There's nothing all that complicated about it. You already know about my peculiar sleeping habits when I first arrive at a situation, remember? Well, I did the same thing again last night. After Micah Danvers convinced me there might be something out here that could give us a jump on the next rustlin' attempt, I agreed to meet him today after the cattle had been moved in. I guess you probably know about that, too.

"Anyway, I rode out last night and camped not too far away. It was too dark to see anything by then, but I was up at first light and didn't waste any time coming the rest of the way to give everything a good lookin' over before anybody else showed up. I made my approach about like I did just now, and the first thing that caught my eye was the glint of sunlight off the spent cartridges in the weeds behind some bushes."

"The spot the rifleman was firing from," Buckhorn

said. "That's one of the things I intended to come back and check out today . . . until that proddy Mexican changed my plans."

"Uh-huh. Well, for me, needless to say, comin' across that much ejected brass stirred my interest all the more," Menlo said. "Only one or two reasons I could think of for anybody to be throwin' that much firepower. So I got down on foot and began workin' the length of the hogback, bein' careful not to disturb those hoofprints in the middle that pulled everybody's attention here to begin with. Eventually I came to the spot where the target of all that shootin' left his horse, hit the dirt, and scrambled to cover. What I didn't see was any blood traces or any sign of returned fire."

"There are explanations for that," Buckhorn told him.

"True," Menlo agreed. "But it didn't matter so much. Leastways not compared to what I *did* spot."

Buckhorn hissed an irritated sigh.

"Which I hope you're eventually gonna get to. Maybe even yet today?"

Menlo's thin smile hinted he was enjoying seeing Buckhorn squirm a bit. Gesturing in the general direction of Sarge's front legs, the old ranger said, "You aware the front right shoe on that stud of yours got nailed on at a slight twist? Don't hurt his stride none, I guess, and it's not real obvious. But if you study on it some, it's there."

"So that's what you spotted? And that's what made you conclude it was me all those rifle rounds were aimed at?"

"Am I wrong?"

"You know damn well you're not, or I wouldn't be here talkin' to you about it. But how come you to be familiar with the shoe marking of my horse?"

"When you went out for your little target shoot yesterday morning, testin' to see if your Colt still fired true after usin' it to pound dents in the cement head of Ace Ringwold," Menlo explained, "I sorta tagged along. When I noticed you riding out of town so early, it made me curious. I made sure you didn't see me, but I wanted to know what you were up to. Once I saw, it made sense."

"Thunderation and hellfire!" exclaimed Buckhorn, smacking the edge of his fist down on the top of his saddle horn. "First Obie from the Circle D and now you—was the whole doggone county out there watchin' me that morning? I could've sold tickets and put on even more of a show."

"The one you put on was pretty impressive as it was," Menlo said, a trace of admiration in his tone. "But to go back to your question . . . Following you out from town yesterday was where I first noticed the quirk in your horse's shoe print and how I was able to recognize it again this morning."

Buckhorn scowled and said, "Okay. That takes us back to my earlier question. Once you pieced together that another ambush attempt had been made on me, why didn't you tell anybody?"

"Why didn't you?" Menlo fired right back at him.

"I had my reasons."

"Same here. You want to go back and forth like this all afternoon, or do you want to get to the meat and bones of it?"

"What I want is to not have some lowdown skunk

throwing lead at me every time I turn around," said Buckhorn. "I figured if I didn't let on about this latest try but then somebody else *did*, I'd have me something I could sink my teeth in."

"Sounds reasonable. Only now I'm the one who's come along and let on about it. You gonna sink your teeth in me, Buckhorn?"

"Don't tempt me."

"In the first place, I got no reason to shoot you. Yet. And if I did, I'd never dishonor this badge by back-shootin' somebody from ambush. You'd damn well better know that much."

Buckhorn not only saw but *felt* the intensity behind his words.

"I believe you," he said flatly. "It'd simplify some things if I didn't, but that isn't the case. So I'm left with two tries at bushwhacking me and not only no clue as to who or why but also no idea how anybody could have known I'd be where it was they laid up for me."

"You think the two tries were connected?"

"Each time they seemed hell-bent on trying to get rid of me. Not much doubt there. But, beyond that, I have no way of knowing or even making a good guess."

"So what's your plan from here?" Menlo wanted to know.

"To do what I'm being paid to do—find and bring back Jeff Danvers."

"You can just leave this alone?" Menlo made a gesture, sweeping his hand to indicate the spent cartridges in the weeds. "Even though it happened here where everybody figures another rustling raid is bein' planned, you're willing to turn your back on the cattle-stealin' end of things and concentrate on the missing kid instead?"

"Like I said, it's what I'm bein' paid to do. And 'the cattle-stealin' end of things' has now been taken over by you."

"What if the two go hand in hand? Whenever the subject of either one comes up, most folks mention Dan Riley's name in the same breath."

Buckhorn said, "I'm aware of that. So what are you getting at?"

The ranger eyed him shrewdly for a long moment. Then: "You ever hear of killin' two birds with one stone?"

"Is that some kind of favorite sayin' for you lawmen? Matter of fact, the last person I heard use that phrase was Sheriff Tolliver. Shortly after, you showed up."

"Can't help that. You want to hear where I was headed by usin' it, or not?"

CHAPTER 24

"Who is it? Who's out there?" Obie said in response to the soft but persistent knocking at the back door of his cabin, just off a corner of the kitchen area.

"It's me—Buckhorn. Throw the bolt and keep the lantern turned down, I'd just as soon nobody saw me here."

Outside, dusk was settling fast, shadows lengthening and turning velvety thick. Obie had moved to the edge of the kitchen area, a lantern in one hand, his six-shooter in the other. Recognizing Buckhorn's voice, he set the lantern on the cold cookstove, turned it low, then stepped over to the door and shoved back the bolt. Just in case, he kept a tight grip on the gun, holding it down alongside his leg.

Buckhorn came through the doorway.

"What's goin' on, Powder-burner?" Obie said. "I didn't expect to see you comin' back around for a spell."

"That's how I figured it, too," Buckhorn replied. "But some things have changed."

"How so?" Obie asked as he closed and re-locked the door and then turned back to Buckhorn.

The gunman walked over and took a seat at the table.

"You got any coffee?"

"There's some in the pot. But I'd have to—"

"Cold is fine."

The old-timer filled a tin cup and set it in front of Buckhorn. Then he took a seat, too. The six-gun he'd been carrying around, its holster and cartridge belt previously removed from around Obie's waist for the evening and draped over his easy chair, he rather awkwardly placed on the tabletop.

After Buckhorn had taken a drink of the coffee, a grin tweaked at one corner of his mouth as he tipped his head toward the gun.

"I see you're walking on the careful side."

"This old shack don't see a lot of visitors, especially not at the back door with dark settlin' in," Obie explained. "A little caution never hurts."

"No, it doesn't. And, especially once we're done talking here this evening, I want you to be sure and remember that."

Obie frowned.

"Sounds like you got something mighty serious on your mind, Powder-burner."

"I'll let you decide that for yourself once I've spilled what I came here to talk about." Buckhorn took another drink of the cold coffee, which was thick and bitter but somehow still hit the spot. "Let's start with a simple but important question."

"Go ahead."

"Yesterday, when I went out to that hogback where

Micah and the others found those suspicious tracks, did you for any reason mention to anybody that I was headed there?"

The question clearly caught Obie by surprise. He blinked a couple times, pondering briefly before he answered, "Nope. Not at all. 'Cept for goin' out to the well to fetch a pail of fresh water, I never even left the cabin here during the time you were gone."

Buckhorn listened to the words intently and closely watched Obie's face as he responded. What he heard and saw only confirmed what he *wanted* to confirm, what he'd already concluded. Whatever or whoever was behind the most recent ambush attempt, Obie had nothing to do with it.

"What makes you ask that?" Obie said.

"Because, shortly after I got there, somebody opened up on me with a rifle. They caught me flat-footed, and it was only luck—good for me, bad for them—that they missed with their first shot. I made it to cover, but they kept pouring it on, trying to flush me out and finish the job before they finally gave up and lit a shuck away from there."

Obie's eyes widened.

"Gettin' ambushed is becomin' a real bad habit with you, Powder-burner. Sooner or later your luck ain't gonna hold and one of them rounds is liable to hit its mark. Why in blazes didn't you say anything before this?"

"Because I figured if I *didn't* say anything, it might leave an opening for somebody else to let something slip that could indicate who or what's behind wanting me plugged full of lead so bad."

Now Obie's eyes narrowed. He said, "And since I

was the only one who knew you'd gone out there, you figured I might be included amongst the 'who or what.' Is that it?"

"I'm afraid so," Buckhorn replied, wishing he could dodge the question but knowing he had no choice but to face up to it. "I didn't want to think it, but put yourself in my place. How could the question not cross my mind?"

A flood of expressions conveying different emotions poured rapidly over Obie's face. Indignation, sadness, anger . . . until it finally settled on a begrudged understanding.

"In your place," he said tightly, "I reckon I couldn't hardly keep from wonderin' the same thing."

"It's important you understand and mean that. If I go ahead with these changes that have cropped up, I'm gonna need to be able to count on you more than ever. I can't have you harboring hurt feelings because I had a brief spell of doubt. I'm over that, I've got to be sure you are, too."

"I've been on your side ever since you showed up in these parts, ain't I?" said Obie. "I still am . . . for the sake of Miss Pamela, young Jeff, and the whole Circle D operation that I've put the sweat and blood of over half a lifetime into. Something about you, Powder-burner, makes me think the best chance for it all to end up okay rests on your shoulders. There. That's my piece. I've said it, now it's up to you whether or not you believe it."

Buckhorn nodded.

"Good words. They mean a lot."

"So where do they take us? What's this big change you say has cropped up?"

Buckhorn drank some more coffee. When he lowered the cup, he said, "The idea came from Menlo, the Texas Ranger. It's a bold one, not something I'd likely dream up on my own. But I like it. It'll really spur things along, and it stands a good chance of scalding out a whole passel of answers in mighty quick order."

"You're doin' a good job of sellin' it so far. But are you sayin' you and Menlo have throwed in together on this? How did that come about?"

"You mean on account of him being a lawman and me a hired gun?"

"Ain't exactly a common pairing, you gotta admit."

"Let's just say that Menlo doesn't appear to make a habit of always going by the book. And, like I already mentioned, I know the sound of a good idea when I hear one."

"Fair enough. So go ahead, let me hear the sound of the rest of it."

"Simply put, I'm gonna take my differences with Micah and pile on the shoot-out with the Mexican from this morning—talk of which has got to be making the rounds all over the town and county by now—and play them up as a lot bigger rift than they truly are. Enough of one to cause me to part ways with Mrs. Danvers and the job I hired on to do for her. And then, as a hardcase in need of work and packing a chip on my shoulder for the Circle D, I'll offer my services to Dan Riley. To sweeten the deal as far as giving him reason to take an interest in me, I'll hint that I can tell him all about the trap being set for him and his boys if they make a try on that cattle herd being moved to the far meadow."

Obie gave a low whistle.

"Whooeee. Talk about skippin' barefoot through tall grass set with bear traps! And you're loco enough to say you think that sounds like a good idea?"

"Menlo's got some fancy words for it. Working undercover, infiltrating the Riley gang."

"Gonna take more than twenty-dollar words to keep your hide intact if Dan Riley catches on to what you're up to."

"I thought you're the one who's been telling me that Riley isn't really the bad *hombre* so many others have painted him to be."

"Back a man into a corner, make him feel desperate," Obie said, "what comes out of the corner ain't necessarily the true nature of what you started with."

"Sounds like you're admitting that the Dan Riley of today isn't exactly riding the straight and narrow trail since parting ways with the Circle D."

"Like I said before, from the way he works so hard at hidin' it, it's hard to deny he appears to be not strictly on the up and up."

"All I know is that if he's behind the rustling or has anything to do with the disappearance of Jeff Danvers, then it's not for me to fret over why he made those decisions any more than I care why Gonzalez made the choice to slap leather with me this morning."

"I guess I can understand an outlook like that. Up to a point. I guess it's also what made you the right choice for Menlo to pitch his idea to. You put it to me a little bit ago whether or not you could trust me. How about Menlo? You figure you can trust him?"

Buckhorn hesitated only a second before saying,

"For what's at stake here, yeah, I do. He's made it plain that he doesn't particularly care about the disappearance of Jeff. But when it comes to the rustling, I think he's hell-bent on putting it to an end and smoking out whoever's behind it. That means if Riley's *not* the one, then Menlo isn't looking to hang it on him regardless. What he's out to get is the real culprit."

Obie nodded and said, "I like the sound of that."

"I wouldn't throw in with him and put my neck on the line if I thought otherwise."

With a grunt of effort, Obie shoved to his feet and limped over to the kitchen cabinet against one wall. From it he withdrew a long-necked bottle half-full of amber liquid. Turning back, he said, "That cold coffee might do it for you, Powder-burner. I know you don't favor whiskey. But I hope you don't mind if I have me a snort or two."

"We've covered that before," Buckhorn told him. "Go right ahead."

"Still a little coffee left in the pot—you want your cup topped off?"

"Might as well."

The old handyman returned to the table carrying the pot, the bottle, and a tin cup for himself. Buckhorn relieved him of the pot, re-filled his cup, set the pot over on a corner of the table. After lowering himself back into his chair, Obie wasted no time pouring a generous splash of the whiskey into his own cup and knocking back a big gulp.

"Whoo, yeah. Now we're talkin'," the old-timer declared. Then, eyeing Buckhorn somewhat skeptically, he added, "Figured I might need me a jolt because

I'm guessin' you're finally about to get to the point of what role you want me to play in this scheme of yours and Menlo's."

"All right, here's the thing," Buckhorn said. "If I make it into whatever Riley's operation is—if I infiltrate it, to use one of Menlo's words—then it's not likely I'll start out with the freedom to just come and go as I please. There's bound to be a sort of 'proving out' period for me to show I can truly be trusted."

"Sounds reasonable."

"So I'm looking for some kind of pipeline in case I need to get word in or out while I'm under that kind of close scrutiny. That means I came to you looking for an idea on how I can do that."

Obie made a kind of groaning sound.

"Turns out I was wrong about needin' a jolt from this bottle. You just hit me with a bigger jolt than I wanted."

"I've got a hunch you can handle it."

"Yeah? What if I say nuts to you and your hunch? What makes you think I got any ideas on how to set up anything like this 'pipeline' you're wantin'?"

Buckhorn pinned him with a penetrating gaze.

"Like I said before, I don't think there's much of anything that goes on in these parts that you don't know at least a piece of."

"And what do you reckon a whole lot of pieces gets a fella?"

"Maybe more than you think. Maybe more than you're willing to take a chance on trying to put together."

Obie poured some more whiskey and said, "Since you showed up, that ain't hardly been a problem. You take enough chances so that anybody hangin' around you is apt to get their share and then some rubbed off. And now the ranger sticks his nose in, proddin' you along with more risky notions."

Each man raised his cup and took a drink.

Buckhorn gave it several beats before he finally asked, "Well? Anything percolating in that ornery old brain of yours? Any ideas come to mind I might be able to use?"

"Even if something does, I ain't yet heard me say that I'm willin' to hand it over."

"What do you want—for me to say 'pretty please'?"

A strange expression—part sad, part wistful and faraway—settled briefly over Obie's face.

"What I want," he murmured, "is for things to settle down and be good—as good as they ever can be with Boss Gus gone—for the Circle D again."

"You may not approve of my methods," Buckhorn replied, also speaking in a somewhat lowered voice, "but I'd say what you want and I want puts us working toward the same purpose."

Obie started to raise his cup again, but then paused and put it back down. Expelling a gust of air, he said, "Sure. O' course it does. For a moment there, after you walloped me with that 'undercover' business, I guess I sort of forgot."

"I hope you keep remembering."

Obie gave a quick, faint nod, as if to himself.

"I will. Now, here's about the only thing I can think of, at least for a start, that might give you something on the order of that 'pipeline' you're wantin' to set up . . ."

CHAPTER 25

"A Missouri mule named Sylvester and a chuck wagon cook called Slim Bob. That's all you got for a safety net?"

"That's *what* I've got," said Buckhorn, striking a more positive chord in response to Lyle Menlo's meager assessment of what Buckhorn and Obie had come up with as far as a pipeline in and out of the Riley ranch. "Unless you have something better."

"No, afraid I don't," admitted the old ranger. "We're puttin' this together on the fly, remember?"

"Oh, I remember. All too well. We're also putting my neck on the line on the fly. Remember that part?"

The two men were sitting on the ground before a crackling fire in another of Menlo's outlying night camps. It was full dark now, under a clear sky liberally sprinkled with stars but only a thin slice of moon.

"Okay, let me see if I got this straight," said Menlo as he puffed on a crusty briar pipe. "This Slim Bob is the cook for the wrangler crew at the Slash-Double R run by Milt Riley, Dan's brother. Dan has supposedly thrown in with Milt since he got booted from the Circle D, though he never seems to be around whenever anybody stops by."

"That's the size of it," Buckhorn said. "And just for the record, I had some time to kill earlier, after you and I parted at the hogback and before I went to see Obie, so I used it to do some reconnoitering of the Slash-Double R from a nearby hill. I spotted who I took to be Milt Riley, from a description provided by Obie. But nary a sign of Dan—or his daughter Eve or Jeff Danvers, either."

Menlo sent a cloud of pipe smoke rolling up into the still air and said, "Gettin' back to this Slim Bob . . . According to Obie, who's also usually in attendance, every Wednesday night Bob saddles his mule and rides to join a handful of other old-timers from the area in a weekly poker game held at the home of a former stagecoach jehu by the name of Barstow.

"He lives alone in a shack in the hills somewhere between the Circle D and the Slash-Double R. Gets by on some hogs and chickens he raises, and a smidgen of prospecting he does farther up in the hills.

"And then, on Saturdays after dishin' out breakfast, Bob hitches Sylvester to a buckboard and goes into Barkley to stock up on supplies. So, providin' you wangle your way in with Dan Riley like we're hopin', those will be your only two outlets for gettin' messages in or out. With the help of Obie."

"That's right," said Buckhorn, nodding. His hawkish features were made even starker by the shifting pattern of light and shadows thrown by the fire. "Slim Bob won't have any idea he's doing the transporting back and forth. I'm thinking I can cut a thin slice in the mule's bridle big enough to fit in a tightly folded piece of paper that nobody would spot unless they know to go digging for it. By that means, Obie can get word in to me if and when he wants to and I can send a message out to him—and you, if it's something he needs to pass along."

"Making it an outlet you could only use twice a week."

"It's the best we've got for right now," said Buckhorn. "Besides, how long do you figure this is gonna take to play out."

"It *should* go pretty quick if you're able to convince Riley there's a trap waitin' for anybody plannin' to try and rustle that fresh herd in the meadow. If he does have something in the works, like Micah Danvers and most everybody expects, and he reveals it for certain by holdin' off on account of your warning—well, that oughta nail the can to his tail once and for all and give me all I need to haul him in. If it turns out he don't know what the hell you're even talkin' about, though . . . then we got a whole different kettle of fish to boil. Unless another gang of rustlers is obliging enough to show up and ride into the trap we'll have set."

Buckhorn grunted.

"Yeah, that'll be the day."

Menlo eyed him through a curl of smoke.

"Stranger things have been known to happen."

Buckhorn felt the weight of those eyes on him and said, "You're pulling my leg. Right?"

"Maybe just a little. It so happens, though, that Kirby Peck, the young ranger who took a stab at this case ahead of me, wrote in the notes he left that he was startin' to wonder if there might not be *two* rustler gangs at work in this general area."

"You think he might have seriously been onto something?"

"Not necessarily. Not at first anyway. But it's got around to occurrin' to me that a whole bunch of people—including none other than your Mrs. Danvers—sure have got their minds made up that Dan Riley is the nasty *hombre* behind practically every bad deed that happens hereabouts. There's been other outlawry in the general area, too, you know— rustling raids on other spreads, even a few stagecoach and bank robberies. Could be grounds for what they call 'misdirection.' Mighty handy for another party lookin' to pull a foul deed here and there to get away with it a lot easier and hardly even be noticed when all eyes are busy lookin' elsewhere."

Buckhorn's face bunched into a scowl.

"Now wait just a minute. I hope you aren't saying you suspect Pamela Danvers of—"

Menlo cut him short, saying, "The only person I have reason to suspect—and that's mainly because I've had his name force-fed to me practically from the minute I set foot in town, which is sorta the whole point I'm trying to make—is Dan Riley. All I'm sayin' is maybe it's time to take a step back and cast a little wider look around. Still include Riley in the view, but not quite so exclusively."

"I guess what you're saying makes sense," said Buckhorn, feeling the tightness ease out of his shoulders. "And it doesn't change a thing for the short term, this plan for me to try and get in with Dan."

"Not at all."

"Because the other part of all this, aside from the rustling," Buckhorn reminded the ranger, "is for me to also try and get a line on what happened to Jeff Danvers, not to mention Riley's daughter Eve."

"You know where I stand on that," Menlo reminded right back. "If harm has been done or you turn up evidence of kidnapping, I naturally will get involved. But I didn't come here to mount an investigation into a couple of missing lovebirds. My main focus remains gettin' to the bottom of and puttin' a stop to the rustling. Just so we're clear on that."

"We're clear," Buckhorn said. Then added, "Long as that also includes you understanding what *my* main focus is, and not getting in the way of me doing what I have to for the sake of that."

CHAPTER 26

After sharing Menlo's campsite for the night, the ranger and the gunman rose and parted ways shortly after daybreak.

Buckhorn rode toward the Slash-Double R under a sky that, for the time being, was clear and bright, stretching from the eastern sunrise.

But off to the northwest, a smudge above the ragged horizon was rapidly thickening and darkening into an ominous cloud bank that appeared to threaten rain by midday. Intermittent gusts of cool air stabbing ahead of the thunderhead only served to heighten the sense of an oncoming storm.

Before approaching the main buildings of the ranch itself, Buckhorn once more paid a visit to the hilltop from which he'd done some reconnoitering the previous afternoon. Tying Sarge on the back slope of the hill, he ascended to the crest where he stretched out on his belly and raised a powerful set of field glasses to his eyes.

The layout below was pretty standard for a ranch of any size. Main house; outbuildings and corrals; a bunkhouse and grub shack. It wasn't arranged in a V pattern like the Circle D ranch headquarters, and the latter was notably larger, but otherwise there were many similarities. The main house here at the Slash-Double R was showing some age and wear, though still kept up quite well, and there was a newer-looking addition jutting off one corner that Buckhorn guessed might be an accommodation marking when Dan Riley and his daughter had come aboard.

When Buckhorn had taken his look-see yesterday, most everyone was scattered to handle the day's chores, so there hadn't been much activity to observe. This morning it was different. It was still early enough so that some of the hands were working around the headquarters. Two men were shoeing horses over by an open-fronted building with an anvil and a glowing forge inside. Another was rubbing on liniment and otherwise tending to a sleek roan that appeared to have come up lame.

Buckhorn even caught sight of a tall, skinny gent in a stained white apron—who had to be none other than Slim Bob—throwing a tubful of kitchen scraps out one end of the grub shack. A handful of chickens and a pair of spotted shoats came scrambling to fight over the offering.

On the front porch of the house, Buckhorn again spotted Milt Riley sitting in a sturdy rocking chair enjoying a cup of coffee in the company of a trim, handsome, butterscotch-haired woman who had to be his wife Larraine. He knew, from Obie, that Milt and Larraine also had a daughter just a little older than Eve. Buckhorn couldn't recall her name, not that it really mattered. Particularly since he saw no sign of her, or of Eve or Jeff Danvers, as far as that went.

And no Dan Riley, either.

Buckhorn calculated that when Milt finished the private bit of leisure time with his wife, he likely would rise out of his chair, come down off the porch, and join his crew, prodding them into whatever work was in store for the day. Buckhorn further reckoned that if he waited for brother Dan to show up, he might be there until the approaching storm washed him away or the blizzards of winter rolled in.

So if he was going to get the ball rolling, it looked like his best bet would be to start it with Milt. And, if he meant to do that while the man was right there handy, he'd best quit looking and start doing.

Another of those cold prestorm gusts came rolling up over the crest just as Buckhorn lowered the binoculars and started to push himself away before rising to his feet and descending back down the slope. Amidst the low moan of the cold gust and the whisper of dust granules that carried with it, a voice spoke clear and sharp.

"Hold it right there, mister. Stay on your belly, like the snake you are, and keep your hands right where I can see 'em—in plain sight and empty."

Inwardly, Buckhorn cursed himself. What the hell was wrong with him lately? What was allowing him to be distracted to the point where would-be ambushers were able to get close enough to fire their first shot before he was aware they were anywhere near?

Or almost as bad, for *both* Obie and Menlo to have been able to observe him testing his Colt and target practicing the other day without him having any idea either one was there. And now, yet again, he'd let someone sneak up on him—not only that but, judging by the voice, the s*omeone* was a female!

"And in case you're not inclined to take orders from a gal," the voice added, as if reading his mind, "then you might like to know that I have a Winchester aimed square at you. You might also like to know that I'm a darn good shot. But even if I wasn't, I could hardly miss blowing your spine in two from this close, no matter how bad I was."

"Actually," said Buckhorn, his face so close to the ground that his breath puffed up miniature dust clouds when he spoke, "I wouldn't like to know any of those things because I'd rather not be in a position where I *need* to know 'em."

"Then you ought not be trespassing where you're not wanted and crawling on the ground like a rattlesnake or a lizard to spy on folks!"

Before Buckhorn could make another reply, the Winchester behind him roared and a chunk of ground less than a foot from his left hand kicked into the air as a slug tore into it.

A wild thought streaked through Buckhorn's brain. Could it be that the girl was *not* the markswoman she claimed and she'd shot at him and missed?

Before that possibility could sink in, there came the sound of another round being levered into the firing chamber followed instantly by the Winchester being triggered again. This time a slug tore into the ground close to his right hand. Buckhorn dug his fingers clawlike into the earth and refused to jerk his arm away. The rifle spoke again and a third round sizzled just above Buckhorn's head to bury itself into the ground only inches ahead of his face.

The gun went silent. And only then did Buckhorn fully realize what had just happened. The girl had issued a warning signal, three rapid-fire shots, to those below. At the same time, by planting the slugs so closely around him, she had demonstrated to Buckhorn that she could just as easily have riddled him with lead.

To confirm his realization, Buckhorn was able to lift his face slightly and see, even without the binoculars, a sudden swarm of activity down among the buildings of the Slash-Double R ranch headquarters. Milt Riley had bounded off the porch and was trotting toward his men who were jabbering excitedly and pointing upward toward where Buckhorn was flattened on the ground.

"Long as you're willing to keep holdin' still, I'm willing to not shoot you," said the female voice behind him. "But we're going to have visitors in a few minutes and I can't make no promises for them."

"Judging by the bowler hat and the Indian look to him, he's got to be the hired gun we heard about Pamela Danvers bringing in," said the girl—who'd introduced herself, while they were awaiting the arrival of the others, as Milt's daughter Josephine. "I was out for an early ride before the day turns stormy, wanting to run some more of the rough off that new mare we just broke in," she went on, explaining to her father and the two wranglers who'd come along with him to the top of the hill. "I was pushing her hard across some high ground off to the south when I happened to catch a glint of sunlight off this jasper's field glasses as he was squirming into position."

"Why didn't you hightail it back to the ranch and fetch me and some of the boys right away," her father demanded, "instead of sneaking in on this owlhoot alone? You could have got yourself hurt."

"I did all right, though, didn't I?" There was a smugness to the tone of Josephine's reply. "Before he had a clue I was behind him, I got close enough to slap that silly hat off his head if I'd wanted to. I was afraid if I rode down to warn you he was lurking up here, he'd be looking on and sniff out what I was up to. Then he'd've had the chance to get away before anybody could circle around on him."

"I didn't come here to turn tail and run," said Buckhorn, from where he still lay on the ground. "I came here to talk."

"*Talk*, you say?"

Milt Riley stepped around in front of him. Buckhorn cranked his head back and lifted his face to get a better look at the man. He wasn't overly tall, but massive through the chest and shoulders. Big, thick-fingered hands gripped a Winchester Yellowboy like it was a twig. He glared down at Buckhorn with green eyes set deep in a broad, fleshy face bracketed by thick sideburns the color of old rust. It was a face that looked like it could be as quick to humor as it was to anger. But the latter was definitely holding court at the moment.

"You got some fancy way of strikin' up a conversation from atop a far-off hill? Is that how you set out to have a talk with somebody?"

"I was looking the layout over before I came the rest of the way on down," Buckhorn explained. "Since you already seem to know about me, then you ought to know that folks have been poking guns in my face or tryin' to ambush me ever since I showed up in these parts. I was just aiming to be cautious."

"But you weren't cautious enough, were you?" said Josephine, definitely with a taunting lilt to her voice. "You let me move up behind you."

Buckhorn felt the burn of embarrassment crawl onto his face.

"Afraid there's no getting around that," he muttered.

"So what's this talk you're lookin' to have that made you think you had to be so careful about comin' forward with it?" Milt wanted to know.

Buckhorn started to answer but then stopped short. His humiliation suddenly flared to a spurt of anger and he said instead, "I've said all I'm gonna say lying here on the ground like a worm. You want to hear any more, let me get to my feet. Otherwise, to hell with you."

One of the rifle-wielding wranglers who'd accompanied Milt up from the ranch took a step forward and said, "You'd better watch your mouth, mister, or you're gonna find it mighty hard to do *any* talkin' out of it."

Milt raised a hand, holding the wrangler in check. He returned his glare to Buckhorn, seeming to consider, then said, "Okay. Go ahead and push yourself up as far as your knees. Real slow. Remember you got four guns trained on you, so keep your hands out away from your body or you're apt to make one of us twitchy."

Buckhorn did as instructed.

"Now, even slower, unbuckle your gunbelt and push it back behind you."

Again, Buckhorn complied.

"All right. Get on up the rest of the way. Just be sure to do it—"

"I know. Real slow," Buckhorn finished for him.

As he rose to his feet, Buckhorn swept his gaze over the rest of those arranged in a semicircle before him. Milt remained directly in front. To either side of their boss stood two lean, leathery-looking wranglers, both appearing to be in their middle to late twenties, with nothing to mark them as particularly distinct or memorable.

Farther to Buckhorn's right, comprising the tip of the semicircle on that side, stood the girl, Josephine. In addition to being the only female in the group, there was plenty else that was distinct and memorable about her. Early twenties, Buckhorn judged her to be, nicely filled out with mature, all-woman curves that not even her simple attire of corduroy riding skirt and plain white blouse could subdue. She had her father's penetrating eyes, though blue in her case, dominating a finely sculpted face surrounded by a spill of blond hair touched with traces of red.

She, too, held a Winchester in a leisurely, confident manner, and the set of her jaw along with the way those blue eyes met and challenged Buckhorn's appraising gaze gave every indication she wouldn't hesitate to pull the trigger again.

Slowly, first with one hand and then the other,

Buckhorn reached up and brushed the dust from the front of his clothes. Then he raised both hands and adjusted his hat.

"There. You're on your feet and primped up good and proper," Milt said. "Now let's hear whatever it is you came here to get off your chest."

"Actually," said Buckhorn, responding to Milt while feeling the expectant looks of the others also trained on him, "the talk I came here to have is with your brother Dan. So, since I can see you've got important ranch chores hanging fire, it'd save time and re-telling if you just took me to him direct."

One side of Milt's mouth lifted in a sarcastic sneer.

"Well, it sure is nice of you to worry about me and the boys being kept from our ranch work. And don't think we don't appreciate it. But you let me worry about that part of it. You got us real curious about what you came here to say, and we're anxious to hear it, even if we have to listen twice."

Buckhorn shrugged.

"If you say so. Seems like a waste of time, though, if you ask me."

"Nobody did," Josephine pointed out.

"Besides," Milt said, "you ain't gonna be talking to my brother any time soon, anyway. Happens he's not around. He's off on—"

"A business trip," Buckhorn cut in, finishing the lie for him. Then he added, "I've heard all about those frequent business ventures your brother seems to be away on whenever anybody comes around."

"That may be." Milt's expression was turning more suspicious. "But so far I ain't hearin' where his business is any of yours."

"We still got time to get to that." Buckhorn shrugged again. "But it sure sounds to me like you're gettin' the shitty end of your partnership. Dan goes sportin' around on business trips all the time while you're stuck here in the heat and dust with all the hard labor and the day-to-day grind. That's a mighty poor bargain, especially with you being the older brother and the original owner of the ranch and all."

That struck a sour chord in Milt. He took a step closer to Buckhorn, baring his teeth as he said, "You let me worry about that, Mr. Big Mouth. What you'd better start worryin' about is—"

Milt's display of anger was a mistake on two counts. First, his uncharacteristic outburst jerked the focus of his wranglers and his daughter to him and away from Buckhorn. Second, he stepped within Buckhorn's reach.

Exploding with greased-lightning speed, Buckhorn shot his left arm forward and then swept it upward, knocking the barrel of Milt's Winchester high and loosening his hold on it. In the same motion, Buckhorn twisted his upper body to his left, reaching with his right hand and clamping his own iron grip just ahead of the rear stock. Sliding his left hand down the barrel and grabbing there, too, he yanked the weapon away from Milt, pulling him another step nearer at the same time. As the rancher leaned in, now fighting for balance, Buckhorn's right elbow swung up and across in a slashing blow to the older man's jaw. Milt was knocked backward, his feet tangling as he toppled away.

Letting his momentum whirl him farther to his left,

Buckhorn quickly re-adjusted his grip on the rifle until he was holding it similar to a soldier preparing for a bayonet thrust. Which was exactly how he used it, ramming the muzzle forward at an upward angle and driving it under the chin of the wrangler who'd been standing on that side of Milt. The head of the young man, attempting to brace himself as he raised his own rifle, snapped back from the impact and he emitted a sharp gagging, hacking sound as he dropped the gun and twisted away, knees buckling.

Without hesitation, Buckhorn spun back the other way, to his right, where the remaining wrangler was bringing his Winchester to bear. Buckhorn continued his hard turn. As he did, he released his left hand's grip on the front stock of the confiscated rifle and, wielding it only right-handed now, extended his arm and swung the edge of the barrel as hard as he could, slamming it against the side of the young wrangler's head. The heavy *chunk!* of metal against meat and bone came just an instant ahead of a discharge from the wrangler's gun, but the impact of the blow was enough to divert the weapon's aim and thereby send the round harmlessly into the dirt.

That left the girl, Josephine, as the only one still standing against Buckhorn. Even as he'd rifle-whipped the second wrangler he feared that his attempt to turn the tables on those who had the drop on him, as smooth and fast as his moves had been, had taken too long, was going to come up short.

Except for the one thing that wasn't in his calculation. Emotion. Josephine's instinctive concern for her father, seeing him knocked to the ground by the elbow smash, had overridden what became her secondary instinct, to retaliate against Buckhorn. Vaguely, he recalled hearing her cry of "Father!" as he was wheeling away from throat-thrusting the first wrangler.

As the second wrangler was hitting the ground, Buckhorn spun to face Josephine full on. He found her just starting to correct herself from the lunging step she had automatically taken toward her father, instead stopping short and now, realizing her mistake, beginning to bring the aim of her rifle back to Buckhorn. But it was too late and Buckhorn was too fast.

He batted her Winchester away with a sideways swat of his own, at the same time stepping close, wrenching the gun from her grasp with his free hand, then throwing a hard shoulder bump that backed her up three jerky steps.

Regaining her balance, her hands balled into trembling fists that she held at her sides, Josephine glared at him and hissed, "You dirty, sneaky bastard! Look at those men—you hurt them bad!"

"Man pulls a gun on me," Buckhorn replied, his voice like a file scraping on rock, "I usually hurt him to death."

"What about women? You gonna hurt me bad, too—or are you gonna go ahead and just gun us all down? Like you probably came here for to begin with!"

"Lady, if I came here to gun anybody," Buckhorn told her, "I'd do it face on and it would be all over by now."

They stood there glaring at one another. Josephine was breathing hard from exertion and stress. It was hard for Buckhorn not to let his eyes linger on the rapid rise and fall of her breasts.

The wrangler who'd taken the muzzle thrust to his throat was squirming a bit on the ground, inhaling and exhaling noisily, raggedly. Milt, who'd received the least amount of punishment next to his daughter, was pushed up on one elbow and doing some groaning of his own. The other wrangler was out cold.

Buckhorn recalled that the ranch boss hadn't been wearing a sidearm. Jerking a thumb, he said to Josephine, "Go to your father. Circle wide, don't even think about trying to pick up any hardware on the way."

While the girl was doing as told, Buckhorn gathered up the fallen rifles and stripped the two fallen wranglers of their gunbelts. All of this he put in a pile and then took time to strap his own gunbelt back on. That made him feel better, whole again.

Leaving Milt and Josephine huddled together, Buckhorn went to check on the wrangler he'd struck in the throat. The fellow was breathing noisily and with some difficulty.

"Just stay still and take it easy," Buckhorn advised him. "You'll be okay." He turned to father and daughter. "What are they expecting down at the ranch?" he asked of them. "You got any more signals set up?"

They both just glared at him some more.

"Don't be stupid," he told them. "Unless you want to see more people hurt, tell me what it will take to put everybody else at ease until we can all go down there and I'm given the chance to say what I came here for."

After hesitating, Milt said, "Three more shots, spaced like Joey did before. That's the all-clear."

"What about the wild shot your man got off?"

"That'll be okay, as long as they get the all-clear before much longer."

Buckhorn motioned to Josephine—"Joey" her father had called her.

"Get up there in that open spot where they can get a good look at you. Wave your arms up over your head while I fire off the rounds."

"You love spoutin' orders, don't you?" she said, not moving.

"Do what he says," Milt told her. "If he wanted us dead, he'd have done it by now. Let's try to make it through this like he said, without anybody else gettin' hurt."

Sighing, Joey went to the open spot and began waving her arms. Edging up behind and off to one side, where he could peer down through some bushes, Buckhorn triggered the blasts from his Colt. Down below, he could see everyone who had been intently looking up at the crest abruptly appear to relax and otherwise show signs of relief in their body language.

"Okay, that's enough," Buckhorn said to Joey. Then, as his hands automatically began punching out and replacing the three spent shells, he added, "Go grab a canteen off one of the horses your father and his men rode up on. We can use it to roust the two injured wranglers. The sooner we get them on their feet, the sooner we can go down and get this over with."

Joey's eyes burned into him as she said, "This ain't gonna be over with, mister—not completely—until I get you under the muzzle of my gun. Comes to that and I put you on the ground again, I guarantee you won't be getting back up a second time."

Buckhorn met her fiery gaze and let one corner of his mouth twitch momentarily upward.

"I'll be sure to keep that in mind. Now go get the canteen."

CHAPTER 27

It wasn't until they were well within the confines of the Slash-Double R ranch headquarters before those awaiting them started to catch on that everything wasn't quite right, in spite of the all-clear signal.

The battered condition of the two young wranglers drew the attention of Slim Bob and the men who'd been shoeing horses. They came forward, just curious and rather slowly at first, but then, with frowns deepening at what they saw, their steps quickened.

As for Larraine Riley, all she had to do was take one look at the expressions on the faces of both her husband and daughter in order to sense they were unsuccessfully trying to mask some kind of trouble.

"What is it, Milt? What happened?" she asked, moving close as he reined his horse at a hitch rail in front of the house.

"What the heck happened to Tully and Sweetwater? Who's this here other fella you brung with you?" Slim Bob wanted to know, his tone more strident and demanding.

It was Buckhorn, riding up just behind Milt, who

answered. "Before you worry too much about *who* I am," he said, "you might want to take note of *what* I am—and that would be the *hombre* who has a drawn Colt .45 resting atop my saddle horn, aimed square at your boss. Something else probably worth noting is that your friends here have all been disarmed. Now if everybody else just stays calm and hears me out, none of that will really matter. But if any of you take a notion to get excited and maybe overreact, then it won't turn out good."

Slim Bob's long, weather-seamed face pulled into a scowl that made the seams even tighter and deeper.

"You see here, you. Nobody just rides up and—"

"Back down, Bob," Milt interrupted him. "Do what he says, for the reasons he says. I don't want anybody hurt worse, not if we can help it."

"But what about those men who obviously are *already* hurt?" Larraine demanded.

"That's a fair point," Buckhorn said. "If somebody wants to ease those boys down out of their saddles and make 'em a mite more comfortable, I won't object. But, before that, you in the red shirt"—he tipped his head toward one of the pair who'd been shoeing horses, a yellow-haired gent wearing a gun on his hip—"shuck that gunbelt of yours, real slow and careful, and fling it away. *Then* you can help with your two injured pards."

As far as Buckhorn could see, neither Slim Bob nor the other horse-shoer was armed. Once the yellow-haired man had done as instructed, the three of them gently lifted down Tully and Sweetwater and laid them on the ground. Larraine went over to help tend the men.

As this was taking place, Buckhorn backed Sarge off a few paces and turned him so that everyone was directly before them, where Buckhorn could effectively cover anybody who might be foolish enough to try something.

All the while, he was keenly aware that Milt and Joey were back to glaring at him. Buckhorn didn't take either of them for being foolish, but the hate in their eyes made it plenty clear that, if given a fraction of a chance, they'd love nothing better than to nail his hide to the wall.

"All right," Milt said, his voice harsh. "Ain't it about damn time you spilled what this is all about? If you think you can go up against my brother and continue getting away with these kind of tactics, then you're in for a rude awakening!"

"That's the part you've got all wrong," Buckhorn told him. "I'm not looking to talk to your brother because I'm out to go *against* him. Not anymore. What I'm aiming for now is to *join* him."

"You expect anybody to believe a load of bull droppings like that?" snapped Joey. "You heard me say that we know all about you hiring out to Pamela Danvers. Everybody in the territory knows how much she hates my uncle. Can't be any doubt what she brought in a hired gun to do."

"And you've made it plenty clear how willing you are to live up to your reputation," Milt added.

Buckhorn heaved a ragged sigh and said, "I also *tried* to make it clear that if I'd come here to do gun work, those two over there would be dead, not just busted up."

"It might be one and the same if we don't get these boys some medical attention," Larraine said anxiously, from where she was on her knees beside the injured men. "They're hurt bad and they surely deserve better care than they can get lying here on the ground!"

Seeming to ignore her, Buckhorn kept his focus on Milt.

"Appears you aren't keeping up with things near as good as you think you are, not when it comes to my hire-out to the Widow Danvers. Happens I had to shoot and kill one of her wranglers yesterday morning when he prodded me into a showdown. On top of that, Micah, the cocky little puke she calls a son, was in my face right from the first . . . until I had to pull a gun on him, too. Long story short: my service to Pamela Danvers and the Circle D is over."

Milt's reaction was a look of surprise followed quickly by one of suspicion.

"Come to think on it," spoke up Slim Bob, "a couple of our fellas who'd gone into town last night said something at grub this mornin' about hearin' of a shoot-out over at the Circle D yesterday. The sheriff and undertaker even got called out."

"That's right," said Buckhorn. "They tried to sic the law on me. Not only the sheriff, but also that Texas Ranger who showed up the other day."

Milt scowled.

"Texas Ranger, you say?"

"Uh-huh. The boys mentioned something about that, too," confirmed Slim Bob.

Milt found someone other than Buckhorn to aim his glare at.

"Jumpin' blazes, Bob! You ever think about passin' on some of these things you hear?"

"I'd've got around to it," Slim Bob said defensively. "The day is still young and you only came down from the house a bit ago when we heard Joey's signal shots."

Speaking of Joey, her father's hard look may have been diverted from Buckhorn, but hers hadn't wavered. She addressed him now, saying, "None of this explains why you're so secretive, yet all-fired determined to meet with Uncle Dan, mister."

"And none of it is helping these poor boys, either," added her mother.

"All right," said Buckhorn through gritted teeth. "I'm gonna state one more piece of my business and that's it. The reason I'm being so-called 'secretive' is that it's *my* damn business. A man has a right to conduct his own affairs—in private, if he chooses—don't he? That's what I'm lookin' to do with Dan Riley.

"The Widow Danvers convinced me to come here and now has stiffed me. I need a job, a payday. I have some information that I think will be of interest to Riley, so I'm aiming to parlay that into doing some work for him instead."

"My uncle's not in the habit of hiring professional gunnies to do his dirty work for him," Joey said.

"That's for him to tell me, not you," Buckhorn responded. He paused for a beat, his eyes scanning, touching the faces of all before him. Then: "I don't believe for a minute that Riley is gone on some kind of extended trip. I believe he's somewhere not far from here—maybe holed up for some reason. Let's not pretend we don't all know about the suspicions of rustling and other outlawry where he's concerned. But never mind any of that. For now, all I want to know is if one of you is gonna help put me in touch with him . . . or if I have to do it the hard way."

CHAPTER 28

As they rode away from the Slash-Double R headquarters, Buckhorn was still having trouble believing he had gone along with this arrangement. The only thing that balanced it somewhat in his mind was the belief that Milt Riley must be wrestling inwardly with the same thoughts. Nevertheless, the agreement had been reached and now it was in motion.

Riding at Buckhorn's side as they put the ranch buildings behind them and angled to the north and west, was Joey Riley. She was the one setting the course—the course that allegedly would take them to her uncle Dan.

That was the deal that had been struck. Buckhorn had refused to wait at the ranch like a sitting duck and have Riley brought to him. Milt had refused to simply tell Buckhorn where he could find Dan and then leave his brother the sitting duck for Buckhorn to go after unexpected and unannounced.

Plus, the latter, from Buckhorn's perspective, could have meant sending him on a wild goose chase that would have provided the chance to warn Dan so he could go on the defensive or perhaps even take up the offense. The compromise was someone accompanying Buckhorn, leading the way and also serving as an intermediary to make sure no traps were sprung by either side.

Selecting Joey as said intermediary was not arrived at without a good deal of contention. Buckhorn saw her as a risk who might turn on him the first chance she got. Milt and Larraine were understandably not comfortable at the thought of their daughter riding out with a notorious gunman.

But Milt himself was not an option; he needed to stay with the ranch and his diminished crew. Larraine was out of the question. Neither Slim Bob nor any of the other remaining able-bodied men would hold enough sway over Dan to ensure he heard Buckhorn out before possibly reacting rashly at the first sight of him—plus those men also needed to stay at the ranch, especially if it was deemed necessary to haul their injured pards into town to the doctor.

So that left Joey, who knew how and where to reach her uncle, was a competent horsewoman, and was willing to fill the role. A little too willing, the way Buckhorn saw it. But, above practically anything else, he wanted to keep what he'd undertaken in motion and he wanted the face-to-face with Dan Riley. So he'd capitulated, said Joey was okay with him. After that, the others grudgingly gave in, too.

Before they'd ridden out, however, Milt had leaned in close at one point and said to Buckhorn, in a low and very intense voice, "You may be out of my league as far as a fighting man and gunslinger and so on. But if you do anything to cause my little girl harm . . . I'll come after you, no matter how long or how far it takes, and see to it you pay hard."

The storm that was moving in was coming fast and they were riding straight toward the heart of it.

"We gonna make wherever we're headed before that thing hits us or we hit it?" Buckhorn wanted to know, his words tossed around on the buffeting wind that was growing steadily stronger.

"Gonna be close," Joey replied. Her long hair was streaming straight back from her stern and determined expression. Abruptly, she turned to face Buckhorn and flashed a crooked grin. "What's the matter, Mr. Big Bad Gunman? You're not worried about a little storm, are you?"

"I worry about anything I can't stop with a bullet," Buckhorn answered flatly.

For some miles, the terrain they covered was all good graze land, mostly flat with a few low, grassy hills that occasionally rose to sharper, pine-studded ridges. Here and there the ground was split open by shallow, washed-out gullies.

Eventually, though, the land began to change. It became rockier and more rugged, the grass thinning. The rolling hills rose up sharper, turned ragged looking and only sparsely sketched with brownish-green scrub brush. The gullies deepened into narrow, twisting arroyos. Buckhorn calculated these changes were an extension of the same broken land he'd seen reaching away to the north of the hogback and lush meadow on Circle D property.

"We still on Slash-Double R land?" he asked Joey.

"Not sure," she replied offhandedly. "It's such crappy ground I don't think anybody pays much attention."

A short time later, the storm hit. They saw it coming in time to reach shelter under a rocky ledge that protruded sharply outward near the top of a rubble-strewn slope. Even at that, they weren't in time to totally avoid the first slashing waves of cold rain that blew flat and hard ahead of the main deluge.

Dismounting, Buckhorn and Joey clambered as far back into the recess as they could and squatted there, sleeving the rain from their faces and shaking it off their hats. The horses were too tall to fit far enough under the ledge for complete protection, but they were still considerably better off than out in the open, so they munched from clumps of scrub brush and seemed content with that.

Meanwhile, the black, boiling storm clouds had turned the afternoon nearly as dark as night. In contrast, the frequent pitchforks of brilliant lightning illuminated everything with crystal clarity. The wind-driven sheets of rain, caught in these bursts of light, looked like gleaming silver sword blades slicing across the landscape. The rapidly repeating peals of thunder rolled with a force of their own, at times shaking the ground so hard that having the slab of rock over their heads almost seemed like more of a threat than a salvation.

From his war bag, Buckhorn pulled a heavy gray rain slicker that he proceeded to shroud himself in. Looking over at Joey, he said, "You got one of these?"

She shook her head.

"Didn't think to grab one."

Buckhorn produced a second slicker, mustard yellow in color and showing some patches, that he held out to her.

"Here. Pull this over yourself. Leaks a little, but it'll keep you a lot drier and warmer than you will be otherwise."

Joey didn't hesitate to pull the garment over herself. Then she said, "Thanks. But why do you care if I'm warm or dry or comfortable in any way at all?"

"Don't, particularly," Buckhorn said. "But if you were to drown or catch pneumonia, it'd make it harder for me to link up with your uncle. Plus, I'd have your father on my neck."

"I should have known that plain old chivalry didn't play any part."

Buckhorn gave her a look.

"*If* I had any chivalry in me . . . and I'm not saying I do . . . it'd still be kinda hard to dredge it up for somebody who threatened to blow my spine in two when she had a Winchester aimed at my back. Sorry, Miss Riley, but, as a damsel in distress, you fall a little short."

"Fine by me," Joey declared. "I can ride and shoot as good or better than most men, making me plenty capable of taking care of myself. What's more, all that fawning, moony-eyed junk that goes with a gal and a fella sniffin' around one another has always been about as appealing to me as a case of saddle rash. So I'm *glad* to hear I fall short as the damsel in distress type."

The full intensity of the storm began to abate somewhat. The lightning pops and crashes of thunder came less frequently, but the rain continued to pour down and, by the look of the churning, still-bloated clouds, wasn't likely to quit any time soon. The ribbon of flat, sandy ground they had been following along the base of the slope was swirling wildly with thick, muddy brown run-off.

"Looks like we won't be going anywhere for a while yet," Buckhorn noted as he reached once more into his war bag. He brought out a handful of beef jerky strips wrapped in oilcloth. After taking one for himself, he placed the open pack on the ground between him and Joey and said, "Help yourself, if you've a mind. Probably won't gain any favor for myself if I let you starve, neither."

"It's hardly been that long since breakfast," Joey said. But she nevertheless took a piece of the jerky. After snapping off a bite, she added, "What would really go good right about now would be a cup of coffee."

"No argument," Buckhorn agreed. "Unfortunately, what little bramble there is within reach is too wet to burn and wouldn't make enough fuel to boil a pot anyway."

They sat quietly for a spell, chewing and gazing out at the rain.

At length Joey looked over at Buckhorn, and for the first time her expression was one more of curiosity than annoyance or anger.

"What is it you're *really* up to with all of this, Buckhorn?" she said.

Buckhorn wagged his head and told her, "I've explained it as clear as I know how and about as damn often as I intend to. What's so hard to understand? Getting fired by the widow left me in a tight. I need a job, money. I figure I've got something to offer your uncle in return."

"Because you believe the stories about him being a rustler and an outlaw." It was a statement, not a question.

"Well, in case you didn't notice, I didn't pitch my services to your pa. It's not cowpuncher work I'm looking for."

Joey took another bite of jerky and regarded him some more. Buckhorn decided it made him less uncomfortable when she was glaring at him. He'd gotten used to that.

"I just might believe you," she said, "if it wasn't for one thing."

"And that would be?"

"You mentioned Micah Danvers. Everybody knows what a jackass he is. But what about his brother—Jeff?"

Buckhorn sensed this was some kind of test. And how he responded was going to go a long way toward how far Joey would be willing to trust him from here on out—and, in turn, how far he might be able to trust her.

"The young fella who's gone missing, you mean?" he said simply, aiming to coax out a little better idea of what she was angling for.

"That would be the one, yes. Pamela's youngest. Hard to believe she'd hire you to look into her rustling problem without including Jeff's disappearance as something also for your consideration."

"She mentioned it, naturally. I could see she was plenty distraught over it, and she made sure I knew most of the details so I could keep an eye peeled for the boy." Buckhorn spread his hands. "But you've got to remember, I was only part of the picture for a pretty short time, and doing detective work isn't exactly my strong suit. Maybe she meant to crowd me more into searching after the missing boy but just never got around to it before everything fell apart."

"You'd think a missing son would be her first priority."

"*If* that was the main part of why she sent for me. Like I said, detective work isn't exactly what I'm known for. Especially now that she's got a Texas Ranger on the scene. Kidnapping is one of the many things that are right up their alley."

Joey's eyebrows lifted. She said, "Is that what they're calling Jeff's disappearance now? Kidnapping?"

Buckhorn gave it a cautious beat before saying, "I guess I can't claim to have heard anybody else use that word. But the son of a rich ranching family suddenly comes up missing . . . Am I the only one who thinks of kidnapping as something that's likely behind it?"

Now it was Joey who hesitated before responding. Buckhorn was pretty sure she was trying to get him to admit he knew something about her cousin Eve and how she might be connected to Jeff's disappearance. But Buckhorn was holding fast to his pretense.

Finally, Joey said, "From what I understand, Jeff has been missing for several days. If it was kidnapping, don't you think a ransom note would have shown up by now?"

Buckhorn frowned and said, "You're right. I guess I didn't think of that."

"So Pamela never mentioned anything about a note?"

"Not to me."

Joey turned to look at him full on, eyeing Buckhorn more sharply than ever.

"You're either denser than I'm ready to believe, or one hell of a good actor who's got something up his sleeve. Or maybe you're actually on the level. I can't make up my mind which."

Buckhorn tried a disarming grin.

"Take your time. Maybe you'll find I'm a little bit of all three."

In that moment, a burst of lightning cast the hawk-like features of his face in a pattern of contrasting brilliant light and inky shadows that made Buckhorn look more threatening than disarming. And yet, judging by the look in her eyes, Joey no longer felt threatened by him. Not at all.

CHAPTER 29

"Well, there they are. Finally," Micah Danvers said. "Where we've been wanting to get 'em for two blasted days."

"I wish it *had* been two days ago," Hank Boynton lamented. "Or yesterday . . . or even tomorrow. Any time but right now with this frog-strangler of a storm pourin' down on us."

"Aw, quit bellyachin'," Micah said. "If this all works out the way it's shapin' up to, then a little rainwater down the back of your neck is gonna be a minor inconvenience. It'll be worth this and more."

They sat their horses under an overhang of dripping cottonwood branches on a slope of high ground. Below them, spread across the oval meadow, shiny and slick looking from the sheets of rain being wind-whipped across their backs, were just short of seven hundred longhorns milling and bawling under a sky of roiling dark clouds cut by forks of lightning.

Dave Millard came riding up and joined them under the minimal cover provided by the cottonwood canopy. Thunder rolled around his words when he spoke. "They're good and tired from the drive up here. The men will stick with 'em for a while, but I think they'll hold in place pretty good, even with the storm."

Micah nodded.

"I think so, too. The rain may last for a while, but the bluster of the storm will move on fairly soon. That'll help keep 'em settled."

Dave grinned in the dim afternoon light.

"And once they get a taste of that sweet graze down there, they ain't ever gonna want to leave."

"For sure not on account of no stinkin' rustlers. Us and that Texas Ranger are gonna see to that. Right, Micah?"

Micah didn't answer right away. He was gazing out across the meadow, and for a moment his expression shifted into a strange, faraway look, like he could see something through the rain that the others couldn't. Then he said, "Indeed we are, Hank. Indeed we are."

On the far side of the meadow, Lyle Menlo squatted warm and dry under the canvas tarp he had spread between clumps of bramble brush in anticipation of the storm's arrival. As was his habit, he had taken up his position well in advance of both the first drops of rain and the first heads of cattle to show up. From where he was, he could not see the three men on the slope across the way. He expected they were present somewhere, involved in driving the cattle, but didn't know exactly where. For their part, they were unaware of his presence at all.

In the pops of lightning, as the arriving herd

spread wider and wider across the meadow, Menlo caught glimpses of wranglers on horseback passing near him as they worked the cattle. But none were Micah Danvers or his two closest cohorts whom Menlo had never caught the names of.

Not that the ranger cared one way or the other. Especially not right at the moment. He was in no hurry to confab again with Micah, though he knew he had to eventually. For now, though, he was simply enjoying the show being put on by the longhorns filling up the meadow.

One of these days, when his badge-toting was behind him, Menlo aimed to have a small cattle ranch of his own. Nothing big, just a few head to chase and raise; to move back and forth between the best graze until they were sufficiently fattened up for shipping off to market, and then start all over again with a new bunch.

Although the cards that laid out his fate had never turned up a chance for Menlo to work on a cattle ranch, that had always been his dream. He loved the notion of ranching and working cattle. That was why he hated the notion of sneaky, lowdown rustlers and why he'd earned a reputation for shutting down more rustling rings than practically any ranger on the force.

Looking at the fine bunch of young beef accumulating before him now—slick and mud spattered and rain blurred though they might be—only strengthened the old ranger's resolve to keep his rep intact by chopping short the ropes of any wide-loopers looking to strike again here.

That he would succeed at this, Menlo was confident. The areas where he was less certain lay with those he'd allied himself with. To say he had some reservations when it came to Micah Danvers would be an understatement of no small proportion. Nor was his fellow lawman, the dense-seeming Sheriff Tolliver, particularly inspiring.

Ironically, the individual he was counting on the most—his hole card, so to speak—was Joe Buckhorn. A hired gun. A man with his own reputation—one that, until not so very long ago, ranked him as little more than a paid assassin. And yet, in the here and now, there was something about him that Menlo found . . . solid.

In the West, it wasn't uncommon for a man to put his past behind him and become something different. Sometimes for the better, sometimes for the worse. Buckhorn, Menlo sensed, was the same man he'd always been but something *within* him had changed. For the better, if only slightly.

But only slightly would do just fine for the situation at hand. Considering the circumstances Menlo had encouraged him to thrust himself into, it wouldn't do for Buckhorn's dangerous edge to be blunted too much. Not if he wanted to make it back out alive.

Pamela Danvers stood on the open front porch of her house and gazed out at the rain lashing down on the grounds and buildings of the Circle D ranch head-quarters. Occasional cold drops would spray in and reach her under the roof overhang, but she appeared not to notice. Her expression was intense, almost as dark and turbulent as the angry sky.

Everything was in motion, she tried telling herself.

So much of what had been plaguing her of late, the pressures that had been building up around her, had been placed in competent hands and were now being directly addressed. Complete with the buy-in and participation of Ranger Menlo, Micah's plan for confronting and trapping the rustlers (that traitorous damn Dan Riley!) seemed to hold real promise for success. And Joe Buckhorn was locked solely on finding out what had become of Jeff and hopefully bringing him back home safe.

Hopefully.

That was the trouble. Too much of it depended on hope. And undermining Pamela's ability to remain positive and hopeful were doubts she could not ignore. Dan Riley and his gang had been getting away with their rustling raids and other outlaw acts for a long time now. What was the likelihood that this time—even with an assist from a Texas Ranger—would be any different? And as competent and fierce as Joe Buckhorn had proven to be, were those the proper skills for getting to the bottom of Jeff's disappearance?

Moreover, beyond the simple doubts, lay the down-deep, personal truths that were even harder to try and face up to.

Her son Micah had serious character flaws. On some level, Pamela had known it for a long time, but she had looked away, ignored it, and when she couldn't do that she had convinced herself that in time, with maturity, he would change, would come around to finally being the man you'd expect a son of Gus Danvers to be.

But his attitude and actions lately had only served

to demonstrate a seething, disturbed side that seemed bent on pulling him farther away from her. Even if Micah succeeded in playing a major role when it came to finally putting a stop to the rustling, would it change him for the better or only make him more arrogant and demanding? There was no way of knowing the answer for certain, yet Pamela had a sinking feeling that she *did* know.

And what of precious, gentle Jeff? Also very unlike his father, but not in such a distressing, threatening way. No matter how hard Pamela tried rejecting the thought, there was no denying that the length of time he'd been missing without contacting her was not a promising sign. The sinking feeling she had where Micah was concerned was even deeper and more agonizing when it came to Jeff and any potential for his safe return.

The single thread of hope she *did* manage to cling to was the one connected to Buckhorn. Whether or not his skills were the proper or ideal ones, Pamela somehow felt—no, *knew*—that the best chance for the safe return of her son rested with the intense, hawk-faced man. Maintaining this belief, this knowledge, would see her through.

It had to.

From his cabin window, Obie watched Pamela as she stood on the porch of the main house. Even through the rain, he could make out the forlorn look on her face and it pained him to see that.

Obie hated seeing Pamela hurt or unhappy. He wished he could take her in his arms and protect her from every unpleasant thing for the rest of her days. He knew that could never be, of course—no one could be shielded from all the harsh things to be found in life.

And the chances of him ever being wrapped in an embrace with Pamela the way he had longed for since practically the first moment he laid eyes on her was an equally impossible fantasy. On his best day, he'd never been worthy of someone like Pamela. And especially now, now that he'd become just an old cripple, a shell of his former self, it made him disgusted with himself to even think such thoughts.

Yet the longing would always be there. It was something he'd grown to accept, to live with, and to settle for just being near Pamela.

But the part about not seeing her hurt, that he would never give up on. Not as long as there was a breath in his body and there was anything, even the most minimal contribution, he could do to prevent it.

Right now, as far as Obie could see, that meant floating his stick with Buckhorn. The powder-burner. There was a strength about the big ugly cuss that made Obie think of Gus Danvers . . . and, to a somewhat lesser extent, Dan Riley.

Buckhorn's bold plan to infiltrate (the ranger's twenty-dollar word) Dan's alleged "gang" appealed to Obie on several counts. First and foremost, what he *hoped* it would reveal was that Dan wasn't behind the rustling and other outlawry he was thought by many to be responsible for. Even though Dan's elusive and suspicious ways over the past couple years made it hard not to think he must be up to something shady,

Obie remained stubborn in his belief there must be other reasons behind his behavior.

If Dan Riley was guilty of anything, Obie feared, it would turn out to be some involvement in the disappearance of Jeff Danvers. And maybe Eve, too, considering nobody seemed to have seen her, either, not since Jeff had gone missing with the announced intent of the two of them stealing off together. A young buck shows up meaning to claim the daughter of a hard, stubborn man like Dan Riley, a man with reason to harbor ill feelings against the upstart and his whole family, tempers flare . . .

That scenario, with various unpleasant endings, had been running through Obie's head for days now. It was the only explanation he could think of for young Jeff going away and staying away and not contacting his mother.

And now Buckhorn was putting himself in a position to either find an answer to the disappearances—along with the rustling and other suspected misdeeds—or at least lay to rest whether or not any of it had gone along the lines of Obie's nightmare version. And then, of course, there would be the nagging little detail of the powder-burner making it out alive in order to report his findings.

Unfortunately, however all of that played out, perhaps the biggest threat to Pamela's future happiness would still remain . . . Micah. As he'd told Buckhorn, Obie had recognized long ago there was something twisted and wrong inside the boy. He kept hoping that the offspring of the two people he revered most in the world would somehow, some day grow out of it, come to his senses and earn the right to take over the reins of the Circle D.

His hopes for that ever taking place were diminishing more each day. He had a hunch that Pamela was finally starting to realize the shortcomings in Micah, too, but he had doubts as to what or how far she'd be willing to go to face that reality full on. Especially lacking the safe return of Jeff. Losing both of her sons—one to misadventure, the other to a black twistedness inside him—would be devastating to Pamela, to any mother. And no matter how badly Obie wanted to protect Pamela from such devastation, he feared it was an impossible task.

"What I want is for things to be good—as good as they ever can be with Boss Gus gone—at the Circle D again."

Those had been Obie's words to Buckhorn only a short time ago. They'd been as sincere as any words he'd ever spoken. He'd told them to the powder-burner because, for some reason he didn't fully understand, he had a strong sense that if anybody *could* help make that happen, it would be Buckhorn. Today, in the gloom of the storm, with his gaze locked on Miss Pamela's lovely face wearing its forlorn expression, his feeling about that wasn't so strong.

Yet, even still, he insisted to himself, if anybody *could* . . .

CHAPTER 30

"Gotta tell you, Joey, I don't like this very much. Matter of fact, I don't like it worth a damn. I'm surprised at you and your father both for going along with such a thing."

"Maybe you ought to at least hear him out before you make up your mind that you're right and everybody else is wrong."

"What more do I need to hear? You already told me he's a hired gun working for Pamela Danvers. That makes it plain enough he's somebody working *against* me."

The man doing the talking was none other than the elusive Dan Riley. Ordinarily he would have come across as a taller, blockier version of his older brother. At present, however, he was recovering from a gunshot wound. Sitting on the edge of an old cot, torso bared except for the thick wrapping of bandages around his middle, he was pale and weak looking. The slackness of his flesh indicated recent and rapid weight loss, and his frequent pauses to catch his breath further suggested that he still had a ways to go before he'd be completely healed.

Once the storm drained itself to a point where the gray cloud cover was starting to break up and only spitting infrequent spatters of cold drops, Buckhorn and Joey had emerged from under their protective rock ledge. With Joey again leading the way, they'd proceeded on across the broken land, much of it now pocked with puddles of brownish water and smeared with streaks of a sand/mud mix where the rock base was less solid. In addition to the ground evidence deposited by its passing, the storm had also left behind a gusty breeze that had a chilling bite to it until the clouds cleared the rest of the way and allowed the sun to emerge fully.

The shadows of late afternoon had begun stretching long in this wash of sunlight when the riders abruptly came to the edge of a jagged rim and found themselves looking down on a small, bowl-like valley ringed by pine and cottonwood trees with a mix of shaggy brush and faded grass spread across its bottom. On the far side, tucked back in where some long fingers of rock extended out horizontally from a high, wide cliff, stood a sun-bleached old house and a handful of outbuildings.

"There's our destination," Joey had said. "All that's left to show for the gut-bustin' work some stubborn fool put into trying to make a go of a hardscrabble farm in this lousy soil. Failed and gone so long ago nobody even remembers his name."

"That's where Dan Riley is holed up?"

"If you want to put it that way. It's where we'll find him, yeah."

"How do we get down there off these high rocks?"

"Only a couple passable cuts that lead in or out." Joey jabbed a thumb. "Nearest one is over this way. Follow me."

Less than fifty yards down into a narrow, twisting, gradually descending gap between deeply seamed rock walls was where they'd gotten jumped. More accurately put, it was where Buckhorn had gotten jumped.

The faint sound of two whirling lassos cutting the air on either side of the gap was the only warning. A moment later the twin loops had sailed out, at a perfectly timed interval from one another, then dropped down over Buckhorn's head and shoulders. They were immediately yanked tight so that his arms were pinned to his sides, preventing him from reaching for his Colt. An instant later, a man stepped out of a rock crevice directly in front of Buckhorn and pointed a sawed-off shotgun at him.

"Stop tryin' to jerk free, mister, or I'll stop you permanent-like. You're captured. Accept it. You ain't smart enough to see that, you'll just make it harder on yourself."

The man with the shotgun had stepped out between Sarge and the rear end of Joey's horse. The girl twisted around in her saddle, looking back, as the shotgunner spoke. There was a look of mild concern on her face—but not for herself. She clearly was under no threat from this turn of events.

"What the hell's the big idea?" Buckhorn had demanded of her.

"Just a precaution," Joey was quick to explain. "The

entrances to this valley are closely guarded. Nobody
from the outside gets in without being challenged.
These men know me, but not you. They're making
sure I brought you here willingly."

"So, did you?" said the shotgunner. He was a tall
black man, shirtless, wearing just a fringed buckskin
vest above the waist. His exposed dark skin rippled
and bulged with smooth, powerful muscles. A single
bandolier loaded partly with shotgun shells and partly
with .45 cartridges was draped across his wide chest.
A Colt .45 that could have been a twin to Buckhorn's,
if not for more ornate grips, was holstered low on
his right hip. On the outside of his left leg, where his
denim trousers were stuffed into high-top moccasins,
the bone handle of a Bowie knife thrust up from its
sheath sewn inside the leather.

All in all, it was a rather showy display to convey the
image of a fighting man. But Buckhorn's instincts
quickly concluded it was more than show. It told the
truth.

As the black man's inquiry into Joey's willingness
for bringing a visitor had hung momentarily in the air,
the two men who'd thrown the lassos slipped down
on either side of Buckhorn. One was a lean, typical
wrangler type, not too far past twenty, clad in dusty
denims and boots, packing a sidearm. The second
lassoer had the distinction of being half again as wide
through the shoulders, deep chested, yet still narrow
waisted with a fancy black leather gunbelt buckled
around it. Above his chaps and jeans he was clad in a
panel-front shirt that was also a cut above standard
wrangler wear.

Not waiting for Joey's answer, the burly gent in the panel shirt had reached to relieve Buckhorn of his Colt and then stepped back, looking up at the hogtied captive with a taunting glint in his eye.

After what seemed like an inordinately long pause, Joey said, "Yes, I brought this man to see Uncle Dan. He has some important information to deliver and he's looking for a job. You can loosen those ropes on him."

"The ropes stay. And we got all the help we need," the black man said.

"As we just made plenty clear," added Panel Shirt, spinning Buckhorn's Colt possessively.

"I think that's for Uncle Dan to decide," Joey had reminded them in a flat tone. "And I've got a hunch he wouldn't like hearing he was kept longer than necessary from getting the information I mentioned while you jaw-jackers wasted time pretendin' you had a say in the matter."

The black man gave her the narrow eye, but Joey held her ground without flinching. Buckhorn had barely been able to suppress a wry grin, thinking that, when it came to glaring, the big *hombre*'s size and muscles and weaponry still didn't necessarily make him a match against Joey.

"All right," the shotgunner grunted. Then, to the two wranglers, he added, "But strip his gunbelt off and cinch those ropes good and tight. They stay on the ugly cuss until Dan says otherwise."

"What about my hat?" Buckhorn wanted to know, jerking his chin to indicate his bowler lying on the floor of the arroyo, where it had fallen after being dislodged by the lassos.

"Never mind. You're better off without a stupid-lookin' thing like that on your head anyway," said Panel Shirt.

"Grab his damn hat," said the black man. "Don't you recognize high style when you see it? Besides, we don't want him catchin' a cold due to our careless-ness, do we? Wouldn't be neighborly."

From there to the cluster of buildings across the valley there hadn't been any more talk. Once the five of them reined up in front of the patched-over old farmhouse, Joey and the black man had dismounted and gone inside. Buckhorn and the two lassoers stayed in their saddles. Buckhorn could feel eyes on them from inside some of the other buildings.

Whenever the captive's gaze fell on Panel Shirt, the burly lassoer would twirl his commandeered Colt and flash another taunting grin. Buckhorn promised him-self that, no matter what else, before he was done here he was going to introduce that grin to his fist. More than once.

It hadn't taken long before the black man re-emerged from the house and motioned for Buckhorn to be taken down off his horse. The lassoers did so, none too gently. Then, leaving the ropes in place, the black man told the others to wait where they were and he pushed Buckhorn—again none too gently—on into the house. Once inside, they'd made their way to a room at the back where an obviously wounded Dan Riley was waiting, seated on the edge of his cot ex-pressing his displeasure to his niece for her judgment.

Without waiting for an invitation, Buckhorn jumped right in on the conversation by saying to Riley, "You're about a day and a half wrong on what you think is so plain. I *was* workin' for the Widow Danvers and I *was* fixin' to head out against you. That all changed when I got fired."

The black man dug his fingers under the ropes still cinched around Buckhorn and gave a hard jerk.

"You speak when you're spoken to, bub."

"There's no need for that kind of treatment," Joey objected. Then, focusing directly on her uncle, she said, "Those ropes don't even belong on him. He's not some horse or mule. His name is Joe Buckhorn. I brought him here, I vouch for him. Doesn't that mean anything?"

Riley couldn't hold up under her withering look, especially not in his weakened condition. He released a gusty sigh and motioned to the black man.

"Go ahead, Ulysses. Take the ropes off him."

"You sure that's a good idea?"

"I said so, didn't I? Do it."

"You've got him stripped of his gun," Joey said pointedly. "What more do you want?"

"Where is his gun?" Riley wanted to know.

"Perlong's got it," Ulysses said. "Outside."

Riley nodded and said, "Good. That's a fine place for it." He cut his gaze to Joey. "We'll not be giving that back to him just yet."

"Fine by me," said Buckhorn. "When it's time, I'm sorta lookin' forward to retrieving it from Mr. Perlong my own self."

Ulysses made no attempt to simply untie the ropes knotted around Buckhorn. Instead he leaned over and pulled the Bowie knife from its moccasin sheath. He stepped around directly in front of Buckhorn and, with a wide smile, held the long, gleaming blade up for him to get a good look at. Buckhorn smiled right back, until the black man's faltered and then turned into an attempt at a face-saving sneer. It took barely a touch of the razor-sharp blade to part the ropes. They loosened and fell away.

Ulysses stepped back. Buckhorn promptly began bending and flexing his arms to work the kinks out.

A barely audible groan escaped Dan Riley. Then, sighing raggedly, he said, "Okay, Buckhorn. Let's hear why you think you're fit to join my outfit . . . and what this nugget of information is that will make you even more so."

CHAPTER 31

Before Buckhorn could go into his spiel, he was interrupted by the arrival of two additions to the gathering. First there was the sound of footfalls out in the other room and then the pair entered without announcement or ceremony. A slender, pretty strawberry blonde in a gingham dress came first, and following her, somewhat more tentatively, was a tall, thin young man with familiar dark eyes. Buckhorn knew instantly that he was looking at Eve Riley and Jeffrey Danvers.

Confirming at least part of this, the girl went straight to Riley and said, "Father, you shouldn't be sitting up like that, not without being propped on pillows. Look at you. You look tired and paler than you were just this morning. You're not resting like you should and I'll bet your wound is leaking again. I came to check on it; now I'll have to open your bandages and re-dress it for sure."

"Doggone it, gal, you fuss over me like I was a toddler still in diapers," grumbled Riley. "Don't you believe in knocking? Can't you see I'm in the middle of a business discussion here? Your nurse-maiding is gonna have to wait until—"

"No, it's not," his daughter cut him off with finality. "You're going to let me change your dressing and look at that wound. Then—maybe, if I think you're up to it—you can finish your talk."

"Oh, for Pete's sake! You'd think—"

"I already told you what I think, and that's the way it's going to be." Eve stepped closer, bunched up the pillows at one end of the cot, and then placed her hands on her father's shoulders. "Now lay back against these pillows and relax while we get fresh bandages ready. There's no sense arguing with me because you're weak enough I can out-wrestle you if I have to. Plus I have plenty of reinforcements if I need them. Now lay back."

Riley did as he was told, grumbling all the while. As she was getting him settled, Eve said over her shoulder, "Jeff, get that bag of bandages and the salve out of the cabinet there, will you please?"

Straightening and turning to the others in the room, Eve then said, "Hi, Joey. I thought that was your pinto at the hitch rail out front. Sorry to barge in and interrupt like this, but I guess you know how these Riley men are. You've got one of your own back at the ranch."

"I sure do," Joey replied. "But I've got the advantage of having Ma to help ride herd on ours—the two of us can always gang up on him if need be."

"Well, I wish I still had my ma around for a lot of reasons. But helping to ride herd on this stubborn old goat is sure one of 'em. When it comes to this gunshot, he's not behavin' worth a darn."

"How bad is it?" asked Joey.

Eve scrunched up her face.

"Oh, it's actually healing up pretty good. He's almost as tough as he is stubborn. Just not as tough as *he* thinks he is."

"Don't count on it," growled Riley.

Eve turned back to face him. Jeff held out a bulging carpetbag that he'd taken from a cabinet over against the wall.

"Is there anything I can do?" Joey said.

"You can leave. Go in the other room, all of you," Riley responded bluntly. "This ain't something I want a damn audience for."

"Probably just as well," Eve agreed. She looked at Buckhorn and Joey. "You two are a little bedraggled and still damp. You must have gotten caught in that storm a little while ago. So you likely could use some coffee. There should still be some hot coals in the cookstove out there, and there's cups and coffee fixin's in the pantry area right next to it. Jeff can show you. This'll take a while, but I can handle it by myself okay. Unless he passes out on me."

"That'll be the day," Riley said.

The rest of them departed as suggested. Jeff pulled the bedroom door partly shut behind them, leaving it open far enough to hear Eve if she called. In the kitchen area there was a large wooden table with a half dozen mismatched but sturdy-looking chairs gathered around it. Just beyond was the cookstove and pantry.

Buckhorn and Ulysses pulled out chairs for themselves. Joey went to the stove and lifted the lid on the chamber that still had some hot coals in it. Jeff brought her the coffee makings and then, from behind the stove, some chunks of split wood to get a hotter fire going.

Ulysses, who had been keeping the sawed-off handy and never aimed very far away from Buckhorn the whole while, now seemed to be studying him with a renewed interest.

"Joe Buckhorn," he said at length, putting equal emphasis on each syllable. "I've heard some about you."

Buckhorn returned his gaze flatly. "Uh-huh. And, unless I miss my guess, you'd be Ulysses Mason."

"You've heard of me, too, eh?" A corner of Ulysses's mouth lifted, pleased at the thought.

"Like you said . . . some," Buckhorn allowed.

"Coupla hardcases like us . . . Ain't that many of our kind around no more."

"If you say so. I don't keep particular track."

"You should. Always a good idea to keep track of the competition."

"I didn't know we were in competition."

"You figure on signin' on to this outfit, I expect we will be." Ulysses's mouth twitched again in another half smile. "You see, the top spot around here, next to Riley, has already got my notch in it. And I don't reckon you're the type to settle very long for havin' somebody else's notch above yours in any outfit you're part of."

"Could be," Buckhorn said. "But I don't quite know how you could come to that conclusion seeing as how I haven't ever made a habit of being part of any outfit in the past. Leastways, not for long enough to speak of."

"That's another thing. How is it, after all these years of operatin' mostly on your own, you're lookin' to throw in with an outfit like ours, anyway?"

"I told you. I'm in a tight. I need a job, money. Gun work is what I know. So the stories I heard about the Riley gang made it sound like the nearest spot I could ply my trade and earn a payday. Plus, like I've also been saying, I picked up a piece of information I believe Riley will be mighty grateful to hear."

"Information that, strictly on its own, he might be willin' to pay for? Is that what you're hopin'?"

"If he wants to throw down a bonus when he hears what I've got, I sure as hell won't object," Buckhorn replied. "But you heard me say I'm willing to *earn* my pay."

"Yeah, you did at that," Ulysses allowed. He continued to study Buckhorn. "This piece of information . . . you come across it while you was workin' for the Widow Danvers, did you?"

At the mention of his mother's name, Jeff Danvers wheeled about and took a step toward the table.

"What was that? What did you say about my mother?"

"Take it easy, Jeff-boy," Ulysses was quick to respond, holding up a hand. "Nobody's bad-mouthin' your ma. Buckhorn here just came from bein' hired on at the Circle D for a spell. That's all."

Jeff's eyes cut to Buckhorn.

"Is that true? Were you there recently?"

Buckhorn nodded and said, "For a fact."

"Did you happen to see my mother? Do you know how she's doing?"

"Besides being worried sick about you, you mean?"

Buckhorn hadn't intended to let his tone and words convey how he felt at finding Jeff here, unharmed and apparently of his own free will. But having seen Pamela's torment over her missing son, the gunman's anger at such thoughtless, uncaring behavior on the boy's part got the better of him.

Jeff's expression fell.

"I . . . I regret putting her through that. I really do. But . . . I have my reasons."

Ulysses chuckled nastily. Then, to Buckhorn, he said, "I guess there's some things you don't know about Jeff-boy, just like there's things he don't know about you. What it boils down to, see, is that Jeff's, er, extended stay with us ain't necessarily been on account of that's how he wanted things. After he shot Boss Dan, though, we sort of insisted on him sticking around."

Buckhorn normally kept a pretty tight rein on showing his feelings. But once again, like a moment ago with his anger at Jeff, the jolt of surprise carried by Ulysses's words hit him harder than he was able to completely contain.

Seeing this, Ulysses's chuckle deepened.

"After he did what he did, most of us was ready to fix it so the boy stayed here in this valley permanent-like, if you get what I mean. It was Dan himself who insisted we hold off on anything so drastic. So that's sorta where we're still at. Still holdin' until we're sure Dan is gonna pull through okay. If he does, he's got the final say. If he don't . . . well, it ain't very likely Jeff-boy is gonna pull through, neither."

"Real friendly, how you grow so fond of folks who

come to your valley that you never want 'em to leave," said Buckhorn dryly.

"Ain't it, though? Something you might want to keep in mind."

"Coffee'll be ready in a couple minutes," Joey said, walking over from the stove and laying out some cups on the table. "In the meantime, it sounds to me like the two of you are snorting and pawing over things that aren't gonna play out until Uncle Dan has his say over them. So, in the meantime, why don't you try acting civil until Eve says she's ready for us to come back in there."

Neither Buckhorn nor Ulysses put up an argument. Both Ulysses and Jeff, who'd pulled out his own chair and sat down, went into a kind of sullen silence. Buckhorn stayed quiet, but his mind was racing with dozens of questions he wanted to ask young Danvers about the shooting allegation and other matters. But now was not the right time or place to try to get into any of that.

While they waited for Joey to pour some of the coffee, Buckhorn took the opportunity to study Jeff more closely. The dark eyes he shared with his brother were a match to the painting of his father in the main house back at the Circle D. And, if you looked close enough, some of the same delicate lines to be found in his mother's facial features were present in his.

Where Micah was roguishly handsome, Jeff was good looking but in a way that was less bold. Physically, he was taller, but much leaner and less muscular. Such features, combined with the lad's meeker tendencies—especially compared to his brother and father before him—no doubt went a long way toward his mother (and others, more than likely) tagging him with having that "gentle side."

That could just as well be a sign of shortsightedness on the part of anybody who didn't take note of the intensity in the young man's eyes, Buckhorn judged. He *did* take note and suspected that, if angered or backed into a corner, Jeff might prove very un-gentle and capable of displaying a surprising kind of toughness.

Not to mention making an unexpected choice like shooting the overly protective father of the gal he sought to marry.

When the coffee was ready, it came hot and strong, just the way Buckhorn liked it. Joey filled cups for everybody, including herself, and then took her own seat at the table where they all sat in rather awkward silence until Eve called from the other room and said it was okay to come back in.

CHAPTER 32

"So the herd is in that pasture now?"

"That was the plan last I knew. They were gonna move 'em in this morning. You gotta keep in mind, though, that I've been gone from the Circle D since early yesterday."

"That's when you shot and killed the Mexican. And then the Widow Danvers fired you."

"That's right. Gonzalez drew on me; I did what I had to. Plus there was a little more to it than just that. Me and Micah rubbed each other wrong right from the first. I saw fit to put him in my sights more than once. Even though I held off, I guess it added up to once too often."

"Too bad. You pulled the trigger on the wrong one," Dan Riley said bitterly. "That waste of mother's milk Micah shoulda been shoveled to the bottom of a shit pile before he was old enough to break in his first pair of boots."

"I know some about this Gonzalez," spoke up Ulysses, breaking into the exchange that up until then had been taking place only between Buckhorn and

Riley. "He was supposed to be good with a gun. Real good." He paused and then added, "A greaser with greased lightnin' in his gun hand, that's what everybody claimed."

"Lot of claims bein' made around here," muttered Riley. "I could claim to be the King of Sheba if I wanted. But could I back it up? That's the thing."

"Some of our Slash-Double R riders were in town last night and heard talk to back up the business about Gonzalez getting shot by a man named Buckhorn—and that was long before Buckhorn here showed up at our ranch this morning," pointed out Joey. "The sheriff went out to bring the body back in. He was accompanied by the Texas Ranger who Buckhorn can tell you more about also."

Buckhorn would have preferred to parley with Riley under much more private conditions. But trying to hold out for that, if it could have been arranged at all, would have been difficult and would have only eaten up more time than the gunman was willing to burn. So when he and the others returned from the kitchen and Riley indicated he was ready to get on with their talk, even with everybody present, Buckhorn decided to proceed.

Riley looked markedly better than he had earlier, before his daughter tended to him. The bandages around his middle were clean and fresh and there was more color in his cheeks. The cup of amber liquid he held in his lap, whiskey from the whiff of it that Buckhorn picked up, likely also played some role in that.

"Wasn't exactly news that the widow had gone and hired herself a gunman to come in and help with her troubles. We'd all heard about that," Riley said. "I guess Gonzalez wasn't smart enough to respect that a hired gun gets paid because he's good with the tool of his trade."

"Ulysses can speak to that as well," Joey said. "From the way they were talking in the other room, he and Buckhorn know each other by reputation."

Riley's interest was clearly piqued. He glanced at the black man and asked, "That so, Ulysses?"

Ulysses shot a displeased scowl at Joey and then said, with some reluctance, "Reckon so."

"He any good?"

Ulysses shrugged.

"S'posed to be. We never crossed paths directly before."

Riley turned to Buckhorn.

"And you've heard of our Ulysses here. Is that right, Mr. Buckhorn?"

"Same as he has about me," Buckhorn allowed.

Riley took a drink from his cup. Lowering it, he said, "Well now. With both of you on board, the 'Riley Gang,' as everybody insists on calling us, would surely gain increased status as a force to be reckoned with, wouldn't it?"

"Father," said Eve, "you know that whole 'gang' thing has been blown way out of proportion."

"Has it really?" her father said. "Then again, whether it has or not, maybe it's time for us to start taking ourselves as seriously as others insist on. Maybe *we* should be the ones to take our reputation by the horns and blow it out of proportion even more."

"If you're going to start talking ridiculous, then I've got better things to do than hang around and listen to it." Eve headed for the door, adding over her shoulder, "Come on, Jeffrey!"

Jeff Danvers clearly did not want to leave. His eyes flicked plaintively to the other faces in the room. Then, reluctantly, he turned and followed Eve.

Riley waited until the pair were out of earshot before rolling his eyes dramatically and saying, "Not meanin' to be indelicate with Joey still here, but there's a term for a fella who fawns over and follows every whim of a gal like that. Even though the gal's my daughter and I sure wouldn't stand for her bein' with some lowdown who argued with her and knocked her around every chance he got. But good God, that boy needs to grow a backbone!"

"Didn't he show enough of one when he shot you?" said Buckhorn.

Riley arched a brow.

"You heard about that, did you?"

"Some. Gotta admit I'm curious to hear more."

"Yeah, I bet you are. Tell me . . . When the Widow Danvers hired you to come in and help with her troubles, was it mainly the rustling problem? Or did she also mention her missing son?"

Buckhorn nodded and said, "She did for a fact. I tried to explain to her that I wasn't no kind of detective for tracking down lost boys, but she wanted me to know about it and insisted I keep an eye peeled all the same. The way she saw it, the two would end up somehow tangled together on account of she was convinced you were behind both."

Riley's expression tightened in an odd way, almost like a spasm of pain or sadness had passed through him.

"That sounds like her. Bitter and blaming me for every bad thing that ever came down the pike."

Buckhorn was tempted to point out that Pamela's blame hardly appeared misplaced. Although restrained somewhat loosely, Jeff certainly was being kept here against his will—at least as far as not being able to contact his mother. And so far no one had bothered denying the widespread rustling allegations.

Riley took another drink of his whiskey, a long pull this time. After swallowing, he expelled his breath in a ragged hiss.

"So there's no denying we've got the boy here. You've seen that for yourself. We ain't got him chained up like a dog or anything, but he's not free to leave this valley, either. Not yet. Maybe never."

"Because he shot you or because he tried to steal away your daughter?" Buckhorn asked.

"Both," Riley said quickly, bluntly. He paused, released another sigh, and when he spoke again it was in a much mellower tone. "Although these past few days have reminded me that, when it comes to two young fools in love, there really ain't no 'stealing away.' Not by one over the other, not when the both of 'em are bent on slipping off to start a life together. And considerin' the situation they find themselves in around here, caught like they are between two families so full of hate for one another, who can blame them for wanting to light a shuck for somewhere else?"

"Lightin' a shuck is one thing," said Ulysses. "But shootin' you on the way out, Boss, can't hardly be excused so easy."

Riley's mouth curved in a rueful grin.

"I said I wanted the kid to show some backbone, didn't I? When I caught on to what they was up to, I came roarin' out to confront 'em. It was half-dark, the middle of the night. I said some pretty rough things, threatened to turn Jeff into a gelding right there on the spot. Took a swing at him. As he fell back, he jerked out a gun to defend himself. Hell, I'm twice his size. I don't think he meant for it to go off, though. When it did, I think it surprised him even more than me."

"Lucky it didn't surprise you to death," Ulysses muttered. "He shoulda put up his fists and fought you like a man."

"To give him his due, he didn't bolt like a yellow dog. He stuck around and immediately went to work with my daughter to tend the wound. Might even have saved my life with their quick attention."

"Yeah, *after* he dang near took it to begin with. That don't exactly balance the scales to my way of thinkin'. I still say we shoulda strung him up that same night."

Riley replied, "In case you never noticed, Ulysses, I think the milk of human kindness might be seriously curdled inside you."

Ulysses just grunted.

"I guess it's partly my own fault for sayin' I was curious to hear more about the Danvers boy bein' here, how he came to shoot you and all," spoke up Buckhorn. "But we've drifted kinda far off the track of why I'm really here. What's it gonna take for you to make up your mind on hiring me as part of your crew? And do you want to hear more about that outlying meadow and the surprise that's gonna be waitin' there for anybody lookin' to try and make off with the herd they've moved in?"

Riley regarded him thoughtfully for a long moment, then said, "You've got a lot of brass, that much is obvious. And, from all reports, you're handier than average with a gun. That might be a combination I'd be interested in, but then again it might *not* be. We'll let my answer to that percolate for a little while longer.

"As to the meadow you're referring to, I'm very familiar with the spot. Matter of fact, I tried to add the piece of land around there to Circle D range clear back when I was ramroddin' the place. But Goetz, that tight-assed old Dutchman who owned it, wouldn't deal. Truth to tell, when I heard last winter that he finally made the sale it galled the hell out of me that somebody else was able to get it done. It's damn good land, and that meadow is the prize part. I figured Micah wouldn't waste any time puttin' some cattle in there first thing this spring."

"So you've had some of your boys keepin' tabs on it, right? Watchin' for the move to take place?"

"That was the general idea."

"Next time you do something like that, I'd suggest you tell your scouts to be more careful about leaving sign," Buckhorn said. He went on to explain how the fresh prints on the hogback had been spotted and how Micah had reacted.

"Hell, that shouldn't have come as any big surprise," Riley said. "Did they expect that stickin' a fresh herd in an outlying spot like that would do anything else *but* attract the interest of any rustlers workin' the area?"

Buckhorn shrugged.

"Don't know what they would or wouldn't have expected under different circumstances. But in this case, with a Texas Ranger fresh-arrived in the county, they got powerful anxious to use the lure and location for settin' a trap."

"And the ranger bought in?"

"That he did."

Riley's expression pulled into a frown.

"That's damn poor luck. Those rangers don't miss a lick, and once they sink their teeth into a thing they stay clamped tight as a hound dog on a bone. And you don't dare shoot one of the devils or the rest of the outfit will be on you for the rest of your born days!"

"Since they only just moved the cattle in this mornin'," said Ulysses, "what are the chances they'd have their trap ready to spring right away on the first night?"

"What difference does it make whether they do or not?" Riley grumbled. "Either way, we ain't ready to take action on such short notice."

"Oh, I don't know," Ulysses countered. "We still got two or three hours of daylight. Then another stretch before midnight. Ain't like we've never wide-looped a bunch of beef before. We put our heads together and do some hurry-up thinkin' and plannin' I don't see why—"

"No," Riley said with a firm shake of his head. "Our way ain't ever been to rush into a thing half-cocked. That's why we've been successful and never got caught. We ain't gonna change that now, especially with a Texas Ranger in the picture."

Ulysses's nostrils flared. He clearly wanted to argue

his point some more. In the end, though, he held his tongue.

"But what we *are* gonna do," said Riley, "is put our new friend here to the test." He jerked a thumb to indicate Buckhorn though his eyes stayed on Ulysses. "Once it's full dark, take a couple men—men who know how to move like shadows and have eyes like hawks—and go check out that meadow. See what's waiting there in case we *would* have tried something tonight."

"What about him?" Ulysses asked, gesturing toward Buckhorn.

"As long as he's unarmed, he'll be all right to stay here where we can keep an eye on him," Riley answered. "I've got my brace of Navy Colts right here by my bed, and the gals can give a holler if he tries anything funny. Tell the other men to keep an eye on the house but not to interfere unless they're certain of trouble. I don't think there will be, though. I haven't made up my mind yet exactly what this bird is up to, but it's something more elaborate than just marching in here and shooting up the place."

"Thanks for the vote of confidence," Buckhorn muttered.

Now the wounded man's eyes swung to Buckhorn.

"Don't get too cocky, mister. After I've heard what Ulysses finds in that meadow, then I *will* make up my mind about you. But it's not a done deal yet."

CHAPTER 33

With the darkness of evening descending outside, Buckhorn took supper with Joey, Eve, and Jeff Danvers. In his weakened condition, the afternoon's discussions and activity had exhausted Dan Riley to the point where he'd nodded off as soon as things quieted down. Choosing to let him rest, Eve had prepared a plate and set it aside for him to eat when he woke later on.

Ulysses Mason also left Riley undisturbed when he, along with two men of his choosing, had faded off to go check out the Circle D meadow.

Conversation during the meal was minimal and somewhat strained. When they were done eating, the women shooed Buckhorn and Jeff away while they cleared the table and did the dishes. The two men made their way outside and found themselves faced with the first opportunity for just the two of them to talk without anyone hovering in close proximity.

That didn't mean they weren't still being watched, however. Buckhorn had felt eyes upon him, either directly or covertly, every second since he'd arrived at this place. It wasn't those whose presence he could discern openly that bothered him—not Riley or his daughter or Jeff, not Ulysses or even the two lassoers from the pass—but rather the shadowy observers who hung back inside the murky recesses of the old farm's other buildings. Buckhorn had caught furtive movements, heard more than a few soft bootscrapes of sound. He knew they were there, had no doubt about it. He just couldn't tell how many there were or why the need for such ghostly behavior.

"It's creepy, ain't it?" said Jeff, as if reading his mind. "Knowing they're there, knowing they're watching your every stinkin' move. That's how they did me at first, too. I think it's like a game. Meant to unnerve you, keep you on edge . . . What made the game all the more fun for me was the thought that for every set of unseen eyes there was a hangman's noose dangling and eager to tighten around my neck."

"Thanks for painting that cheerful picture," Buckhorn said. "I hadn't been thinking anything about a hangman's noose."

They'd each lowered themselves to take seats on the edge of the porch, leaning back against gray, weathered posts.

"You're probably safe from worrying about a noose," Jeff said. "Me, I'm the dummy who showed up aiming to seduce away the boss's daughter and ended up shooting him in the attempt. You, you're just lookin' to get hired on as part of the gang."

"Yeah, but if I *do* get hired, I didn't figure that lurking around like some damn ghost would be part of the job."

Jeff grunted and said, "Still might be a chance for

me to end up a lurking ghost, too—only I'd be the
real deal."

"From the look and sound of things, I think you're
pretty well past that threat. Riley says he likes men
with backbone, men willing to fight for what they
want. I'd say you showed that kind of grit by shooting
him. Plus you happen to have a pretty little ace up
your sleeve in the form of the daughter he adores and
who, in turn, seems plenty adoring of you."

"I sure hope so," Jeff said. "The way I've botched
things up, I wouldn't blame her if she changed her
mind about her feelings for me."

Thinking, among other things, of how his own
situation wasn't taking shape exactly as hoped for,
Buckhorn said wryly, "You've hardly got a patent on
botching things up, kid. You can take my word on
that."

"I hope you're right on that score, too. I've got to
admit that, if I can come out of it alive, there's been
some things I ran across here that I don't all the way
regret. I've had my eyes opened to stuff that . . . well,
are a lot different than I believed before."

Buckhorn's eyes blazed. He was intrigued to know
what the young man meant by that. He wanted to
press him hard for the answer. At the same time,
though, he knew he had to approach it with the right
amount of caution.

"Hey," he said. "I'm angling to try and join this
outfit. Remember? I know they're outlaws and all, so
that hardly makes me some lily-pure soul who's shy
about mixing in a little rough business. But if their
game is something too far on the rotten side, that
might be good for me to know before I get—"

"No, it's nothing like that," Jeff interrupted. A thin, lopsided smile touched his mouth. "Comes to that, they're just common grade rustlers and robbers. Involved in standard 'rough business,' as you put it. What I ran across, the stuff I'm talkin' about . . . well, it's more of a personal nature."

Once again Buckhorn wanted to pounce on that statement and hear more about what was behind it. But, as before, he knew he had to handle it just right, not appear too eager.

He said, "I only worked for your ma for a short time. But it was long enough to see that—apart from her immediate concern for you and your safety since you've gone missing—she's still deeply troubled and bitter about the way Riley turned on her and the Circle D. If you found out something that would ease her mind about that, at least allow her to understand it better, you're right about that being something not to regret."

Jeff's expression turned forlorn.

"That's just it. I *can* ease her mind about why Big Dan did what he did. But in order to do that, I'd have to hurt her, break her heart, in a whole different way. One that's sure to be even harder on her."

Buckhorn stayed quiet. Waiting. Hoping that the young man would continue on without prodding.

Thankfully, he did.

"The night I shot Dan, you see, he said some things right afterward that hit me almost as hard as my bullet hit him. It happened at his brother's ranch, the Slash-Double R. That's where him and Eve were staying, where I'd gone to fetch her. I didn't even know about this place—we didn't come here until two or three days later, when it seemed safe to move Dan and he insisted on being brought here to recuperate.

"But that first night everybody thought his wound was worse than it was. Even Dan. There was so much blood and pain he thought it might be mortal. That's when he grabbed me by the shirtfront and told me some things he said I needed to know and needed to tell my mother. Back when he got driven off the Circle D, he swore he'd never done any of the things he was accused of. He insisted he was set up. And, although he wasn't able to prove it—not then, not since—he's convinced my brother Micah was behind it all."

In his gut, Buckhorn immediately believed what Jeff had just said. Believed what Jeff was claiming, believed the accusations by Riley that were behind it. *Micah*. Snake mean and ruthless beyond reason.

But, to avoid the appearance of buying in too easily, the gunman said, "That's quite a story, kid. Only thing is, and I hate to break this to you, but practically every *hombre* who's ever gone down the owlhoot trail has some kind of excuse or sad tale of woe about why he made his bad turn."

Jeff shook his head vigorously.

"No. Not in this case. Don't you see? This was practically the same as a deathbed confession—the kind of thing that would stand up even in a court of law. Dan genuinely thought he might be dying. Before he did, he wanted me to know the truth."

"And you believe him? About your own brother?"

Jeff looked away and said, "You don't understand.

There's always been a dark side to Micah. Twisted and cruel for no good reason. Devious, too."

"And what about all this?" Buckhorn said, gesturing. "This hideout valley and the gang of rustlers and robbers he's got gathered around him . . . Is this all staged by Micah, too? Piling on the evidence to keep making Riley look bad?"

"The way Dan explains it," Jeff answered, "once his name had been dragged through the mud and pretty much ruined, he decided to hell with it—if people were so willing to believe he'd turned outlaw, then he'd by-God be one."

"And so that's what he's been working at ever since."

"I guess that's the size of it."

Further discussion of the subject was interrupted by Eve and Joey emerging from the house. It was full dark by now, and the air, still damp from the afternoon rain, carried a deepening chill. Both women were wrapped in shawls and Eve was carrying a candle.

For the first time, Buckhorn noticed there were traces of lantern and candlelight starting to show in some of the other buildings, thin seams of illumination leaking out around what he took to be pieces of burlap covering the windows.

"Brrr. It's cold out here," Eve said. "I think I changed my mind about sitting out here with y'all for a spell. Let's go back inside, maybe even throw a couple logs on the fire. I'd better check on Father, too. He'll be needing an extra blanket."

Jeff rose to his feet.

"Sounds like a good idea."

But Joey lagged.

"I think I'd like to stay out here and enjoy the fresh air for at least a little while," she said. "If Mr. Buckhorn is willing not to leave me all alone, that is."

"Wouldn't think of abandoning you that way," Buckhorn assured her. "Pick yourself a slice of porch and have a seat."

"Do you want me to leave the candle?" Eve asked, looking somewhat reluctant to proceed with her departure now.

"No, that's okay," Joey told her. "The moon is on the rise. And we won't be all that long."

"Very well. Please don't overdue it. You'll catch your death in this damp air."

Eve and Jeff disappeared inside.

As soon as they were out of sight and earshot, Joey laughed softly and said, "She is such a little worry wart. She told me that she thinks you are an incredibly menacing desperado, and I can tell she is officially horror-stricken at the thought of leaving me out here alone with you. I predict it won't be five minutes before she finds some excuse to pop back out to check on us."

"Maybe she'll bring hot cocoa and a blanket."

"Wouldn't surprise me a bit. The really silly part, of course, is thinking she's leaving me alone with you when she knows darn well that there are a half dozen or more of Uncle Dan's thugs watching your every move. Furthermore, most of them are cut from cloth exactly the same as you. Well, maybe not *exactly*, considering you could probably shade any two of them. Except maybe for Ulysses. You want to talk about a menacing *hombre*? I don't think you'd have to look much farther."

"Yeah, I sorta noticed that, too . . . especially during the time he was waving that sawed-off scattergun under my nose."

"Which came after I led you into the pass where I knew some of Uncle Dan's men would be waiting. That's the part you're leaving unsaid but surely must be thinking. Right?"

Buckhorn gave a one-shouldered shrug.

"Now that you mention it . . ."

"I was just doing what you wanted. What you more or less insisted on. Keep that part in mind, too. And, if you got a little scuffed up as a result, well, I hadn't forgot that you'd done your own share of scuffing up a couple of our boys back at the ranch."

"Not denying that," Buckhorn said. "And I'm not complaining about you leading me into that pass. We had to get down here somehow and, like you said, it's what I wanted." He paused, grinned a little. "Besides, it was an improvement over when, not so much earlier, you were threatening to blast my spine in two. Way I saw it, we were making pretty good progress."

Joey showed her own smile. A three-quarter moon had crested the horizon, and the faint silvery light it cast played across her features in a very flattering way.

"You take a surprisingly optimistic view of certain things."

Buckhorn rolled his head on the porch post and fixed a direct gaze on her.

"Seriously. You could have made things a lot tougher for me since we got down into this valley. You even spoke up and vouched for me at one point. Don't think I don't appreciate that."

Joey held his eyes for a long moment, then looked

away. She heaved a sigh before saying, "I just hope I'm not making a mistake. I hope my reasons for helping you are the right ones."

"What *are* your reasons, Joey?"

Her eyes came back to him.

"Whatever you truly came here for, I don't believe it's simply to join my uncle's gang. Nor do I believe you came here to do him harm. If I thought that, you can bet I *wouldn't* be helping you. And if it turns out I'm wrong and you *do* hurt him, then we'll be right back to me looking to put a bullet in your spine."

"Hold on, let's not start backsliding here," said Buckhorn, holding up one hand in a warding-off gesture. "If you don't think I'm out to hurt your uncle, what do you think I'm after?"

"It's Jeff," Joey said, her eyes brightening with conviction. "I think you came here looking for some answers—or even just some clues—to Jeff's disappearance. And you ended up practically stumbling over him. Richer pay dirt than you dared hope for."

"So you think you've got it all figured out."

"I saw it in your eyes when you practically *scolded* him for worrying his mother so bad because he hadn't made any contact with her. Then I saw it again in your reaction when you heard he'd shot Uncle Dan."

"Okay. If you're on such a roll, what's the rest of it?"

"What do you mean?"

"According to you, all of that has fallen into place. So where do I go from here? What's my next move?"

Joey eyed him coyly and asked, "Are you admitting I'm right so far?"

"You seem convinced you are," Buckhorn hedged.

"That should be enough for you to go ahead and answer the question."

Joey considered for a moment, then said, "All right. But first—are Ulysses and his men going to find a trap waiting at that meadow?"

"I expect so."

"Will they get caught in it?"

"Not if they're good enough. Not if they go about checking it out the way your uncle told them. They'll just confirm it's there."

"So you're on the level about that much. That was your bargaining chip for getting in good with my uncle, just like you said. But I still can't see you being truly interested in joining the gang. Not for the long run. I remain convinced you came here mainly to find out about Jeff. So does that mean you don't care about the rustling one way or the other?"

Buckhorn shook his head.

"Not particularly. Not what I'm bein' paid to care about. That's in the hands of others."

"So, for you, it *is* all about Jeff. And that must also mean you're still in the employ of his mother."

Buckhorn grinned in a curious way.

"There's an old story about a young Indian buck who went out on a big hunt with other men from the tribe. He wanted badly to impress them. Came a point where they'd chased a bear into some bushes and had him surrounded. The young buck went ahead and charged straight in all by himself. The other hunters heard a lot of growling and thrashing around for a few minutes, until it went kinda quiet and the buck called out: 'I got the bear!' So the others hollered in:

'Then bring him out!' To which the young buck hollered back: 'What if he don't want to come?'"

By the time he paused, Joey was smiling, too. She said, "Anybody ever tell you you've got a strange way of going about confirming or denying something? And you're not exactly a *young* Indian buck, by the way. But I think I see enough other similarities to get the point of your little story."

"Good. Then be sure to let me know if and when you come up with any ideas for how I'm gonna get the bear out of the bush."

CHAPTER 34

It was well short of midnight when Ulysses Mason and the two other men got back. They came riding hard across the valley floor and reined up in front of the house, their arrival announced by pounding hooves followed by the snorting and blowing of the horses. Ulysses dismounted, waved for the men who'd ridden with him to take care of the animals, then went on into the house.

Inside, Eve had just finished giving her father a back rub after her latest check of his bandages. Riley had awakened and eaten his supper earlier. The tray and plates were still at his bedside. Joey, Jeff, and Buckhorn were again occupying seats around the kitchen table while Eve was tending the patient. But when Ulysses came in they all got up and followed him into the bedroom.

Riley didn't waste time with preamble.

"Well? Are they there?"

Ulysses nodded and said, "Yup. They're there all right. Thick as bugs on a sugar cookie, hid back out of the way behind every rock and bush and tree to be found. Damn near thirty of 'em, by my count. I even managed to catch a glimpse of the one with a star-in-a-circle Texas Ranger's badge pinned on his shirt. And I think Sheriff Tolliver was in amongst 'em, too."

"That figures. That hump-backed law dog," Riley said through gritted teeth. "He wants so bad to find favor in Pamela Danvers's eyes that he'd squat all night in a pile of buffalo droppings if he thought it'd gain him anything." After the words were out, his eyes darted quickly to Jeff. "Meanin' nothing off color toward your ma, Jeff-boy. Her and I may be at serious odds, but I'd never imply anything that way about her. I'll even give her credit for havin' enough sense not to be swayed by any of Thad Tolliver's drooling advances these past few years."

Jeff kept his expression impassive, made no reply.

"All I know," Ulysses said, continuing his report, "is that if any rustlin' party had ridden into that meadow tonight, they would have found themselves in a mighty sorry situation."

"So there you've got it," stated Buckhorn. "Ulysses just backed up everything I told you about that business. That oughta give credit to my word. Now how about the rest, the part that's still unfinished between us?"

Riley eyed him sharply.

"You mean my decision on whether or not I'll take you into my outfit?"

"That's right."

"Maybe you oughtn't be so pushy, mister," suggested Ulysses.

"To hell with that," Buckhorn replied with a shake of his head. "I think I've been patient to a more than reasonable degree. If you're not interested in adding me as another man, just say the word and I'll ride out of here at first light. But, either way, I want my gun and my gear back. I've earned the right to that much. Now."

Ulysses returned the negative head shake and said, "That ain't gonna happen."

"Stop and think," Buckhorn insisted. "If I was out to raise hell from within your ranks, I had all the chances I needed right here tonight during the time you were gone." He cut a glance over at Riley and continued, "No disrespect, but while you were asleep I could have snatched your Navy Colts and, if my purpose was to do damage to you and your operation, they'd've more than provided me the means."

"That's big talk," snarled Ulysses. "But it don't change nothing . . . not unless you want to give everybody a demonstration by trying to take my weapons from me."

"Just hold on a minute," said Riley, his gaze whipping back and forth between the two men. Buckhorn was somewhat surprised to see an odd gleam, what looked almost like a heightened level of excitement showing in his eyes. "I'll admit, Ulysses, that a nagging little voice keeps whispering inside my head that our Mr. Buckhorn here is up to something other than what he's telling us. Like I said before. But I don't know what it is. Still, lacking any proof and considering that he's done us a service by warning us about the meadow trap, our continuing ill treatment of him—depriving him of his personal belongings and such—does seem a bit harsh."

"So what are you sayin'?" Ulysses wanted to know.

"Who did you mention before as having taken charge of his gun?"

Ulysses didn't answer right away. Something shifted in his eyes, too, and Buckhorn could have sworn he saw the hint of a smile briefly touch his mouth. Then he said, "Why, I believe Perlong still has it."

"That's right. I remember now." Riley looked over at Buckhorn. "And I believe I also remember you saying, Mr. Buckhorn, something about how you wanted to personally retrieve your gun from Perlong. Ain't that right?"

Buckhorn nodded.

"You remember real good."

Riley spread his hands.

"Very well, that settles it. Ulysses, how about you tell Mr. Buckhorn where he can find Mr. Perlong. At the same time, advise Perlong that Buckhorn wants his gun back. We will then leave it to the two of them to, er, *negotiate* the terms for returning the property."

Now Ulysses was definitely grinning, and not trying to hide it.

"Whatever you say, Boss. But I gotta tell you, I think Perlong has grown kinda fond of that gun. He thinks it goes awful good with that dressy rig of his. I got a hunch he's gonna hate to give it up."

"As I said, we'll leave it up to him and Buckhorn to work out the details of the transaction."

"Oh, this is shaping up real slick," Buckhorn said. "In other words, you're inviting me, unarmed, to go take my own gun away from that smiling ape while he's armed not only with my Colt but also his own six-gun, not to mention however many of his cronies will be waiting out there to back his play."

"You try takin' something away from Perlong that he don't want you to have," said Ulysses, "I think you'll find him quite a handful strictly on his own."

"What's more," Riley pointed out, "only just a few minutes ago you were explaining how much of a ruckus you could raise around here strictly on *your* own, Buckhorn. Sounds to me like you'll be entering those negotiations on pretty even footing."

"But not if the other man has a gun, or more than one," protested Joey.

"I can't believe you're encouraging something so unfair!" wailed Eve.

"Oh, stop the caterwauling," Riley said. "If this turns into a fight—and I agree that it sounds like it may—then it will be *for* a gun, but nobody's encouraging a shoot-out. If Perlong refuses to give up Buckhorn's property, then it will be up to him to hang on to the gun but without using it to give him an unequal advantage. You understand what I'm saying, Ulysses?"

"I understand."

"Good. I expect you to control things accordingly. Now go roust Mr. Perlong and advise him of the situation."

"Won't have to go far to roust him. He's one of the men I took with me when I rode to check out that meadow. He'll be just outside, takin' care of the horses."

By then, Buckhorn clearly saw what was going on. Dan Riley liked men who showed backbone, and what he was pushing for here was the chance for Buckhorn to prove his, to test his mettle against the burly Perlong who apparently had a reputation within the group as a scrapper who could hold his own with just about anybody.

Buckhorn not only saw what was going on, he found himself actually liking the idea. He remembered all too vividly Perlong's taunting grin after he'd claimed the Colt and the way he kept spinning it to make the point of it now being in his possession even more chafing.

Buckhorn remembered, too, how badly he'd wanted to drive his fist through that damned smirk. And now it looked like he was about to get the chance.

"Let's not keep Perlong waiting," he said. "My gun, neither. It's probably getting lonely by now, wanting to come home where it belongs."

CHAPTER 35

They quit the house with Ulysses leading the way, Buckhorn right on his heels. After a brief show of reluctance and uncertainty, Joey, Eve, and Jeff followed. The two women brought lanterns.

Perlong was just emerging through the gate of a rickety corral constructed between the house and one of the sheds where Buckhorn had sensed the presence of other men and seen light seeping out from the windows. A second man, the other lassoer who'd gotten a loop on Buckhorn back in the narrow pass, was walking behind Perlong.

Over at the shed, the front door was now standing open. Backlit by a lantern pouring illumination out from inside, a couple of tousle-haired men, apparently made curious by the sounds of Ulysses and his men returning, were peering out.

Looks like we're going to be putting on a show for the whole bunch, Buckhorn thought to himself.

"What's goin' on, Ulysses? You look like you got something in your craw," said Perlong, frowning, as he watched the approach of the black man and Buckhorn and the others trailing behind.

"More like it's Buckhorn here who's got something in his," replied Ulysses. "He figures he did us a good deed by settin' us straight on that trap they got waitin' over at the Circle D. For that, he figures he's earned the right to have his gun and the rest of his gear back."

Perlong squinted, considering. He said, "You think that's a good idea?"

"Not sure if it is or ain't. But Boss Dan kinda sees it as Buckhorn's got the right to ask. And, since you're the one who gathered up his stuff, the boss suggested he come take up the matter with you."

"He did, did he?" Perlong's gaze shifted to Buckhorn. "Then why ain't the 'breed speakin' up for hisself?"

"You want it, you got it," Buckhorn grated. "But here's the thing . . . I'm not *asking* you for my gun back. I'm *telling* you it's time to hand it over."

Perlong rasped, "Oh? Well, here's the thing from how I see it. Number one, I've grown real fond of this here .45." He tapped the fancy holster on his hip, where Buckhorn's Colt now resided.

The instant the burly man's hand started to reach down, something like an electric current shot through Buckhorn. His right shoulder dropped and his hand streaked for . . . the empty space over his right hip where his holster and gun had been stripped away. Buckhorn straightened up and went momentarily rigid as a cold rage built pressure inside him.

"Always wanted a .45 of my own," Perlong drawled on. "Especially after seein' the one Ulysses likes to sport around. This is damn near a twin to his, so it really fills the hankerin'. Plus, it goes doggone nice with this gunbelt of mine, don't you think?"

Buckhorn clenched his teeth, said nothing.

"Number two," said Perlong, "that makes it flat-out too good a gun for a lowdown, stinkin' half-breed. And number three, no dog-eatin' 'breed is *ever* gonna tell me what to do!"

"The only thing that leaves then," Buckhorn said, his voice barely above a whisper as he started around Ulysses, "is *making* you do it."

"Hold it," said Ulysses, extending his arm, blocking Buckhorn. "You two go right ahead, do all the ground-pawin' and chest-thumpin' you want. You can even pound knots on one another. But Boss Dan made it clear he don't want no gunplay. This might be *about* a gun, the way he put it, but it ain't about anybody usin' one." His eyes bored meaningfully into Perlong for a moment, then swept over the other lassoer and the men in the doorway of the shed. "Everybody clear on that? This is strictly fist and foot between these two men, and none of the rest of you are to interfere. I'm here to make sure none of you do."

"That's fine by me," Perlong declared as he stripped away his gunbelt and handed it off to one of the other men. "I don't like things too crowded, anyway. I need me lots of fightin' room."

"More like you'll need lots of room to roll when I knock you ass over elbows," Buckhorn told him, taking a minute to peel off his jacket and vest and remove his hat. Then he shoved away Ulysses's arm and bulled forward.

And so it was on.

The wash of bluish-silver moonlight pouring down from above made a curious color blend with the pale gold splashes thrown by the lanterns. Yet the combination succeeded in providing sufficient illumination for the event underway, casting long, distorted shadows from the combatants as they closed on one another.

As he began to circle with Perlong, Buckhorn was aware of the shed door opening wider and men starting to emerge. He counted five. No surprise there, that they were drawn by the loud talk and interested in watching the action.

What was a bit more of a surprise, though, was that, off the other way, he saw the form of Dan Riley appear in the doorway to the house and lean against the frame, also watching.

But Buckhorn's main focus had to stay on the burly Perlong. The man was lowered into a half crouch with his fists balled and raised in a manner that suggested he might have some genuine boxing skill to go with the raw strength and rough-housing tactics that were to be expected. He was several pounds heavier than Buckhorn and possibly a bit more powerful. But some of the weight was fat, whereas Buckhorn was all hard, tight muscle honed for flexibility and quickness as well as endurance.

Perlong made the first move, lunging forward not with a big roundhouse like many big men were prone to open up with but rather snapping two crisp left jabs. Buckhorn bent sideways at the waist, dodging the twin pokes. Still leaning to his right, he planted his right foot, twisted his hips, and swung his left leg in a whipping motion that crashed half its length hard across Perlong's midsection. The big man was caught leaning into it, pulled partially forward by the jabs he'd thrown, increasing the force of the impact. Air gushed out of him, mingled with a loud curse.

Buckhorn straightened up, danced away a couple steps. Then, when he was balanced and ready, he quickly moved in again and landed a solid right cross to the side of Perlong's jaw before the burly man had gotten all the way straightened up from the blast to the gut.

The punch knocked Perlong away, turning his whole body. Acting on instinct and rage, he kept right on turning. Quickly and unexpectedly, he whirled full around, extending his thick right arm and lashing out with it—blindly at first—until it whirled in nearly a three-hundred-sixty-degree flat arc and at its completion brought his fist crashing against the side of a wholly surprised Buckhorn's head. The momentum built up by that big swing made the impact hard and loud and sent Buckhorn staggering.

The men outside the shed emitted whoops of approval.

This smattering of cheers only added to Buckhorn's anger at himself for getting caught by such an unorthodox move. But this fueled him to recover and retaliate even quicker than he otherwise might have. Wheeling about to face Perlong once again, Buckhorn saw the burly man also re-centering himself, getting balanced and ready.

The two charged together without hesitation, throwing a whirlwind of smashing, savage punches, some missing, more landing. The rat-a-tat-tat of fists on meat and bone was intense. Finally, Buckhorn shoved in close enough to try a head butt. Perlong jerked his face away at the last second, taking only a glancing blow on the side of his bull neck.

Before Buckhorn could pull back, he was caught in a bear hug by his opponent's powerful arms, pinning his own arms momentarily, threatening to crush him. Memories of the lasso loops closing around him rushed through Buckhorn's brain, frantically urging him to do something. Not letting those arms get cinched tight, the way the lassos had, Buckhorn instantly went slack, dropping his full weight downward, managing to slip loose from Perlong's grasping arms.

As his knees hit the ground, Buckhorn threw two punishing hooks, first a right and then a left, into Perlong's ribs. He heard bone and cartilage crack, and this time when the air came gushing out of Perlong there were flecks of blood in it.

Buckhorn rolled away. He sprang back to his feet as fast as he could, knowing he hadn't yet delivered enough punishment to keep Perlong down or make him quit. His assessment was immediately confirmed when he saw the burly man lumbering toward him, hands reaching clawlike, elbows tucked protectively close to guard his ribs.

Buckhorn went to meet him. But he gave his opponent plenty of time to take the next swing, calculating it would come slow and somewhat restrained by the damaged ribs. When the punch sailed out—a more predictable roundhouse right this time, though still delivered with surprising zip—Buckhorn ducked under it.

As he did, he kicked out with another leg whip, this one sweeping low and crashing into the backs of

Perlong's legs, just below the knees. The burly man buckled and toppled backward, landing heavily and driving even more weak wheezes of air out of him.

Buckhorn was on him in a flash. He dropped a knee to Perlong's stomach once, twice, and then took a step back and stood looking down, wanting to assure himself there was no chance the man was going to rise up again anytime soon, not without help. Buckhorn's own breathing was coming in rapid huffs, and for a little while that was the only sound.

And then, slowly, Buckhorn turned his head and looked all around. The men over by the shed were silent, not moving. Eve and Joey were looking on aghast. Jeff was wide eyed, appearing a bit stunned.

When Buckhorn's gaze came to rest on Ulysses, his field of vision also included Dan Riley, still in the doorway of the house. Ulysses's face was stone, expressionless; the distance and the shadows blurring his countenance made Riley's face even more unreadable.

"You can see that Perlong can't speak for himself right at the moment," Buckhorn said. "But does everybody else agree I've come out on top in these negotiations and have the right to reclaim my property now?"

Nobody answered right away until a voice quavering slightly with a mix of outrage and uncertainty said, "No. Aw, hell no!"

Buckhorn looked around again, and this time his eyes fell on the one person he'd skimmed past before: Perlong's cohort, the other lassoer from the pass. In the course of things, Buckhorn had never caught his name. But, abruptly, this got taken care of.

"Now take it easy, Lowe," Ulysses told the man. "You

heard how I said it was gonna be. The way Boss Dan
wants it. Perlong had his chance to play it different,
but he chose not to. He made his call and came up
short. That's the way it is."

The man called Lowe shook his head.

"No. No, that ain't good enough. You can't just
leave it go at that. Look at poor Perlong layin' there,
busted half in two by this damn 'breed. And all you
can say is 'That's the way it is'?"

"What I say *is* the way it is," Ulysses said flatly.

"No, that ain't good enough," Lowe said again. He
glanced down at the gunbelt he was holding—the
one containing Buckhorn's gun in its holster, the rig
Perlong had stripped off and handed to Lowe preced-
ing the fight.

"Don't even think it," Ulysses warned.

Lowe's eyes went to him again.

"But it ain't right not to do something, Ulysses.
Perlong was my best pal. He was one of *us.*"

"I'm warnin' you."

Lowe's mouth curled like it was going to issue a
snarl, but no sound came out. His eyes shifted back
and forth between the weapon he was holding and
Ulysses. In the open distance between the two men,
Buckhorn's eyes also whipped back and forth. He was
too far away from Lowe to rush him if he tried to
bring the Colt into play. If it came to that, Buckhorn
knew he would nevertheless make the attempt. But he
also knew his only real chance in that event rested
with Ulysses.

Lowe made the decision to put the question to its
ultimate test. A snarling curse finally escaping through
his curled lips, he seized the Colt and yanked it free

even as he let the rest of the gunbelt drop down and away. But before he could bring the muzzle to bear, Ulysses drew and fired his own Colt with blinding speed and deadly accuracy.

A single .45 slug screamed through the night air and slammed into Lowe's chest, just to the left of his sternum. He fell back against the rickety corral rails, hung there for a moment, then collapsed the rest of the way to the ground, Buckhorn's gun slipping unfired from his grasp.

Buckhorn was still standing there. Ulysses strode past him and walked straight to the fallen Lowe. He stood over the body, once again stone faced as he gazed down upon it. Then, holstering his Colt, he turned away.

"Obliged," Buckhorn said.

Ulysses glared at him.

"I don't want your damn 'obliged.' Two of my men are down—one of them permanent—because of you. Nothing you can say is gonna fix that."

"You didn't have to kill him."

"Hell I didn't. Wasn't time not to. Besides, I won't have somebody who can't take orders."

From the doorway of the house, Riley called, "Is Lowe dead?"

"Afraid so, sir. Couldn't be helped," Ulysses responded. Then he added, "It's not over, though. There's more I have to do."

So saying, he pivoted sharply and lashed out, swinging his fist in a whistling backhand that caught Buckhorn flush on the side of the jaw. The punch was so unexpected and powerful that it sent Buckhorn once more to the ground.

He jackknifed quickly to a sitting position and sleeved a trickle of blood from the corner of his mouth, scowling fiercely up at Ulysses as he watched the black man shrug out of his bandolier and begin unbuckling his gunbelt. "What the hell's the idea?" Buckhorn wanted to know.

Ulysses leaned over and placed his gear on the ground, also pulling the knife from his moccasin boot and adding it to the pile. Straightening up, he said, "Just like I won't have somebody who can't take orders, neither will I have somebody who thinks they can operate outside the rules. So I'll have to finish the job that Perlong started but wasn't able to get done."

"In other words," said Buckhorn, climbing back to his feet, "what you're really worried about is maintaining your notch at the top of the pecking order."

"Say it however you want. Point is, I got to make sure that everybody"—Ulysses's eyes darted meaningfully toward the men over in front of the shed, then back again—"is clear on who's the he-goose callin' the shots around here. I lose that, I got nothing."

"You force me to break you in half like I did Perlong," Buckhorn pointed out, "you'll make it a certainty."

Ulysses smiled a thin, cold smile.

"Guess I'll have to be sure I don't get busted in half then, won't I?"

CHAPTER 36

The two men slammed together like a pair of warring buffalo bulls—the bare-chested, heavily muscled black and the leaner, more sleekly muscled half-breed. Eyes fierce, teeth bared, all the skills and instincts of two warriors tested and tempered by many previous battles were fully in evidence. Punches were thrown and blocked, kicks were deflected, attempts to clamp and hold were slipped.

But they fought on relentlessly, knowing it was just a matter of time before somebody wore down or made a mistake and there would be an opening.

Even in the cool, damp night air, Buckhorn felt the sweat start to flow freely down his face. He saw it shine on the face and bulging shoulders of Ulysses, too.

Back and forth they went. Slugging and shoving, grabbing, twisting, ducking, until their breathing began to chug like a set of steam engines.

When Buckhorn's foot slipped and he nearly sagged to one knee, Ulysses lunged close and tried to clamp on a headlock. Buckhorn's sweat-slick hair and quick pulling-away action saved him from getting caught securely by the hold.

As he jerked back, he took advantage of the way their bodies were momentarily positioned and drilled two hard punches into Ulysses's left kidney area. The big man's grunts of pain and the *feel* of each impact told Buckhorn he had scored solidly.

He got a little too eager and tried to close again less cautiously than he should have, wanting to take further advantage of the first real damage he'd been able to score. For his trouble, he caught a vicious backward-thrusting elbow smash to the mouth that rocked him in his tracks.

Ulysses wheeled around, exhibiting some over-eagerness of his own as he sought to take advantage of the damage *he* had caused. Buckhorn was waiting to make him pay for his eagerness. Leaving himself wide open for a fraction of a second in the midst of his turn, Ulysses's solar plexus became the target for a perfectly timed and placed left hook. The nerve-numbing blow immediately took him to his knees.

Buckhorn dropped his right shoulder and launched himself straight into the black man's middle. The thud of their bodies colliding was like the sound of distant thunder. Ulysses was bowled over backward and Buckhorn went with him, the two of them rolling into a tangle.

A lesser man than Ulysses would have been finished at that point. But even though Buckhorn landed on top, when he tried to pull free he felt the fingers of Ulysses's left hand clutching his hair, trying to hold his head still while the black man's right fist clubbed against the side of his face.

The blow didn't have a lot of force behind it now, though. Buckhorn blocked a second attempted punch and jerked his hair free with a curse. He raised his own right fist high and was ready to bring it crashing down, ready to end this once and for all.

This time the cannon-like boom was much closer and more directly related to firepower. All eyes snapped around and locked on the sight of Dan Riley, having taken two or three steps outside the doorway of the house, one of his Navy Colts pointed skyward. With everybody looking on now, he fired a second shot, yellow flame and another crash of sound erupting from the muzzle.

"Enough!" Dan hollered. "Stop it, Buckhorn! Stop it, for God's sake. You've made your point; enough damage has been done. Let it be finished."

Buckhorn had frozen at the sound of the first gunshot. Like everybody else, his attention was on Riley. Now, as the man finished speaking, Buckhorn realized he was still holding a balled fist over the pain-etched face of Ulysses. He slowly lowered the fist.

When he attempted to push away and stand up, he discovered his legs were as weak and unsupportive as two pieces of string. Instead of standing, he edged off to one side and rolled over onto his back.

I'll just lay here a minute and catch my breath, he told himself . . .

More than an hour had passed.

Lowe's body was wrapped in a canvas tarp and temporarily placed in a wagon along with his personal gear. Since he had no kin that anybody knew of, it was planned for him to be buried here in this valley at first light. Dan would read over him, as he'd done for others in the past.

Perlong and Ulysses were brought into the house, and their wounds—mostly bruises and cuts once they got their breath back—were tended to by Eve and Joey. Perlong's cracked ribs amounted to the most serious of the injuries. The women tightly wrapped his middle in a wide bandage to control his breathing, and then some of the other men helped him back to the bunk shed where he'd announced to one and all his plans to further medicate with a bottle of whiskey.

Buckhorn, having sustained the least damage, was the last to receive attention. He'd already done some tending to himself, washing up at a watering trough outside and putting his vest and jacket back on— along with his gunbelt and holstered Colt, which did more than anything to make him feel healed and whole again.

He insisted nothing more was really necessary, but Joey wouldn't hear of it. She plopped him on a chair before a basin of hot, sudsy water on the kitchen table and began dabbing at the cuts around his mouth with a damp cloth. Eve, seeing there was no need for her to lend a hand, excused herself to go check on her father, who'd returned to his room. Jeff trailed after her.

"Lord, your skin is like leather," Joey muttered as she worked. "It's a wonder it could be split open with anything short of a bayonet."

"Well, I thankfully didn't see any bayonets flashing at me out there. But I guess one of those boys still managed to get the job done anyway."

From the kitchen doorway, a voice said, "Yeah, I only *wish* I woulda had a bayonet . . . and maybe a line of infantrymen to go with it. Then maybe I wouldn't be standin' here now feelin' like *I* was the one who got trampled over by 'em."

Buckhorn and Joey both looked around to see Ulysses Mason leaning wearily against the door frame, a crooked half smile on his face.

"You two aren't going to start up all over again, are you?" Joey said anxiously.

"Heck, no. Leastways I hope not," Ulysses assured her. "My arms feel like they weigh a young ton each, and if I didn't have this door frame to lean against I wouldn't be standin' here upright."

Buckhorn nodded.

"That's good to hear. I made it far enough to drop down in this chair, but I'm sure not in any hurry to push back up off it."

Ulysses's expression sobered.

"You're a fightin' sumbitch, Buckhorn . . . pardon my language, ma'am." The last he included as a quick aside to Joey, then continued addressing Buckhorn: "For whatever it's worth, I wanted you to hear that from me. I'd be proud to ride with any outfit you're a part of."

Buckhorn regarded him, accepting the words. Then he said, "But what about Lowe?"

"Lowe was a weak link. I'd seen it and known for some time he was gonna have to be dealt with. He wouldn't've lasted as long as he did if not for ridin' on Perlong's coattails. Tonight just brought to a head what was bound to happen anyway."

"And the rest of the men, after all that happened tonight?"

"They saw how it went down. They got no problem havin' you in the outfit."

"Even though I'm a half-breed?"

"We got men of a lot of different stripes and from all kinds of backgrounds here. Hell, in case you ain't noticed, I'm a black man. They been ridin' *behind* me. If Boss Dan calls it that way after tonight, they'll ride behind you."

Buckhorn shook his head.

"Ain't gonna be like that. Be too crowded. You're the top notch around here; they're gonna stay ridin' behind you."

Ulysses held his eyes for a long moment before saying, "Obliged for that." Then, the crooked half smile returning, he added, "And I hope you're smarter at acceptin' obliges than I was a little while ago."

"Consider it done."

Ulysses straightened up in the doorway, jabbed a thumb over his shoulder.

"When you're finished there, Boss Dan wants a word with you."

"I see you got your gun back."

Buckhorn nodded.

"Along with the rest of my gear."

"You negotiate pretty convincingly," Dan Riley allowed.

"Done my fair share of that kind of negotiating."

"Not to mention the kind strictly involving gunplay."

"There was a share of that kind tonight, too," Buckhorn pointed out.

"Yes. I guess I should say that was regrettable, but I'm afraid Lowe had other shortcomings that made him overdue for culling out regardless. I suppose that makes me sound harsh," Riley said, "but these are harsh conditions we find ourselves living under."

This time it was just the two of them in the room. The door was closed. Buckhorn had waited until Eve and Jeff came out, after the girl had finished the latest examination of her father's wound. When he'd entered in their place, Riley had motioned for him to shut the door.

As far as Buckhorn could tell, getting to his feet and venturing outside during the fight—an act Eve found very concerning—hadn't left the wounded man looking any worse for wear. His mood and tone, however, were decidedly sober.

"Speaking of harsh," Riley went on, "I suppose you think that whole business of making you fight to get your own gun back was pretty harsh, too."

"You run the show around here. You got a right to call the tune however you want it played. Those who don't like it don't have to stick around and listen to the music."

"And yet you still want to join our outfit."

"What I came here for."

"Is it really?" Riley regarded him closely for a long count. "I'm damned if I can make up my mind about you, Buckhorn. I like you, so help me. You got brass, you got grit . . . But that little voice keeps yappin' inside my head. Tellin' me there's something off about you, warnin' me not to buy the whole package."

Buckhorn held his eyes levelly.

"Man ought to go with his gut," he said. "If something plain don't feel right, you're probably better off not seein' it through. I got nothing more to say, nothing more to show. I thought revealing that meadow trap gave me a reasonable bargaining chip. If it wasn't enough, then that leaves riding on the best thing for me."

"You'd do that?"

"You not fully trusting me would only bleed into others not trusting me and me not being able to trust anybody in return. What chance would that have of working?"

"You know," Riley said, "what you said a minute ago about anybody who don't like the way the tune is played around here not having to stick around and listen to the music . . . that's not exactly accurate. At least, that's not how it's been."

Buckhorn said nothing. Waited.

"As you got a taste of on the way in, we keep this valley pretty carefully guarded," Riley continued. "That means from the outside and also from the inside. Having this place to come to, to hide out if you want to put it that way, has been what's allowed me to keep operating and keep the law off our backs. Should be obvious, I guess, why we want to keep outsiders out. On the flip side, letting somebody who's seen our operation here, maybe even ridden with us for a spell, decide they want to leave and venture off on their own . . . well, surely you can see how that might not sit real well, either. Especially if said person might be leaving as the result of being disgruntled or dissatisfied in some way."

"I think I'm seeing the picture plain enough," Buckhorn said.

With what looked like a long, genuinely sad face, Riley said, "Fortunately, that kind of situation has only come up a time or two in the past."

These words made Buckhorn recall the talk he'd heard earlier about how Boss Dan would read over the grave of Lowe—*like he'd done for others in the past*—after they buried him in the morning.

As if of its own volition, Buckhorn's body tensed, became poised in a barely perceptible way, like a wild animal that's been alerted to danger.

"So," he said, his voice a knife blade sliding down a honing stone. "What I'm hearing is that I can't be trusted to join your outfit and can't be trusted to leave your valley. That about the size of it?"

Riley raised one hand, palm out.

"Now take it easy. Don't get all coiled tight like a rattler gettin' ready to strike. And you can relax the hand you got half-clawed over the Colt you just got back. You think I'm stupid enough to invite you into a closed room with me and then threaten you now that you're freshly re-armed?"

Buckhorn let the question hang in the air. Once again said nothing, just waited.

Riley lowered his hand and said, "As far as men not riding out of here after they've seen our operation, what I said was that's how it *has* been. Sooner or later, you run across an exception to every rule. I'm thinking that fits you in this instance. What you did here tonight ought to earn you something. And you also alerted us to that trap waiting in the Circle D meadow and how there's a Texas Ranger now involved. So, first thing in the morning, you're free to ride out." Riley paused and his gaze took on a deep earnestness. "I still don't know exactly what your game is. I just hope to hell you don't betray me and make one or both of us regret me taking the gamble of letting you go."

CHAPTER 37

It was only a few short hours to daybreak. Buckhorn knew he had to act fast. He had no intention of waiting around until then before making his departure from the valley, nor did he have any intention of leaving alone.

In an almost omenlike stroke of luck, when he came out of Riley's room it was Joey who was waiting to show him where he could catch a few winks of sleep.

"They've been keeping Jeff locked at night in a lean-to room just off the kitchen," she explained. "You know, to discourage him and Eve—who sleeps upstairs, right above her father's room—from getting together and making another attempt at running off. Also from getting together and . . . well, you can figure it out, I'm sure." She flushed in the glow of the lantern she was holding, clearly embarrassed. "Anyway, Ulysses said I should point you back there with Jeff for what little time you have to rest before morning. He already put your war bag and bedroll in there and the room won't be locked for tonight."

"Did Ulysses tell you I'll be leaving at daybreak?" Buckhorn asked.

Joey looked away from his gaze.

"He said he thought that's the way Uncle Dan was leaning, but he wasn't positive."

"Well, that's the decision," Buckhorn confirmed. "Leastways that's the way it's *supposed* to go."

Joey's eyes came back, looking up at him.

"What do you mean?"

"I mean I'm not sticking around that long. I don't think the old man's all the way convinced that letting me go is the smartest move, and I can't risk waiting in case he changes his mind."

They'd moved away from Riley's room and edged toward the kitchen, talking in low voices with the old house silent and empty feeling all around them.

Joey nipped a corner of her bottom lip between her teeth, then said, "Sounds to me like you'd just be trading one risk for another."

"Maybe. But there's only one of them I can plan for and control. And that's also the only way I can make it about more than just myself."

"I don't understand."

"You should. You're the one who figured out what I came here for," Buckhorn told her. "I was looking for information about Jeff, and like you once put it, I ended up stumbling over the actual person. Now that I found him, I don't intend to leave without him."

"That will only add to your risk. What's more, how do you know he'll even want to go with you?"

"If it comes to that, I'll have to see to it he understands he doesn't have a choice. Consider this: with your uncle's policy about men who've seen and been part of this operation not ordinarily being allowed to leave, what does that mean for Jeff's chances of ever making it out of here in one piece?"

"I've thought about that, too. Worried about it. But Uncle Dan would never do that to the man his daughter is in love with!"

"Wouldn't he?"

Joey chewed her lip some more.

"What about Eve? Do you plan on taking her, too?"

Buckhorn shook his head. "She'd never come, not with her father still needing care for his wound. The only way would be to knock her unconscious and drag her, and *that* I don't have the time or patience for."

"But you think Jeff will somehow be more persuadable?"

"Jeff's got more reasons for wanting to break free from here than just to save his own skin," Buckhorn said. "Once he takes care of some things on the outside, he can always come back after Eve."

"And you'd be the one to help him do that, wouldn't you?" Joey said, peering intently into his eyes.

"Only if the money was right," Buckhorn said. "Don't try to read more into me than what's there, gal—I'm a hired gun, plain and simple, not somebody willing to stick my neck out simply for the sake of doing a good deed."

"I think there's more of that in you than you're willing to admit," Joey insisted.

"Go ahead and think that all you want, but you'll be thinkin' wrong." Then, softening his tone, Buckhorn added, "Only that doesn't mean I'm not hoping there's some good deed doing left in you."

"What are you getting at?" Joey wanted to know.

"Look, you've been covering my tail ever since you led me down into this valley. I'm not exactly sure why, especially considering the rough start we got off to. But I think—particularly after you guessed what I was really up to—it's because you want to see the romance between Eve and Jeff get a fair shake, have a chance to work out. You could have burned me more than once, but you didn't. For that, like I already told you, I'm grateful . . . but now I need to ask you for even more."

"Can't I even say good-bye to her?" Jeff Danvers asked.

"No," Buckhorn said bluntly. "We can't take time for that and we can't risk the fuss she might put up. After we're gone, Joey will explain to her why you had to take off so suddenlike, that I'm forcing you. Later, once we've seen to what needs taken care of on the outside, you can come back for her."

"If she'll *want* me to come back," Jeff said as a gloomy expression covered his face.

"If she doesn't, then she wasn't ever the right gal for you to begin with. But, in the meantime, there's another gal who for sure wants and needs you to come back—your ma. She badly needs to know you're alive and safe. And, no matter how painful it might be for her, she deserves to hear the truth about Dan Riley and the hand Micah played in it."

"I've been avoiding even thinking about those things. Instead, I've been leaning on the excuse of not knowing how I could escape from here to try and do anything about them, no matter how bad I wanted to."

"Well, the time for excuses and avoiding what has to be done is over," Buckhorn told him. "We need to ride hard outta here and start setting some things straight."

This conversation had been taking place in the cramped, shadowy lean-to room where Jeff had been confined each night. Buckhorn had barged in and wasted no time laying things on the line for the tormented young man. Overcoming his initial surprise and reluctance, Jeff was now showing signs of being up to seizing the opportunity and subsequent test that was suddenly being thrust upon him.

"You're right. It's time for me to grow up," he said with sudden resolve in his voice.

Buckhorn snapped a quick nod.

"Good. Joey should have the horses ready by now. Let's go join up with her."

They walked the horses a couple hundred yards out from the farm buildings before climbing into their saddles. The long day, the natural letdown after a high peak of excitement, and the prospect of having only a short amount of sleep available left everybody in their wake slumbering deeply. This worked to the favor of those slipping away as far as being able to do so without raising any alarm, but there was no sense failing to take reasonable precautions.

Also working to their favor was the dimming of the moon and stars that came with the approach of dawn. The floor of the valley was awash in gray murkiness.

They made their way across it slowly but steadily, sticking to the higher grasses and frequent stands of brush so as to make themselves as inconspicuous as possible.

As they neared the gap that would give them passage up to the rim and beyond, Joey said, "Best let me ride ahead a little bit, so I can give the signal."

"Signal?" Buckhorn questioned.

"That's right," she replied, smiling somewhat sheepishly. "The one I *didn't* give the first time I brought you through. It's a whistling sound, a quick series of notes that lets the guards on duty know that a friend is approaching."

"I'll be damned," Buckhorn muttered under his breath.

Only a couple minutes later, as they started their ascent up through the narrow pass, Joey emitted a shrill whistle that tapered off in an odd way at the end. It was promptly answered, and then, a couple minutes after that, two men stepped out to block the way of the trio on horseback. One of the men held up a lantern; the other held a Winchester at the ready.

"Name yourselves," said the man with the lantern in a gruff, sleepy-sounding voice.

"It's Joey Riley," Joey answered. "One of the men with me has been badly injured and Uncle Dan sent us to get him to a doctor."

"At this time of night?" said the man with the Winchester.

"Accidents don't necessarily wait for a convenient time to happen," Joey said tersely. "Now this man is hurt bad so we can't afford a lot of chin wagging over it. Let us by so we can get him some help."

"I'd better have a look for myself," said the man with the lantern as he stepped toward Jeff, who was sagging convincingly in his saddle to sell the appearance of someone who'd been hurt. "What the heck happened anyway?"

When the man was right beside him, lantern held high, Jeff suddenly straightened up and shoved the barrel of a previously concealed six-gun practically against the tip of the lantern-bearer's nose.

"Nothing compared to what's going to happen to you, mister, if you don't quit yapping so much and do exactly as you're told."

Lightning-quick, Buckhorn had his Colt drawn and aimed at the man with the Winchester, who'd made the mistake of relaxing and lowering the rifle's barrel because he was trying to also gawk at the injury when it fell within the illumination of his pal's lantern.

"Same goes for you, *hombre*," Buckhorn said. "That rifle barrel raises one twitch, your head's gonna make a lumpy, bloody mess rolling down the trail after I blow it off your shoulders."

To make it clear he understood and had no intention of trying anything, the rifleman dropped his Winchester and let it clatter to the rocky ground.

"Good." Buckhorn waggled his Colt. "You and your partner get over there against the rocks, keep your hands where I can see 'em plain. You, Missy"—he motioned to Joey—"get down off that horse and get over there, too, now that you've served your purpose."

Joey did as instructed, putting on the act of firing one of her famous glares at Buckhorn as she did so.

"My uncle will get even with you for this, you can count on that," she said through gritted teeth.

Ignoring her, Buckhorn said to Jeff, "Take charge of that lantern and then strip the men of their guns while I keep 'em covered. Give anything you find a good fling off into the rocks. We're in no hurry to have them found again."

"What are you gonna do to us?" asked the former lantern bearer after he'd been disarmed.

Buckhorn swung lightly from his saddle and walked over to stand close to the man.

"Turn around and face the rocks, all three of you," he ordered. When that was done, he said, "Now, as far as you guards, I'm gonna do you two big favors—I'm gonna let you live and I'm gonna give you permission to take a little nap while on duty."

So saying, he swung two rapid strokes with the butt of his Colt and knocked each of the men unconscious. They crumpled into heaps on the rugged ground.

Re-holstering his gun, Buckhorn said, "Okay, it looks like we got away with it. We're pretty much in the clear now."

"What about me?" Joey asked.

"Without your help we never could've pulled it off, that's what about you," Buckhorn told her. "You know how beholden I am. If you don't, I haven't got the words to say more."

"I don't mean that," Joey said, shaking her head. "I mean what about the condition you're going to leave me in? If we're going to finish selling the notion that you forced me this far—and I'll be in a tight spot if we don't—then you're going to have to make it look good by knocking me out, too."

"Aw, come on," protested Jeff. "We can't do that."

Buckhorn scowled and said, "No. She's right. We have to do it . . . for her own good."

"Yes, you do." Joey squared her shoulders, lifted her chin. "But first, there's something I need to do."

Abruptly, she took a step closer to Buckhorn, reached up and placed her palms on either side of his face, then pressed her lips hard against his. When the kiss was over, she let her hands slip away and took a step back.

"What the hell was that for?" Buckhorn asked, feeling a little stunned, as if somebody had just walloped *him* on the head with a gun butt . . . although the kiss was a lot nicer than that.

Joey smiled coyly and said, "I've been wondering what it would be like, that's all."

Buckhorn was clearly a bit flustered.

"And?"

"It could use a little work. If we had more time, I'm sure we could get the wrinkles smoothed out. But, for now, there are more important things to take care of." She lifted her chin again. "So go ahead and do what you have to. I know you've already got the wrinkles smoothed when it comes to knowing how to knock somebody out . . ."

CHAPTER 38

"Well, that was a long, cold night wasted," grumbled Dave Millard as he slumped wearily in his saddle.

"You can say that again," chimed in Hank Boynton, riding along beside him.

"No, he can't," Micah Danvers snapped irritably from where he rode just ahead of the pair. "I heard enough bellyachin' out of the two of you all through the night. More than enough to last me for a good long spell, so knock it off with any damn more."

The three men, along with Ranger Menlo, Sheriff Tolliver, his deputy Bud McKeever, and three more Circle D wranglers were on their way back to Circle D ranch headquarters. The sun was less than an hour old in the eastern sky.

All of the riders sat their saddles with an exhausted slump to their shoulders and an air of frustration about them. The long night's vigil over the remote meadow had been fruitless as far as catching even a whiff of rustlers in the trap they'd been primed to spring.

The other *hombres* who'd manned the trap with

them—a handful of wranglers from neighboring ranches and a few men from town who'd been willing to come out and lend a hand—had branched off separately and were also on their way back home. Four relief men from the Circle D had shown up to take over standing watch just after daybreak. No one expected a full-on rustling raid to be attempted during the daytime hours.

"You don't suppose we could be wrong about that, do you?" said Thad Tolliver abruptly. "About the rustlers tryin' something today, I mean. I know it's never usually done that way, but the surprise factor might be exactly what some wide-loopin' scoundrel decides to count on."

"By 'wide-looping scoundrel' you mean Dan Riley, right?" said Micah.

"Sure, that's who we're figurin'. But it could be anybody in the rustlin' business."

"How many rustlin' gangs you figure you got operatin' around here, Sheriff?" asked Ranger Menlo somewhat sourly.

"Exactly one. And it's run by Dan Riley," Micah was quick to answer. "And I can't see him—or anybody else, if you want to stretch the point unreasonably—tryin' to move a stolen herd in the daylight. Especially not with our neighbors on all sides, some of whom were on watch with us last night and have lost cattle themselves, alert for anything suspicious."

"Sounds like pretty tight figurin' to me, Sheriff," allowed Menlo. "I don't think there's much worry about that herd, or any other as far as that goes, gettin' snatched in the daytime."

"So we go back and do it all over again tonight?

And the next, and the one after that . . . until the thieves finally show up?"

Micah sighed.

"Only if we want to catch them, Sheriff. Unless you know a way to get 'em to make an appointment."

"I don't appreciate the sarcasm, Micah." Tolliver scowled. "The point I was working toward was that me and Bud here can't leave Deputy Scanlon taking care of the town all by himself every night for who knows how long. Not to mention who'll cover daytime duties if we're all three working nights. We're gonna need some sleep sooner or later."

"I'm sure Micah understands that," Deputy McKeever spoke up. "It would've been nice if those skunks had been accommodating enough to hit this first night. But since it looks like they might be draggin' it out before they make their move, we'll just have to figure out a way to drag out our coverage, too. Comes down to it, I could do the watches out here while you and Harold take care of the town. Something like that."

"And, just incidentally, in case anybody forgets," said Menlo, "I'm also on hand to help represent the Law. Me and my outfit, a little group you might have heard of called the Texas Rangers, are actually considered pretty good at this sort of thing."

Tolliver rolled his eyes.

"Just what I need . . . more sarcasm."

When they got to the ranch, Micah directed Dave and Hank and the other wranglers to hit the grub shack for a big breakfast and then some much-deserved shut-eye. The lawmen had already been invited to join Micah for a separate breakfast up at the main house. Since no good news had been relayed back to the ranch any time during the night, both kitchens would be prepared for the return of disappointed but hungry men.

The aromas of fried ham, bacon, fresh biscuits, and more that assailed their nostrils as the men came up the front porch steps of the house quickly confirmed this expectation. Pamela Danvers—looking lovely as usual though somewhat wan and hollow around the eyes, as if she also had gone without sleep—was waiting to greet them. So alluring to the weary, hungry men were the aromas and the vision of their awaiting hostess that none of them took much notice of the two horses already tied at the hitching rail out front even as they'd secured their own mounts right beside them.

Pamela directed the new arrivals first to an area off one end of the porch where they could wash up, then told them to rejoin her in the dining room.

As the men filed into the dining area they were greeted by the sight of a long table set with plates, utensils, cups, carafes of coffee, and pitchers of buttermilk and water. In the middle of the table were platters of ham, bacon, biscuits, and jars of honey and jam. Pamela motioned everyone to sit wherever they pleased, and as this was taking place, Helga appeared with two additional platters heaped with piles of steaming scrambled eggs.

"On second thought," Sheriff Tolliver said, "maybe it wouldn't be such a hardship after all if layin' in wait for those rustlin' scoundrels *does* drag on for a bit. Not if there's gonna be breakfasts like this waiting for us on the mornings after we stand watch."

"But if you're forced to stay in town to handle duties there, you'll miss out," Deputy McKeever was quick to point out. "Me, bein' on assignment out this way, will just have to shoulder whatever responsibilities comes with that part of the duties."

Tolliver grinned good-naturedly and responded to the rib, saying, "Careful, or you might get yourself re-assigned awful suddenlike. Something *could* occur to me that'd make it necessary for me to send you rushing right back to town this very minute."

"That ain't even funny," McKeever groaned in mock horror.

The men waited to claim their seats until Micah had held a chair for his mother. Only then did they sit.

Taking his own seat at the head of the table, Micah scanned the spread before all of them and then arched one brow questioningly.

"I notice other places set, Mother. Are you expecting more . . . oh, I suppose Obie will be joining us, too."

"Yes," Pamela said in a carefully controlled tone. "Obie should be here any second. Along with some other guests who arrived a short time ago."

"At this early hour?" Micah said.

"Considerin' how long I've been absent," said a voice from across the room, "you could say it's more like I'm actually kinda late."

The clink of glasses and the scrape of spoons ladling food came to an abrupt halt as the men filling their plates sensed something unsettling in the air. All eyes cut to the doorway where Jeff Danvers stood. Behind him loomed Buckhorn, with Obie at his side.

The facial reactions showed varying degrees of surprise, but none as extreme as what Micah displayed.

"Jeffrey!" he exclaimed, his voice strained almost to a croak.

"Mornin', Micah," Jeff said casually. "You look a little frazzled. Guess that comes from havin' been out all night hoping to spring a trap on some no-good rotten rustlers, eh? Too bad you came up empty."

Micah blinked several times as if in disbelief before finally finding his voice again and saying, "Me? Never mind about me. Good God, we've all been so worried and . . . What about you? That's the question everybody wants to hear the answer to."

Murmurs of concern mingled with the surprised expressions still being worn by almost everyone else in the room.

"It's like a miracle, isn't it?" said Pamela, smiling broadly. "That Jeffrey is back and that he's returned safe and sound!"

"Yeah, a miracle," Micah echoed, though lacking his mother's enthusiasm. He rose to his feet and came around the end of the table, reaching to shake his brother's hand. "You have got a story to tell, mister. Where the devil have you been all this time?"

"Funny you should ask," Jeff replied, taking Micah's extended hand but accompanying his grip with a penetrating look that conveyed little in the way of friendliness. "Although it admittedly wasn't what I set out for, I also ended up becoming involved with a rustler and lawbreaker."

"Well, sure," said Micah, grinning somewhat uneasily. "I mean, if you set out to run away with Eve

Riley you should have known there was the risk of tangling with her old man."

"Heavens, Jeffrey," said Pamela. She looked genuinely concerned, but at the same time, her automatic bitterness for any mention of the Riley name showed on her face, too. "Is that what happened? Did you run afoul of that treacherous Dan Riley? There's so much you haven't had the chance to tell us yet."

"As a matter of fact, I did run across Dan Riley," said Jeff. "And he'll be the first to admit that he's been involved with rustling and probably plenty of other misdeeds as well. But he wasn't necessarily who I was talking about. Because he wasn't the only rustler and outlaw I ran across—or learned about, I guess I should say—while I was gone."

"Holy cow, little brother," Micah said, the uneasy grin spreading wider. "How much territory did you cover while you were away? And are you gonna tell us the rest in riddles, or have you got something to say flat out?"

Jeff didn't reply right away. First his eyes went to his mother. An unmistakable sadness settled over his face as he said, "I'm sorry to spring this on you without any warning, Mother. There wasn't enough time between when I got here and now. And I wouldn't know of a good way to break this, no matter how long I had or might've taken."

The concern on Pamela's face only deepened.

"What are you trying to say, Jeffrey?"

"Yeah. What kind of song and dance are you mumbling and stumbling over? Make some damn sense," demanded Micah impatiently.

Looking on, Buckhorn was poised and ready for

any reaction that might appear to be a threat to the truth about to be exposed or to the young man getting ready to reveal it. In the short time he'd been around Jeff Danvers, he'd grown more and more impressed by him—a sharp contrast to the downward spiraling opinion he'd had of Micah almost from the beginning.

"This isn't exactly rustling related," Jeff said, reaching inside his jacket and withdrawing an object. "But I think it makes for a good place to start. How about *you* offer an explanation that will make sense of *this*, Micah?"

Jeff tossed the object onto the tabletop where it landed between platters of food and unfolded, proving to be a canvas sack with a heavy metal clasp at the top. Stenciled lettering on the face of the sack read: HAWTHORNE & HALSEY.

"Hawthorne and Halsey," said Sheriff Tolliver. "That's the stage line that runs out of Basin City off to the south. That's one of their money sacks for carryin' payrolls and the like."

"Ain't that also the line," said Ranger Menlo, "that's suffered some robberies over the past year or so?"

"Sure is," said Obie. "As recently as only a few days ago."

"Well, hallelujah, we got us a couple lawmen who can read and an old goat with a good memory." Micah scowled fiercely and raked his eyes across everyone gathered around the table. Returning them to Jeff he said, "So what the hell's a dusty old stagecoach money sack supposed to mean to me? What kind of explanation am I supposed to offer for it?"

"How about starting with how it got in your room? That's where Buckhorn and I found it just a few minutes ago."

"That's a lie!"

Jeff shook his head.

"No, it's not. You had it hid in the back of your closet."

Micah's eyes turned angry, started to go a little wild.

"I never saw that thing before in my life. If you found it in my closet, then somebody planted it there for the sake of trying to hang something on me." He thrust an arm out, pointing a finger. "It's that damn half-breed! He's had it out for me ever since he showed up in these parts. He must have stuffed it in that old boot when you weren't looking, Jeff, and then made sure you *did* take a look so you'd be sure to spot—"

"How do you know I found it in a boot, Micah? I never said that. All I said was that I found it in your closet."

Micah's eyes grew wilder, bouncing from face to face.

"He's right, son," Ranger Menlo pressed in a low, even voice. "He never said anything about the sack being in a boot."

"This is some kind of trick. A trap," Micah protested. He looked pleadingly in the direction of Pamela. "You believe me, don't you, Mother? It's all some kind of crazy mistake. Why on earth would I be mixed up in anything like a stagecoach robbery?"

Pamela's face was gripped by shock and confusion.

"I . . . I don't know what to think," she murmured.

"I'm sorry, Mother, but there's really only one thing you *can* think," Jeff told her. "When I excused myself to go up to my room a few minutes ago, I took the opportunity to also take a peek in Micah's. I don't know exactly what I was even looking for. But I know what I found, and it's right there on the table. And I'm afraid that's only the start. In addition to—"

"That's enough!" Micah shouted, his right hand diving for the six-gun on his hip.

But the gun hadn't lifted more than a fraction of an inch out of its holster before Buckhorn's Colt was drawn and aimed, muzzle locked unwaveringly on the desperate brother.

"Raise that hogleg another whisker and your brains will plumb ruin that platter of scrambled eggs in front of you," the gunman said.

Micah froze like a statue.

Pamela gasped audibly.

But then, only a second later, there was the unmistakable sound of the hammer of a revolver being thumbed to full cock directly behind Buckhorn. "You go ahead and stroke that trigger, 'breed," snarled a voice from the same spot, "but the insides of *your* skull will be taking their own trip on a bullet if you do."

Scarcely had those words been spoken before there came the thud of a heavy blow and, immediately to Buckhorn's right, Obie's twisted form pitched forward and hit the floor.

"Same for the cripple!" declared a second voice.

The only sound for a long moment was the tick of the clock on the wall. With agonizing slowness, Buckhorn lowered his arm.

"All the way. Drop the gun," said the voice behind him.

As soon as Buckhorn's Colt clumped onto the floor, Micah came out of his frozen pose. He finished drawing his gun and then covered the distance to Jeff in a single long stride. He swung the gun barrel viciously, slamming it against his younger brother's jaw and sending him sprawling alongside Obie.

"Micah! What madness is this!" said Pamela shrilly.

"Shut up, Mother!" Micah responded. "For once in your life just keep your damn mouth shut!"

Sheriff Tolliver couldn't contain himself. He shot to his feet saying, "You snot-nosed little bastard! Anybody who'd talk that way to his own mother don't—"

Directly beside the sheriff, Deputy McKeever also rose suddenly, one hand streaking to the pistol on his hip. For an instant, Buckhorn thought the young fool was making some kind of suicide play to try to save the situation. But instead of turning his gun on Micah or the men who'd gotten the drop on Buckhorn, the deputy jabbed the muzzle hard into the ribs of Tolliver, cutting short his words.

"You shut up, too, you lovesick fool!" McKeever barked. "If you wasn't such an idiot, you would have caught on months ago that there was a second outlaw gang operating practically in your backyard. So it's a little late for heroics from you now."

Tolliver looked more stricken by the harsh words than the jab to his ribs. He said, "Bud? I don't understand. What th—"

"Shut up, I said!"

Micah finally got around to looking over and acknowledging the two men who'd come up behind Buckhorn and Obie. Buckhorn took the opportunity to glance around and have a look for himself. As he should have guessed, he saw it was Dave and Hank, the two wranglers who seemed to be Micah's near-constant companions.

"I don't know what brought you two rowdies over here," Micah said, grinning ruefully, "but it was damned good to see you slide up in back of that stinkin' half-breed."

"Over at the grub shack, Cookie mentioned how he'd seen Jeff and the 'breed ride up a little while ago and come right to the house," explained Dave. "We thought that sounded like it might mean trouble so we figured we'd best slip over for a look-see."

"Well, that was mighty good figurin' and don't think I ain't grateful."

"I just hope you didn't scrape the bottom of the barrel on good figuring," said McKeever. "Because, in case it ain't occurred to nobody but me, now that the beans have been spilled on what's been taking place behind the scenes around here, we're gonna have to do some quick, smart figurin' on how to play things next."

"Ain't like we haven't known this day was comin' sooner or later," Micah replied. "For starters, I think a smart move would be to make sure these *hombres* are all stripped of their weapons and then corralled somewhere secure so we can do the rest of the figurin' we need to do. Line 'em up against the wall over there and make sure they keep their hands in plain sight. All except my lovin' little brother, that is. Leave him layin' for now. When we get the others taken care of, we'll bring him around so me and him can have a real intense talk about a few things."

"He may be hurt bad," Pamela protested. "You can't just leave him lying there!"

"Shut up, Mother. I don't aim to keep sayin' it over and over," Micah told her. "Number one, I just said we're gonna roust him up in a minute, didn't I? Number two, in case you haven't figured it out by now, you all of a sudden don't have any say around here anymore. *I'm* the one running the show from now on!"

"You're a disgrace."

Micah heaved an exaggerated sigh.

"Yeah. Well, if you'd been payin' closer attention, that really oughtn't come as a big surprise to you by this point." He turned away from her and waggled his gun at Dave and Hank. "Herd those men over against the wall, like I said. Then you two keep 'em covered while McKeever strips 'em clean of their weapons."

Holding his hands at chest level, Buckhorn started shuffling toward the wall with the others. His mind was churning, enraged, looking desperately for some kind of opening. But the quarters were too close and too crowded. And there were the women to consider. If he attempted anything and gunfire resulted, there was the risk of one of them catching a bullet. No, all he could do for right now was go along, try to keep alive, and hope for a better chance to turn things around.

As he turned toward the wall, Buckhorn stopped to help Obie get to his feet.

"Leave him alone!" Micah barked. "Let the old cripple haul himself up; it'll make for a good show."

Buckhorn couldn't hold back. He kept the grip he

had clamped on Obie's arm and his face snapped around, glaring at Micah.

"To hell with you! I'm helping this man."

He heard somebody—Dave or Hank, he couldn't be sure which—say, "But who's gonna help you, you mouthy stinkin' 'breed?"

Then fiery pain exploded on the back of Buckhorn's head. He felt himself pitching forward, and all of a sudden there was only blackness around him, swallowing him whole.

CHAPTER 39

Slowly, painfully, consciousness returned to Buckhorn. But the blackness remained. His eyes were open, he was certain of it. He rolled them around, blinked a few times. Yet everything was still dark.

"I think he's coming around," somebody said.

"Thank God," said a different voice. Female . . . Pamela Danvers.

Buckhorn could smell dirt. Damp earth. He was lying on the ground, partly on his side. He tried moving his legs and they seemed to work okay. He pushed himself up on one elbow.

"Take it easy. Don't get too rambunctious there, Powder-burner. You took a hell of a wallop to the head." Obie's voice.

"Why can't I see?" Buckhorn demanded, annoyed, maybe a little panicky.

"You're in a cellar. Underground. There's no light. Your eyes will adjust in a minute and you'll be able to barely make out some shapes and such, but that's about as good as it'll get." This voice was recognizable as belonging to Ranger Menlo.

Buckhorn pushed himself the rest of the way to a sitting position. The pain in his head poured down through the back of his neck and shoulders. But that was okay, he could stand a lot of pain. As long as his vision hadn't been seriously damaged.

"What cellar? Who's down here with me?"

"It's a storm cellar out back of the main house." Pamela's voice again. "They shoved all of us in here to lock us securely out of the way—you, Obie, Ranger Menlo, Thad, Helga, and me. Everybody but Jeffrey."

"I'm afraid that poor lad is havin' a pretty rough go of it," said Sheriff Tolliver's voice. "Micah kept him at the house to beat more information out of him."

Buckhorn was starting to be able to make some things out now. Thin lines of light leaked through the seams between the wooden boards of the sloping cellar door that covered the recessed area into which he and the others were crowded. By those slivers of illumination he could discern blurred ovals that were faces, a few patches of lighter-colored clothing.

"Have they got guards stationed on us?" he asked, lowering his voice from before.

"Not as far as I can tell," answered Menlo. "There's really no need. Once they dropped a bar across those doors on the outside, they've got us pretty well contained."

"How long was I out? How long have we been down here?"

Again it was Menlo who answered, "About twenty minutes all told. They had the sheriff and me drag you out here with the rest of us right after you got pistol-whipped."

Buckhorn reached up and gave an experimental push against the underside of the cellar door. There wasn't much give.

"It's solid as a damn rock," said Obie. "Oak boards on the two door halves, hinged at the outside, a four-by-four barred across the middle. I was in on the buildin' of it years ago. We made sure it was good and sturdy."

"How far away from the house?"

"Fifty, sixty feet. Thereabouts."

"In the year or so right after we built the house, there was a series of bad summer storms," said Pamela. "One of our neighbors dug a storm cellar but he put it too close to the other buildings, and when a storm hit his place it blew part of a roof over the shelter and trapped him and his family for several days before anybody found them. Gus wanted to be sure we put ours a good distance out."

"Look, we all know the basics of a storm cellar so we should recognize the fix we're in here," said Menlo somewhat impatiently. "That's *what* we got. But I'd like to hear a little more about the *who* behind it. You need to fill us in on what happened when you went after Jeff, Buckhorn. How did you find him so quick and how did he find out about Micah's outlaw activity? What else does he know that Micah is so anxious to try and force out of him?"

"I wish everybody would quit talking about that part," Pamela said with a touch of shrillness in her voice. "I know what Micah threatened to do in order to get more answers out of Jeffrey, but I'd rather not keep hearing it over and over again. Still, what Menlo says has merit, Buckhorn. What answers can you give us?"

So Buckhorn laid it out for them, holding back only the scheme he and Menlo had cooked up to warn Dan Riley about the meadow trap for the sake of Buckhorn winning his way into the gang. He concluded by saying, "But the business about Micah and his bunch also being in on stagecoach robberies came as something brand new right here this morning. It happened just like Jeff told it. For some reason he had an urge to take a quick look through Micah's room while there was the chance, and we turned up the money sack."

"So not only has Micah put together some kind of gang and has been robbing and rustling and pulling God knows what else practically right under my nose," Tolliver said, "but one of my very own deputies is in the thick of it with him. Hell, for all I know, Scanlon might be part of it, too."

"At least you haven't been betrayed by your very own blood," Pamela said. "I wasn't totally blind, I certainly saw there were flaws in Micah . . . But I kept thinking, hoping . . . And I surely never . . ."

"Let it go. Never mind all that for right now," Buckhorn said. "There'll be plenty enough blame and self-pity to go around if we manage to get out of this. But *that's* the main thing to concentrate on right at the moment. Blood kin, friends, coworkers, none of that matters. These are ruthless, dangerous *hombres*— each of us has to think of them in only that way."

"Buckhorn's right," said Menlo. "We can't expect them to give us any quarter. So we can't allow ourselves to think any other way in return."

"Well, that's real tough minded and all well and good," said Tolliver. "But it doesn't change the fact that we're bottled up and pretty much helpless to retaliate against 'em at all. No matter how unforgiving we mean to be."

"You're never helpless as long as you're alive," Buckhorn said through gritted teeth. He began moving around as best their confines would allow, groping, searching as he was able with his eyes as well as his hands. "Didn't anybody think to place any kind of provisions down here?"

"Yes. We stored a sack of candles and matches. And some canteens of water," Pamela said. "But they took all that out when they locked us in here."

"I've got some matches if you want a quick look," said Menlo, the pipe smoker. "But I've already burned a couple and I can tell you there's not much to see. It's a hole in the ground on the slope of a hill, all that a storm cellar is supposed to be."

"I'll take you up on burnin' a couple more of those matches," Buckhorn said. "I'd like to take a look for myself, if you don't mind."

Menlo struck a match. Buckhorn looked away from the initial flash so as not to distort his vision again, but then, after the Lucifer tip had dimmed to a meager flickering flame, he used its weak, temporary illumination to quickly scan their surroundings. He was concentrating on some rubble at the rear of the cavity when the flame died out.

"What's that looser pile of dirt at the back?" he asked.

"I took it as part of the rear wall just crumbling loose," said Menlo.

"No. Wait a minute, I remember now," said Obie. "Been so long since we dug this blamed thing and then never did use it but once or twice over the years that I all but forgot. The thing was, after we got this here part dug, Boss Gus still worried about gettin' trapped if we ever had to use it in the event of a bad storm, on account of that neighbor Miss Pamela spoke of. Anyway, he fretted over it so much that he decided to add a second escape hatch just to be sure."

"I never knew that," Pamela said.

"It's a fact," insisted Obie. "Might've went a little fuzzy in my memory for a while, but I remember good now because I'm the one who got stuck doin' most of the diggin'."

"Wait a minute," said Buckhorn, not wanting to get over-eager but at the same time feeling a surge of excitement. "Are you sayin' there's another way out of here, a tunnel or some such?"

"That's right. A tunnel. Runs back another forty feet or so and comes out in the middle of what used to be a fruit orchard," confirmed Obie. Then he added, "Leastways it did. Like I said, ain't nobody hardly been down here but once or twice, and not for a lot of years at that. The way it looked in that match light, it must've—"

Buckhorn didn't wait for him to finish.

"Let's try another one of those matches, Menlo. Over here closer."

Bodies shifted around in the cramped, near-total darkness. When Menlo snapped another match to life, Buckhorn already had his hands on the loosened pile of rubble at the rear of the cavity. In the brief illumination, he began scooping and dragging away handfuls of dirt and sand.

"Yes," he said just before the match winked out. "Yes, there *is* a tunnel here!"

An excited, wordless murmur passed through the group.

But then Tolliver lamented in a dull tone, "But it looked all caved in."

"Right here at the mouth, yeah," Buckhorn said, continuing to drag handfuls of dirt away from what he could feel to be taking shape as a roundish secondary cavity dug at the base of the larger area's back wall. "But maybe for only a short distance. Maybe most of the tunnel is still clear. Damn it, man, it's something to hope for, to *try* for."

"He's absolutely right," Menlo said. "The rest of us can help by scattering around this loose dirt he's pitching out. It's obvious our captors either forgot or never knew about the tunnel. In case they check on us before Buckhorn breaks through, we don't want to make it obvious what we've discovered by leaving clumps of fresh dirt for them to spot."

"You heard the ranger, Thad," Pamela said sharply. "Start helping to scatter this fresh dirt. Do *anything* but just moan and complain."

A moment later, a previously unheard voice spoke up, saying, "Excuse me, Mr. Buckhorn, but perhaps I have some items here that would help with your digging?"

It took Buckhorn a second to realize that it was Helga talking. In his visits to the Circle D main house, he further realized, he had never heard the stout, elderly woman say anything before. She had a surprisingly soft, sweet voice.

"What is it you're referring to, Helga?" asked Pamela.

"If the ranger would light another match please, I can show you. In all the excitement, I'm sorry I was too frightened to think about these before. When I am preparing and cooking meals, you see, I often drop utensils in my apron pocket to keep them handy for further use until everything is ready and served."

When another of Menlo's matches flared it revealed Helga holding her flower-patterned apron spread open before her and in the shallow scoop of material lay a large serving spoon and a spatula.

"Blazes, gal, that's practically a treasure trove!" Obie exclaimed.

"I'll say," agreed Buckhorn, reaching for the items while there was still light to see what he was grabbing. While not quite on the level of a pickaxe and shovel, the spatula and spoon were certainly a step up from bare hands for digging out the collapsed tunnel.

"Miss Helga," said Menlo in a deeply sincere tone, "to say you have very possibly proven to be a lifesaver to all of us would not be an exaggeration."

"What a wonderful revelation, Helga!" Pamela added.

"If it wasn't so dark that I'm afraid I might grab Obie by mistake," Buckhorn said, "I'd reach out to give you a big hug and kiss, Miss Helga."

"Paugh!" Obie said. "If'n you was to grab me the wrong way, bub, you'd need more than that spatula and spoon to scoop your way free of the clawin' and kickin' I'd do in return! Now get back to diggin' and don't bring up no more o' those disgustifyin' notions!"

CHAPTER 40

"I will sure enough be damned," said Micah, stepping back to catch his breath and sleeve sweat from his forehead. "I never thought the delicate little nance had anywhere near this kind of tough streak in him. Stubborn blasted fool."

From where he stood nearby, watching, Hank leisurely held out a half-full bottle of whiskey. Micah took it and tipped it high.

Directly in front of Micah, tied to a straight-backed dining chair, slumped Jeff. He'd once again been rendered unconscious by the blows Micah had been raining on him with gloved fists. The beaten man's head hung forward, chin resting on shallowly rising and falling chest, strings of blood and snot dripping from the corners of his mouth and from the flattened nostrils of his pulverized nose. His eyes were narrowed to nearly invisible slits within swollen bulbs of flesh, ugly purplish in color.

Micah handed back the bottle. Turning to the dining room table behind him, he snatched up one of the napkins from a plate of cold food and used it to wipe the streaks of blood from the tight black gloves he was wearing.

Heaving a frustrated sigh, Micah said, "Everything's out in the open now about the gang we've put together and the robbing and rustling we've been doing. Not to mention how charitable we've been about giving all the credit to Dan Riley in addition to the stuff he does on his own. So why be so damn stubborn when it comes to clearing the air on one final detail? He spent time with Big Dan, he played footsie with sweet little Eve, he buddied up with that damn half-breed . . . Why can't he tell *me*, his own brother, the simple thing I want to know?"

"I think he's close, Boss. I think he was darn near ready to spill before he passed out this last time."

Micah frowned.

"But what if he passes out one too many times? What if he passes out and don't come around again? I mean, I don't care if the little puke dies. I figure on seein' to that anyway. I just don't want it to be before he tells me what I want to know."

There was the sound of the front door opening, and seconds later Dave came clomping into the dining room.

"McKeever back with Kelso and the boys yet?" Micah asked him.

"No. I wouldn't expect 'em for a while longer." Dave tipped his head to indicate Jeff. "Get the rest of what you wanted out of him?"

"No luck yet," Micah muttered.

"Remind me," said Hank. "What's left that we need out of him again?"

Micah shook his head in exasperation.

"How many times do I have to explain it to you? Jeff spent most of those days he was missing with Dan Riley. That means he must know where Riley and his gang go to hide out between jobs. Just like Kelso and our boys have got that hideout camp up in the hills where they lay low. Understand?

"And the reason we need to know where Riley's got his hideout is because, now that the cowflop has all of a sudden hit the fancy carpet, we need to go there and wipe 'em out. After we do that, we're gonna bring back enough of their bodies to stage it like they showed up here and got in a big shoot-out with the ranger and the sheriff and all the other people who now know too much—thanks to Jeffrey. The whole bunch who could make it bad for us will be dead. And the only survivors left to tell the bloody awful tale of what happened, backed by McKeever as an eyewitness officer of the law, will be us."

"But the truth is that we'll be the ones who did all the killin'. Right?"

"Now you got it."

Hank scrunched up his face and asked, "Even your own ma?"

"Afraid that's how it has to be," Micah said with a shrug.

Hank wagged his head admiringly.

"Boy, you have got one thick layer of bark on you, Boss."

"Speakin' of your dear mum," Dave said to Micah. "Has it occurred to you that she might be a useful tool to help get that last bit of info you want out of Jeffy-boy?" He strode over and held out a hand for Hank to fork over the bottle. After he'd taken a swig, he lowered it and added, "Your baby brother is provin' tougher than you expected when it comes to holdin' out . . . but how long could he hold out if it was your ma takin' the punishment?"

Micah eyed him narrowly.

"You got a nasty, lowdown mind, you know that?"

Dave took another slug of whiskey, said nothing.

"But I like it," said Micah, nodding, a ghost of a smile flicking across his mouth. "We'll roust Jeff-boy and give him one more go. Hank thinks he's almost ready to spill. If he don't, we'll drag Mother back in here and try your idea."

Buckhorn slowly lifted the wooden barrel lid that covered the exit of the storm cellar's escape tunnel. He closed his eyes and sputtered against the layer of dirt and dried leaves that dislodging the lid disturbed, causing much of it to spill down onto him. Once the spillage had ceased, he opened his eyes again, allowing them to adjust to the daylight, and carefully scanned in all directions.

At ground level, all he could see was a carpet of more leaves, tufts of grass poking through, and the bases of several surrounding tree trunks. He was in the grove of fruit trees, as described by Obie. No buildings were in sight, and no one appeared to be anywhere close by.

Buckhorn shoved the barrel lid all the way off to one side, thrust his head and shoulders up through the opening, and sucked in deep mouthfuls of fresh air. It was the sweetest taste he'd ever experienced.

The escape tunnel had proven to be seriously collapsed in only a couple of places—at the start and about halfway through. Buckhorn had dug relentlessly through the obstructions, aided considerably by the spoon and spatula provided by Helga. His fingers and hands were nevertheless scraped and bloody, but the accomplishment of clearing the passage was well worth it.

The task now was to come up with the best plan for proceeding from here. Buckhorn had been thinking about that all the while he was digging, but he knew that any ideas he had would have to be discussed with the others. So, instead of quitting the tunnel entirely, he replaced the barrel lid cover and crawled back to the main cavity to discuss their altered situation with the rest of the group.

"Believe me, I understand how badly everybody wants to get out of this hole in the ground," he told them. "It looks pretty clear out there in the immediate vicinity of where the tunnel empties. But if we all go clambering out at once, we'll run a greater risk of drawing attention."

"So what are you suggesting?" Tolliver wanted to know. "That *you* go and leave the rest of us behind?"

"Quit your damn whinin', Sheriff, and let the man talk," growled Menlo. "If he wanted to take off and leave the rest of us on our own, he wouldn't have come back in the first place."

Buckhorn said, "I think our best bet would be groups leaving at staggered intervals, with each group having a specific destination and a plan for when they go."

"Sounds okay so far," Menlo allowed. "Who would make up the groups and what would be their destinations?"

Buckhorn rubbed his jaw.

"Well, that depends. Pamela, are there any guns in the house? Besides the ones we left behind in the dining room, I mean?"

"There's a good-sized gun cabinet in what used to be Gus's office. Everything in there is pretty much the way he left it. The cabinet has about a half dozen rifles. And a shotgun, I think. There are two or three handguns, too. And boxes of ammunition."

"Where is this office?"

"Off the front parlor, to the left, when you first go in the house."

"There's a narrow hallway from the back of the kitchen pantry that goes in there, too," Helga reminded her.

"Yes, that's right."

"How about your cabin, Obie? You've got guns in there, don't you?" Buckhorn asked.

"You bet I do."

"And what about the bunkhouse and the different sheds and outbuildings?"

"Heck, you know how it is around a ranch. There's varmint guns stashed in practically every corner of the different buildings. I think Cookie even keeps a shotgun in the grub shack. And you can bet there are plenty of shootin' irons amongst the personal belongings in the bunkhouse."

"I suppose Cookie is bound to still be poking

around the grub shack," Buckhorn mused. "But the bunkhouse should be empty this time of day, shouldn't it?"

"There were three Circle D men out on watch with us last night," pointed out Tolliver. "They've likely had breakfast by now and are sacked out in the bunkhouse, I'd expect."

Buckhorn was quiet for a minute, thinking. Then: "Okay. There's no way of knowing who among the Circle D crew is just a wrangler working for wages or which ones are also tied to Micah's outlaw bunch. So the only safe thing is to figure anybody you run into once we leave here has got to be treated like a threat. That means you take 'em down fast and hard. I know that probably sounds harsh, but it's the only way to be sure. So, keeping that in mind, here's a way I think might work . . ."

CHAPTER 41

"Aw hell, he's out again. This is gettin' us nowhere."
Micah removed his bloody gloves and flung them disgustedly to the floor at the feet of Jeffrey, still tied to the dining room chair and once more lapsed into unconsciousness. Stepping around the battered victim, Micah went to the long table still set for breakfast. He reached out and picked up a pitcher of water from amidst the plates and platters of now cold food. After removing his hat, he lifted the pitcher and poured half its contents over his head and face, drenching away the hard sweat he'd worked up. Using a clean napkin from the setting, he wiped his face vigorously and then slicked back his hair before replacing the hat.

"McKeever's gonna be back here with Kelso and the others and we ain't gonna have nowhere to lead 'em because we ain't gonna have no better clue where to find Dan Riley than we did when I sent McKeever out." Micah flung the wet napkin to the floor, too, and strode back around to stand in front of his brother again. In frustration, despite Jeff being in no condition to feel or hear anything, Micah gave him a vicious kick to the shins and hollered, "You stubborn damn fool!"

"You might as well face it," drawled Dave from where he sat in an easy chair in the front parlor, his head cranked around to watch the proceedings. "You're gonna have to change tactics if you ever want to get anywhere. You want me to go fetch your ma now?"

Micah sighed heavily as he continued to glare down at his brother.

"I gotta admit I ain't really crazy about the idea," he said, still a little short-winded from his exertions. "But I also gotta admit that you're right about needing to try something different. So, yeah, go ahead and get her. Take Hank with you and make damn sure you keep the others in their place while you drag her out. Above all, keep an eye on that stinkin' half-breed."

Hank grunted and said, "I doubt he's even come to yet. I hit him an awful hard lick. Might've even settled his hash."

"If you did, you did. I was looking forward to makin' that dog-eater whimper some before pinchin' out his wick," said Micah, "but we're probably runnin' out of time for that anyway. So, either way. But hurry up and haul my ma in here; I want to get the business with her over with as soon as possible."

Dave and Hank started out the front door but then stopped short.

"Hold on a minute," said Dave. "You got a visitor ridin' up out here."

"Who is it? You recognize him?"

"Ain't a him, it's a her," said Hank. "She looks kinda familiar. But I ain't sure . . ."

"It's that Riley girl," said Dave.

"You mean Eve?" asked Micah. "The one Jeff is sweet on?"

"No, not her. The other one. Not Big Dan's daughter, his brother Milt's."

Micah swore under his breath.

"Anybody with her?"

"Not that I can see."

Micah swore again and said, "What the devil would she be comin' here for? Listen, you're gonna have to step out on the porch and stall her for a couple minutes. I can't let her see me all bloody like this. Tell her that Ma ain't here, has gone to town or is visitin' neighbors or something. I'll be out as soon as I change my shirt."

Approaching the Circle D's main house, Joey Riley was relieved to see Buckhorn's horse, along with the one Jeff had ridden away on and three others, tied at the hitch rail out front. Somewhat surprisingly, she noted no activity around the corrals or outbuildings as she rode up. But that was just as well. She didn't know how welcome her visit was going to turn out to be, so the fewer people she encountered the better.

Reining up, she was disappointed to see two men she didn't recognize emerge from the house and step out onto the front porch. On closer examination, she decided she may have seen the pair around town on one of her infrequent visits there but, since there was nothing in particular to distinguish either of them from any of the dozens of other wranglers who drifted in and out of Barkley, it was hard to say for sure.

One of the men, the youngest of the two and borderline handsome but with a piercing stare that Joey found unsettling, pinched his hat and said, "Mornin', ma'am. Can we help you with something?"

"I'm looking for Jeffrey Danvers and a man named Joe Buckhorn," Joey said. "I have a rather urgent message for either or both of them."

The man with the unsettling eyes looked thoughtful for a moment.

"Buckhorn, you say? That's a kinda unusual name, one I reckon I'd remember if I ever heard it. But I haven't, so I don't guess I know the man you're askin' after. As for Jeff, it seems you ain't heard that he's been away for some time. Nobody's sure where, though, and the whole family is mighty worried. So if your message has something to do with his whereabouts, I'm sure it would . . ."

The look on Joey's face caused the man to let his words trail off. The lies pouring out of the man's mouth were so blatant and so stupid—what with Jeff's and Buckhorn's horses tied right there only a few feet away—that Joey was immediately alarmed. And her alarm became so evident that it made the man realize his blunder. When that happened, those eyes that Joey had found unsettling from the get-go became even more so when they suddenly narrowed into dangerous slits above a menacingly snarling mouth.

"You done screwed up, Dave," said the second stranger on the porch. "I'm supposed to be the dumb one, remember?"

"Shut up and grab her!" hollered Dave as he lunged forward.

Both men sprang from the porch and ran toward Joey. She instantly wheeled her horse and tried to get away, but the distance the men had to travel was too short and they were all over her before she could get her horse turned. They fanned out to either side and began frantically grabbing—at the reins to restrain the horse, at the saddle, at her legs. Joey kicked and struggled desperately to break free. When she reached down to try to lift her rifle from its saddle scabbard, the man on that side clamped on to her wrist and forearm and pulled her down.

Joey hit the ground hard, jarring the breath out of her. She nevertheless had the sense to go into a roll, partly to get free of the stamping feet of her frightened horse and partly still intent on trying to get away from the two men. She didn't get far, though, before both of them grabbed hold of her, by her hair and clothes, and started to haul her to her feet.

But they didn't get far in their efforts, either.

When a voice shouted "Hey!" Joey's eyes automatically snapped in the direction of the sound. Through the tears welling in her eyes from the pain and humiliation and fear, she caught only a glimpse of a shape coming around the corner of the house. A shape with hawklike facial features framed by gleaming black hair above the gold-orange muzzle flashes of a Winchester talking business.

The hands gripping her so roughly suddenly let go and then, as she dropped once more to the ground, Joey was aware that the bodies from which those hands extended were jerking and spasming above her in concert with the meaty thuds of bullets tearing into flesh and bone.

The plan laid out by Buckhorn and agreed to by the others called for him to be the first one to leave the storm cellar by the exit tunnel. If all went without discovery or some other unexpected trouble, he would make his way to the back of the main house, enter through the kitchen area, and proceed by the hallway off the pantry to Gus Danvers's old office. There, he would arm himself from the gun cabinet and also gather additional weapons for Menlo and Tolliver.

Still barring no trouble, Buckhorn would leave the house the way he'd gone in and meet up with the two lawmen who were scheduled to make their own exit from the tunnel fifteen minutes after his. With all three of them armed, they would cover the house and grounds until Obie and the two women left the cellar and went to Obie's cabin where they would hole up, also arming themselves, while Buckhorn and the others turned their attention to confronting Micah and the men siding him.

That was the plan.

Buckhorn made it to the office and its gun cabinet without a hitch. Along the way, although he never had a vantage point where he could see clearly out into the dining room, he could hear Micah, Dave, and Hank talking. He could also hear the sounds of Jeff being savagely worked over. As much as it galled him, however, he was in no position to try to put a stop to that right at the moment.

Buckhorn had gathered up the desired weapons and ammo and was ready to slip back out when Joey showed up in the front. He first heard Dave warning the others about a visitor and then, edging to the office's window and carefully peeking out, he saw her for himself.

Damn!

By the time Micah was instructing his cohorts to go out and stall the girl, Buckhorn was already in motion. Part of his brain was telling him that, like he'd restrained himself from interfering with what was happening to Jeff in the other room, he really shouldn't risk trying to do anything concerning Joey. But at the same time, he knew damn well he couldn't hold back in this case.

Bursting out the back of the house, he was glad to discover that Menlo and Tolliver had jumped the gun a little on their fifteen-minute wait before quitting the tunnel. He could see them making their way cautiously down the slope that led up to the fruit orchard. After motioning for them to come on, to hurry, he made sure they could see the guns he'd selected for them as he placed the weapons on the ground before he wheeled and went tearing around the corner of the house.

Buckhorn raced to the next corner, at the front. As he reached it, he could hear the sounds of Hank and Dave cursing as they dragged Joey to the ground and struggled to control her.

Buckhorn stepped out around the corner and raised the Winchester Yellowboy he'd taken from Gus Danvers's gun cabinet.

"Hey!" he shouted.

Hank and Dave looked up, startled by the shout. Doubly startled to see Buckhorn standing there. They dropped the girl and immediately grabbed for their guns. Buckhorn levered five rounds into them before their fingers ever touched the grips and sent them into spinning, staggering dances of death before they toppled to the ground.

Running forward, Buckhorn reached his free hand down to Joey and said, "Come with me! Hurry!"

But the urging wasn't really necessary. Joey grasped his hand tight and sprang to her feet, following eagerly as he tugged her back to the corner of the house. This came not a second too soon. As they scurried to make the turn, gunshots barked from inside the house, and the front window exploded outward under the impact of slugs sent after the two fleeing forms.

Still tugging Joey after him, Buckhorn hurried back toward the kitchen entrance. Menlo and Tolliver were waiting there, prominently displaying the rifles Buckhorn had left for them.

"What the devil's going on?" Menlo said.

"Joey? What in blazes are you doing here?" Tolliver wanted to know.

"No time for details right now. I cut down two of 'em out front," Buckhorn told them. He added, "Micah is still inside. Along with Jeff who, from what I overheard, has been getting worked over pretty bad. We need to try and—"

His words were cut short by the shriek of a horse followed quickly by the sound of pounding hoofbeats fading away from the front of the house.

"Damn!" cursed Tolliver. "He's getting away!"

* * *

Micah was coming down the stairs from his room, still buttoning the front of a clean shirt, when he heard the voices out front grow suddenly louder and contentious. Drawing his gun, he edged out into the parlor just in time to see, through the front window, Dave and Hank go into convulsions as slugs tore into them in conjunction with the rapid-fire booms of a Winchester rifle. Seconds after his two pals bit the dust, Buckhorn streaked into view, leaning down to help to her feet the strawberry blonde who'd ridden up only a few minutes earlier.

That trouble-making half-breed!

That meddlesome Riley bitch!

With no more thought than that, Micah raised his pistol and began blasting at the pair. Unfortunately, he was a second too late to hit anything but the window glass, which shattered and blew outward. And he was definitely too late to do anything for either Dave or Hank.

What the hell was going on?

How had Buckhorn gotten loose from the storm cellar? And if he was loose, that must mean the others were out, too! Where were they? If Buckhorn had gotten his hands on a rifle, did that mean Tolliver and Menlo—two seasoned lawmen—were also armed?

Micah thought he heard voices at the back, out through the kitchen.

What if they were all armed somehow and were surrounding the house? Micah started to panic. Suddenly realizing he was all alone, he panicked even more. He'd be trapped, hopelessly outnumbered.

No, he couldn't allow that. If they were working their way around from the back, he only had one chance.

Out the front door Micah raced. Straight into the saddle of the first horse he saw, Joey's horse, invitingly standing there not even tied to the hitch rail. Spurring the animal hard, Micah was relieved to find it was responsive and fast. Still, he hunched his shoulders tight as he pounded away, half fearing that a bullet might catch up with him.

The thought of a bullet made it occur to him that he should have taken time to plant one in Jeff before he rode away. Damn, he wished he would have thought of that!

CHAPTER 42

The shouting and shooting naturally drew the attention of Cookie and the men from the bunkhouse, the three wranglers who'd participated in the all-night vigil over the meadow. All four came running out with guns drawn and ready.

Fortunately, seeing that the sheriff and the ranger were still present was enough to calm them down. They didn't stay that way for very long, however, when—acting on Buckhorn's advice that none of the Circle D crew should be trusted until there was time to thoroughly sort out allegiances—the two lawmen promptly disarmed them, slapped on handcuffs, and left them chained to their bunks until further notice.

While that was being taken care of, Buckhorn stood guard out front of the house, eyes scanning in all directions. Inside, Obie and the women were tending to the badly injured Jeff.

When Menlo and Tolliver came walking back from the bunkhouse, the sheriff asked, "How's the boy?"

Buckhorn's face was grim as he said, "He took a

hell of a beating. Busted nose for sure. Probably jaw, too, and most likely some ribs. Maybe tore up on the inside. He'll definitely need to be gone over by a doctor as soon as we can get him to one. But, for right now, he's holding his own."

Tolliver shook his head.

"That damn Micah. His own brother! I always knew there was a bad streak there, only I never guessed it ran so deep."

"Seems to be a common refrain," said Menlo somberly. "Too bad somebody didn't take it a little more seriously."

If the ranger's remark was meant as a dig at the sheriff, Tolliver didn't seem to notice.

"I'd better get in there, see if there's anything I can do," he said. "Pamela's got to be beside herself."

After the sheriff disappeared inside, Menlo came over and stood next to Buckhorn. His eyes followed the line of the gunman's gaze as it swept out over the surrounding landscape.

"You expectin' Micah to come back?"

"I'm thinking it's a possibility," Buckhorn admitted.

"The way he lit a shuck out of here sure didn't look like anybody who'd be too quick to want to come back. Thing is, he was alone. What do you suppose happened to the other fella, the deputy?"

"The only thing I can think is that he must've left out earlier . . . to somewhere. For some reason."

"You're thinkin' about Micah's gang, ain't you?"

"Tell me you're not?" Buckhorn said right back to the ranger.

Menlo heaved a sigh.

"Well, we know they're out there. The way things have all of a sudden blown up on Micah, it wouldn't seem outta line if he wanted his full force around him."

"Which means," said Buckhorn, "if they're on the way back here, we're not exactly sitting pretty."

"Makin' a good case—on top of needin' to get that boy in there to a doctor—for hightailin' it out of here."

"Except for the risk of maybe running smack into who we'd be looking to hightail it away from. They catch up with us out in the open, we'd be sitting even less pretty."

Menlo gave him a sidelong glance.

"So what are you saying? Hole up here for a spell until we see what rolls in with the tide? Maybe send a rider out for the doctor and some backup of our own?"

Buckhorn tipped his head to indicate Obie's cabin.

"Could do worse than to fort up in Obie's place. It's sturdy and small enough for us to effectively guard all sides. Got a pretty good-sized open area around it, an unprotected killing field that anybody wanting to get at us would have to cross."

"Jesus." Menlo's expression turned sour. "You make it sound like we're preparin' for a battle."

Buckhorn gave him a look and said, "Micah returns and comes boiling in with a couple dozen men, what would you call it?"

Before the ranger could reply, Obie poked his head out the front door and said, "You gents oughta come in here and have a listen to this."

Inside, they had cut Jeff's bonds, stripped away his

bloody shirt, and moved him to an easy chair in the parlor where his various wounds were being administered to. He'd regained a semblance of consciousness and was trying to talk through split, swollen lips, and broken teeth.

"McKeever gone for : . . Kelso . . . and gang . . . Micah wants them to attack . . . kill . . . Big Dan and all of us . . . blame it all on Riley."

"So that explains why McKeever was already gone and Micah was by himself when he took off," said Menlo.

"Anybody know the name Kelso?" asked Buckhorn.

"There was a Bray Kelso hangin' around these parts a while back," said Tolliver. "He struck me as a bad *hombre* and we kept a close eye on him whenever he came to town. But I could never turn up any papers on him that gave me legitimate cause to run him off. He eventually solved that himself by driftin' on . . . or so I thought. Maybe he's the same Kelso runnin' Micah's gang."

"Bray Kelso. Yeah, I've heard that name here and there," allowed Menlo. "But, like you say, not any time lately."

"Seems like I overheard Micah mention the name Bray once or twice over the past months. But I never knew who it was or what it was in regard to," added Pamela.

"Well, if Micah's gang is on its way here with killin' in mind," pointed out Buckhorn, "it doesn't really matter if Kelso's leading them or even who he is. The thing is, we got a lapful of trouble on the way."

"It may be even worse than that," spoke up Joey.

All eyes swung her way.

"It's what I came here to tell y'all about, but haven't had the chance yet," she explained. Her gaze settled on Buckhorn. "My uncle and his men are on the way here, too. He's got blood in his eye for you, Buckhorn—for crossing him the way you did. And he means to take Jeffrey back, too."

"My God," breathed Pamela. "I can't believe all of this is happening!"

"Uncle Dan sent me away, told me to go back home," Joey further explained. "But I came here to warn you instead."

"Well, we're grateful for that," said Buckhorn. "It gives us a chance to adjust our plans accordingly."

"Lettin' the two gangs shoot it out ain't necessarily a bad thing," Tolliver suggested.

"It depends on who gets here first," said Joey. "If it's Micah's bunch and then my uncle shows up and rides right into the teeth of their gunfire, you'll have to excuse me if I *do* find that a bad thing!"

"Joey's right," Buckhorn said. "Big Dan is only out to get even with a couple of us. Micah's outfit is coming on a flat-out killing spree. Picking a side between the two seems pretty clear to me."

In a rather odd, somewhat faraway tone, Pamela said, "If I hadn't let Micah mislead me so badly, Dan Riley wouldn't be looking to get even with anyone."

"But he is, all the same. At least at the outset of when he shows up, he will be," said Tolliver. "That puts us in the middle of a bad situation, no matter how you slice it. I say we need to get the hell out of here."

"Jeffrey's in no condition to be moved, especially not in a rush," Pamela was quick to respond.

"And if we *did* try riding out," Buckhorn said, "we'd risk running smack into what we were hoping to get away from. Me and Menlo already hashed this over. We propose sticking right here and forting up. And now that we know both gangs are on their way and will likely be blasting hell outta one another, that makes even more sense."

"All I know is that I need to ride back and warn my uncle," said Joey.

"I just told you that riding out isn't a smart idea for anybody," Buckhorn insisted. "Besides, you lost your horse."

"We're wastin' too much time yappin', you ask me," said Obie. "If we're gonna fort up and get set proper, which I agree is the best idea, then we need to get that took care of pronto, before we get visitors. Strikes me that the most suitable place to do that is my cabin rather than all the space we'd have to try and cover here."

Buckhorn flashed him a grin.

"Don't let it build your hopes too high, but now you're startin' to think like me."

Obie made a face.

"Paugh! That's a disgustifyin' thing to tell a body."

Relocating to Obie's cabin went quickly and orderly. Buckhorn and Tolliver picked up Jeff's easy chair with him in it and carried the whole works over with minimal disturbance to the victim. The others brought guns, ammo, canteens, other containers of water, and various other items in the way of supplies.

The men locked up in the bunkhouse had to be dealt with, too. Buckhorn still didn't trust them, but if they *weren't* part of Micah's gang, there was a chance they'd be ruthlessly slaughtered when the killers showed up. He wasn't going to abandon them to that fate, so he and Menlo went to the bunkhouse, where the ranger unlocked the handcuffs while Buckhorn covered the men.

"You fellas get your horses and light a shuck out of here," he told them when they were free. "You're not getting your guns back, though, and if I see any of you with Micah's bunch later, I'll take special care to gut-shoot you so you'll be a long, hard time dying."

"What I'd suggest," said Menlo, "is headin' for the hills until all this is over."

"Is that an order, Ranger?" asked one of the men.

"Yeah, make it an order."

The man looked at the others, nodded, and said, "I reckon we ought to take off for the tall and uncut, then."

The others agreed, and as soon as they could throw saddles on horses, that was what they did.

Lagging slightly behind the rest of the group on the last trip from the main house with supplies, Pamela caught everybody by surprise when she suddenly bolted and ran to the horses still tied at the hitch rail. She quickly loosened Sarge's reins and swung into his saddle.

As she wheeled the big gray around, Tolliver ran out from the front of the cabin, shouting, "Pamela! What on earth are you doing?"

"This is my fight yet everyone else has been taking

all the risks for me," she called in return. "Joey was right about needing to warn Big Dan, and it's time I held up my end. Take care of my boy—I'll be back!"

With that, she touched her heels to Sarge and they thundered off, horse and rider flowing smoothly together.

Standing beside Buckhorn, Obie said in a hushed, somewhat awed tone, "Look at her go. Told you she could ride like the wind when she took a mind to. And that's the first time in near two years I heard her say Big Dan and not cuss the Riley name when she spoke it at all. Maybe there's still a chance for those decent times to return to the Circle D after all, Powder-burner."

CHAPTER 43

Maybe conditions at the Circle D *could* return to the way Obie longed for. But there remained some bad business that had to be settled first.

In case any among those now forted up in the handyman's cabin hoped to avoid that unpleasant detail, they found out it wasn't going to happen when Micah showed up again less than a half hour after he'd ridden away with his tail tucked between his legs. Thanks to the two dozen grim-faced, heavily armed men thundering in behind him, his tail was no longer tucked, but appeared quite high and feisty.

Riding to Micah's left and back just slightly was Bud McKeever. On the other side, similarly positioned, was a blue-jawed specimen marked with the stamp of a hardcase. He had a milky left eye and a ragged whitish scar running down from the center of a whiskered cleft chin, reaching like a pitchfork of lightning until it disappeared behind the right-side collar of his shirt. One glance was all it took for Buckhorn to know that he was looking at Bray Kelso.

The riders fanned out to four or five abreast and

slowed their horses to a cautious walk as they moved between the outbuildings and corrals and approached the main house. Most of them had rifles prominently displayed, shoulder stocks resting on hips, barrels jutting up and out at forty-five degree angles. Those not showing rifles, like the three in front, held their gun hands poised close and ready over their sidearms.

When they'd drawn close to the house, Micah checked the horse he was riding and raised an arm to signal for the others to halt as well. His eyes, narrow and sullen, swept back and forth across the width of the house. The bodies of Dave and Hank still lay off at one end of the porch, where they'd fallen when gunned down by Buckhorn. The house seemed as dead and silent as they were. There was no sign of movement through any of the windows, no sound of any kind seeping outward.

"Mother!" Micah called out. "Are you in there?"

The house responded only with continued silence.

Micah called again. "It's foolish to try and hide, Mother. I know you're around somewhere; you couldn't have all fled in the short time I was away. You might as well get it over with. Come out and face the music!"

More silence.

"Damn it, this is nonsense! Where's your big, bad hired gun? Where's the sheriff or that representative of the mighty Texas Rangers? Is the whole bunch gonna keep tryin' to hide like scared little school-girls?"

After another stretch of silence, Kelso drew his gun and said, "Maybe we oughta give 'em some incentive to come on out of there."

Micah considered for a moment, then nodded and drew his gun, too.

"Maybe we oughta at that."

"You mean blast the hell out of your own house?" asked McKeever.

Micah's expression was flat and cold as he replied, "This place has never felt like a home to me—just somewhere I could come to when I had nowhere better to go."

So saying, he set it off. A blistering volley of shots, joined in by Kelso and McKeever, that blew out windows and tore randomly, recklessly through the inside of the house. As soon as their guns were emptied, the trio began reloading. But, through the haze of bluish smoke and dust kicked up by the smashing bullets, the house remained stubbornly silent.

"Want me to go in and have a look?" said Kelso. "I think maybe the joint *is* empty."

"Go ahead. Watch yourself."

Not bothering to dismount, Kelso nudged his horse forward. While he was doing that, Micah twisted in his saddle and called to those in the group behind him, "Some of you men back there, peel off and check out the bunkhouse and grub shack. The sheds and barns, too. Be careful."

A handful of the men began doing as instructed.

By then, Kelso had prodded his horse up onto the front porch and, ducking low in the saddle so he could clear the top of the doorway, right on into the house. They could hear him bulling around in there, the horse's hooves clumping loudly on the floor, furniture and lamps and so forth being knocked aside, some of it crashing into wreckage.

After a few minutes, Kelso reappeared. He gigged his horse down off the porch. He was busily chewing something and in one hand he held two thick, crisp strips of bacon.

"Ain't nobody in there that I can see," he announced. "But, man, there's a whole table of food gone cold and left for waste. And what a shame that is if it's all as tasty as this bacon."

"They've got to be around here somewhere," Micah said.

"Well, if the cook is still around," said Kelso single-mindedly, "I vote we consider keepin' her alive for when you take over everything. Be worth it for the cookin' and if she happens to look like anything on top of that, well . . ."

"Get your mind off food and out of the gutter," Micah snapped. "The old German lady who cooked that bacon and the rest is nearly as wide as she is tall and about seventy years old."

"So what?" Kelso took another bite of bacon. "I got nothin' against fat gals. And sometimes those older babes really know how to—"

"Knock it off, I said."

As he continued looking around, Micah's eyes raked across Obie's cabin. He did a double take, returning his gaze to the structure and locking it there. And all of a sudden he knew with crystal-clear certainty where their quarry was.

Buckhorn calmly sighted his commandeered Yellow-boy through a cabin window that he'd already broken the glass out of.

"One stroke of this trigger, I can send Micah straight where he belongs—to hell."

"You can't do that," Joey was quick to protest.

Tolliver backed her up, saying, "Gunnin' him out in the open like that, basically the same as cold blood, would make us just as bad as him."

Buckhorn turned his head to look at them, not surprised by their reaction but at the same time not understanding it.

"If I'm the one who pulled the trigger, wouldn't be no 'us' to it. It'd be strictly me," he told them. "And, no matter what else, the main thing is that it would make us a hell of a lot better off if I cut down Micah and one or both of those right beside him before they knew what hit 'em."

There was some empathy in Menlo's tone when he said, "I can't stop you. But it ain't the ranger way, son."

When Buckhorn's gaze fell on Obie, the oldster didn't say anything but the same conflict was also evident on his face.

There was a time when these kinds of reactions from others, even though predictable and expected, wouldn't have made any difference. Buckhorn would have said to hell with them and gone ahead and done things his way.

But those days and the way he'd gone about things back then were past. Mostly. And the slim chance at redemption Buckhorn figured he *might* still have a shot at was enough to make him reconsider moments like this.

All of which became a moot point in this particular instance when Micah suddenly sensed those present in the cabin. Looking back out the window, Buckhorn was quick to see the realization and the shift in attention that ran through the rest of the body of men out there.

"Well, in just a minute or two I calculate that it's gonna be a matter of *returning* fire. I hope you won't object to me doing that much."

With some quickly barked commands and a good deal of arm-waving, Micah got the men backing him to spread out in a different pattern, all now focused directly on the handyman's cabin. Several of them dismounted and scurried in behind corral fencing and feed bunks.

Micah, McKeever, and Kelso stayed on their mounts, swinging them to face the cabin and then advancing a few yards toward same.

"All right, your little maneuver threw us off for a minute or two," Micah called. "But everything is plain enough now. And it ought to be plain enough to you that you don't have a chance if you try to make a fight of it. My men will blast you to shreds. All I want is my brother and that stinkin' half-breed. Give them up, I'll let the rest of you live!"

Ranger Menlo cracked open the front door of the cabin and responded, saying, "And we're supposed to believe that?"

"What you can believe for damn certain is that you'll die if you don't cooperate," Micah told him.

"We've sent a rider to town to bring back reinforcements and to wire ranger headquarters with your name and what you've been up to in these parts," Menlo claimed. "You kill me, not to mention these other folks, you won't be able to run fast enough or far enough to escape the full wrath of the rest of the rangers. Your best bet is to give up and opt for a fair trial. Maybe you won't swing. If you insist in makin' a fight of it, we can hold out until help from town gets here. In the meantime, there'll be no negotiatin' with the likes of you!"

"Now who's tryin' to get who to swallow a load of hogwash?" Micah said with a sneer. "You're a damned liar, Ranger, and you'll die with that dishonor to your badge."

"I've talked all I aim to with scum like you." The anger was building hot in Menlo and it was evident in his voice. "I'll give you to the count of three to either clear out or commence the fight. One—"

"Wait a minute! I want to talk to my mother."

This time it was Buckhorn who replied. "She doesn't want to talk to scum like you. But I've got a .45 caliber message from her that I'll be happy to deliver as a free-of-charge bonus to what she's already paying me. You sure you want to hear it?"

Micah's face flushed purple-red with rage.

"You go to hell, you interferin' bastard. You want to talk bonuses? I've got one right here for you—" As he said this he was ripping the gun from the holster on his hip, so much anger surging in him that his words came out a high-pitched shriek. "And I hope your black soul chokes on it!"

An instant after Micah's bullet slammed impotently against the side of the cabin, a full foot above Buckhorn's window, it seemed like every other gun on the property erupted at once. Tongues of orange-gold flame licked out of muzzles, blue smoke puffed and rolled into a thick cloud, and the air sang with the whine and sizzle of bullets.

Micah's frantic clawing to get his gun drawn jerked his body in such an unexpected way that it caused Buckhorn's first shot to miss. By the time he levered and fired again, Micah had pitched from his saddle and was scrambling for cover behind a nearby well. Buckhorn managed to punch a slug through Micah's right heel before he got completely out of sight behind the piled stones of the housing, but his target's loud curse and howl of pain was nowhere as satisfying as his death gurgle would have been.

Elsewhere out in the open area, McKeever also kicked free of his horse and found cover with Micah behind the well. Kelso wheeled his mount back toward the house and sprang from the saddle onto the front porch, firing over his shoulder as he ran in a ragged pattern and plunged through the open door, gaining his own cover inside. The rest of the gang members had all scattered over and back toward the outbuildings, ducking in behind corral rails, watering troughs, and a couple of wagons. Two who hadn't quite made it lay sprawled motionless in the dust.

Bullets relentlessly hammered the cabin and answering lead spat back from every window and opening. Menlo and Tolliver had tipped Obie's sturdy wooden table onto its side and shoved it a few feet outside the open door, providing room for each of them to hunker down behind it and spray lead in a wide pattern over the buildings and corrals. Joey hovered close behind them, reloading as necessary, throwing out shots of her own when she had a break.

Buckhorn and Obie manned the two windows positioned along the walls of the kitchen area, providing them the vantage points necessary to keep Micah and McKeever pinned down behind the well and make it hot for Kelso inside the main house. Helga and the battered Jeffrey were hunkered down safely back by the fireplace.

Just under two miles away, Dan Riley raised a hand to signal a halt to the riders coming hard in back of him. As the twenty horses were reined up, dust swirling from behind and rolling over them, Pamela Danvers, who was mounted to Riley's left, said anxiously, "What's wrong? Why are we stopping?"

Riley didn't answer right away. He sat his saddle slightly cocked to one side, obviously in considerable pain despite the heavy wrap of bandages around his middle and the plain grit driving him from deeper within. His eyes were narrowed as he gazed out ahead, concentrating on something.

"Listen. Don't you hear it?"

"I do," said Ulysses Mason, mounted on the other side of Riley. "It's the sound of heavy gunfire."

With the pounding of horses' hooves now quieted, the distant sound—a faint, erratic crackling—became discernible to all.

"It's started," said Pamela somewhat breathlessly. She turned her head and looked imploringly at Riley. "Do you believe me now?"

He returned her gaze, and there was a softness there that hadn't been present for a long time.

"I never *didn't* believe you," he said. "After you came in search of us, after you admitted finally acceptin' the truth about Micah . . . well, painful as that was for you, it was all I needed to hear. What I've *wanted* to hear for years. When it came, I sure wasn't gonna turn it away with doubt."

"That's all well and good," Ulysses prodded. "But if we're gonna do any good for those folks under fire, we need to do more than just sit here talkin' about it."

CHAPTER 44

"I think we need to get somebody up in that loft window," Obie called over to Buckhorn amidst the whine and crash of the continuing gunfire. "Other than the back door off the kitchen, it's the only view on that side. Right now we're blind to anybody comin' at us from there."

"With all the lead we're pouring on to keep 'em pinned where they are, what are the chances of anybody getting around that way?" Buckhorn wanted to know.

"Slim, maybe. But not impossible. Some of those varmints back by the bunkhouse could circle wide, wormin' through the high grass, and come in that way. And this Kelso character in the house all of a sudden ain't throwin' much lead. I don't think I hit him, so that gives me a hunch maybe he squirted out the back and is tryin' his own luck at wigglin' around and blindsidin' us."

"I'll go," said Joey, who'd overheard the exchange. "I can shoot as well as anybody and from that high window I'll have prime pickings."

"She's makin' sense," Menlo said from the doorway. "The shooting out this way has slowed some. Sounds like we need her guardin' our backside worse than we need her loadin' for me and the sheriff."

"If Kelso makes a break for back there, I still might have a crack at him from here," said Obie. "But havin' the girl up there would give us double for-certain coverage."

"Okay. Do it, then," Buckhorn agreed. He locked eyes with Joey. "Just be damn careful."

She held his eyes and grinned.

"Good to know you care."

Buckhorn was caught off guard once again by her boldness, and didn't know how to respond. So he said nothing and just returned to pouring lead out his window.

"We sure put ourselves in a shitty position by droppin' here," lamented Micah, still pinned down behind the well housing. "And that stinkin' 'breed put a hole in my foot—which hurts like hell, by the way—so I can't even make a run for something better."

"You got anything else you want to bellyache about?" said McKeever, hunkered beside him.

"You got something better to do? Like cough up a brilliant idea, maybe?"

McKeever bared his teeth.

"Yeah, maybe I do have a better idea. I ain't got no bullets in me. Yet. I'm thinkin' maybe I oughta take a chance at makin' a run for it and then just keep hightailin' as far as I can go. There flat ain't no future here no more. Not for any of us. In case you ain't figured it out, Micah, your big plans for wipin' out your family and the Rileys and you bein' left to take over the whole territory are burnin' up out there in little pops of gunfire. There's too many loose ends. Even if we're left standin' after this skirmish, none of the rest of it has any chance of holdin' together."

"Shut up! There's always a chance."

"Go ahead. Have one of your temper tantrums. That's always your answer. But this time it ain't gonna solve anything, and you know it."

Suddenly Micah's gun was aimed at McKeever from a distance of less than one foot.

"You try runnin' out on me, you chicken-livered ingrate, and see how fast I can solve that."

With guns still blasting all around them, the tense, heavy breathing of the two men seemed like the only sound for several seconds. Until, straining to control his voice, Micah said, "Now. If you look back behind us a little ways you will notice that some of our men are shooting from behind the cover of a wagon. See it? Do you also see that the wagon is loaded with a fair amount of straw? Good. Now, do you happen to have any matches on you? If so, give me one."

His eyes shifting nervously between Micah's eyes and the gun still aimed at his face, McKeever produced a match and handed it over. Taking it, Micah said, "You don't see where I'm going with this, do you?"

"I . . . I'm not sure."

"Do you want to stick with me and find out? Or do I have to shoot you?" Micah asked matter-of-factly.

McKeever swallowed and said, "I'll stick."

"Good." Micah lowered his gun and turned toward

the men behind the wagon, emitting a shrill whistle and motioning to get their attention. When he had it, he held up the match for them to see. Flicking the match to life with his thumbnail, he pointed at it with his free hand. From there he pointed to the wagonload of straw they were squatted behind. And next, in a sweeping gesture, he pointed from the wagon to Obie's cabin.

"Hell yeah!" said McKeever. "We'll roast the stubborn fools like pigs on a spit!"

"Something fishy going on out there," said Buckhorn from his window. "All of a sudden these two birds I got pinned down behind the well aren't throwing anything back at me."

"Nothing more out of Kelso yet, neither," offered Obie.

"We still got incoming over here, but it's definitely slowed down some," Menlo reported.

A moment later they caught a whiff of something. And then they saw the gray ribbons of smoke curling up out of the straw in the wagon bed. Next hungrily licking orange flames crawled into view.

At the same time, the wagon started in motion, slowly at first but steadily building speed, the wagon tongue on the back end simultaneously being used to push and steer—straight for the little cabin and those within.

"Fire!" shouted Buckhorn. "They're gonna try to burn us out!"

"Shoot under the wagon," hollered Tolliver. "Aim at the legs of the men pushing it!"

Unfortunately, the sheriff got too eager to follow his own suggestion and carelessly exposed himself in his attempt to shoot the legs out from under the wagon pushers. Almost immediately he caught two slugs. One split his sternum, the other slammed in an inch to the left. He was knocked backward several feet, heels rapping a death kick on the bare wood floor before he hit flat on his back and shoulders and lay totally still.

The flaming wagon kept rolling closer.

Seeing Tolliver go down, Obie turned away from his window and limped over to help Menlo at the front door. He called to Joey up in the loft, "The back side is all yours, gal. Keep a sharp lookout but keep your head down."

Out behind the well, Micah was excited to see that his plan with the wagon looked like it was going to succeed. The rolling ball of fire was only a few dozen yards from the cabin and closing fast.

It occurred to him then that the cabin occupants would be forced to flee out the back, an area his gang had not encircled. To rectify this, he began shouting and making urgent motions with his arm.

"Around back! Around back!" he called. "Mow 'em down when they make a break for it!"

But just as Tolliver had done in the cabin doorway, he got carried away with issuing his instructions and failed to keep sufficiently behind his cover. Buckhorn was ready to take advantage of that. His Yellowboy roared and the slug punched into the side of Micah's neck, under and slightly back of the left ear, then out the other side in a thick gout of blood. Micah tipped over like a bottle target and hit the ground.

After he fell, the well again blocked Buckhorn's view. He could not see that Micah, somewhat miraculously, was still alive. He lay writhing in the dust, moaning in agony.

"My God, I think he's killed me. Oh, my God . . . Don't leave me, McKeever. Don't abandon me."

"Sure. Whatever you say, Micah," the crooked deputy told him. Yet, even as he was saying the words, he was glancing around and eyeing the remaining horses, all saddled and ready, still tied to the hitch rail in front of the main house. As soon as the burning wagon hit the cabin, he calculated, those inside would suddenly be too busy with the fire to worry about him. At which time, he told himself, you bet he *did* mean to abandon Micah and this whole scene that had fallen into such chaos.

In the cabin doorway, Menlo and Obie continued to pour lead at the oncoming wagon and its load of hellfire. But it was no use. There was no chance to turn or stop it. What was more, Obie saw some of Micah's men slipping around on one side, sticking to the high grass and bushes, obviously meaning to try to make it to the back. But there was no chance to stop them, either.

"Stand clear!" bellowed Menlo. "She's gonna hit!"

And hit "she"—meaning the flaming wagon—did. Any impact against the side of the cabin would have been damaging. But, as luck would have it, the rolling fireball hit right on the open front door. Which meant that the sudden, crashing halt caused the momentum of its load to carry on, pitching forward straight through the open door. In a matter of seconds, the interior of the cabin was boiling with flames.

"Out! Out the back!" Buckhorn ordered.

"But remember Kelso is somewhere out there," Obie added. "And there's some other jaspers workin' their way around, too. So keep your eyes peeled and your shootin' irons ready!"

Still ducked low behind the well, McKeever watched the wagon hit and almost instantly saw the flames spreading inside. That was his chance. He spun and started for one of the nearby horses.

"McKeever!" called Micah, continuing to writhe on the ground. "Don't leave me, damn you!"

McKeever didn't even bother to look around. But he should have. Because Micah was still clutching his gun. With his last heartbeat of strength and life, Micah raised his arm, aimed, and fired. The slug entered in the back of the fleeing deputy's head and exited high in his forehead, just under the hairline. The surprised expression on his face froze there in death and was ingloriously mashed into a pile of horse droppings after he staggered several steps and then finally fell.

Inside the cabin, it was a scramble to get everybody out. Buckhorn helped Helga and Jeffrey. Obie exited first to cover their departure on the back side, along with Joey who remained for as long as she could in the loft window. Menlo covered on the inside, in case any of the wagon pushers tried to follow up by shooting through one of the abandoned windows. There was no chance to try to remove Tolliver's body because a heap of the burning straw that pitched in on impact had landed directly on him.

Once everybody else was safely outside, they quickly agreed to regroup behind the cover of a large, partially stacked woodpile that was about halfway between the cabin and the main house. They were in the process of doing exactly that when the mysteriously absent Bray Kelso made his reappearance. He rose up from behind one of the stacks of wood and without hesitation opened fire on the knot of people moving directly toward him.

Obie caught a slug and went down. Buckhorn, who was supporting, half-carrying Jeffrey, was unable to bring his Yellowboy into play and also took a hit. He and Jeff both toppled to the ground.

Kelso's luck ran out at that point, however, when a simultaneous flurry of shots from Menlo and Joey riddled him mercilessly and dropped him into a leaking heap amidst some of the split wood.

But barely had that round of gunfire subsided when a handful of Micah's gang members came charging out of the high grass and bushes just beyond the far end of the burning cabin. Menlo and Joey each dropped to one knee and raised their rifles. They'd scarcely stroked a trigger, though, when the air filled with a great roar of discharging guns and the advancing men were almost literally cut to pieces by a rain of lead pouring down on them.

Somewhat awestruck, Menlo and Joey turned their heads and stared up the slope of higher, tree- and brush-studded ground that rose behind both the cabin and main house. A thick haze of gunsmoke hung in the air partway up the incline. And then, as they watched, several men and one woman emerged out of this haze and descended toward them.

"Uncle Dan! Miss Pamela!" Joey said breathlessly. "Thank God!"

CHAPTER 45

Three days had passed.

Two members of Micah's gang were taken alive and jailed, two had escaped, the rest were killed in the shoot-out. The bodies of the deceased were hauled away from the Circle D and buried in unmarked graves in Barkley's boot hill cemetery. After much soul-searching and a good deal of discussion between Pamela and Jeffrey, the body of Micah was buried in the family's private plot on a hill overlooking the ranch headquarters, in a far corner removed from Gus's grave.

Thad Tolliver's charred remains were taken back to Barkley and buried in the main cemetery. The service was attended by folks from far and wide, one of the biggest local crowds ever to gather for the funeral of a single person.

The four men who'd been sent to watch over the remote meadow at daybreak that fateful morning were determined to have had no connection to Micah's gang and so were invited to stay on; three accepted the offer, one decided he would drift on to new territory.

Cookie returned as well, saying that the three men who had fled with him just before the battle started had decided to rattle their hocks out of this part of the country without ever looking back.

Whether or not they had ever been part of Micah's gang would remain a mystery, but as long as they were gone, Buckhorn figured he could live with not knowing.

Aiding the three cowboys who remained in the work that had to be done as far as clearing the damage left by the shoot-out and the host of regular chores related to keeping the spread going, were most of the men from Riley's crew. They all had ranch experience from some past point in their lives, so the duties were quickly understood and resumed with minimal trouble.

Wounded representatives from those who'd fought for the Circle D tallied up to: Jeff, Obie, and Buckhorn. Also included was Dan Riley, who received no new wounds but whose incompletely healed bullet hole from days earlier had opened anew during the ride from his hidden valley to settle scores with Buckhorn and Jeff.

A doctor was brought out from town to assess the injuries and administer accordingly. Eve Riley, who'd been left back in the valley camp and ordered to stay there by her father when he rode off, had once again demonstrated her rebellious side by showing up at the Circle D less than an hour after the shooting was over. This made her available to do some nursing before the doctor arrived and to earn her some compliments from the medic for what she'd been able to do, particularly the prior care she'd given to her father.

The bullet that had put Obie down turned out to be a strike to his already deformed hip, resulting in considerable pain, some blood loss, and a few fragments that needed to be dug out for the sake of avoiding possible infection. Beyond that there was no lasting damage, causing the crusty old-timer to remark, "Can you beat that? The durn fool wasted a perfectly good bullet on what was already wrecked."

Buckhorn's wound was little more than a bullet burn to the outside of his left thigh, slicing a furrow through meat and a shallow layer of muscle. It didn't even bleed a significant amount. The doctor applied some salve and a bandage, which he suggested reapplying daily for a few days, again mainly to guard against infection.

That left Jeff, whose suffering at the hands of Micah came to no small amount of damage. Broken nose; dislocated jaw; cracked ribs; concussion; possible internal bleeding; and cuts and bruises too numerous to count. The doctor strongly suggested he be taken to town and kept in the back room of his office, the closest thing the area had to an actual hospital, for a number of days. But Jeff, backed by his mother as well as Eve, refused that.

So the main house at the Circle D became the second closest thing to an actual hospital in the area, its size coming in handy to accommodate the healing of all the wounded men even as the surrounding ranch was undergoing its own healing.

* * *

On the morning of the fourth day, Buckhorn and Menlo stood talking and drinking coffee on the front porch. Menlo had his pipe going.

"So you'll be riding out today," the ranger was saying. "That your intent?"

Buckhorn nodded.

"That it is . . . unless you're fixing to tell me you've got some kind of objection."

"Nope." Menlo puffed some smoke. "Ain't anxious to see you go—and me sayin' that is something I'd just as soon not get around, for the sake of my reputation—but I could see it comin' and I got no basis to try and stand in your way."

"That's good to hear."

"Thing I regret the most is never bein' able to see that mule-carrier message scheme in action—you know, the one Obie and you put together for gettin' word in and out for the time you expected to be out of touch once you were infiltrated into Riley's gang."

Buckhorn grinned ruefully.

"What a bust that turned out to be, eh? Took us longer to dream up the scheme than the amount of time I ended up being infiltrated."

Obie came limping out to join them and asked, "Did I hear my name bein' taken in vain a minute ago?"

"You did for a fact," Buckhorn admitted. "You, me, and a mule named Sylvester."

Obie grunted and said, "Reckon I been linked in with worse company."

"Yeah. But what about the mule?" said Menlo.

They all had a chuckle over that and then Obie turned serious.

"So. You still figurin' on headin' out today, Powder-burner?"

"Way I got it figured."

"Not surprisin', I guess," said the old handyman. "Gotta admit I hate to see you go, though. You've made things mighty interestin' since you showed up, and you've done a lot of good."

"Hey," protested Buckhorn, "I've got a reputation to think of, remember. I'm a hired gun, not a do-gooder. I did a job, got paid, it's time to move on. That's the way it works."

"Yeah," said Menlo, squinting against a curl of smoke as his gaze swept across the Circle D grounds. "We were all part of seein' to it that plenty of men—not to say that most of 'em didn't deserve it—paid for gettin' that job done. Paid in blood . . . Reckon that, among other reasons, will have me feelin' my own urge to move on before long."

Pamela and Dan Riley came out to join them on the porch.

"What's all this talk about everybody moving on?" Pamela wanted to know. "I've got a ranch to build back up, a crew to fill out. There's plenty right here to occupy anybody who's willing to pitch in."

Buckhorn replied, "Speaking strictly for myself, and in addition to me not being the cowpuncher type to begin with, your new ramrod there"—he jabbed a finger at Big Dan—"already turned me down for one job and then, last I heard, was looking for me with blood in his eye. Somehow that doesn't sound like real solid ground for starting a new career."

"If you'd quit remindin' me of all the past reasons I got to be sore at you," said Riley, "I might forget about 'em on account of all the new stuff I got on my plate to get this ranch up and runnin' smooth again. Just like the ranger there has indicated my fresh start has him willin' not to dig too deep into the accusations of my past, er, business dealings."

"Something else on your plate—on *both* of our plates," Pamela reminded him, "is the upcoming marriage of your daughter and my son as soon as Jeff is healthy and on his feet again."

"There's another thing I'd rather not be reminded of," Riley muttered, though not too seriously.

"I got a marriage of sorts I'm not so sure I want to be reminded of, either," remarked Menlo with a scowl. "And that's your man Ulysses pinnin' on a deputy's badge for Barkley's newly elected Sheriff Scanlon."

Riley shrugged.

"What can I say? Ulysses ain't the cowpuncher type, neither. Whether he's lawman material or not remains to be seen. But I'll tell you what . . . while he's finding out, I bet the town of Barkley will be tamer and quieter than it's ever been."

An hour later, Buckhorn found himself alone in the Circle D stable, aiming to slip away without further fanfare. His trail supplies were replenished, and Sarge was saddled and ready to ride. A moment before slapping foot to stirrup, however, he found out he wasn't alone after all.

"Planning on leaving without even saying good-bye?" said a soft voice behind him.

He turned to see Joey standing there, the morning sunlight streaming through the stable door and turning her blond hair molten.

"Thought it would be best . . . or at least easiest," Buckhorn admitted.

"Not even interested in another try at smoothing out those kissing wrinkles?"

"That definitely would not make leaving easier."

She moved closer to him and said, "All the more reason to work on it then."

The kiss was long and lingering. When their lips finally parted, Joey leaned back and gazed up at him.

"Now *that* was already a step in the right direction. But it wasn't enough, was it? Not to keep you from going."

"Like I said, it's for the best. The best for you." Buckhorn's voice had an added huskiness now. But also a firmness. "You quit threatening to shoot fellas in the spine," he added, "and you'll find the right one for you. One you deserve. And he'll be the luckiest son of a bitch in the world."

With that, he pushed her gently away. Turned and mounted Sarge, rode off. He didn't look back, knew he didn't dare to.

But she stood looking after him until he was just a speck in the distance . . . and then gone entirely.

TURN THE PAGE FOR AN EXCITING PREVIEW!

From America's greatest storytellers comes the first in an explosive series featuring a new hero of the Old West— in an epic fight for justice that begins as so many legends do: in a hailstorm of bullets . . .

After spending most of his young life driving cattle from Texas to Nevada, Will Tanner is ready to wash the trail dust from his throat. Maybe it was fate that brought him to the Morning Glory Saloon on the border of Indian Territory—or just plain bad luck— because no sooner does he sit down than three rough-looking characters walk into the bar with vengeance in their eyes, guns at their side . . . and fingers on the triggers. The trio's target is the famous U.S. Deputy Marshal Dove who arrested one of their kin—and who's sitting in the bar near Will Tanner. Seeing that Dove is facing losing odds, Will Tanner makes a decision that changes his life forever. He draws, takes aim, and saves the deputy's life. Tanner has himself a new job, a badge, and enough grit to make him a legend on the American frontier.

New York Times and *USA Today* **Bestselling Authors**
WILLIAM W. JOHNSTONE
and J. A. Johnstone

**WILL TANNER,
U.S. DEPUTY MARSHAL**

CHAPTER 1

"You're just lookin' for trouble, Boss," Shorty Watts cautioned as Jim Hightower put his boot in the stirrup. "You better let Will take the starch outta that one."

"You just hold on to his ears till I get in the saddle," Hightower replied confidently. He knew Shorty might be right. He was getting too old to try to break the really rank ones, and this horse must have been gelded much too late because there was still a helluva lot of stallion in him. He was a handsome devil, though, a blue roan, about fifteen hands high, and Jim couldn't help admiring him. But so far, no one had been able to saddle-break him, and Jim thought it would be the perfect way to cap off his farewell to the cattle business. He decided he could use one more good ride on a bucking horse before he retired to the rocking chair.

Walking out of the barn, Will Tanner called out, "Hey, Boss, why don't you let me ride that one? Shorty's right, he's got a mean streak in him." The horse did have a mean streak, and it had been at least a couple of years since Hightower had decided his bones were getting too brittle to dust his britches on the hard ground of the corral. Will was usually the man to break the ill-tempered horses, but he hadn't gotten around to this one.

"Too late," Hightower said as he settled his weight in the saddle. "I'm already on him. Let him go, Shorty." Shorty shook his head, concerned, but he released the roan and backed away. The horse remained motionless, surprising all three of them. "Well, I'll be . . ." Hightower started. "I believe he's just a big bluff."

"Watch him, Boss," Will warned when the roan's ears pricked up and he raised his tail, even though there was no other indication that he was going to move away from the rail. The words had no sooner left his lips when the horse exploded. Bucking stiff-legged, it slammed Hightower against the corral rails repeatedly before rearing back so violently that it seemed about to fall on its back. His leg already shattered by the corral rails, Hightower tried to hold on to the saddle horn, but the horse bucked so violently he was thrown to the ground, landing hard on his back. Still bucking insanely, the horse reared up over the stricken man and came down fiercely with his front hooves on Hightower's chest, crushing the life out of him.

Will was quick to climb over the rails, but it was too late to help his boss. It had happened so suddenly, and the horse almost seemed intent on killing the man. Shorty managed to back the horse away to the other side of the corral, where it stood calmly with no sign of violence other than the wild look in its eye and the flared nostrils. Will knelt beside the broken body of the man he had known as a father figure since he was a boy. Looking at him lying there in the dust of the corral, his eyes flickering like a candle about to go out, and blood trickling from the corner of his mouth, Will wanted to cry out in anguish. Devastated by his inability to help, as he witnessed the last feeble gasps of breath leaving the dying man, he said his silent farewell to a man he loved and respected.

Jim Hightower had taken in a fatherless boy, the son of a drunken whore, and taught him how to work with cattle and horses. He seemed to delight in the boy's natural ability to ride and rope. And when Will developed into the kind of man a father could be proud of, Jim made him his foreman. This was in spite of the fact that he was younger than most of the men who worked for him. The decision proved to be a wise one, for there was never any doubt among the men concerning Will's qualifications. He was just as proficient in handling an unruly cowhand as he was a bad-tempered horse. But now, on this tragic day, he was as gentle as if working with a newborn foal when he carefully lifted Jim's body up in his arms.

"Go on up to the house and tell Miss Jean," Will said to Shorty. "Tell her that I'm bringin' Boss."

"Is he dead?" Shorty asked anxiously as he hustled to open the corral gate. Will nodded solemnly. "My Lord . . ." Shorty declared, at a loss for words. "I swear . . ." He stood there and held the gate for Will. Then he closed it again and hurried up ahead of him to the house to alert Jim's wife.

Jean Hightower, affectionately known to the men of the J-Bar-J as Miss Jean, was not the typical pioneering woman often found standing shoulder to shoulder with her trailblazing husband. In fact, Miss Jean was a rather fragile woman, the daughter of a

Presbyterian minister in a little town east of Fort
Smith, Arkansas. As Will expected, she almost collapsed when told of her husband's tragic death. She
was fortunate to have the support of her longtime
cook and housekeeper, Sally Evening Star, an Osage
woman. Sally helped her clean Jim's body and lay him
out in the bedroom in his one suit coat. Miss Jean
would sit with her husband's body all night, saying her
farewells before he was buried in the morning.

Will was grieving privately for the loss of the man
who had given him a life, but he was angry, too. He
found it difficult to understand how Jim Hightower's
life could be snuffed out so suddenly, and at a time
like this, when the man was retiring. Jim was planning
to take Jean back close to her people in Arkansas.
Most of the cattle had been sold. There was only a
skeleton crew left to take care of the ranch—Shorty,
Cal, Slim, and himself. There were no buyers for the
small ranch there in northeast Texas, so Boss had
planned to leave it to Will. And now Will wasn't sure
he wanted it. He didn't even know if he wanted to stay
in the cattle business or just sign on with another
rancher. He had lost his desire for it. And he was
angry, damned angry, because he had been really
happy that Boss could retire while he was still young
enough to enjoy it. *He had to try to ride that one devil
horse*, he thought.

After Will and Shorty did all they could for their
grieving mistress, they returned to the barn.
"Whaddaya want me to do about that horse?" Shorty
asked as they approached the corral. The roan was

still standing where Shorty had tied it. "Want me to pull the saddle off?"

Will took a long, hard look at the horse before answering. "No, you go find Cal and Slim and a couple of shovels. Miss Jean said she wants Boss buried over near the creek, close to those willows where that bench is. I'll take care of the horse."

When Shorty went inside the barn, Will went to the corral gate. He stood looking at the big blue roan for a long moment, then he opened the gate and went into the corral. He walked purposefully toward the horse, looking it in the eye as he untied the reins from the rail. The roan did not resist when Will led him away from the side of the corral. "Now, you evil son of a bitch, I wanna see if you're really a killer," he said, and stepped up in the stirrup. Just as before, the roan made no move when Will settled down in the saddle. Then, also as before, the horse exploded suddenly, but this time the rider was not taken by surprise. Around and around the corral they went, the roan bucking and rearing as if to fall over on its back, then landing stiff-legged to buck again. Time and again, it tried to pin Will against the side rails of the corral, only to have Will pull his foot from the stirrup and raise his leg, further frustrating the belligerent beast.

Hearing the pounding hooves and the horse's squeals, Shorty ran to the barn door to observe the contest between man and horse. "My Lord," he muttered as he watched the battle of wills on display, neither man nor horse willing to yield. He was certain that he was witness to a ride like he had never seen before, or was likely to see in the future. Will drove the horse relentlessly on until it began to take pauses between its violent attempts to throw the demon on its back. But Will would not let him rest. Shorty stood spellbound, holding a shovel in each hand, for a solid three-quarters of an hour before the final surrender, when the roan stood defeated, its head and tail drooping. Will kicked his heels into the roan's sides, forcing it to a slow trot around the corral. Then he reined the horse to a stop and dismounted. He was not satisfied that the horse was really broken, however, sensing an evil streak that was inborn.

"I'll get a pick and help you dig that grave," Will said as he walked past Shorty. "We'll let that devil horse rest for a spell, then one of you take him for a little ride to make sure he's fully broke."

By the time the three men had dug Jim's grave, the blue roan had had plenty of time to become rested, so Slim volunteered to try him out. Will's instincts had been right about the horse, however, and when Slim got on him, the horse repeated his attempts to maim his rider. Slim escaped the fate that had befallen Jim simply because, like Will had, he managed to get his leg out of the way before it was shattered. He could not prevent being thrown, however, and barely escaped being trampled by the belligerent horse's hooves. Rolling over and over, he scrambled to his feet and went over the side of the corral just before being bitten.

"That damn horse is a man-killer," Slim gasped breathlessly. "He's out to do you in, and that's a fact."

"I'm afraid you're right," Will said. He thought about it for a long moment before deciding what needed to be done in regard to the wrathful beast. It was a hard decision, but he finally went inside the corral and approached the leery horse. It backed away, rearing up on its hind legs, its front hooves pawing the air as if daring the man. When it dropped its hooves to the ground again, Will grabbed the reins. Holding the bridle, he forced the roan's head down, so he could look him in the eye. "Go back to hell where you came from," he said. "You killed a good man today." Then he drew the .44 he wore and put a bullet in the horse's brain. Stepping back to keep the horse from falling on him, he turned and walked back to the gate.

Slim was still standing, speechless, when Will came out of the corral. In over four years riding for the J-Bar-J, he had always known the young foreman to be kindhearted when it came to horses. Fair and even-tempered as a rule, Will Tanner could be riled over some things after all—if they were important to him. Slim learned that today.

"You or Cal hitch up a team and drag that damn carcass outta the corral. I'm gonna ride in to Sulphur Springs and see if I can get the preacher to come out and give Boss a proper funeral in the morning."

Jim Hightower was buried before noon the next day. Thanks to Will's diligent efforts the night before, Sam Harvey, barber and undertaker, drove a wagon carrying a pine box and the Reverend Edward Garrett out to the J-Bar-J. With Will's help, Harvey placed Jim's body in the simple coffin. Before he nailed the lid on, Miss Jean came in and said one final good-bye to the man she had been married to for thirty-one years. She placed a scented linen handkerchief in

Jim's cold hand. "So that something of me will always be with him," she said tearfully. Acting as pallbearers, Will, Slim, Cal, and Shorty carried the coffin out to the willows by the creek, and Reverend Garrett delivered a fine eulogy, considering the deceased had never set foot in his church. Will compensated Sam Harvey for the pine box, but Sam said there was no charge for the four-mile trip from town to deliver it. Reverend Garrett graciously accepted a donation to his church. When it was all done, Will had spent fourteen dollars of the money he had saved up over the last few years. He didn't begrudge the expense and felt good about spending the money.

After the eulogy that turned into a sermon, Jim was lowered to his eternal rest on two lengths of ropes held by the pallbearers. Miss Jean expressed her appreciation to the reverend and Sam Harvey for making the eight-mile round-trip, and to all the cowhands involved. After the funeral party was fed one of Sally Evening Star's beef stew dinners, and the wagon departed for town, Miss Jean pulled Will aside. She wanted to thank him for his thoughtfulness in arranging a real funeral for her husband. "I know Jim appreciates it," she said. "You know you've always been someone very special to Jim and me, and I'm just sorry that we didn't have something to leave you besides this ranch. I do have a little bit saved back, though, and I want to give you money for what you've spent for the funeral. I know it cost you a lot to get them to come out here, all the way from town."

"No, ma'am," he insisted. "It didn't cost nothin' at all. The preacher don't charge, and that coffin was one Sam had already made. They were glad to do it for Boss 'cause he was such a fine, upstandin' man, they said."

She smiled gently, obviously pleased by the sentiment. "Will," she said, "you're a man any father would be proud to call his son—and such a splendid liar."

The next couple of days were sad and worrisome days for Miss Jean as she went through the process of closing out her life on the J-Bar-J. In preparation to leave for Arkansas, Jim had already closed out their bank account and settled up with anyone he owed in Sulphur Springs. So she was left with the question of how best to go to her family's home, now that her husband was no longer there to take her. It was possible to go by train, but it would require a long, round-about journey to make railroad connections. And it would also mean she could not take most of the possessions she had planned to carry by wagon. She was spared the sorrow of leaving her precious keepsakes when Will told her that he would take her to Arkansas. It was what she had counted on, but she still questioned his decision. "Won't you be needed here at the ranch?" she asked.

"No, ma'am, not really," he said. "Shorty and the others can handle everything here. There aren't but a handful of cattle left to worry about, and the horses. They don't need me."

So it was settled, then. The wagon was packed with the sentimental keepsakes Miss Jean was fond of, as well as the cooking supplies needed for a trip that Will figured to take close to three weeks. Planning to keep one of the team of horses to use as a packhorse on his return trip, he put a pack saddle rig in the back of the wagon. When all was ready, the party prepared to depart early one June morning. Will had planned to drive the wagon, but Sally Evening Star insisted that she knew how to drive a team of horses. That was good news to Will, because he preferred to ride his buckskin gelding instead of sitting on a wagon seat for three weeks. It also meant a little more room in the wagon. The three remaining cowhands stood by to wish the travelers a safe journey, each one stepping forward to shake Miss Jean's hand. "We'll make sure Boss's grave don't grow up in weeds," Cal assured her.

"I know you will," she said. "Jim was always talking about how pleased he was to have you boys working for him."

"What about you?" Shorty asked Will after he helped Miss Jean up on the wagon. "The ranch belongs to you now. Anythin' you want done while you're gone?"

"You know what needs to be done," Will said. "Just take care of things like you usually do. The ranch is yours till I get back. Run it like I ain't comin' back." It was not an idle suggestion, because he had given the possibility serious thought. "In fact," he said, the idea suddenly striking him, "I'm making you my partner, if you want it. Half owner, whaddaya say?"

Totally flabbergasted, Shorty blurted, "Hell, yes, I want it!" He immediately offered his hand to shake on it. "What about Cal and Slim?"

"I'll tell 'em," Will said. The two hands were good men, but Shorty had been working the J-Bar-J since Will was a boy, and he was the most capable to run the ranch. Will led his horse over to Slim and Cal and told them that they were working for Shorty now. They had already assumed as much. That done, he stepped up into the saddle. "Let's go to Arkansas, ladies," he sang out, and started out to the northeast, toward the Red River.

The journey that Will had figured to take three weeks stretched into a month, because of a spell of bad weather that delayed them and forced a detour miles out of their way to find a ferry crossing. The two weary women gratefully rolled into Fort Smith on the Fourth of July amid that city's celebration of the holiday. Miss Jean had planned to stay one night in a hotel to give herself the opportunity to recover from the grueling trek through Oklahoma Indian Territory. Because of the celebrations, however, she was unable to find accommodations in the better hotels. So she decided to push on to camp overnight east of town. They found a camping spot by a creek where she could bathe and freshen up before meeting her brother and sister-in-law at the family farm near a little junction called Ward's Corner, named for her father, Henry C. Ward.

Not one of the three travelers was happier to see Miss Jean's old home place than Will Tanner. He felt satisfied knowing that Miss Jean and Sally had been safely delivered, with all the contents of the wagon intact. But he was weary himself after the wagon's slow pace of travel. It had given him many hours to reflect on his life to this point, however, and to decide if he was content to return to the little ranch near Sulphur Springs. In spite of this, he had still come to no decision, primarily because he didn't know what else he wanted to do. So he put it aside to deal with later.

It was a short trip to the Ward farm the following morning. They arrived before noon to the surprise of Marjorie Ward, Miss Jean's sister-in-law. She had expected them, but not until the end of summer. Shocked to hear of Jim's death, she greeted them warmly and sent her daughter to the fields to tell her husband that his sister was home. Watching the reception Miss Jean received, Will was satisfied that she was truly welcome. Since this was really his only concern, he was eager then to be on his way. Even though Marjorie insisted that he surely must stay for supper, Will lingered only long enough to meet Henry junior when he came from the fields. Not one to normally turn down the offer of a good meal, he somehow felt a little awkward in the sad reunion. He was no longer a part of Miss Jean's life, so he respectfully declined the invitation, got his pack saddle from the wagon, and took his pick of the wagon team to use as a packhorse. Miss Jean caught him as he was about to leave.

"You're not getting away from here without giving me a hug, Will Tanner," she declared. He grinned and accommodated her. "Thank you for taking such good care of me," she said. "Take care of yourself just as well, you hear?"

"Yes, ma'am, I will," he said, and stepped up into the saddle. Touching his forefinger to the brim of his hat, he bid a final farewell to a woman who had been such a big part of his life. Then he turned the buckskin toward the road that led back to Fort Smith.

CHAPTER 2

Approaching Fort Smith, Will decided that he had earned a drink of whiskey and maybe a good supper, but first he needed to take care of his horses. So when he came to a stable on the east side of town, he pulled up and dismounted. "How do," the owner greeted him when he led his horses toward the corral.

"Howdy," Will returned. "I'm needin' to put my horses up for the night. Whaddaya charge?"

The man looked at the two horses, then took another look at Will. "Tell you what I'll do. I charge fifteen dollars a month to stable a horse, but since you're just wantin' to stay one night, I'll let you have the monthly rate. That'd be fifty cents for the night." He paused to check Will's reaction. When Will didn't protest, he said, "Course, that's for each horse. Since you've got two, that'd make it a dollar."

"How 'bout with a portion of oats?" Will asked.

"Dollar and a half."

"How much if I sleep in your hay barn?" Will asked.

"Two dollars and a quarter."

"Hell," Will said. "How come you charge me more

'n you charge my horse? I ain't gonna eat any hay—I'm just gonna sleep on it."

"Two dollars even," he said, and waited for Will's response.

"All right," Will said, reaching into his pocket. It seemed a little steep to him, but he thought maybe prices for everything in Fort Smith might be high. He counted out two dollars and handed them to the owner.

"Yes, sir. Thank you, sir," he said when he had money in hand. "My name's Vern Tuttle. This here's my livery stable. You in town for the Fourth celebration?"

"Nope," Will said. "I'm just passin' through, I reckon. Thought I'd stay over and get me a good meal and maybe a drink of whiskey. You got any recommendations for either one?"

"Sure do," Vern replied. "Mornin' Glory Saloon for both of 'em. You can't go wrong there. They got a cook there that's every bit as good as any of them in the hotel dinin' rooms, and it's in easy walkin' distance from here."

"That sounds like what I'm lookin' for," Will declared. "Think I'll give it a try as soon as I put my horses away."

Vern pointed up the street. "The Mornin' Glory's right up there. You'll see the sign. Come on, and I'll help you settle your horses and show you where you can put your saddle and stuff." He turned to lead him into the stable. "What's your name, young feller?"

"Will Tanner," he answered.

"Glad to know you, Will. If you ain't ever been in Fort Smith before, I'll just give you a little advice. This is a bad town to raise hell in." He paused. "Not sayin' you look the type, but just thought you'd like to know. We got more law in this town than we know what to do with. We got a sheriff and deputies, but Fort Smith is the headquarters for the Western District of Arkansas U.S. Marshals Service, too. So there might be a dozen deputy marshals in town at any one time."

"Thanks for the information," Will said, "but I just want a drink and a meal."

"Just sayin', that's all. No offense."

"None taken," Will said.

The Morning Glory Saloon was a little longer stretch of the legs than Vern had said, but Will didn't mind. It was good to work his legs a little after so many days in the saddle. The saloon's sign was not as obvious as Vern had promised, either, but that may have been because of the fact that the nails had evidently backed out of one end of it, causing the sign to hang vertically. Judging by the weathered boards on the facade of the building, Will figured it must have been one of the oldest drinking establishments in town. That notion was further strengthened by the obvious fact that most of the newer buildings seemed to be centered more to the north of town. *But there are a few horses tied at the hitching rail out front, so somebody must think it's as good as Vern says,* he thought.

"Howdy, stranger," bartender Gus Johnson greeted him cheerfully when he walked up to the bar. "What'll you have?"

"Howdy," Will returned. "How 'bout a shot of whiskey to settle the dust?" While Gus reached for a bottle to pour his drink, Will took a moment to look the room over. The large barroom was about half-full. There were a couple of customers at the end of the bar, but most of the crowd were seated at the tables arranged around three sides of the room. As Will casually scanned the tables, he took note that only a few of the patrons were eating supper. That could be good or bad news, but better than no one eating, he decided. His gaze skipped quickly over a table in the back corner of the room, then was drawn back for a second look. One man sitting at the table had his back to the wall. He was one of the diners. A large man, judging by the width of his shoulders, he hovered over his plate of food, which seemed to have captured his full attention. He was drinking coffee, but there was a bottle of whiskey on the table as well. The sound of a shot glass on the bar brought Will's attention back to his drink of whiskey.

"Here you go, young feller," Gus said as he poured. "I ain't ever seen you in here before."

"Reckon not," Will said. "I'm just passin' through."

"On your way to where?" Gus asked.

Will hesitated before answering. When he did, he almost surprised himself. "Damned if I know."

Thinking that Will might have found him too nosy, Gus quickly explained, "It ain't none of my business. I was just makin' conversation. I figured maybe you were in town to watch the hangin' tomorrow."

"No problem atall," Will quickly assured him. He chuckled then and confessed that he really wasn't sure where he was going. He tossed his drink back and waited a few moments to get over the burn before continuing. "I didn't know there was a hangin'."

"Yep," Gus said. "Judge Parker sentenced a young boy named Troy Gamble to hang for shootin' a feller over in the Nations."

"Is that a fact?" Will responded, not really interested. "Vern, over at the livery stable, told me I could get a decent supper here. Is there any truth in that?"

Gus laughed. "You bet there is. We got us a dandy cook, and she's cooked up one of her specialties tonight, cowboy stew."

"Well, I reckon I'm lucky I came in on a night she cooked her specialty," Will said.

"Yes, sir," Gus went on. "What makes Mammy's cowboy stew so good is because she makes hers with real cowboys instead of beef." He laughed harder than Will, obviously enjoying a joke that he had told countless times before.

"Well, I don't reckon I can pass that up," Will said.

"You won't be sorry," Gus assured him.

Will heard a soft voice behind him, and turned to meet a solemn-looking woman, almost as tall as he was. "Evenin', cowboy. You lookin' for some company?"

"No, ma'am," Will said. "Thank you just the same, though."

She immediately turned away. "That's Lucy Tyler," Gus said. "She's one of our regulars."

"I'll have one more shot of that whiskey," Will decided. "That last one didn't quite cook my whole throat." He watched Gus pour his drink. "Who's the big feller sittin' at the back corner table? I noticed a couple of your other customers speakin' to him when they walked by."

"Him?" Gus replied. "I expect about everybody in town knows him. That's U.S. Deputy Marshal Fletcher

Pride. He always takes supper here when he's in town." When Will didn't appear to recognize the name, Gus continued. "Pride's the oldest and best-known deputy marshal in the territory. Matter of fact, he's the one brought Troy Gamble in to be tried by Judge Parker. You ain't never heard of Fletcher Pride?"

"Nope, I can't say as I have."

"Where are you from?" Gus asked, incredulously.

"Texas," Will said.

"Well, I'm surprised you ain't heard of him down there 'cause I'm sure he slips over into Texas from time to time."

"Reckon I just ain't been breakin' the law," Will said.

"Reckon not," Gus agreed. "Set yourself down at a table and I'll tell Mammy to bring you a plate. You want coffee with it?" Will nodded.

Picturing Mammy as a rather large woman, Will was surprised when a small, fragile-looking woman with stringy gray hair brought him a plate heaped high with stew. Two thick slices of bread rested on top. *Reckon she doesn't eat her own cooking,* he thought. "Was you the one wantin' to eat?" she asked before setting the plate on the table.

"Yes, ma'am," he replied.

"I'll bring you some coffee," she said. "You want some sugar with it?"

"No, ma'am," he said.

She returned shortly with a large cup of coffee. She set it down on the table, nodded toward his plate, and asked, "Is it good?"

She seemed genuinely interested in his opinion of her stew, so he said, "Yes, ma'am, it surely is." This was in spite of the fact that he thought it a little too greasy. But it sure beat what he would have cooked for himself had he decided to camp by the river instead of sleeping in the hay barn. She gave him an approving nod and returned to the kitchen. Will resumed his assault on the cowboy stew, with no notion that his peaceful supper was about to be interrupted.

Three riders pulled up to the hitching rail of the Morning Glory, dismounted, and looped their reins over the rail loosely, in the event they might find it necessary to make a hasty departure. "How we gonna do this, Pa?" Orville Gamble asked. "Are we just gonna walk in and kill him?"

"No, dammit," his father said. "I want him to know why we killed him, and who it was that done it. So don't neither one of you pull a trigger till I start the shootin'." Luther Gamble was an angry man. He and his three sons had always operated outside the law in their home state of Kansas. After a bank holdup in Wichita, during which a teller was shot, he and his boys slipped over to Oklahoma Indian Territory to lie low for a while. It was purely bad luck that his youngest, Troy, got into a little scrape with a Cherokee policeman and had to shoot the son of a bitch. Maybe Troy was a little hotheaded, but he didn't deserve to be hanged for killing an Indian.

Luther was determined to kill the man who tracked Troy down and brought him to the gallows. He knew he had no chance of saving his son, because of the army of lawmen that guarded every hanging in Fort Smith. But he could put a bullet in Fletcher Pride's head to even the score. He looked at his two surviving sons, Orville and Simon, and felt a sense of satisfaction in knowing they were as mean as their old man. "Let's go have a visit with Deputy Fletcher Pride, boys," he said, and stepped up on the narrow porch.

Busy working on his supper, Will paid little attention to the three men who walked in the door of the saloon. He continued to ignore them until they walked past his table, moving toward the back of the room, and he took a good look at them. He decided then that they had to be a father and his two sons, for there was a definite resemblance—all three appeared to have the same mean streak showing. Spread out, and walking in a single line, they advanced slowly on the big deputy marshal at the corner table. All three were resting their hands on the handles of their pistols. Will suddenly realized the scene that was about to unfold, as did most of the other customers in the saloon. There followed an exodus of most of the men seated at the tables, anxious to avoid being caught in a hail of gunfire.

Pride glanced up from his plate when he realized the three men, with pistols now drawn, were advancing toward him with the clear intention of doing him harm. He made no sudden moves, but studied the three as they silently came to a stop some five paces from his table. He slowly put his knife and fork down beside his plate and dropped his hands in his lap. His heavy, gray eyebrows arched slightly as his gaze went from one man to another, settling on the older man who bristled with anger. "You'd be Luther Gamble, I reckon," Pride said. "I never had the pleasure. I heard you've been pretty busy up in Kansas, though."

"Never mind who I am, you son of a bitch," Luther spat back. "I know who you are, and that's a piece of bad luck for you."

"And these must be your other two sons," Pride went on. "Fine-lookin' young men. I bet you're proud of 'em. Too bad about Troy, though. I reckon that's why you're in town, to see Troy hang, so these other two sons will see that crime don't pay."

"What are we waitin' for, Pa?" one of the boys blurted anxiously. "He's talkin' crazy."

"Shut up, Simon," Luther growled. "He's tryin' to talk his way outta the grave. But that ain't gonna work, lawman," he shouted at Pride. "It's eye for eye. You mighta brought my boy in to hang, but by God, you're gonna go with him."

"That don't make a lotta sense," Pride said, still calm, "when you've got all these guns aimin' right at you and your boys."

"What?" Luther started, looking right and left, seeing no one. "What guns?" He feared for a moment that he might have walked into a trap. "There ain't nobody but you, and I'm tired of hearin' you talk."

"Maybe you better listen to what he's tellin' you," a voice behind him said.

Startled, Orville reacted immediately, spun around, and fired at Will, his bullet tearing a chunk out of the table Will had taken cover behind. Before he had time for a second shot, a bullet from Will's .44 smashed into his chest, driving him several steps backward to collapse on his back. Before Luther could react, a bullet from the .44 in Pride's lap cut him down. Caught in the confusion that had suddenly exploded, Simon Gamble couldn't decide which gun was the most critical. He turned to shoot at Will, only to be cut down by a second bullet from Pride. After the explosion of gunfire, the room was suddenly silent until Pride called out, "You all right, partner? You didn't get hit, didja?"

"No," Will answered, "but I lost half of my supper when I turned the table over."

Pride chuckled as he got up from his chair. "We'd better check these fellers, make sure there ain't no more bite in 'em." It took only a minute to determine there was no longer any threat from Gamble and his sons. Simon was dead, as a result of Pride's bullet to the head. The other two were still alive, but sinking fast. "Best just let 'em lay," Pride said as he kicked their weapons out of their reach. Then he looked toward Gus, who had just surfaced from behind the bar. "Gus, send somebody over to get Doc Peters." Bringing his attention back to Will again, he extended his hand. "Partner, I'm sure glad you joined the party. I was in a tight spot there, and I doubt I coulda got out of it without at least one of 'em puttin' a bullet in me. Are you one of the deputies from up Kansas way? I heard a couple of you fellers might be here for the hangin'."

"No," Will said. "I ain't no deputy. I just came in to get a drink and some supper."

"Well, I'll be . . ." Pride started. "You ain't a lawman?" Will shook his head. "If that don't beat all," Pride exclaimed. "Then I reckon I really owe you my thanks. Hell, everybody else ran out the door."

Will shrugged modestly. "It just didn't seem like a fair fight, and you bein' a lawman and all." He paused to look at the three men on the floor. "What would you have done if I hadn't been here?"

"Died, I reckon," Pride said with a laugh, then on a more serious note, he confessed that he wasn't sure what he would have done. "I knew for sure that I was gonna get the old man, and maybe one of the boys."

"I reckon it's a good thing they didn't just come in blazin' away before you had a chance to do anything," Will said.

"As soon as I looked up and saw who it was, I figured I had a chance," Pride said. "I knew the old man would wanna see me sweat a little and make sure I knew why he was killin' me. So I tried to talk him up as long as I could to keep him from pullin' the trigger— thought maybe he wouldn't notice I was cockin' my pistol."

"You always eat with your pistol in your lap?" Will asked.

"Not always, but I thought it might be a good idea today, with the hangin' goin' on tomorrow. Trouble is, I got into Mammy's stew too deep to see what was goin' on. If I'd seen those three when they walked in the door, I'da had my piece out and cocked before they got this close."

With the shooting over, the frightened patrons crowded back inside to view the bodies and talk about what a close call they had just had. Gus was happy to give them his accounting of the gunfight as first one and then another leaned close over the victims to get a better look. Pride snorted, amused. "It was kinda hard to see hunkered down behind the bar, I expect. Wasn't it, Gus?"

Having hidden in the pantry as soon as she heard

the shots, Mammy came out then to clean up the mess Will had made when he turned the table over. "I'm right sorry, ma'am," Will said as he tried to pick up the coffee cup and plate. "It was real good. I'm sorry I didn't get to finish it."

Overhearing, Pride spoke up. "Fix him another plate, Mammy, and put it on my bill. I'll set down with him and have another cup of coffee." He looked at Will and grinned. "I figure I sure as hell owe you that much."

"It's on the house," Gus chimed in at that point.

"Why, thank you kindly," Will said. "I did work up a little appetite."

Mammy stood for a moment, holding a tray with the dirty dishes she had picked up, until the table was set upright again. Then she spun on her heel and headed toward the kitchen, muttering in disgust, "Men and their guns."

"I ain't never known Gus to give anything away before," Pride teased. "What if Clyde finds out you're givin' away his profits?"

"Clyde might be the owner," Gus replied, "but I'm the one behind the bar when the bullets were flyin'." He turned to take another look at the three bodies. "I expect we oughta drag them out of the middle of the floor."

"Hell," Pride snorted. "They ain't in anybody's way—might as well leave 'em lay till Doc gets here."

"Yeah, but they're bleedin' all over my floor," Gus complained. "I wish they'da waited to jump you out-side."

One of the interested spectators, bending low over Luther Gamble's body, declared, "Ain't nothin' Doc can do for this one. He's dead. Best send for Edward instead."

Dr. Peters walked in the door in time to hear the comment. Only slightly irritated to be called away from home at suppertime, he said, "Might as well examine them, just in case." A quick examination confirmed the customer's diagnosis, and by the time he got to the other two, they were gone as well, so he said that Edward Kittridge could come for the corpses. He looked at Gus and said, "It's gonna cost you a drink of whiskey for my services."

Gus had some of the men help Pride and Will drag the bodies outside to wait on the porch for the under-taker to come for them. Pride relieved the bodies of their weapons and anything of value, explaining to Will that he hoped they had enough on them to pay for their burial. He explained that if a deputy marshal killed a felon, he had to bear the cost of his burial. When he was satisfied that he was compensated, they went back inside to finish their supper.

Pride was interested to find out more about this Good Samaritan with a gun, so he questioned Will so intensely that Will was driven to ask a question of his own. "Are you thinkin' I'm an outlaw or something?"

Will's response brought forth a lusty chuckle from the big lawman. "Well, no, I ain't, but since you brought it up, are you wanted for a crime somewhere?"

"No, I'm not," Will said, "unless you're fixin' to arrest me for shootin' that feller just now."

Still grinning broadly, Pride assured him. "Nah, that was in self-defense. Besides, I officially deputized you to help me arrest them outlaws. I just forgot to tell ya." He paused while Mammy brought out a fresh pot of coffee and filled their cups, then he continued. "So you ain't been doin' nothin' but punchin' cows all your life?" Will nodded, and Pride went on. "Things were happenin' fast back there, but I couldn't help noticin' you were pretty handy with that Colt you're wearin', and pretty cool in the middle of all that shootin'."

Will shrugged indifferently. "I reckon I didn't have much time to think about it," he offered.

"Practice a lot with that Colt, do ya?"

"I don't reckon I practice with it at all," Will said, thinking the man must really have a deep interest in firearms. "Shoot a snake with it now and again. That's about all."

"Well, now you've shot a man with it," Pride reminded him. "How do ya feel about that?"

Will shrugged again. Now the conversation was getting a little strange. "I don't know how I feel about it," he said. "'Bout the same as shootin' a snake, I reckon. Tell you the truth, I hadn't thought about it one way or the other. I didn't go to kill anybody, but the feller shot at me, so I shot him."

"He had it comin', right?"

"I don't know if he did or not," Will said impatiently. "But he shot at me, so I shot him."

Pride sat back in his chair, pleased with his impression of the young stranger. "From what you've been sayin', I take it you ain't sure you're headin' back to drivin' cattle again." As before, the comment was met with a shrug from Will. "You consider workin' for the U.S. Marshals Service?"

"Shoot, no," Will said at once without having to think about it.

"Why not?" Pride pressed. "You said yourself you ain't got no place in particular to go to. So what are you gonna do? I wouldn't have even mentioned it to you, but I ain't ever seen a man with better makin's for a deputy marshal than you—and I ain't known you for longer than about an hour. Do me—and yourself—a favor and think about it. The Marshals Service needs men that think fast and ain't scared when bullets are flyin'." He sat back in his chair again and drained the last of his coffee while he watched Will, who was obviously thinking the proposition over. Pride had refrained from telling his potential recruit one of the main reasons he had been trying to sell him on the service. The mortality rate for deputy marshals was high. His boss, Marshal Daniel Stone, had just been bemoaning the fact that he had lost two deputies in the last month, both victims of ambush by outlaws. He thought about sharing that information with Will, but he had gotten the impression that it would not have been a deciding factor for the young man. On the other hand, it might have been, so why mention it?

"I don't know, Fletcher . . ." Will paused. "That's right, ain't it? . . . Fletcher?" He was sure that was the name Gus told him. Pride confirmed it with a nod, so Will continued. "I sure as hell never thought about being a lawman. I don't know anything about it."

"You don't worry about that," Pride assured him. "We'll take care of that."

"Like I said, I don't know," Will hedged. "Let me think about it for a while."

Thinking that if he had him on the fence, it wouldn't take much to pull him on over, so he asked, "Why? Back there when that Gamble feller shot at you, you didn't have to think about it for a while. Whaddaya say you meet me right here in the mornin' and we'll go talk to U.S. Marshal Daniel Stone? It'll mean a steady paycheck and a few extra bonuses from time to time."

"Wouldn't hurt to just talk to him, I reckon," Will conceded, since he didn't have any plans for the next day. Pride gave him one firm nod, as if putting a period on the conversation, leaving Will to wonder if he was making a smart decision for himself. He finished his coffee and said good night after promising to return in the morning. He thought about the prospect of becoming a U.S. Deputy Marshal, still not finding it a natural job for him. He had never had any desire to protect the people and punish the lawbreakers. But he honestly did not want to return to driving cattle all his life. This thought brought to mind the three men he had left at the J-Bar-J, Shorty, Slim, and Cal. He wondered if he was letting them down, and immediately told himself that he was not. They knew how to manage cattle. They didn't need him to tell them how. As far as possibly building the operation into something closer to the way it was when Jim Hightower ran it, Shorty had a good head on his shoulders. He was as likely to make it successful as Will was, and Will had told him to run it as if he wasn't coming back. If he didn't return, the ranch would be his free and clear. *Hell*, he thought, *what am I worried about it for?*

He slept that night on his bed of hay, his horses fed and watered, and his stomach filled with a good meal. Tomorrow might mean a major change in his life. He wondered what Jim and Miss Jean would think about it.

J. A. Johnstone on William W. Johnstone
"Print the Legend"

William W. Johnstone was born in southern Missouri, the youngest of four children. He was raised with strong moral and family values by his minister father, and tutored by his schoolteacher mother. Despite this, he quit school at age fifteen.

"I have the highest respect for education," he says, "but such is the folly of youth, and wanting to see the world beyond the four walls and the blackboard."

True to this vow, Bill attempted to enlist in the French Foreign Legion ("I saw Gary Cooper in *Beau Geste* when I was a kid and I thought the French Foreign Legion would be fun") but was rejected, thankfully, for being underage. Instead, he joined a traveling carnival and did all kinds of odd jobs. It was listening to the veteran carny folk, some of whom had been on the circuit since the late 1800s, telling amazing tales about their experiences, that planted the storytelling seed in Bill's imagination.

"They were mostly honest people, despite the bad reputation traveling carny shows had back then," Bill remembers. "Of course, there were exceptions. There was one guy named Picky, who got that name because he was a master pickpocket. He could steal a man's socks right off his feet without him knowing. Believe me, Picky got us chased out of more than a few towns."

After a few months of this grueling existence, Bill returned home and finished high school. Next came stints as a deputy sheriff in the Tallulah, Louisiana, Sheriff's Department, followed by a hitch in the U.S. Army. Then he began a career in radio broadcasting at KTLD in Tallulah, which would last sixteen years. It was there that he fine-tuned his storytelling skills. He turned to writing in 1970, but it wouldn't be until 1979 that his first novel, *The Devil's Kiss*, was published. Thus began the full-time writing career of William W. Johnstone. He wrote horror (*The Uninvited*), thrillers (*The Last of the Dog Team*), even a romance novel or two. Then, in February 1983, *Out of the Ashes* was published. Searching for his missing family in a postapocalyptic America, rebel mercenary and patriot Ben Raines is united with the civilians of the Resistance forces and moves to the forefront of a revolution for the nation's future.

Out of the Ashes was a smash. The series would continue for the next twenty years, winning Bill three generations of fans all over the world. The series was often imitated but never duplicated. "We all tried to copy the Ashes series," said one publishing executive, "but Bill's uncanny ability, both then and now, to predict in which direction the political winds were blowing brought a certain immediacy to the table no one else could capture." The Ashes series would end its run with more than thirty-four books and twenty million copies in print, making it one of the most successful men's action series in American book publishing. (The Ashes series also, Bill notes with a touch of pride, got him on the FBI's Watch List for its less than flattering portrayal of spineless politicians and the growing power of big government over our lives, among other things. In that respect, I often find myself saying, "Bill was years ahead of his time.")

Always steps ahead of the political curve, Bill's recent thrillers, written with myself, include *Vengeance Is Mine, Invasion USA, Border War, Jackknife, Remember the Alamo, Home Invasion, Phoenix Rising, The Blood of Patriots, The Bleeding Edge,* and the upcoming *Suicide Mission.*

It is with the western, though, that Bill found his greatest success. His westerns propelled him onto both the *USA Today* and the *New York Times* bestseller lists.

Bill's western series include *Matt Jensen, the Last Mountain Man, Preacher, the First Mountain Man, The Family Jensen, Luke Jensen, Bounty Hunter, Eagles, MacCallister* (an Eagles spin-off), *Sidewinders, The Brothers O'Brien, Sixkiller, Blood Bond, The Last Gunfighter,* and the new series *Flintlock* and *The Trail West.* May 2013 saw the hardcover western *Butch Cassidy: The Lost Years.*

"The western," Bill says, "is one of the few true art forms that is one hundred percent American. I liken the Western as America's version of England's Arthurian legends, like the Knights of the Round Table, or Robin Hood and his Merry Men. Starting with the 1902 publication of *The Virginian* by Owen Wister, and followed by the greats like Zane Grey, Max Brand, Ernest Haycox, and of course Louis L'Amour, the western has helped to shape the cultural landscape of America.

"I'm no goggle-eyed college academic, so when my

fans ask me why the western is as popular now as it was a century ago, I don't offer a 200-page thesis. Instead, I can only offer this: The western is honest. In this great country, which is suffering under the yoke of political correctness, the western harks back to an era when justice was sure and swift. Steal a man's horse, rustle his cattle, rob a bank, a stagecoach, or a train, you were hunted down and fitted with a hangman's noose. One size fit all.

"Sure, we westerners are prone to a little embellishment and exaggeration and, I admit it, occasionally play a little fast and loose with the facts. But we do so for a very good reason—to enhance the enjoyment of readers.

"It was Owen Wister, in *The Virginian*, who first coined the phrase 'When you call me that, smile.' Legend has it that Wister actually heard those words spoken by a deputy sheriff in Medicine Bow, Wyoming, when another poker player called him a son of a bitch.

"Did it really happen, or is it one of those myths that have passed down from one generation to the next? I honestly don't know. But there's a line in one of my favorite westerns of all time, *The Man Who Shot Liberty Valance*, where the newspaper editor tells the young reporter, 'When the truth becomes legend, print the legend.'

"These are the words I live by."

Connect with Us

Visit us online at
KensingtonBooks.com
to read more from your favorite authors, see books
by series, view reading group guides, and more.

Join us on social media

for sneak peeks, chances to win books and prize packs,
and to share your thoughts with other readers.

facebook.com/kensingtonpublishing
twitter.com/kensingtonbooks

Tell us what you think!

To share your thoughts, submit a review,
or sign up for our eNewsletters, please visit:
KensingtonBooks.com/TellUs.